Rain on A Good Day

Anne Comfort

SILVERSMITH
PRESS

Published by Silversmith Press—Houston, Texas
www.silversmithpress.com

Cover Design: Cayla Dodd

ISBN 978-1-967386-28-4 (Paperback Book)
ISBN 978-1-967386-29-1 (eBook)

To my family. Thank you for your love and support.

Chapter One

Rain on a good day is never wasted.

It's a reminder that the pain in life's journey is necessary for the perspective we need. A nudge to hug our children a little longer and more often, and to never go to bed angry with the ones we love.

This was a parcel of wisdom Lauren's grandmother had taught her.

Looking up through the windshield at the wet Irish sky, she remembered her grandmother's words—how she resented them!

Lauren leaned back in the seat, her hands fisting the steering wheel. The pain of the last year hadn't given her perspective, it had damaged her, broken her in ways she couldn't have imagined.

Watching the wiper blades swishing back and forth, she focused on the rhythm they made before closing her eyes. What had she been thinking, coming all this way to Tramore, Ireland?

After a few moments, she looked across the street at the sign that read *Cups and Cakes Bakery*. She couldn't sit in the car all afternoon, but she could turn it around and head back to the airport, back to Tacoma, Washington, where she belonged, where everything was familiar—even though the pain ate at her mercilessly.

The thought of what waited for her at home—nothing—propelled her out of the car. After looking both ways, she bolted across the street in the steady rain toward the bright blue door of the whitewashed building that housed the bakery.

Inside, she was greeted by the smell of freshly baked bread and sweet delights. She looked around the room for a woman matching the description the real estate agent had given her over the phone—blonde hair, mid-fifties, wearing a light-blue coat. There she was in the far corner of the room near a fireplace, seated at a table for two. After shaking off her wet hair and tugging at her damp sweater, she walked up to the woman.

"Mary?" Lauren asked hesitantly.

The woman looked up from her phone. "That's me... Lauren?" she questioned as she stood with her hand held out in greeting.

Lauren shook her hand. "Yes, it's nice to finally meet you."

"Likewise. I hope your flight was uneventful?" The real estate agent's Irish brogue was just as light and lilting in person as it had been over the phone. It reminded her that she was truly half a world away.

Lauren took the seat opposite Mary's. "Uneventful but long. I haven't flown that far since..." Her voice trailed off at the memory.

If Mary was curious about what caused the abrupt end to her comment, she didn't show it. Instead, she said, "I'm just sorry the rain didn't hold up until after you arrived." She glanced at Lauren's sweater then reached down into the bag sitting beside the table to retrieve an umbrella. Placing it on the table in front of Lauren, she said, "I should have told you to pack one of these."

Lauren chuckled. "I did but put it in the bottom of my suitcase. I'm from Tacoma. We get lots of rain too. I wasn't thinking."

"Well, please keep this one; I have more than I can count. I have the paperwork for the rental. The flat is right next door, so we can do the walk through first."

"Oh, I didn't realize it was so close."

"It's in the same building. The bakery takes up one half and the other side consists of two flats, one upper and one lower. Yours is on the first floor. It will either be divine or pure torture living so close to a bakery." Glancing at Lauren's all-too-thin frame, she added, "I imagine you won't be too worried about having a billion calories and carbs at your fingertips."

Lauren gave her a small smile. Food had been a mere necessity the last year. Even now, living next door to a bakery made no difference to her. "I'll do my best to control myself," she replied, just to be conversational.

"Well, glad to hear it. May I get you a drink or something to eat before we head next door?"

Lauren shook her head. "No, thank you. I had a snack on my way to Tramore."

Mary nodded. "All right then, let's go, shall we?"

The entrance to the flat was only a few feet from the bakery's door. Both women rushed from one to the other, not wanting to bother with an umbrella. When they entered, Lauren was pleased with what she saw—a quaint, efficient living space with modern touches. The walls were a soft white, the furnishings a neutral palette of grays and taupes. Pops of color appeared in the form of accessories and artwork, varying in orange, bright blues, and subdued greens. Surprisingly, there were a few touches of floral motifs to soften the modern feel.

"It's really nice!" Lauren said admiringly. "Even better than the pictures from the website."

"It is a pleasing space. I especially like the terrace off the dining room. It faces the street. A great spot any time of the day but especially in the morning when downtown Tramore is quiet."

They walked toward the terrace. "Oh, nice! I love the French doors," Lauren remarked as she unlocked them to draw them open. The frames were the same white as the walls and constructed with a single sheet of glass, with no window trim to obstruct the view of the street. "I also love the planting pots. They're so bright and colorful."

"Do you garden?" Mary asked as she joined Lauren on the terrace.

The younger woman hesitated before answering, "I used to."

"Well, if you decide to plant something, you've arrived at the perfect time. The nurseries will be opening in the next week or so for spring. What are your plans for transportation?"

"I'll mostly bike and walk. I'll use a taxi when I need to. Unless, you know someone who's looking to sell a used, reliable car, something on the inexpensive side."

"Hmm, let me do some checking around, and I'll let you know."

"Thank you. I'll be happy to give you a finder's fee."

Mary tsked. "Oh, nonsense! That won't be necessary. I'm happy to help—and if you need anything else while you're here, you have my number. Please call me."

"I appreciate that, Mary." She gave the older woman a smile.

It didn't take long for them to do the walk through and to sign the paperwork. When they were finished, Mary placed her copy of the contract in her bag and asked, "Would you like help with your luggage?"

Lauren looked out of the window and saw that the rain was still steadily coming down. "I think I'll wait a little bit to see if the rain slows."

"Are you sure? You could be waitin' a good while."

"I'll be fine, but I appreciate the offer. Oh, and here is your umbrella. You'll need it to get to your car."

The real estate agent patted her bag. "I have another one. Keep it."

Lauren gave her a smile of thanks.

"And," Mary added, "if you're interested, there is a group of us who meet on Thursdays for a book club. We'll be startin' a new one in a couple of weeks. You could join us then—sooner if you wish—and listen in on the last couple of sessions of our current book."

"I think I might like that, but I'll let you know for sure."

Mary gave her a parting nod before she made her way to the door. "Oh, I almost forgot to tell you. The owner of the flat provided you with a few things to get you by until you can make it to the market. Enjoy, and I hope to see you at the book club meetings or sooner."

"Yes, until then."

After Mary left, Laruen looked around the flat once more taking in her new surroundings, her home for the next year. Had she really committed to being here for that long? She had and knew it was the right thing to do.

Thinking of her home in Tacoma, she looked at her watch. It was close to 5: 00 a.m., too early to call. She reached for her phone and texted her parents and her in-laws to let them know she had arrived safe and sound and that she would call them soon.

When she was done, Lauren moved to the kitchen. It was a small space but nicely done with white cabinetry, gray granite counter tops, and newer appliances, including a small dishwasher. She opened the cabinets and found a stash of assorted tea. *Barry's* was the brand; one she wasn't familiar with. She reached for the box labeled *Irish Breakfast* and paused. It all felt a little surreal being in this place she had dreamt about for quite a while. Had she finally taken that first step of moving on with the rest of her life?

She shook her head as if to clear it. She didn't want to dwell on the reason she was here. Noticing the tea kettle on the stove, she filled it. While waiting for the water to boil, she thought of Mary and appreciated the woman's professionalism and how she had respected her privacy. She had a good feeling about the older woman and hoped she had made her first friend in Ireland.

Lauren pushed away from the counter and went to the fridge to look for cream. She was pleasantly surprised to find containers of prepared meals and a card with her name on it. She opened the envelope and read the words written in a clear, sturdy script.

> *Hello,*
> *Welcome to Ireland. Please enjoy the refreshments, and I hope you find the flat to your liking. If any problems arise, please contact Mary who's also the property manager. She will take care of things.*
> *Thank you for your business.*

A simple but pleasant note, and so thoughtful. Lauren was only mildly curious that the note didn't contain a name. Mary never mentioned the name of the owner, and Lauren hadn't asked. It was probably some real estate investment company, and for all she knew, Mary had written the note on behalf of the owner. She looked at the three packaged meals; one was a chicken dish, the other beef, and the third pork. It was too early for dinner, but she did find some cream just as the kettle began to whistle.

A few moments later, she was at the dining room

table sipping her tea, and watching the traffic go by on the street. She had no plans, only to put one foot in front of the other like she had done for the last year. Hopefully, the next few steps she took would propel her toward the change she needed, or thought she needed. *No, not thought. There was no question: something needed to change.* For the first time, in a long hard year, Lauren was tired of merely existing.

Chapter Two

It was evening by the time Lauren had finished unpacking, showering, and then sitting down to dinner. When she was done with the meal, she enjoyed one last cup of tea, trying to stay awake as long as she could to help adjust to the different time zone. She placed her teacup on the table and stared at the journal sitting in front of her.

She had never been one to keep a journal. In the past, any time she tried, it had always seemed strange and unnatural to write down the things she already knew and felt. Why put them into words and immortalize them? Lauren purchased the journal while preparing for her trip, something her psychiatrist had encouraged her to do.

"Don't think of it as writing things you already know about yourself. Think of it rather as exploring the thoughts and emotions of the things you can't quite express," Dr. Moore had explained when presenting the idea of keeping a journal while in Ireland. "Use this time to sift through the emotions of the past, your present, and even about the future. Bring into focus what you've lost and what you're afraid of."

Lauren stiffened at the comment. "I beg your pardon, Dr. Moore, but I don't need any help understanding what I've lost."

The psychiatrist gave her a brief nod. "Fair enough. Then tell me, Lauren; tell me what you've lost."

Lauren looked away and stared at a print of Georgia O'Keeffe's painting *Oriental Poppies*. It was the one thing in Dr. Moore's office that she seemed to gravitate to when she didn't know how to express the surge of emotions that consumed her. She would fixate on the black ovaries of the flower. They were as dark as the blackness that had swallowed her whole, a bleakness she felt she would never escape. Lauren didn't know how long she stared at the print before the tears began to flow. "I..." she swallowed hard. "I don't know how to say it, how to put it into words, but I feel it so keenly." She placed her fisted hand on the center of her chest while her voice quivered, and the tears ran their course. "Keeping a journal won't change how I feel."

"Lauren," Dr. Moore said, in her even-tempered way of speaking. "Please look at me. We're at a crossroads, and I need you to understand this."

Lauren almost refused and continued to stare at the painting for a few moments longer before finally refocusing on the doctor.

"This is important. None of this is about changing how you feel. For as long as you live, you *will* feel this. It's about moving your pain to a different level, giving it a new place, and no longer allowing it to be front and center in your life. Taking this trip to Ireland and keeping a journal are steps that can help you find that new place for these very real and permanent feelings. I'm only asking you to try. Can you promise to at least try?"

Again, Lauren hesitated and then finally nodded.

"Good. What's the worst thing that can happen if you don't?"

"It won't work, and I'll be stuck here forever."

"Forever is a long time, Lauren. I believe you're stronger than that."

Lauren wiped away her tears and shrugged. "Maybe."

Two weeks later, she had yet to write anything on the blank pages. She reached across the table to pick up the journal and the pen lying beside it. She opened the front cover and stared at the blue lines. Sitting in Dr. Moore's office that day, she'd understood with her mind what the psychiatrist was trying to say, but she had yet to grasp it with her heart. Was it possible to find a less prominent place for the pain she felt? Was she truly strong enough? Suddenly, Lauren's heart began to race and the pressure in her temples grew as hopelessness began to push to the surface. She slammed the journal closed and shoved it off the table. When it landed on the floor with a solid thud, she began to sob uncontrollably. "Why, why?" she cried out to the empty room before covering her face with her hands and allowing her head to fall to the table in defeat.

The rain had stopped. Brendan Callery looked up from the book he was reading to check the time. It was getting late, and the bookstore would be closing soon. He stood to make his purchase, looking forward to the walk home. It was one of the few nights a month he had to himself, and he savored the moment. Not because he didn't enjoy raising a little girl, but because it gave him time to think and to plan without worrying about things like schedules, appointments, and whether he was doing things right or not.

When he left the bookstore, he stopped for a moment to breathe in the chill spring air. This time of year, when the first shoots of life began surging up from the ground and the air started to warm, it always filled Brendan with a sense of change. It was different than how he felt each fall, which gave him a feeling of celebration as it heralded in the holiday season and the joys that came with it.

Summer filled him with the memories of how terrified he'd first felt about raising a child—the most challenging period of his life. It replaced those carefree feelings of summer and his youth. The fear had swarmed and hovered over the question of whether he could adjust and bear the challenge of raising a girl, a precious little child with a mop of curly brown hair who also had Down Syndrome. Her name was Noirin. She was the daughter of his cousin, Katelyn, and his joy.

That summer, while he'd gained the most important responsibility of his life, he'd also lost so much. Katelyn, who was more of a sister to him, had died. Raised as siblings, Brendan had lost a part of himself. He zipped up his jacket a little higher before his thoughts turned to the other person, he'd lost that tragic summer: Eva, the woman he thought he'd love forever.

Each year, as May turned into June, he tried to stave off the melancholy feelings he now associated with the season that had once been his favorite. There was a time when the smell of cut grass and the warm sea air would fill him with a thrill of expectancy, even adventure. Now, it mostly triggered memories of sadness. That summer of loss had been the hardest. Since then, Brendan had worked diligently to remember how much he loved the warm season, and for Noirin's sake, he had learned to put away his dreary thoughts and make the most of what was proving to be his daughter's favorite time of the year.

Brendan smiled inwardly. Noirin loved every time of the year. She was a joyful child and took pleasure in just about everything. It was what he loved most about her, and the person he had looked forward to seeing the most after moving to Dublin. During the four years he'd lived there, Brendan regularly returned home on the weekends. Tramore was in his blood and always would be. After Noirin had been born, the joy of seeing her continued to tug his heart homeward.

Brendan looked both ways before crossing the street. A part of him missed being in a romantic relationship, having that female companionship, someone who cared for him and someone he could care for. If he were being honest, he missed it more now than he had in a long time.

The first year of raising Noirin had been a blur, coping with his grief, his little girl's grief. Then there was fatherhood.

The second year was when their new life together

had finally found its rhythm. Adjusted to their work, school, and social schedules, Brendan had simply enjoyed his new role. He'd delighted in seeing his little girl growing and learning. And the way she loved him, so unabashedly and exuberantly, still sent waves of pleasure through him. One of the greatest parts of his day was picking her up from school and seeing her squeal with delight at the sight of him. After bending down to her so she could throw her tiny arms around his neck, he would close his eyes in surrender to the waves of love and adoration that filled him to the brim.

And now in his third year of raising Noirin, the longing for someone to love had settled in. He no longer missed Eva but desired the simple things like sharing about one's day over a meal with snatches of kisses in between. He wanted to walk from the bookstore, like he was this evening, holding someone's hand, lingering and savoring the moment of simply being together.

Brendan stopped at the corner of his building, and looked out over the street, quieter now in the later evening. As much as he wanted someone in his life, he accepted the fact that it would be difficult to find that person. Brendan wasn't interested in being in a relationship just to be in one; he wanted what a lot of people desired, someone to share his life with, a life that included his daughter. It was a challenge he didn't think he was quite ready to accept.

He turned toward his building and saw the light on in the flat below his. He noticed a woman with dark hair sitting at the dining room table. He'd forgotten about the new tenant. Brendan watched her for a moment, able to make out only her profile. Just as he was about to walk to the front entrance, he saw her slam a book close and shove it off the table. The action surprised him. He lingered for a moment, then felt his chest tighten when he saw her begin to sob uncontrollably. A moment later, she laid her head down on the table, her chest heaving with the anguish she felt.

Brendan recognized what he saw. It stirred up memories of his own suffering. He quickly walked away, leaving the woman to her pain.

Chapter Three

Lauren halted in surprise when she opened her front door and saw a small white box on the doormat. It had a label on the top that read *Cups and Cakes Bakery*. It was a clever design with a medallion border around the name of the bakery finished in colors of soft browns and pinks. Lauren took a minute to appreciate the artwork. Whoever created the piece had a nice sense of creativity.

She picked up the box. Under the lid, the smell of a freshly baked croissant caused her stomach to growl. She closed it, and after checking to make sure the door was locked, she made her way to the bakery.

When she opened the bright-blue door, Lauren couldn't help but appreciate how wonderful the place smelled of baking dough and sugar, with the rich scent of coffee and cinnamon lingering in the air. Yesterday had been the first time she'd stepped inside of a bakery in over a year, and she'd forgotten what it was like to walk into a place for the pure pleasure of enjoying what it had to offer. She tried not to think about the patisserie that she'd shopped at regularly in Tacoma, a place she'd avoided for the last several months. Her food shopping had been relegated to the local grocery store for necessities only.

Lauren made her way to the counter and was greeted by a teenage boy who smiled politely before asking for her order.

Behind him stood an impressive wall-to-wall shelving system made of natural wood and stainless steel. The shelves were stocked with glass jars of tea with pretty medallion labels identifying the different flavors. While scanning the offerings, she asked the teenager, "I'd like some tea, please; do you have a recommendation?"

"I personally like the *Fifth of November*. It's a blend of Chinese black tea, berries, and gunpowder tea."

"Gunpowder tea? I've never heard of it."

"It's a green tea leaf that has been rolled into a small round pellet and unfurls or 'explodes' in hot water. The tea also has a smoky taste to it."

"That sounds interesting; I'll have some of that. One other thing." Lauren lifted the pastry box she had brought with her. "This croissant was on my doorstep this morning. You wouldn't happen to know who put it there, would you?"

The teenager gave her a bewildered look. "I'm sorry, ma'am. We have so many people comin' and goin' every mornin'. I wish I knew."

Lauren smiled at him before reaching for her wallet. "It's okay. I knew it was a long shot."

When she was done paying, Lauren wondered if it was perhaps Mary who had left her the croissant. The next time she spoke to the real estate agent she would ask her.

Turning away from the counter, she looked around the crowded café for a seat, and took a moment to appreciate the space, something she hadn't had time to do yesterday. The décor was warm. Tall glass windows faced the street, letting in bright light. Each table held a small bouquet of fresh flowers, and copper pendant lights were placed over the service counter and throughout the space. It had a warm but modern feel to it, and the stone fireplace added a wealth of charm, with a mantle that matched the wood used for the tea shelves.

Lauren eyed a table in the far corner on the opposite side of the room from where she and Mary had sat yesterday afternoon. She took the tabletop sign holding the number the bakery worker had given her and made her way to the table. Next to her was an older gentleman who looked to be in his sixties. He was reading a copy of the *Irish Times*.

It would be good to have a paper to read, Lauren thought to herself. A way for her to learn more about the country she would be living in for the next year. And she would rather read a newspaper than stare at the blank pages of the journal she'd brought with her. She forced herself not to think about her emotional outburst the night before.

Instead of interrupting the man to ask where she might find a copy of a newspaper, she pulled out a small notebook from her purse and began making a to-do list. At the top, she wrote *Flowers* and stopped to think about what Mary had said about the nursery opening soon and the colorful pots on her patio. Lauren scratched out the word and paused. *What was she doing?* This is why she was here, to find a way to live again. She may not have gardened in over a year, but she loved it, had always loved it—even as a child when she was *expected* to help her mom in the vegetable garden.

She treasured those moments, sometimes pulling

the weeds but mostly harvesting the fruits of their labor. She remembered the joy of anticipation while running to the garden on the twenty-eighth day of planting radish seeds and pulling up a bright purple-red bulb, ready to be eaten. They were special times with just her and her mother, often with a teachable moment between them while they worked the earth and tended to their crops.

"Do you see these weeds, Lauren?" her mother had asked during one of those moments.

"Uh huh. I don't understand why we have to pull them out. Why can't they just grow alongside the cucumbers and the tomatoes? And some of them are pretty, like the clover with its purple flowers."

Her mother stopped what she was doing to look at her daughter. "Weeds grow much quicker and faster than useful plants. Their roots will choke out our vegetables, and then they will bear no fruit. That's why we have to pull the weeds out, even when they're pretty, so that we have food to live." She paused to wipe her brow. "That's how life is, Lauren. Weeds are like bad choices. If we let them take hold in our lives, they'll overcome us, and we'll bear little to no fruit. Sometimes those choices can be disguised as nice and pretty, like the clover, but they'll do as much damage as any other weed. I want you to always make good choices, sweetheart. Your life will be better because of it. Do you understand?"

"Yes, Mama. You and papa made good choices, haven't you?"

Lauren remembered the smile her mother had given

her, beautiful and bright. "We have; and you, my precious girl, are the best choice of our life. Never forget it."

And she never had, forever treasuring her parents who had chosen her as an infant from South Korea to make her their own. It was a wonderful way to be loved.

Lauren smiled at the memory and felt a little wistful when she recalled the conversation she'd had with her mother, earlier that morning. She missed her parents very much and couldn't wait to see them when they visited her in May.

Her brows furrowed in concern. After talking with her mother, she had called her mother-in-law to let her know she had arrived in Ireland safely. Before leaving Tacoma, she had asked her in-laws, Stacey and Fred, if they would like to visit her. Stacey, who was Irish by birth, had refused. In fact, she had always been tight-lipped about her life in Ireland, stating how there was nothing happy about it, and how she would never go back. Not even her father-in-law knew anything about her past—or he'd never indicated he knew.

When speaking to Stacey that morning, she had asked again if she would reconsider coming to visit her. She hadn't yet told her mother-in-law she was in Tramore. All she knew was that she was traveling in Ireland. It's what her father-in-law had asked her to say. Stacey hadn't been happy about the trip, and Fred suspected she wouldn't be pleased to know Lauren had chosen to stay in Tramore. It was the place he believed Stacey was from.

Lauren sighed. It was all such a great mystery—one

she hoped to try and unravel while she was here. She would do it for Christopher's sake. At the thought of her husband, she glanced down at her to-do list and rewrote the word *Flowers*. Next to the word, she added, *for you, Christopher*, and willed the tears that pricked the backs of her eyes not to come.

"Hello, Miss."

Lauren looked up from her notepad and saw a server holding a tray with her tea. "Oh, thank you," she commented before adding, "Do you happen to know where I might purchase a copy of the *Irish Times*?"

While answering, he placed the pot and cup on the table along with sugar and cream. "We normally carry them here at the café, but we are all out at the moment. They go pretty fast, but you can get a copy at the grocery store just down the road. The bookstore also carries various papers."

"Great, thank you for your help."

She added to her list to pick up a copy of the newspaper when she went to the grocery store later that morning.

"Excuse me."

She glanced up to find the older gentleman seated next to her looking at her.

"Would you care to have my paper? I'm almost done and can give you the sections that I've finished."

"Are you sure?"

He smiled. "I'm certain. My name is Shane Byrne. It's a pleasure to meet you." He reached over and offered her his hand.

She shook it, and said, "Likewise. My name is Lauren Ross."

"You're American?" he asked while handing her the sections of the paper he had finished.

She nodded. "I'm from Tacoma, Washington. And thank you for the paper."

"You're quite welcome. Tacoma aye? I hear it's similar to our fair Ireland, climate-wise."

"Interesting, I was just telling Mary that yesterday."

He nodded. "Ah, Mary O'Leary, the real estate agent."

"Yes, do you know her?"

"I do; we're in the same book club, and we've been friends for a long time," Shane replied while she took another taste of her drink. "How is your tea? What blend did you try?"

Lauren sat her cup down. "*Fifth of November*, and it's really good, very unexpected. We don't have a lot of specialty tea shops in Tacoma, at least not any that are nearby. I'm going to enjoy living close to one. I'm renting the flat next door."

Shane smiled. "I thought that might be you. Mary mentioned that the flat had been rented out to a tenant from America. How long are you staying?"

"I'll be here for a year." She took another sip of her tea.

"Work or pleasure?" Shane asked.

"Neither," Lauren said a little quietly before looking down at the teacup she cradled in her hands.

"I'm sorry, lass, I didn't mean to pry."

She looked up and smiled at him. "No need to apologize. I'm here to find myself."

"And you came all the way to Ireland to do that." The comment was made with a softening of the eyes and full of warmth. "Well, you've come to the right place. I'm not a proud man, but I am truly fond of our little parcel of heaven here on earth. You'll have no trouble findin' yerself in this grand land. She might surprise you a wee bit when you do, but you'll find her nonetheless."

Lauren loved the poetic spin he put on her idea of finding herself as well as his confidence. She hoped he was right. "Thank you, Shane."

"My pleasure. You know, since you live next door, and I am here every mornin' around this time, you could come by and share my paper with me. No need to go buyin' one." He paused and then tsked at himself. "Boy, the newspaper folk would love hearin' me say that, now, wouldn't they?"

Lauren laughed. She liked Shane, already felt a connection to him. "Sounds nice. Yesterday, Mary invited me to the book club. Is everyone around here so friendly?"

"Uncle Shane!"

The sound of the exuberant cry prevented the older man from responding and caused both of them to turn their heads toward the entrance of the bakery.

A small brown-haired child was barreling toward the older man.

"Noirin!" Shane replied just as excitedly, while he held out his arms to her. When the child was in them, he asked, "Where's my *pog*?"

The little girl giggled before planting a loud kiss on his puckered lips.

"Ah that's a good, lass, for I do love your *pogs*. They do my heart good, better than any medicine."

She giggled again. "I'm ready for school."

"Okay, but let me introduce you to my new friend, first." He turned to Lauren who was surprised to see she had Down Syndrome. "This is Miss Lauren, and she's come all the way across the pond from America."

Noirin's eyes grew big with surprise. "America, where they have baseball? Dadai loves baseball." The bright ebullient child turned to look at the man standing behind her.

Lauren hadn't noticed him until now. More than his tallish frame and dark hair, she noticed the look of adoration on his face for the little girl.

Shane ruffled the child's hair. "One of the many things your father and I have in common. Say hello to the nice lady, Noirin."

The little girl turned to her. "Hello, Miss from America."

Lauren smiled at Noirin and reached out to shake her hand. "It's very nice to meet you. Do you like school?"

The little girl's eyes glowed with pleasure. "I love school! Uncle Shane takes me every day, and after the bakery closes, Dadai picks me up in the afternoon. I get to play and read books. I love to read books."

Lauren chuckled. "I love to read too. Maybe you can tell me about the books you're reading?"

"Okay, but after school," she replied and then looked at Shane. "It's time to go."

The older man smiled and then looked at Lauren. "Tomorrow morning?"

She nodded. "Tomorrow."

Both she and the little girl's father watched as they headed out of the door.

"What a wonderful daughter you have," Lauren offered.

He turned to her, his pleasant face glowing with pride. "She is *mo chroi*."

When Lauren gave him a puzzled look at the strange phrase, he added, "Sorry, that is Gaelic for '*my heart*'. I'm Brendan, by the way. It's nice to meet you, Lauren. I see you've already met Shane, and it sounds like you two have a date?" He added the last part with a wink.

Lauren chuckled. "We met over the *Irish Times*. He heard me asking one of the workers where I could get a copy and offered to share his with me. One thing led to another, and now, I have a standing invitation to share his paper with him every morning, if I like."

"And do you like?"

"I do believe so. And by the looks of things, he must be a decent person if you trust him to take your daughter to school every morning."

Brendan gave her an approving look. "Shane has been a family friend since before I was born. I trust him with my life and Noirin's."

"Oh, so he's not her uncle?" she asked.

The handsome father shook his head. "No, but he's like family, so Noirin calls him Uncle. He has known my

29

aunt and uncle for most of their lives. He's from Tramore, like most of us are. What part of America do you hail from?"

"Tacoma, Washington."

"I've always wanted to go to the U.S."

"To see a baseball game?" Lauren added with a grin.

"Of course," Brendan replied with a chuckle.

"Well, I hope you get to, someday."

"Thank you." He looked at her table, and asked, "How is your tea?"

"Delicious," she replied while reaching for her cup.

"I'm glad you approve. I'm the owner of the bakery, and I value feedback. I also live in the flat above yours. I intended to stop by to tell you that if Noirin ever gets too loud, just let me know. She's not much of a jumper, but every now and again she can get a little excited, as you saw for yerself." His Irish brogue was pleasing, deep and lilting.

"She's wonderful, and I'm sure she will be just fine. Your bakery is lovely. I didn't have a chance to try the croissant yet, but I'm sure it will be delicious."

"Well, I hope so. It was nice meetin' you, Lauren. I'm sure I'll be seein' you around."

"Nice to meet you too, Brendan."

As he walked away, she couldn't help but feel a little twinge of envy. How Lauren wished she and Christopher had a child!

Chapter Four

Lauren sifted through the newspaper, but her mind was struggling to focus on the contents. She looked up and noticed that the café wasn't nearly as crowded as she expected. Her second pot of tea had gone cold, and she knew she needed to try to write something in her journal. Her errant thought of envy about Brendan having a child pricked at her. She looked at the blank journal and opened it to the first page. She wrote the first word that came to mind, *Regrets,* and remembered the day she had taken the pregnancy test she was certain would be positive.

Thirteen Months Ago

"Lauren, is everything okay?" Christopher could hear her sniffling on the other side of the door. "Lauren, please open the door." His voice had risen slightly.

He waited for a moment then heard the click. The moment the door opened, she stepped into his arms. "We waited too long, Christopher. Why did I have to wait?"

He noticed the pregnancy test sitting on the counter and couldn't see the result from where he stood. But there was no need. His wife's sadness told him what he needed to know. Christopher pulled back to look at her face, blotchy and red from her tears. The look of anguish filling her features caused his gut to tighten. "We both wanted to wait, sweetheart."

Lauren wouldn't look at him. "Two years ago, you were ready, and I asked for one more year so we could save a little bit more, and now we've waited too long." The tears started again.

Christopher led her to their bed and sat down with her, his back against the headboard while he cradled her in his arms.

Her chest heaved with a sob. After taking a gulp of air, she uttered, "I was so sure this time. I'm late and was convinced I was pregnant." She buried her face in his chest and cried some more.

All he could do was rub her back and press his lips to the top of her head. "Maybe, you are pregnant; maybe something is wrong with the test. What about blood work; aren't there some cases when you need to have blood drawn to know for sure? Let's go see the doctor in the morning."

His words seemed to calm her.

Lauren pulled away to look at him. "And if I'm not pregnant, we'll make an appointment with a fertility specialist? We've been trying for a year, and I'm worried that something's wrong."

Christopher kissed his wife's forehead before answering. "If you're not pregnant, we'll see a specialist. But listen to me, Lauren. I don't regret waiting. I've loved having you all to myself these last seven years. Yes, I want children, and can't wait to have them with you, but I've loved every moment we've had together."

"Every moment?" she asked with raised eyebrows and then sniffled.

The look on his face softened. "Every moment, Lauren, because even when we've disagreed, I've been reminded of how passionate you are, how forgiving, and gracious you can be. And when you've been wrong, I've admired your ability to be humble and to ask for forgiveness. So yes, Lauren, I have loved every moment."

She sat up straighter and leaned into him. "Me too." She smoothed her hand over his chest, and added, "I want so badly to have your baby, Christopher. Do you know why?"

He held her gaze and shook his head.

"Because I can't wait for you to be a father, to give our child the gift of being loved by you. It's quite extraordinary, you know."

It was rare for Christopher to feel the need to cry. On his wedding day, when he'd watched Lauren walking down the aisle, the tears had come. When his grandmother had passed, he couldn't keep them at bay, nor had he wished to. And now, being in this moment with the love of his life, and hearing her words of praise and adoration, he felt them. When she saw the tears gathering in his eyes, she pressed her mouth to his and kissed him, ever so tenderly. She poured every ounce of her love into that kiss, causing him to feel as if he had grown ten feet tall. That's how she always made him feel—invincible and able to slay any demon. This woman was his whole world.

The pregnancy test had been right, after all. Two weeks later, they were scheduled to see a fertility specialist but never made it.

Lauren looked down at the journal and stared at the word she had written—*Regrets.* And then her hand began to move. *I don't regret a single thing when it comes to you, Christopher.*

And then she began to draw, another of her pleasures she hadn't done in the last year. It was a sketch of the coffee shop where she and Christopher had met, the place where it had all begun. They had gone back many times since, too many to count. Every now and again, over lattes, they would remember how they had met—the spilled coffee all down the front of his shirt and pants. Thankfully, it had been iced. The gentle look he'd given her when she'd become distraught. The way he had reached for her hand and cupped it gently in his to reassure her he was fine.

When she had insisted on giving him money to replace his clothes, merriment had filled his eyes. "Do you want to know what would make this all better for me?"

Lauren had nodded eagerly.

"Sit with me, for a few minutes, and tell me about yourself."

She had been surprised by his request, but also quite interested. Once she had gotten over the distress of spilling her drink on him, she noticed what a kind face he had. There was a gentleness about him that drew her to him, a kindness that seemed to exude from his whole being.

Together they sat at that café, while coffee stains

settled into his dress shirt, and told each other about themselves. Two hours later, she had accepted a first date with him. That night, on her way home, Lauren became a believer of love at first encounter. And from that moment on, at every opportunity, Christopher proved it existed.

When she was done sketching the front of their coffee shop, Lauren looked at her rendering and felt the first moments of the thaw. *It had happened.* She looked up from the journal and remembered the conversation she had with Shane earlier and then meeting Noirin, and she knew the thaw had actually started with them. It had felt so normal talking to Shane, Noirin, and then later with Brendan. She had spoken to them with laughter and had felt the joy and humor. She especially remembered her conversation with Brendan and how she had added a touch of wit when he had teased her about already having a date with Shane.

Looking back down at her journal, Lauren placed her fingers to her lips. She then pressed them to her drawing and wrote, *I'll always love you, Christopher.*

Brendan couldn't help but notice the intense look on Lauren's face and wondered what she was thinking. He knew he shouldn't stare, but after speaking with her and remembering how he'd seen her through the window crying at her dining room table, it was impossible not to wonder. He took in her long black hair, her beautiful Asian features, with those large dark-brown eyes set perfectly in a heart-shaped face and knew he would wonder about her for some time to come.

More than being attractive, she had been unfazed when she met Noirin. She had treated his little girl as if she were a perfectly normal child. Something inside of him had stirred when he'd watched their exchange.

"You're a fool, Callery," he muttered under his breath, as he finished adding more baked goods to the display case.

"What was that?" John, one of his servers, asked.

"Nothing, just talkin' to myself. I'm goin' back to the kitchen to work on the rest of the bread for the lunch rush. When Aine gets here, can you ask her to call the supplier about the potato flour we ordered? It never arrived."

The boy nodded.

"Oh, and did you study for your geometry test?" Brendan asked. He'd almost forgotten.

"I did study, and am as prepared as I'll ever be," the teenage boy replied in a matter-of-fact tone.

"Good. Then you'll do fine. Have a good day at school, John!"

"You too, Brendan, and careful there about talkin' to yerself. Someone might think you're a header."

"Too late, but don't go tellin' everyone," he said it with a wide grin and then patted him on the back. He'd known John and his family for as long as he could remember. The O'Carroll family were good people, as were most who lived in Tramore.

Aine, his assistant, would be arriving before John left for school. She handled the front of the house and

36

always came in later and worked till the close so she could take her children to school. Aine had been a stay-at-home mom up until her last child started primary school. Her husband worked at Martin's, an auto shop on the west side of town. Her hours worked perfectly for Brendan.

As he made his way to the kitchen, Brendan's thoughts turned to Lauren, and again he thought what a fool he was if he allowed himself to become too interested in the American. She would be gone in a year. But more importantly, he noticed she wore a wedding ring. There was no sense in stirring up that hornets' nest, but he couldn't help but wonder what kind of fool would let his wife move half-way around the world for a year. He thought about the crying jag he'd witnessed and wondered if they were having marital problems.

Brendan shook his head. Marital problems or not, it was best for him to keep his distance.

When he walked into the kitchen, his cousin Ellen glanced up briefly from the petit fours she was decorating—pastel-colored with iced flowers and bees on top. He was always amazed by her talent. He might be a baker, a really good one, but he'd never been able to master the intricate work of designing cakes, especially miniature ones that could be consumed in one bite.

"Is Noirin off to school then?" Ellen asked while continuing to work on her design.

"Aye, she was excited as always. Shane was talkin' to the American—already asked her out."

"Ha," Ellen chuckled. "He's a real lady's man, that's

for sure. Mother told me she was beautiful and Asian, asked about possibly buyin' a car while she's here. Also said, she had a ring on her finger—can't help but speculate about that."

Brendan shrugged and pulled a tray full of dough out of one of the proofing cases. "There's no point in speculatin', Ellen; we'll know what we'll know. She seemed nice enough—was very normal with Noirin."

Ellen looked at Brendan for a minute before returning to her icing. "I'm glad of that. How did you like the lavender biscotti?" his cousin asked, changing the subject.

Brendan was cutting the dough into balls the size of a small bowl. When baked, the center would be cored and used as a soup bowl. "I loved the biscotti." He stopped what he was doing to look at her. "Ellen, what are you doin' here in Tramore? You have mad skills as a pastry chef. You could be workin' anywhere."

She glanced up from the petit fours to give him a pointed look. "You're askin' me that question? After high school you may have moved to Dublin, but you never really left. You came home every chance you could get. And then when everythin' happened with Katelyn, you didn't even hesitate to move back. I'm here because I love it here, same as you. Why do I have to be in some five-star restaurant to feel accomplished? Are city dwellers the only one's entitled to gourmet food?"

His eyes met hers: "What's his name?"

Ellen sat the icing bag on the counter and narrowed her eyes at him. "Really, Brendan!"

"Really, Ellen. You didn't study at Le Cordon Bleu to work at my family's bakery."

"I did so," she retorted with a slightly raised voice. "And you'll be needin' my help more than ever when you open the second location. I'm challenged. You allow me to be creative. I love what I do. It's the truth—ask mother."

He wasn't convinced, but he would let it go. "I just worry about you, and..."

The softening of his cousin's look told him she understood where his thoughts had travelled—Katelyn. She'd been taken advantage of by her boyfriend and left to raise a child on her own.

"I understand, Brendan, and I appreciate your concern. And when there is a man for you to worry about, you can line up right behind Father, and we'll let the inquisition begin."

"Fair enough. Did you finish the layout for the new kitchen?"

Her face brightened. "Do you realize how excited I am to be designin' my own kitchen?" She looked around the room. "I love this place, but it's been hard to modernize in here and to keep things efficient. Now I'll have a clean slate. And you think I'm not happy workin' in Tramore?"

He shaped the last of the bread bowls from the tray he'd pulled out. "Fine, fine. I believe you're happy, and I'll continue to feel like I've won the lottery with you. I'll build this new bakery, and you can never leave me."

She smiled and then gave him a wink. "Why would I ever want to?"

Chapter Five

Ellen didn't feel guilty about her conversation with Brendan. She might be secretly in love with Donal Kavanagh but she hadn't lied. There wasn't a man in her life, for Donal was eternally clueless about her feelings for him. And Ellen was a little too old-fashioned to make the first move. Or was it her lack of self-confidence that held her back?

She decided it was a combination of both.

The fact that Donal was the pastor of their church didn't help. He had more important, headier things on his mind like leading a congregation and ministering to those who desperately needed help. In addition to being a pastor, Donal was young and attractive, and he had nearly every single God-fearing woman—some not so God-fearing— within a hundred-mile radius of Tramore crazy in love with him. This fact alone exacerbated Ellen's problem. He could have anyone he wanted, so why would he want her? Plain ole Ellen with flour and icing permanently stuck under her fingernails.

One would think that because Donal and Brendan were good friends, it gave her the advantage. But she was ordinary Ellen, void of feminine wiles, impatient and intolerant of women who had them, and more than a little too direct at times.

Knowing her chances with Donal were slim to none, she'd done everything possible to get over him. She'd dated other men and tried to uncover anything about him that would turn her off to him, looking for anything that could annoy her to the point of disinterest. It seemed the harder she tried to find something wrong with him, the harder she fell. Then, a few weeks ago, she decided to find another church, which had proven futile as there weren't many options in Tramore, and she wasn't interested in making an extended trek to Waterford every weekend. So, Ellen decided she would stop attending for a while and ask for forgiveness later.

Her mother and father had noticed and had questioned her absence. She made every excuse possible except telling them the truth. Under no circumstances, would any of her family members ever know how she felt about Donal Kavanagh. Wild horses would never pry it out of her.

Ellen sighed as she bagged up the last of the towels and aprons from the bakery that needed to be washed and made her way to the dining room. There was still another hour of service, but her work for the day was done. She opened and Brendan closed. It was a great arrangement for her early bird self.

As she was leaving, she noticed the American woman sitting at a table by the fireplace. It was impossible not to know who she was, for there were very few Asians in all of Ireland, let alone Tramore.

Her head was bent over what looked to be a book and her hand was moving quickly. Ellen noticed the colored pencils and realized she was drawing. She debated about approaching the pretty woman and introducing herself. Her curiosity won the match.

"Hello," she greeted her tentatively.

The American looked up from what was a sketch-book and smiled at Ellen.

"I'm sorry to interrupt, but I wanted to stop and introduce myself. I'm Mary's daughter."

"Oh yes, Mary, a very nice lady. She's been so help-ful these last few weeks while I've tried to find a place to rent. My name is Lauren. Would you like to have a seat?"

"That would be lovely. My name is Ellen. I'm the exec-utive pastry chef here, and Brendan, the owner of the bak-ery, is my cousin." She reached out to shake Lauren's hand.

"So, you're the one responsible for all the wonder-ful smells."

Ellen smiled. "I am, but I hope they taste as good as they smell."

Lauren grinned. "They absolutely do. I had a crois-sant this morning, and I've never had anything better, not even when Chris... " the American paused for a brief moment, "not even when I went to Paris," she finished.

Ellen was immediately curious about who Chris was and remembered the wedding ring she wore. She wanted to ask about her husband but knew it would be rude. Instead, she said, "That's a pretty amazing compliment since the French are the standard for patisseries."

"Well, it's true. And even your French pronunciation is really good. Where did you learn to bake?"

Ellen gave her a sheepish look. "I studied in Paris, at Le Cordon Bleu."

Lauren was impressed. "Ah, it all makes sense. The petite fours are stunning. I haven't had one yet, so I can't tell you if they taste as good as they look." She added the last part with a wink which caused Ellen to laugh.

When Ellen's laughter subsided, she said, "Please tell me you haven't been sitting here since this morning? Brendan mentioned he'd met you. His comment was more about Shane, and how he'd already talked you into a date."

It was Lauren's turn to chuckle. "How could I resist him?"

"You'll enjoy him. He's good people."

Lauren seemed genuinely pleased. "I did leave the bakery this morning. I ran some errands and then realized I was craving more of the tea I had earlier, the *Fifth of November*."

"Ah, good stuff. It's one of my favorites. You should try our chai. I think you'll enjoy that one too." Ellen glanced down at the sketch book. "Do you draw?"

Lauren nodded. "It's just for fun, like doodling. By the way, I've been meaning to ask about the logo design for the bakery. Who drew it?"

"Shane actually. He's a famous artist here in Ireland. Did he not mention that to you?"

Lauren's eyes opened a little wider in surprise. "No, he didn't, but then we didn't have much of a chance to talk."

43

"Google him tonight. He's quite impressive."

The two of them continued talking, and Ellen lost track of time. When she saw Donal walking through the bakery door, she paused mid-sentence, and then quickly recovered by waving to him.

"Hi Ellen," he said as he made his way to their table. He then looked at Lauren and said, "Good afternoon, my name is, Donal."

"Hi, I'm Lauren."

"Nice to meet you," he added before turning his attention back to Ellen. "I'm here to pick up the leftovers. You're here late?"

Ellen looked at the American. "Lauren and I were talking, and I lost track of time. Donal is the pastor of our church and also a good friend of my cousin, Brendan. He gives Donal the unsold items for the food pantry here in Tramore."

"That's right," Donal said, and then added, "They'll be lined up around the block by the time I get there. They always know what's comin'—the best baked goods this side of the continent."

Lauren smiled. "I can only speak for the croissant I had, but I'd say the best including the continent."

"That's our Ellen," Donal added. He looked at Ellen and his brows furrowed. "I've been meaning to call you. I haven't seen you in a couple of weeks. Your mother and dad said you've been busy. I just wanted to make sure everythin's all right."

Ellen could feel the heat rising to her cheeks. She

hadn't thought about him being concerned, but then what a right moron she was, for of course he would be. He was her pastor! She managed to speak without her voice quivering in embarrassment. "I have been busy with the openin' of the new bakery. But I should be there this Sunday."

She turned to Lauren. "If you'd like to come, we'd love to have you. Our church is North Hill, over on Elm Park." Inviting Lauren was the neighborly thing to do, but she did it to get the focus off herself and the lie she had told.

"You're opening a new bakery?" Lauren asked.

Ellen nodded, trying to ignore Donal. "And a tea room, where we'll serve high tea. We want everyone from all over comin' to our new bakery."

"When will it be ready?"

"In three months. Construction started a bit ago, but with the rains, it's been a little slower than planned."

Lauren looked at Donal, and said, "Would you care to take a seat?"

Ellen's chest tightened. She had hoped he would walk off to fetch the leftovers.

"No, thank you. I have to get to the food pantry or there will be a riot on my hands." He placed his hand on Ellen's shoulder. "I'll see you on Sunday?"

She looked in his direction but focused on his chin as she replied, "I'm plannin' on it," her face flushed once more because of the lie.

He nodded and then said to Lauren, "It was nice to meet you."

Ellen looked at the pretty Asian. "I should be goin' as well. I have some errands to run. It was really nice meetin' you." She stood from the chair and started to add, "On Thursday..."

"There's a book club that meets," Lauren interjected with a smile.

Ellen grinned. "It sounds like you've already been given the invite. You should come. We're finishing up *Faust*, and will start *Jane Eyre* in a couple of weeks."

"Ah nice, the classics. I like the sound of that. I don't know if I will be able to make it this week, but I'll try and plan for the following week."

"Good. It was nice meetin' you. I enjoyed talkin' with you, Lauren, and hope to see you again soon."

"Same here," Lauren replied.

Ellen made her way to her car and prayed for forgiveness for the lies she had told Donal; but she was more determined than ever to find a new church. It was impossible to continue seeing Donal every week and falling more and more in love with him. It didn't help when he said things like he'd said a minute ago, 'our Ellen' and 'the best baked goods this side of the continent.' She shoved the bagged towels and aprons into the front seat of her car and slammed the door shut. Ellen wasn't a swearing kind of girl, but at the moment, she wanted to let go of a whole lot of not so nice things. Unrequited love—it wasn't for the faint of heart.

Chapter Six

"Don't walk too far ahead, Noirin," Brendan called out to his daughter. Shadow, Aunt Mary's chocolate Weimaraner, barked in response as if it to say, 'Don't worry. I've got her.'

"I wish you could have a dog, Brendan," Mary said as they walked along Gallwey's Hill toward Lower Strand, the street that would take them to the beachfront. They were near the turn that would soon put the sea to their right, passing all the colorful buildings, in varying shades of red, blue, yellow, and green.

"I would love to have a dog for Noirin's sake, but I can't swing it right now. I have a lot on my plate with the new bakery. I really appreciate you bringin' Shadow around as often as you can, especially for our walks."

The first year, after losing Katelyn, it was Aunt Mary who started their regular walks from the bakery down to the beachfront. It had become their way of dealing with their grief, and his way of decompressing from the stresses of learning to be a father.

Now on Lower Strand, Brendan took a minute to appreciate the view of the sea. This was his favorite part about living in Tramore. As they continued on toward the Promenade, Brendan was tempted to ask his aunt about the man that had Ellen staying put in their small town. But he refrained, not wanting to intentionally stir things up, especially when his thoughts were only a hunch.

It didn't keep him from worrying though. Too many old concerns came to the surface because of what happened with Katelyn.

His cousin had made her choices, but she'd been manipulated and used by Noirin's father. Promises had been made and then broken. When Katelyn had told the man she was pregnant, he had scattered to the wind like dandelion fluff. The worst part was that no one had known about the man. Katelyn had kept her relationship with him a secret.

Ellen had a good head on her shoulders, and Brendan wanted to believe she would make better choices. But then they had all thought the same of Katelyn. And then there was his birth mother, Glenna, the sister to his aunts, Shay and Mary.

"What's on your mind, Brendan?" Mary asked.

"Secrets."

She turned to look at him, but he kept his eyes trained on Noirin as she walked with Shadow. His aunt quietly waited for an explanation.

"Too many secrets," he said after a few moments.

"Are you thinkin' about Glenna?"

He shrugged. "Mostly about Katelyn, which led me to thinkin' about her, somethin' I don't do very much. And I know she and Katelyn were nothin' alike, but what I can't help but wonder, sometimes, is why some women allow themselves to become pregnant and alone."

Mary sighed. "Glenna is an easy one. We had terrible parents, both of them alcoholics and..."

"But you and mum turned out just fine. Did things the right way. Terrible parents aren't an excuse," he interrupted, his tone slightly frustrated.

"We never turned to drugs like Glenna did. It's a game changer, Brendan. It will put you in places you never imagined goin'."

"I suppose," he said, a hint of that old resignation in his voice. He'd had this conversation before, with both of his aunts, but still found it hard to accept.

"Then what about Katelyn? As far as I know she never used drugs, and we grew up with great parents."

"That one, I can't quite figure out and neither can Shay. Once, Katelyn had mentioned a boy in her last few years of school. He was a real *eejit*, had said some really terrible things about the way Katelyn looked. Maybe she believed him, until the first person to come along took notice of her—the wrong person. We suspect she had a touch of 'bad boy attraction'."

"But why keep her relationship with him a secret?" he added.

"I imagine your folks wouldn't have approved. She knew that and was afraid of losin' him."

"And look what it cost her?"

Mary reached for Brendan's forearm. Knowing she wanted to say something important, he called out to Noirin and asked her to stop and make her way back. He turned to his aunt and gave her his attention.

"What's this all about, Brendan? What's really botherin' you?"

Before answering, he looked to make sure Noirin and Shadow were still making their way toward them. "I worry about Ellen. I want her to be happy, like you and Mum. I don't want her makin' a decision that will cost her, the way it did Glenna and Katelyn."

Noirin reached them and motioned for Brendan to pick her up.

"Use your words, sweetheart."

"Up, please," she obeyed. She did so with her slightly muddled way of speaking, the way most people with Down Syndrome spoke, due to the low muscle tone in their tongues.

Brendan lifted her and kissed her on the cheek before resuming their walk and waiting for Mary to respond.

"Well, you know *I* worry about Ellen. I began doin' so the moment I knew she existed."

Noirin laid her head on Brendan's shoulder while he carried her. The moment he heard about Katelyn's pregnancy, he worried too about his little girl, wondering what kind of life she would have. He knew what it was like not knowing one's parents. Then when Noirin was born and they realized she had Down Syndrome, he worried even more. The fretting continued over the years, and often he found himself worrying about her future. Brendan wrapped his arms tighter around her, and she responded by tightening her hold around his neck.

The three of them walked quietly for a long bit

until Noirin signaled she was ready to be put down again. Shadow wagged his tail with exuberance as he resumed his position by the little girl's side.

Mary was the first to break the silence. "It's almost time, isn't it? Is that what's also got your worry up?"

"Yeah. I hate thinkin' about these next few weeks—the waitin' game. Every time, I feel as if I'm holdin' my breath until the results come back."

Every year Noirin had to undergo heart and leukemia testing, two conditions that children with Down Syndrome were susceptible to.

"When's the appointment?"

"Two weeks from now."

"Want me to come?"

"Mum wants to try and make it. It depends on how she's doin'."

"If she can't go with you, I can stay with her," Mary offered. "I know she'll be worried too." The two sisters were close and had always spent as much time together as possible. Ever since his aunt's diagnosis of multiple sclerosis, they made being with each other a priority.

Mary put her arm around Brendan's waist and hugged him to her side. "I don't know how you do it, love. You have the weight of the world on your shoulders."

He reached over to pat her hand. "It's only by the grace of God, I tell ya. That, and I have big shoulders."

She smiled up at him. "That you do, my boy. You're a keeper, you are. I knew it from the moment I first held you in my arms."

Shortly before Glenna had fled, he thought to himself, a little too morosely. The moment she'd decided he wasn't worth keeping.

Chapter Seven

Lauren couldn't see the sun dipping below the horizon. There were too many buildings in the way, but she could see the effects as the sky changed colors from bright reddish orange hues to deep blue tones. She admired the view from the terrace of her flat. It hadn't rained that day, which had some of the town folk out and about a little later than normal, long after the shops had closed.

She looked around and was pleased with the choice of residence she had made. After leaving the café, she walked the streets making her way toward Summer Hill Road, where she stopped to admire the Holy Cross church, with its asymmetrical tower and spire.

Curious about the interior, she stepped inside to admire the architecture. She was greeted by a parishioner who told her about the style of the church and a little bit of its history. Construction started in 1856 and was completed in 1871. The architectural style was Gothic Revival, and it was stunning. It reminded her of something straight out of *Wuthering Heights*.

The town was positioned on the north-western corner of Tramore Bay, and the church had been built on a monumental site overlooking the town. A tour of the cemetery proved to be insightful, as the parishioner explained some of the symbols on the gravestones.

Lauren's favorite had been the emblem for the band and drum guard.

European military units had popularized the idea of a fife and drum corps, a musical ensemble made up of fifes and drums. When Lauren asked the parishioner what a fife was, she explained that it was a small flute with six to eight fingers and no keys. The corps was employed to provide rhythm on marches but also to help with morale amongst the soldiers.

The Irish band and drum guard served a similar purpose in the Irish military, but were made of drummers and bagpipers, dressed in their clan's plaid-tartan kilts. After she had been left by the parishioner to wander along the gravel path to admire the headstones alone, she thought about music and its significant role in nearly every aspect of one's life.

Music wasn't simply the background noise to life. It made life beautiful. Even in the face of the death and destruction that war brought, music was there to soothe the troubled soul, to give calm and peace to the fearful, to give comfort to the grieving.

It was the one thing she hadn't turned away from during her time of loss. She'd embraced music, held onto it like a drowning woman, and it had helped to keep her sane. It had been the only thing that hadn't changed when her world had fallen apart.

Lauren smiled at a couple who walked by her terrace and waved. She'd finished her dinner a short while ago—something light, salad and chicken. Thinking about music and her time in the cemetery reminded her that she needed to refocus on living. She knew her weight was an issue. She'd lost too much of it the past year and knew she needed to take better care of herself.

She remembered the day her mother-in-law had stopped by the house the second week after Christopher had died and had forced her to eat. She wasn't leaving until Lauren had eaten the bowl of chicken soup dished up for her.

Angry and wanting only to die, Lauren had stormed into her room.

"I'm not leavin'," Stacey shouted through the closed bedroom door.

A minute later, Lauren heard Christopher's mother talking loudly on her cell phone to her own mother. "Hi, Angie. Yeah, I'm at Lauren's and she won't eat." There was a pause. "I know she promised she would, but she's not." There was another pause. "No, she didn't let me in. I used my key. Yeah, I think you should come back to Tacoma. I don't know what else to do."

Lauren opened the door before Stacey could hang up with her mother.

"Wait," Stacey said into her phone. "She's goin' to the kitchen." She paused. "Yes, she's eatin' the soup."

"Lauren," her mother-in-law said as she handed her the phone. "Your mother wants to talk to you."

"I don't want to talk to anyone. I'm eating. Isn't that good enough?"

"For now," Stacey replied, in her matter-of-fact

way, her Irish brogue more pronounced than normal. "It's a start. I'll give you that. But while you eat your soup, I'll make one thing very clear. If you do anythin' so foolish as to waste away to nothin', killing yerself, you won't be doin' yerself any favors. You'll be hurtin' us, the ones who love you, the ones who are still here."

Lauren didn't say anything but sat like a stone statue in the chair staring at the bowl.

"Did you hear that, Angie?" Stacey paused. "Yes, I'll stay until she finishes. I'll call you soon."

Eventually, Lauren finished the soup before quietly going to her room and closing the door behind her.

Her mother-in-law had been right, and it had been enough to keep Lauren alive. Her thoughts turned to the realization she'd had earlier today about the thaw and how it had begun, just as she'd hoped it would.

She pulled out her phone and began Googling recipes that required more than tossing some vegetables, greens, and roasted chicken into a bowl. She wanted to find a dish with butter and lots of it. She landed on a creamy alfredo recipe.

Barking in the near distance caused her to look up from her phone. Noirin and a chocolate Weimaraner were walking toward her terrace. The sweet girl was waving and smiling at her.

"Well, hello, Noirin. How are you?" she asked as she stood from the chair and approached the gate. "Who do you have with you?"

"His name is Shadow."

Lauren was now on the sidewalk. She bent down to pet the excited dog. "Hello, boy. How are you?"

The dog grew more excited as she spoke to him.

"He likes you," Noirin said with a giggle.

"Ooh, and I like him." Lauren paused to look at the little girl. "And I like you too," she added while gently tapping Noirin's nose with her finger.

The girl giggled louder. "I like you too, Miss America."

Lauren smiled. "Please call me Miss Lauren."

"Would you like to see some of my books?"

Lauren remembered their conversation earlier that morning about reading and loving books. Before she could answer, Brendan and Mary approached.

"Da," the little girl spoke excitedly. "Can Miss Lauren come up to look at my books?"

Brendan smiled at Lauren before reaching down for his little girl. "How about another time *a leanbh*?" He saw the confused look on Lauren's face and translated. "*A leanbh* means 'my child' in Gaelic."

Lauren nodded in understanding. "Are you fluent in Gaelic?"

"I am. My parents insisted I learn. Same with my cousin—right Aunt Mary?"

"Yes," the older woman replied. "Although my Ellen wasn't as diligent about learnin' as you were."

Brendan turned his attention back to his daughter. "It's gettin' late, Noirin, and you have school in the mornin'."

"Tomorrow?" the girl insisted.

Brendan looked at Lauren. "If it works with Miss Lauren's schedule, we can make that happen."

Noirin clapped her hands together, gleefully. "You'll love my books, Miss Lauren. Won't she, Aunt Mary?"

The older woman grinned and ruffled her grand niece's hair. "That she will, sweetie." Looking at Lauren, she asked, "How've you been?"

"Good, getting acclimated to Tramore. I met your daughter this afternoon. We had a good long talk. She's very nice."

A proud smile pulled at the corners of Mary's mouth. "She's a wonderful girl. I'm glad the two of you met. Oh, I almost forgot. I found someone who might be interested in sellin' his car, cheap. It's a manual transmission. Do you know how to drive one?"

Lauren's face fell briefly. "Unfortunately, not. I wonder if I could learn?"

Mary looked at her nephew. "Brendan knows how to drive a manual. You wouldn't mind teaching her, would you? You could go over to the parking lot off Cliff Road and practice there in the evenings. I'll watch Noirin."

"And Shadow," the little girl inter-jected enthusiastically.

Mary gave Noirin's chin a gentle squeeze. "Of course, Shadow will help."

All three of them looked expectantly at Brendan. "I'd be happy to teach you. Do you plan to travel much while you're here in Ireland?"

"Yes. I'd like to see as much as possible, of both

Ireland and Northern Ireland." She and Christopher had had a plan: Dublin, Belfast, but always the less travelled places like towns up in the western part of Northern Ireland.

"I'd also like to travel to Paris." *To remember*, she thought to herself. To remember the ten glorious days she'd spent there with the love of her life.

Brendan nodded approvingly. "Just Paris?"

She nodded. "So far, my primary interest is Ireland. I'm also here in Tramore to do some family research."

Mary looked pleased. "So, you have a touch of the Irish in you, do you?"

Lauren laughed thinking about her completely Asian looks. "I doubt there's any of the Irish lurking around in these genes," she replied with both fore fingers pointed at herself.

"You never know," Mary said with a wink.

They all laughed, and Lauren didn't elaborate about what the family research was for. Neither did Mary or Brendan press for an explanation. She liked them even more for it.

"Tell your contact, that I'd be interested in taking a look at the car. Do you have a mechanic you can recommend to look at the engine?"

"I do," Brendan offered. "My coworker's husband is the assistant manager at Martin's Auto Care."

"Terrific," Lauren replied.

Mary looked pleased. "I'll call my contact in the morning about a time to meet."

Brendan looked at Lauren. "I'll let you know about a time tomorrow to look at books."

At the mention of books, Noirin squirmed in her father's arms in excitement. "Books, tomorrow!" she echoed with glee.

Lauren felt a tightness in her chest for the little girl she was quickly growing fond of. "It's a date," she agreed, smiling at Noirin. She then looked at Brendan. "Speaking of dates, I have my first one with Shane in the morning at the café. We can talk about timing for books then." Turning back to Noirin, she asked, "May I join you and Shane as he takes you to school?"

The little girl clapped her hands in joy. "Yes!" she exclaimed.

They all said goodbye. Lauren watched them turn to leave, thinking again about the thaw. Surprisingly, it felt good.

The next morning when she opened the door to leave for the bakery, there was another pastry box waiting for her in the empty hallway.

She bent down to pick it up. This time, a cheese Danish greeted her. The crust looked flakier than the croissant she had the day before, if that were possible. Lauren thought about the grocery list in her bag with ingredients for chicken alfredo and smiled. She was off to a good start putting back on the weight she'd lost.

When she walked into the café, she looked for Shane in what appeared to be his normal spot and smiled when she saw him. He happened to look up and waved at her. She motioned toward the counter signaling she would place her order before joining him. He nodded.

After greeting the young man at the counter, she said, "I found another pastry box in front of my door. A cheese Danish. I don't suppose you remember anyone who may have ordered one to go?"

He looked apologetic. "I'm sorry, ma'am."

"Ah well, it was worth a try. I'll take a pot of your *Fifth of November*, please."

After paying, she made her way to Shane's table. "I have a bit of a mystery on my hands," she remarked as she removed her bag from her shoulder and placed it on the floor next to her chair.

"Is that right? I hope it's not too serious?"

"Someone has been leaving pastries at my front door. Yesterday it was a croissant and today a cheese Danish."

"Both are really delicious," Shane commented as he handed her a section of the newspaper he'd already folded and set aside for her.

"Thank you," she murmured while glancing at the copy of the *Irish Times*. "You wouldn't happen to know anything about the pastries, would you?"

"It wasn't me," he said.

She looked stumped. "It's probably Mary. I forgot to ask her when I saw her last night. She'd been on a walk with Brendan and Noirin."

"No, it wouldn't be Mary. She only gets up this early if it's an emergency. She works a lot of evening hours."

She reached in her bag for her journal, a sketchbook, and colored pencils and placed them on the table. "Is there a town welcoming committee I haven't heard of?"

"Not unless they've recently started one and forgot to mention it. What do you have there?" Shane asked while eyeing her pencils.

Lauren shrugged her shoulders. "Just some doodling."

"I'd love to see," he offered.

She didn't make a move to offer him her sketchbook. Instead, she said, "Ellen told me you were a famous artist."

"She exaggerates."

Lauren offered him a bemused smile. "I don't think so. I Googled you."

Shane's eyes twinkled. "You did, did ya?"

"You're amazing! No exaggeration. Have you always been an artist?"

"I've loved art for as long as I can remember. But it didn't pay the bills. So, I worked the family fishin' business and dabbled. Twenty-five years ago, I received my first big break, a showin' at a gallery in Dublin. And the rest, as they say, is history."

Lauren knew this succinct summary of Shane's life wasn't all there was to his story. Looking at his paintings the night before, she had seen every range of emotion flowing from his hand to canvas and knew the wells of his life ran deep. There was a lot of living in those paintings, pastorals, and seaside villages. And then there was the portrait of the elderly woman. The lines of her face expertly detailed, the skin appeared so soft that Lauren felt as if she could actually reach out and touch her face and it would feel like rose petals. While looking into the woman's bright blue eyes, she had felt as if she were staring into the depths of her soul. The painting was titled *Life in Shadows*. Appropriate, she thought.

"Is the elderly woman in your painting *Life in Shadows* your mother?" she asked her new friend.

For the first time since meeting him, Lauren saw the first of Shane's own shadows as his eyes turned slack, the brightness gone momentarily. It was a familiar look, one she had seen staring back in the mirror for the past year.

"I'm sorry I asked," she said and laid a hand on top of his.

He turned his hand over and gave hers a comforting squeeze before letting go. "You didn't do anything wrong, lass. I'll tell you about her one day. But for now, I am curious to see what you've drawn with those colored pencils." The smile and light were back in his eyes.

She couldn't help but return the warmth of his look and added in a teasing tone, "It will cost you."

"Is that so?" he asked with raised eyebrows, the lined skin of his elderly face crinkling with the effort.

"I'd love to have a lesson with you. I'll pay you, of course."

"Well, that's an easy price to pay for seeing your

work, and I won't accept your money. Now let me see what you've drawn."

Lauren hesitated for a moment before handing him her sketchbook. The first page was the coffee shop where she and Christopher had met. She'd redrawn it in the sketchbook she had purchased yesterday morning during her shopping trip.

"Colorful realism, with colored pencils," Shane commented. He looked up at her. "You do good work."

Her eyes lit up. "Really?"

"Really," he replied with a nod. "What inspired you to start this medium?"

"An artist by the name of Susie Tenzer." Lauren paused thinking of the art show she and Christopher had attended while visiting California on vacation. It had been a spontaneous stop as they had walked around the city of Brea, a few miles outside of L.A. They noticed a sign for the art show and decided to step inside. That's when she'd fallen in love with pencil art.

Lauren reached down into her bag and retrieved her tablet. She made quick work of bringing up Susie Tenzer's website to show Shane. "She specializes in architecture, which I've always loved. We did a commission with her, and sent her a picture of our house." Lauren paused when she noticed Shane glancing down at her wedding ring. The words *we* and *our* must have caused him to wonder who she was referring to. Like him, she wasn't ready to talk about someone so close. It still hurt too much. He sensed her hesitancy, understood, and didn't press for an explanation.

She continued, "And as you said earlier, the rest is history. History being that, unlike you, I dabble and do it for fun with no expectation of doing much more. I simply love it."

"You have talent. And I would never tell you that unless I meant it."

Her eyes brightened once more, pleased by the older man's compliment.

Shane continued. "But I don't do pencil drawings. I paint." He was referring to the lesson she had wrangled from him.

"Oh, that's okay. I want to learn something about painting too."

"What do you do for work?"

"I'm an accountant."

"Really?"

Her tea arrived before she could respond. "Thank you," she said to the bakery worker. She began to add her cream and sugar and said to Shane. "Do you think I'll grow tired of this tea before the year is out?" she asked before taking a sip of the steaming hot blend of goodness.

"I don't think so. I've been drinking the chai here for years. So, what made you decide to become an accountant? It seems so left brained for an artist."

She gave Shane a mock look of reproach. "First, I'm not an artist, just a dabbler, and now you generalize and stereotype?"

He chuckled. "Don't we all?"

She laughed while reaching for the box that held the

Danish. Tearing the pastry in half, she placed one piece on a napkin and gave it to her new friend.

"Thank you," he said.

"You're welcome, and yes, all of us generalize and make stereotypes. I'm sure there's been about half a dozen swirling around the café since my arrival in town."

He must have known she was referring to her eastern looks because he said, "It's not often we see Asians in Tramore and most of the time they're from that part of the world. I think you're the first Asian American, I've met in our fair city. And I've been around a long time."

"I'm sure. I did my research about Asians in Ireland before coming here. And when it comes to stereotyping, I'm guilty of it too. I arrived here with my own notions about the Irish."

"Is that right?" Her older friend looked amused. "And what might those be?"

"Well, the food of course. Everyone knows the Irish aren't known for their cuisine."

"And have we proven the stereotype true?"

Lauren took a bite of her Danish and looked thoughtful as she chewed and savored the sweet morsel. "Well, let's see, I know this Danish was made by Ellen, who is as Irish as they come, and it is incredibly delicious. But she was trained at Le Cordon Bleu, so this doesn't count. I'd have to taste real Irish cooking before I could either deny or confirm the stereotype."

Shane gave a hearty laugh. "Ye'r somethin'

fierce, lass. Well, your painting lesson will include some Irish stew."

She gave him a smug look. "Not too shabby for a left brainer. A painting lesson and a free meal."

He laughed again before taking a bite of the Danish.

They continued talking, the newspaper forgotten, both lost in the pleasure of getting to know one another. Being with Shane caused her to miss her father. After they walked Noirin to school, she would call her dad and tell him she missed him. She'd tell him about her new older friend and how Shane reminded her of him, and how she couldn't wait for him and her mother to meet the artist when they arrived for their visit in May. After so much grief, Lauren's father would be pleased with the touch of joy he would hear in her voice. The truth was, she was pleased to hear it too.

Chapter Eight

During their walk, Lauren felt her heart slipping toward adoration for Noirin. She had never met a more wonderful child. The little girl had immediately taken her hand and then Shane's in the other and held them both all the way to school, chatting as she walked between them. She talked about the latest book she was reading, and Shadow. Her love for the dog was as bright as it was for the people in her life.

Toward the end of the walk, Noirin mentioned her upcoming doctor appointment and how it was to make sure her heart was healthy. The words had caused Lauren's gut to clench in concern. After dropping Noirin off, with big hugs and even a goodbye kiss on Lauren's cheek, Shane explained how Noirin had to be checked annually for potential heart conditions and leukemia due to her Down Syndrome.

When they arrived at the bakery and saw Brendan, Lauren's heart grew heavy at what she knew this father must be going through. Oblivious to what they had been discussing, Brendan greeted them with a smile. "Thank you for walkin' with Noirin, Lauren. It's all she talked about before bed and when she woke up this mornin'."

Lauren's heart slid further toward adoration and verged on the edge of love for the child she had just met.

"You are so blessed to have her, Brendan." There were a million unsaid meanings behind those words—regret that she didn't have the same, sorrow at the potential loss of this bright light in a dim world, and the fear of growing to care for someone she might lose again.

He nodded as if he understood the hidden meanings behind her words. "I do love her somethin' fierce. How was your mornin'?" he added glancing between the two of them.

They both smiled. "I managed to finagle an art lesson and a free meal out of Shane."

"Is that so? You two sound serious." There was a teasing look in Brendan's eyes.

"She told me that we Irish don't know how to cook."

"Hey," Lauren protested, "that's not true, I said it was a generalization, not a truth." She looked at Brendan. "He agreed to prove me wrong."

"You and Noirin should join us," Shane offered Brendan.

"When?"

"On Saturday."

"I think we can manage. What's on the menu? I'll bring somethin'."

"Stew, so bring some of your soda bread. World famous," he said to Lauren.

She gave Brendan a pleased look. "Do I have to wait until Saturday to try some?"

"First, Shane exaggerates—like most of us Irish do. And how about I bring a loaf from the bakery, and you can have some this evenin' when you come by to look at Noirin's books?"

"That sounds great."

They talked about a time and then Lauren had to say goodbye. She had an appointment with the man who was selling his car. They were scheduled to meet, mid-morning, at Martin's Auto Care.

Brendan and Shane watched Lauren leave.

The older man had a wistful tone in his voice. "I would have loved having a daughter like her."

Knowing his friend's history, Brendan continued to watch Lauren, and said, "I know you would have. Thank you for being so good to Noirin."

Shane looked at Brendan. "Thank you for letting me be a part of her life."

"I wouldn't have it any other way."

They stood there watching the door till Lauren was no longer in sight. After a few moments, Shane spoke. "She's wonderful, Brendan. I want her for you. You're the son I've never had, and she would be perfect for you."

Brendan's gut clenched from the shock of his friend's words. He hadn't wanted to hear them; to face them. The feelings had been stirring around since the moment he'd seen her weeping through her window, but he'd tried to ignore them. He had submerged them every time he'd spoken with Lauren. While Brendan felt excited about the prospect of seeing her tonight, so she could look at Noirin's books, he squashed the longing that rushed forward. When she had looked at him a moment ago and told him how blessed he was to have his daughter, knowing there was far more behind the words than he understood, he panicked. When he wanted to turn down the invitation to dinner with her and Shane, and had said yes instead, he wanted to take it back.

"There's a problem with your wantin', Shane. She has a ring on her finger."

The older man looked at him. "Her husband is gone."

"How do you know?"

He paused. "Because I know."

Brendan saw the flash of pain wash over his face, a look that rarely made an appearance. But when it did, all those closest to Shane knew the history behind his sorrow and who it was reserved for. With his voice low, Brendan said, "You may be right, but for her, he's still here. I won't put myself through that again."

Shane simply nodded. "I understand. I'm glad you accepted my invitation for Saturday. No backing out. I won't play matchmaker; that wasn't my intent in invitin' you, but I also won't let you avoid her. She's my friend, and I plan to enjoy every moment I have with her until it's time for her to return home."

"Well, you need to talk to Aunt Mary, because she already has me givin' her drivin' lessons on a manual transmission, if she buys that car."

"I'll do what I can, but you know your aunt. Speakin' of aunts, I'm on my way to see your folks before I'm off to Dublin. Do you need me to take them anythin'?"

The thought of his ailing aunt brought about its

usual twinge of sadness. "No, I'm goin' there after I pick up Noirin. Dad is makin' dinner."

Shane nodded. "Oh, and Lauren is an accountant. Your dad is lookin' to sell his accounting firm in the next year or so. There might be a reason for her to stay."

Brendan gave him a pointed look.

Shane held up his hands, and said, "I'm only pointin' out the possibilities. It's not the same as matchmakin'."

Brendan shook his head in exasperation and turned to leave. "I'll see you tomorrow."

"The day after. I'm stayin' over in Dublin."

"Does Lauren know? Won't she be lost without you tomorrow?" The teasing was back in Brendan's voice.

"I told her, and she was devastated. Have John save my paper for her in the mornin'. I told her he would."

"Yeah, yeah, of course you did. Be safe," he added as his friend left the bakery. The good mood that had started off Brendan's day was gone. He wouldn't think about the woman who had captivated his daughter and was chipping away at his defenses.

Ellen stood outside Lauren's door and hesitated for just a moment before knocking. She wasn't sure if she was home and would be okay if she wasn't. Ellen felt a little awkward about inviting the American, out of the blue, on her trip to Dublin to visit with the tea supplier.

It had been her mother's idea. Mary had explained

how Lauren was looking to explore Ireland while she was here and how she would feel better if Lauren made the first trip to Dublin with someone she knew. What perfect timing. And since Ellen and Lauren seemed to hit it off, why not invite her?

Holding the pastry box in one hand, she knocked with the other. *Here goes*, she thought to herself as her insecurities bubbled to the surface.

She heard movement behind the door and felt her nerves kick in a bit.

When Lauren answered, she smiled and then looked at the box and said, "Oh, it must be you leaving the pastries for me in the morning."

Ellen gave her a bewildered look, which caused Lauren to add, "Or not. Come in."

"Hi," Ellen greeted, as she entered the flat. "Someone has been leavin' pastries by your door?"

Lauren nodded. "What a nice surprise! Have a seat." She pointed to one of the chairs by the fireplace. "The first morning I was here, it was a croissant, and this morning it was a Danish. No note or anything."

Lauren didn't seem to mind the unannounced visit, and it caused Ellen's nerves to subside. "Well, it must be one of our regulars. Maybe it's Shane."

"Nope, I asked him already and he says it's not him. How many other regulars do you have?"

"Too many to count."

"Hmm, well we'll see what happens."

"I'm sure it's just someone in town excited to have

a long-term visitor from America. Word spreads quickly around here."

"I suppose. So, how are you? It so nice to see you again."

Ellen smiled and held out the pastry box. "I brought you some of my petit fours."

"Ooh, that sounds wonderful! How about I make some tea. It's about that time, isn't it? Let's go into the kitchen, and we can talk in there while the tea is brewing."

Ellen noticed the fresh pasta on the counter. "Did you make your own pasta?"

"I did. Hey, are you free tonight? Would you like to join me for dinner? Later, I'm going upstairs to look at Noirin's book collection. She invited me last night and we have a date. You could come with me."

The last trace of the tension in Ellen's shoulders left with Lauren's invitation. "I would love to have dinner with you, but I'll have to take a rain check on the book review. I have to be up super early for work."

"That's right; I forget how early bakers start their days. Well, I'm glad you can at least stay for dinner."

They chatted about how Lauren was adjusting to Tramore while the tea was steeping. The conversation continued toward gardening while they drank and ate the petit fours.

"Are you sure you wouldn't mind me taking up a section of your garden to grow my own vegetables?" Lauren asked.

Ellen's parents had some acreage on the outskirts

of town and grew their own produce for the family and the bakery. Brendan purchased the herbs and vegetables from them.

"We have plenty of space, and Mum and Dad would be happy to have you use some of it. I moved back home when I finished at Le Cordon Bleu. When the second bakery opens in late summer in Dunmore East, I'll be movin' there. It's only about a twenty-minute drive."

"Are you excited about the new bakery?" Lauren asked before taking a sip of her tea.

"Beyond excited. It's what I've dreamed of since startin' at Le Cordon Bleu. I love Brendan for givin' me free rein and total trust. He didn't even bat an eye when I told him I wanted to do high tea."

"It's nice that the two of you are so close."

Ellen gave her a hesitant look. "Do you have siblings?"

Lauren shook her head. "I was an only child, and my cousins lived on the east coast, so we didn't see each other often. I have lifelong friends I grew up with, but when I moved to Tacoma, we couldn't see each other as often."

"That must have been hard. When Brendan moved to Dublin, which is such a short drive, it just about killed me I missed him so much. I can only imagine how hard it must have been for you. How far is your home from Tacoma?"

"Far. I'm from a town called Hammond, Montana. It's not really a town, but we do have a post office. The area is ranch land. My parents are cattle ranchers. The nearest town to us has a population of four hundred and sixty-eight people, last census count."

Ellen raised her eyebrows. "And here I thought Tramore was small."

Lauren chuckled.

Ellen sat her teacup down and asked, "So, what took you to Tacoma?"

"School. I went to the University of Washington. Studied finance. I went from population almost nothing to over two hundred thousand people—and that doesn't include Seattle right next door."

"Sort of like me moving to Paris."

Lauren looked wistful for a moment. "That must have been terribly exciting?"

"It was. Admittedly, I was a nervous wreck, but it didn't take long to adjust. I was so focused on school. It was tough, so I didn't have much time to be nervous."

"Do you miss it?"

"Parts of it; but Tramore is my home. I always intended to come back. Brendan doesn't believe me. He can't figure out why I'm bakin' in his store when I could be anywhere in the world." She shrugged. "It's sort of like him movin' off to Dublin. He never truly left home. He came back every chance he could and then when everythin' happened to Katelyn." She paused at the sadness that always seemed to surface.

Laurens expression grew thoughtful. "Is Katelyn Noirin's mother?"

Ellen nodded.

"How long were they together?"

"Noirin was four when Katelyn passed."

"I'm so sorry," Lauren said, her voice soothing and low. "And how long were Brendan and Katelyn together?"

Ellen blinked for a moment in surprise and then realized Lauren didn't know the full story. "Oh, I'm sorry. I forgot that you probably don't know. Katelyn was our cousin."

It was Lauren's turn to look surprised.

"We all grew up together, Katelyn and Brendan were more siblings than cousins. He was raised by Katelyn's parents, Shay and Quinn. My Aunt Shay is my mother's sister."

"I had no idea."

"Aunt Shay was diagnosed with multiple sclerosis two years before Katelyn died. After the accident, it was too difficult for her and Uncle Quinn to care for Noirin full time. He had to keep his accounting firm and the bakery afloat to pay for the medical bills and Aunt Shay was declining faster than expected. But Brendan, who had loved Noirin from the moment he laid eyes on her, gave up his career in Dublin and came back to Tramore to raise her and take over the bakery. He was happy to do it. His heart was never in Dublin."

Lauren sat back in her chair. She looked stunned by what Ellen had told her.

Ellen was slightly puzzled by the American's reaction to her family's story. She sensed there was some of her own pain coming to the surface, but Ellen wouldn't pry.

After a few moments, Lauren spoke. "I was adopted, born in South Korea and placed in an orphanage a couple of days after I was born. I don't know the story behind my birth mother, but I can't help but wonder what would have happened if a relative of hers had loved me enough to keep me."

Lauren shook her head as if to chase away the errant thought. "But then I wouldn't have been loved by two of the most amazing people I've ever known."

Ellen's look softened. "So, you were happy then as a child?"

"Mostly." Lauren paused. "I couldn't have asked for better parents, but I won't deny how hard it was growing up in an area where no one else was like me. I was never treated badly by neighbors or friends, but I was different and there was no avoiding it.

"I don't blame my parents. They wanted a child so badly and were moved by the stories they heard about children in foreign orphanages needing homes. They never thought about how different I would feel living in Montana.

"My parents tried hard to help me embrace my heritage by teaching me about my roots and the culture of the country I come from. Things like introducing me to Korean food, which I never liked, mainly because they made it and didn't know what they were doing. After I moved to Tacoma, I fell in love with the food." Lauren smiled. "I've never told them this but their efforts to embrace my nationality only made me feel more different."

Ellen gave Lauren a look of understanding. "You never wanted to hurt their feelings because what they did for you was born out of love."

Lauren nodded.

She sighed. "Thank you for sharin'. I've always struggled with my looks. I feel totally insecure about them."

Lauren looked genuinely surprised by her comment, and Ellen could have hugged her right on the spot—would have, if she knew her better.

"What's wrong with the way you look? I think you're beautiful."

Ellen's eyes watered because she knew Lauren meant it. It was nice to hear it from someone besides her mother who had to say it. "It's silly but I have always felt too plain, too little—no height." She looked down at her chest. "And I missed my chance to wade through the size C cup gene pool."

Lauren couldn't help but smile and Ellen was glad she did. "Well, I think you're beautiful. You remind me of a little fairy, like Tinkerbell, and I just want to put you in my pocket."

It was Ellen's turn to laugh. "I wish I looked like you, exotic and gorgeous."

"Ha," Lauren said. "The first time a guy told me I looked exotic, I immediately thought of a stripper or a call girl. Not a pleasant thought." She smiled at Ellen, "I know it's stereotyping, so thank you because you meant it as a compliment. Unfortunately, I have a bad habit of taking things and holding them up to my issue of being different."

"I get it," Ellen reassured. "Did you feel that way when you moved to Tacoma?"

"No, not as much. There are a lot of Asians in the Sea-Tac area and where I went to school. It was a good move for me. Hard to be away from my parents, but good."

Ellen couldn't help but ask the next logical question. "So how are you doin' then in Tramore with the lack of Asian influence?"

"I'm good. I'm a visitor, so it's different. Even if I were Caucasian, people would still wonder about me, simply because I'm from America."

"Well, I'm glad you're here. I'd like to be friends."

Lauren's face lit up. "I would like that too, very much."

Ellen smiled and was no longer nervous about asking Lauren to join her on her tea trip to Dublin. "Mum mentioned that you wanted to go to Dublin. Brendan and I are scheduled to go in a couple of weeks to meet with our tea vendor. We have plans to put together some blends for the new bakery-tearoom. I'd love it if you could come. During our free time we could show you around."

"I would love that, and since I have idle hands, I'd like to help with the new bakery. I heard you mention to your pastor that you've been very busy with the work."

Ellen felt the flush of heat rise to her face and knew Lauren could see it because she asked, "Oh! Did I say something wrong?"

Ellen shook her head. "I uh, sort of, uh lied to Donal."

Lauren's eyebrows rose in surprise. "Oh, yeah?"

"I mean, I'm not a liar." *Great*, she thought to herself. Here she was trying to befriend this wonderful person, and she was setting herself up as a liar. "I uh, have been looking at different churches, but didn't want him to know—not yet. So I made up the first thing that came to mind."

There was a look of understanding in Lauren's eyes. "I understand. Does he know how you feel about him?"

It was Ellen's turn to look surprised before it was replaced by one of defeat. "Am I that obvious? Please, no one can know, especially Brendan. They're really good friends, and it would be so awkward."

Lauren reached over to place a reassuring hand on hers. "I promise I won't say anything. But have you thought about telling him how you feel?"

Ellen gave her a mortified look. "Are you kidding me? He has women throwin' themselves at his feet. Gorgeous women and he treats me like I'm Brendan's sister. I'm just an acquaintance to him, and he's never looked twice at me. No, I'm just better off findin' a different church and gettin' over him."

Lauren sat back in her chair. "Okay, if you're sure."

"Oh, I'm sure. And now, time to change the subject. How can I help you with dinner?"

It was the right thing to do. Donal was truly out of her league and Ellen was better off moving on.

Chapter Nine

"That was really good, Dad," Brendan complimented as he patted his full stomach. Noirin, who had finished her food and then climbed into her grandfather's lap, had quickly fallen asleep.

Quinn looked down at her. "Is she doin' all right?"

Brendan knew where the question was coming from. Fatigue was always a worry, worry that something more might be wrong. "She's good. She's just had a lot of excitement."

His Aunt Shay spoke up. "Mary and Shane told us about the American rentin' the flat next to the bakery, and how Noirin has taken a likin' to her."

"She has, like a duck to water. Lauren is very nice. Asian. I'm sure you'll meet her soon. As you know, she's become friends with Shane and had a nice chat with Ellen."

"Well, it's good to know she's friendly enough," his father commented as he cradled his sleeping granddaughter.

"How are you doin', Mum?" Brendan asked.

"I'm grand. Takin' things one day at a time."

He knew that one day at a time for her could be an undertaking. Her nerves had rapidly deteriorated since her MS diagnosis, and she now spent most of her time with a walker.

"I just wish I could do more to help at the bakery," she added.

His aunt was missed at Cups and Cakes. For as far back as he could remember, she was the lifeblood of the store, not only because she was a phenomenal baker, but because she had the personality to match, always the life of the party—that pull-yourself-up-by-the-bootstraps-and-forge-ahead kind of person.

As the oldest of the three Stewart sisters, she'd been the force that propelled them through their harrowing childhood. It saddened her that Glenna, Brendan's birth mother, hadn't made it through to the other side, but Aunt Shay wasn't so self-deprecating that she blamed herself. No, their parents held that honor—full responsibility for their broken family.

Before moving to Dublin, his aunt had told him that while she'd done everything possible to help Glenna, losing her had been her greatest sorrow. That had been before Katelyn's tragic accident and her own diagnosis of MS. Still, Aunt Shay was thankful for every day she had with those she loved, those who remained.

Brendan thought about his conversation with Shane earlier that morning and knew he should take a lesson from his aunt's playbook and her fearless, indomitable spirit. He knew he needed to try to be more like her.

"I know you miss goin' to the bakery every day, Mum. We miss seein' you. But you have a lot of people who love and care for you."

It was true. His aunt and uncle had many friends,

and despite her illness, they had a full social calendar and spent as much time as they could with their granddaughter.

"I do have a lot of people who love me," Shay replied, "but especially you, sweetheart. I'm blessed." She smiled at her nephew.

He leaned over and kissed her cheek. "I do love you, very much. I'm still plannin' to grow up and be like you, just like Dad always told me to."

She laughed. "I wouldn't change a thing about either of you. You're perfect the way you are."

He kissed her again before leaning back in his chair.

"I'm still plannin' to go with you to her appointment," she said.

"I'd like that. I can come by and pick you up."

"Quinn blocked off his calendar."

"I'd like to be there too," his uncle added.

"Well then, it's a plan."

They chatted for a while longer before Brendan cleaned up and packed away the leftovers. Content to have her grandfather hold her, Noirin continued to sleep.

When it was time to go, they woke her, and with a flourish of hugs and kisses, said goodbye before making the short walk to their flat.

A half hour later, there was a knock on the door. Brendan's gut clenched with awareness and anticipation at seeing Lauren again. He berated himself, and before he could even open the door, Noirin squealed in delight, "Lauren!"

"Yes, *mavourneen*, she's here."

Brendan's breath caught at the sight of her.

She was wearing gray slacks and a light blue blouse with a subtle floral print. Her long black hair was pulled back into a ponytail.

"Hi," she greeted with a smile.

"Hello, come on in."

She'd barely made it through the door before Noirin ran up to her and tugged at her hand to lead her to her room where her books were.

"You're here!" the small girl cried excitedly.

"I am. What book are you reading now?" Lauren asked as they entered Noirin's room.

"I'm reading *Peter Rabbit*."

"Ooh, that's a good one, one of my favorites. Tell me what's happened in the story so far."

Brendan leaned in the doorway for a moment longer listening to his daughter chatter away like a magpie and watched Lauren as she listened with rapt attention.

Standing there, watching her, Brendan knew it was only a matter of time before he lost the battle. He stepped away from Noirin's room and went to the kitchen to prepare her lunch for school. Later, he would pack her overnight bag for her sleepover with his parents the following night.

It was their Thursday night ritual. Brendan went to the book club meeting, enjoyed an evening of literature while Noirin spent the night with her grandparents. In the morning, Uncle Quinn would drop Noirin off at the bakery on his way to work. He paused while slicing up carrots for his daughter's lunch and remembered he would have to take her to school the next day because Shane was out of town.

The chatter from the other room kept him company while he finished Noirin's lunch and then emptied the dishwasher. When he was done, he took stock of the fridge and pantry and made a list of items to pick up at the store.

After a while, he realized that the chatter had stopped and he could only hear Lauren's voice, a soft cadence. He put down the pen and made his way to his daughter's room.

The picture before him stunned him. Lauren sat against the headboard with Noirin drawn to her side, her little eyes drooping in slumber. It's what he'd always dreamt of for himself: that *one-day family* with someone to walk alongside him, caring for the children they would have. Then he had a child, Noirin, and after a while, he learned to dream the dream again. This was the closest he'd come to seeing it as a reality. But this wasn't reality: it was a mirage that included a married woman, who was only here for a year.

Shane was probably right about her husband having passed away, but it was clear she was unavailable. Yet, he still wanted her, wanted this picture that filled all his senses, like a stunning painting at an art museum, like one of Shane's paintings.

She must have sensed his presence, for she looked up from the book and glanced toward the door where he stood. Lauren held his gaze for a moment before glancing down at Noirin.

"It seems, I'm putting her to sleep."

"It's your voice, very calming. Here let me get her." When he lifted her into his arms, he said, "Noirin, sweetheart, let's go brush your teeth."

"But Lauren is readin'," she protested in a sleepy voice.

"And you're fallin' asleep. Let's get you ready for bed."

When he returned with a still groggy child, he found Laruen straightening up her books and some of her toys. She had turned down the bed.

"Thank you," Brendan said as he placed his daughter on the soft sheets.

"Of course."

"Hugs," Noirin said to Lauren after Brendan had kissed her goodnight.

Lauren knelt beside the bed and hugged her for several long seconds. "Goodnight, Noirin. Thank you for letting me see all your books."

"Will I see you tomorrow?"

"I'm planning on it," Lauren answered while sweeping away the brown curls from her forehead. "I'll see you in the morning," she added before placing a brief kiss on her cheek. Lauren stood and gave Brendan an uncertain look before leaving the room.

He followed her out and closed the door.

Lauren stood in the hallway fidgeting with her hands. "I hope you didn't mind that I kissed her? I just reacted."

"Noirin has that effect on people." Not all people. Certainly not Eva who had bolted the minute she found out he was assuming custody of his cousin.

Lauren seemed to relax.

"I have some of my soda bread," he offered.

"Ah, the world-famous soda bread. I can't wait to try some."

"Would you like some tea or coffee?"

"Coffee sounds good. Thank you. May I help?"

"Sure. You can slice up the bread while I make the coffee."

After giving her a bread board and a knife, he set the kettle to boil and began measuring the coffee into a French press. "I hope Noirin hasn't been too loud for you below?"

"I haven't heard anything. How long have you two lived here?"

"For almost three years. My aunt and uncle own the bakery and the building. It's been in Uncle Quinn's family for two generations."

She paused mid slicing to look at him. "So, you're my landlord?"

"Yeah, don't worry. I won't hover or be too demanding."

She smiled. "I wasn't concerned about that. I'm just surprised that Mary never mentioned it."

He shrugged, as he spooned clotted cream into a small dish. "I didn't see the point in having her tell you. But since you've gotten to know my family, I didn't want to keep it from you either."

"That makes sense. Why make me aware if we never saw each other?"

"Right."

They chatted about the flat and what she liked about it while the water boiled.

"The coffee is ready," he said after pouring the hot water into a French press. "If you want to grab the bread board, I'll carry the tray."

Brendan led her to the dining room table. When they sat down, he poured her coffee. "How do you take yours?"

"Cream, please."

He handed her the cream and a small teaspoon, then plated a piece of soda bread for her. "You should have some of this clotted cream and jam with it. Would you like to try?"

"That sounds really good."

Brendan waited for her to take a bite before fixing his own slice.

She closed her eyes in pleasure as she chewed the bite and then opened them when she finished swallowing. "Wow! That *is* really good. I've never had Irish soda bread before. Are these raisins?"

"They're currants," he answered while slathering some of the cream on his slice. "When I make some for Noirin, I have to make them without the currants. I didn't even think about that when I set aside a loaf this morning. I gather you like them?"

"I love fruit any way it comes."

"Good to know."

"The coffee is good too. Thank you for this. Oh, I forgot to mention, I agreed to the car. Your friend, Peter, gave it a clean bill of health. He recommended some new tires, so I left it at the shop. Are you still up for some lessons?"

"Of course. Do you need me to pick it up for you tomorrow?"

"You don't mind?"

"I'd be happy to. I have to be somewhere tomorrow evening, but I could start teaching you Friday, after work, if Aunt Mary is free to watch Noirin."

"That sounds great. Is it difficult to learn how to drive with a manual transmission?"

"Not really. Once you get comfortable with easing your foot off the clutch, knowin' when to shift is a piece of cake." Brendan took another bite of his soda bread, then took a sip of his coffee. "How are you likin' it here?"

"Everyone is so friendly and inviting. I had a nice conversation with your cousin this afternoon. She came by for a visit."

"She's good people."

Lauren looked down at her cup, before glancing back up at Brendan. "She told me about Katelyn. I had assumed that you were Noirin's biological father."

It was his turn to look down at his cup. "It was hard hearin' about Katelyn's pregnancy. She wasn't married. The loser took off the moment he found out." He paused, and then looked back up at her. "When the test results came back showin' that Noirin had Down Syndrome, it was even more difficult. I think that's when Noirin became so special to me.

"There was no question she would be loved. It didn't matter to any of us if she had been born with two heads, we would have adored her. But knowin' she would have special needs, it did somethin' to me right here." He placed his hand over his heart. "She quickly became the light of our lives."

Brendan looked thoughtful for a moment. "Katelyn was a wonderful mother. For a while, she was ashamed of how foolish she'd been, but we never held it against her, and we all gained somethin' wonderful because of it: Noirin. And then—Katelyn died." He swallowed hard and held Lauren's gaze. The compassion in her eyes—it melted him a few degrees. "Did Ellen tell you how she died?"

Lauren shook her head.

"A sailin' accident. Katelyn loved the water and her boat, a sixteenth birthday gift from my aunt and uncle. She'd misjudged the weather that day. Her boat turned up empty a few miles down the shoreline."

"I'm so sorry, Brendan."

He nodded. "A couple of days later, we found her another mile down. It was the hardest time of my life. I'll never forget all that happened. I can still remember every detail. The phone call. The frantic drive from Dublin back to Tramore, searchin' all along the shoreline."

"Who found her?"

"One of the coast guard officials. I'm so glad it wasn't Uncle Quinn. He was ridin' with Shane on his boat.

I was with another friend also searchin'. Aunt Shay was strugglin' with her multiple sclerosis and couldn't help us look for Katelyn. She was at home with Noirin and Aunt Mary." He leaned back in his chair. "I'll never forget the phone call from Uncle Quinn tellin' me they'd found her and how I needed to get home to Aunt Shay. I could barely understand him through his sobbin'. He was too far up north and was afraid the news would get to her before either of us could be there.

"I was devastated. We all were. But we managed to pull ourselves together and got busy pourin' every ounce of ourselves into Noirin. She still talks about Katelyn. We watch videos of her. We don't want her to forget her mother."

"I'm so glad you all do that for her. It's important. And how wonderful of you to be there for her, to be her father! You do it so naturally and with so much love."

"Noirin makes it easy. She's an unaffected child, good tempered, so lovin'."

Lauren smiled. "She is wonderful." Her look sobered. "While walking her to school, she mentioned her doctor's appointment. On the way home, Shane explained that children with Down Syndrome are susceptible to heart issues and leukemia. I had no idea."

He felt the worry tighten in his chest. "Every year, the weeks leadin' up to her appointment, I feel like I'm holdin' my breath. I try not to worry, but it's impossible not to when you have a child. You worry about everythin'."

Lauren's lips parted slightly as if she wanted to say

something, but she didn't. Her look softened in understanding, but she waited for him to continue.

"But worryin' never changes anythin', so I try to put it aside, as much as possible, and focus instead on being in the moment." He glanced down and then back up. "Easier said than done."

"So true," she finally commented. "I couldn't help but notice the painting in your living room. Is it one of Shane's?"

"It is. Do you want to look at it?"

"Does the sun rise every morning and set in the evening?"

Brendan laughed. "I guess that's a yes."

He followed her as she made her way to the painting and watched as she looked at their friend's work.

Lauren was quiet for several long moments while she studied the painting. Finally, she spoke, "It's Katelyn and Noirin."

"Yes," he said as he looked at the painting of his cousin and daughter dancing in a field of red poppies, the sun shining brightly down on them, joy filling every space of the canvas.

Lauren continued to stare at the painting while she spoke. "While looking at his work online, I could feel the emotion." She paused. "Seeing one in real life, it—it leaves me speechless." She turned to him then, her eyes wet. "I'm so sorry for your loss, Brendan." Her voice trembled as she spoke. "Thank you for, everything. I'll see you later," she added, before she made her way to the door and left.

Brendan stood in the middle of his living room, his own emotions a mess as he stared at the closed door. Loss. It was a hard path to cross, like hovering over the edge of a steep gorge with a raging river beneath and a fire-breathing dragon at your back, knowing that escape lay on the other side. Brendan was even more certain Lauren had set upon her own path of loss. Was she close to the other side?

Chapter Ten

Lauren lay on her bed face up staring at the ceiling. She didn't cry. Sometimes she felt as if she'd already shed a lifetime of tears and that no matter how much harder life got, she wouldn't have any more to let go of.

The poppies. Staring at Shane's painting and seeing them reminded her of her own pain, all those moments in Dr. Moore's office when she'd stared at the Georgia O'Keefe print, wondering how she would take her next breath. Seeing Shane's painting had shifted her own suffering, backdropped it, as it were, against the pain that Katelyn's family had endured, a family she was growing to care for. Their suffering was like hers, and it scared her.

She turned onto her side and thought about her conversation with Ellen earlier that afternoon. Lauren had enjoyed every minute of it. It had felt so good to talk to another person about one's insecurities and then laugh over them. Cooking dinner with Ellen had been a further unexpected pleasure. It had been easy to be herself because no one knew about her pain. Her family, her friends, her co-workers back home, for each of them her suffering was an open book. They walked on eggshells around her, careful about what they said, how much they shared about their lives, because they were living theirs while she remained stuck in her grief.

For the longest time, she'd stopped being herself. But today she remembered how much she enjoyed who she was, what she was like and was beginning to relish the wholesome feelings it produced. The joy she had felt, it was genuine.

Then she'd seen Brendan with Noirin, something that always managed to tie her up inside. The tenderness he showed his daughter and the unwavering love, it exuded from him like rays of sunshine. It left her wanting and afraid of the wanting.

When she started this journey, her goal had been simple: to want again. To want to live, to want to experience what life had to offer. She hadn't anticipated the fear that would accompany the wanting. When she heard the details of Katelyn's death, it reminded her that life was also about losing. It would always be about losing.

Life is a gift. Lauren blinked rapidly as the thought pulsed through her mind, trying to reach down and push past the fear. It caused her to think about the gift Christopher had given her, the gift that unknowingly had prepared her for this journey, this passage through the grieving that still haunted her.

Six Years Ago

"So, where are we going?"

"It's a surprise. I'm not telling you," Christopher replied with merriment in his eyes as he put the car in gear.

All he had told her was to pack a weekend bag. He

had woken her early, in his sweet gentle way of doing so, with a soft kiss to her forehead, then to her nose, ending with a tender caress along her arm.

While she readied herself for the day, he had prepared breakfast to go, egg, bacon, and cheese sandwiches with coffee in travel mugs.

It was their second wedding anniversary, and Christopher had told her a couple of months ago he had plans... a surprise.

She could tell by the direction they were driving they were headed for the coast.

"We're staying at a bed and breakfast in Ocean City?" she guessed.

He tossed her a sideways glance. "Would you stop trying to guess. You're not getting even a hint."

"Not even one tiny little one?" she coaxed.

"Nope."

"I have ways of convincing you, Christopher." Her voice grew low and sultry.

He took his eyes off the road to look at her before reaching for her hand and lifting it to his lips, shifting his gaze back on the road. He continued to hold her hand; their fingers intertwined while he maneuvered the car onto the highway. Lauren gave up trying to pry their destination from him and simply enjoyed the anticipation.

For the rest of the drive, they listened to their play list, enjoyed the scenery, and talked about their future.

When they arrived at the coast, it wasn't a bed and

breakfast Christopher had arranged but the rental of a small yacht.

"It's wonderful!" Lauren exclaimed as they stood on the dock staring at the blue and white Monterey bobbing in the water.

"I thought we'd sail south."

Lauren turned to him, a pleased smile on her face. "This is a nice surprise, baby. Thank you." She stood on her tip toes to kiss him.

When they went below deck, they took a few moments to survey the details of the small, cozy space. The cabin was done in white leather and cherry wood finishes, with a small kitchen and a king size bed with a moon roof for star gazing.

She looked inside the stocked refrigerator and pantry and realized Christopher had planned everything including the meals for the trip. On the end table, she saw a stack of their favorite board games, and copies of their favorite movies.

"You thought of everything!"

"Are you excited?" he asked while reaching for her.

"I am, but you know it's going to be hard leaving it all behind."

"If we like it that much, we'll start saving for our own."

"Oh, I think we're going to like it," she agreed with a grin.

After unpacking, they set out for the open sea and made their way south, looking for signs of whales and sea lions along the way.

As the sun began to dip in the western sky, they went below deck to make dinner. After they finished the shrimp and lobster stir fry, with basmati rice, they took their food above deck to enjoy it while watching the sun set. For dessert, they fed each other coconut ice cream topped with mangos, and added a few stolen kisses in between bites.

It was the eve of their anniversary, and they celebrated by making love under the cover of darkness with only the stars above and the fish below for company. They touched and tasted as if they had all the time in the world.

Spent and content, they held each other in the warm balmy night and savored the moment, the luxury of their surroundings and the vast open sea.

Easing up on her arm, Lauren looked at Christopher who had his eyes closed, his breathing still slightly labored. She kissed his mouth and placed her hand to his chest where she could feel the beating of his heart, a comforting feeling, something she often did after they made love.

"Thank you, sweetheart."

He opened his eyes to look at her, saw the look of adoration behind her gaze, and smiled. He turned to his side and propped his head on his hand. "I love you," he said.

She closed her eyes at the rush of emotion that filled her. How she loved him, desired him, wanted to be like him!

He kissed her eyelids. "You make me so happy, Lauren." When he saw the tear escape from beneath her closed eyes, he caught it before caressing her cheek.

She buried her face into his neck, savoring the scent of his skin. "Is it possible to be this happy? I want this forever, Christopher. Every day I get to wake up with you by my side, and I know that everything is right with my world. You're everything I ever hoped for. When I think about how we might have never met, it kills me."

"We would have met, eventually." His hand stroked the small of her back.

"How can you be so sure?"

"Because we were made for each other. I'm convinced of it. If it hadn't been for spilled coffee, it would have been something else, like simultaneously reaching for the same piece of fruit in the grocery store or standing in line at the bakery and realizing we ordered the exact same thing. Somehow, we would have known, would have been drawn to each other. But we don't have to worry about that," he added, "because we're here together and completely in love with each other."

Lauren smiled. "I do love you."

Christopher kissed her forehead before rolling onto his back and drawing her to his side so they could gaze up at the stars and pick out the different constellations.

The next morning, over blueberry pancakes, Christopher gave Lauren her anniversary gift, an envelope wrapped in a bow.

"What's this?" she asked while shaking the envelope, playfully, as if it might give her an indication of its contents.

He laughed before giving her a brief kiss on the lips. "Happy anniversary, sweetheart."

"I have something for you too." She reached into her beach bag and pulled out a gift-wrapped box.

"You first," he insisted.

Lauren smiled as she removed the ribbon and then opened the envelope.

"It looks important," she remarked as she removed the piece of paper. She paused and looked up at him. "Is it a trip to Ireland?"

He shook his head.

She unfolded the document and stared at the contents for what seemed like forever. When she looked up at her husband, her lips were trembling, and she couldn't speak.

His eyes were filled with tenderness. "If anything happens to me, Lauren, I want to know that you're taken care of, that you have the ability to live life to its fullest."

The paper fluttered from her hand. She watched it fall and stared at it lying on the floor of the Monterey.

Christopher reached for her hand. "Lauren," his voice laced with concern. "Lauren, please look at me."

When she did, there were tears in her eyes. "I can't think about this, Christopher. I'm supposed to die before you. I can't think about this. Why, why would you give me this? I don't need a life insurance policy for you. I need you." The last few words were said with force and more tears before she raced down the stairs to the cabin.

He sat above deck—stunned and dazed. It wasn't the

reaction he had expected, but then how foolish of him to think she would be happy! It had seemed like a good idea at the time, this urge to know that his wife, the woman he loved more than anything, would be cared for, should something happen to him.

Christopher waited a few moments before going below deck.

He found Lauren lying face down on the bed sobbing into the pillow.

He sat beside her and rubbed her back, wanting to take away her sorrow, something he had never meant to cause.

"I can't lose you, Christopher. I'll die if anything happens to you."

He felt the tension tightening in his neck.

"Lauren, look at me, please."

When she didn't turn over, he asked her again. After a third time, she finally complied.

"Lauren, you can't say things like that. If anything were to happen to me, I need to know that you will live." His voice was tight, his brows furrowed in concern.

Panic coiled in her eyes. "How? How?" she cried.

He reached for and held her in his arms. "You would find a way, and you would do it because you love me, and because I would want you to, need you to."

Lauren cried for a while longer, grief filling her as if she'd already lost him.

"I'm sorry for making you sad, sweetheart. I only wanted to give you a gift that would last beyond our time together."

As he held her and comforted her, she prayed, desperately prayed that her time to depart this world would come first, for she truly didn't know how she would manage to live without him.

The memory of that day haunted Lauren frequently since Christopher's death. He had wanted her to live. When she finally came to terms with his gift on that second anniversary of their life together, he'd made her promise that if anything did happen to him, she would live, no matter what. That she would use the gift he'd given her to forge a new life for herself.

It had been a long, difficult place to arrive at. But she was fulfilling the promise she had made that day in the belly of the Monterey while it bobbed on the currents of the Pacific Ocean. A part of her was happy, while the rest of her simply missed her husband even more. But then she would always miss him, and nothing would ever change that.

Chapter Eleven

Life *was* a gift. Holding Noirin's hand while she walked with her to school helped to remind Lauren of what Christopher had meant.

That morning, she had gone to the bakery at what was becoming her usual time for tea and to enjoy what was becoming a daily gift. Today what greeted her by the door was a queen ahmahn, a French butter cake that was more like a caramelized croissant but shaped differently. It was exquisite, and while on a break, Ellen had stopped by her table to give Lauren the history of the queen ahmahn, a pastry from the Brittany region of France.

She had chatted with Ellen for a few minutes before the pastry chef headed back to the kitchen. Lauren returned to the newspaper Shane had thoughtfully instructed John O'Carroll to give her when she arrived. He was a nice kid. She realized that on weekdays he worked from opening up until it was time for him to leave for school, and then all day Saturday. The bakery was closed on Sundays. Lauren had also met Aine Doyle and realized she was Peter's wife, the mechanic who had inspected the car she'd purchased.

Lauren hadn't been sure if she'd see Noirin since Shane wasn't there to walk her to school and was pleasantly surprised to see her running into the bakery at her regular scheduled time.

"Miss Lauren!" the little girl greeted her with such happiness that it tugged at her heart.

Brendan was right behind her. "She insisted on seeing if you would be here, before she went to school," he said.

Lauren smiled with pleasure at Noirin before bending down to the child's level and taking her hands. "I'm here, angel."

"Dadai says that Mommy is with the angels. So, am I one of her angels too?"

"You are absolutely the best angel that your mother has. Do you know why?"

Noirin shook her head, her eyes growing slightly wider.

"Because she needs you to take care of your dad and the rest of your family while she's with the other angels. It is the most important job of all."

At the thought, Noirin wrapped her arms around Brendan's hips and pressed her face into his thigh. "I'll take good care of you Da," she concluded before looking up at him.

He reached down to draw her up into his arms. "You already do a fine job, *mavourneen*. I love you," he added before giving her a kiss.

Standing to her full height, Lauren basked in the love between father and daughter and then received an invitation from Noirin to join them on their walk to school. How could she refuse?

They walked the first few minutes talking about the

weather, which looked as if it would pour any minute. The adults had come prepared with golf-size umbrellas, while Noirin wore wellies and a raincoat. She looked sweet in her waterproof boots decorated with pink peonies, and her green and white polka dotted raincoat.

"Do you always walk to school?" Lauren asked.

"Yup," Noirin replied. "Shane likes to walk."

Brendan looked at Lauren. "Unless it's pourin' down sheets, Shane prefers to walk than drive. A lot of our rain is that steady trickle, which is actually quite nice to stroll around in."

"My first day here it poured most of the day, but I'm used to it. So, what are you two doing tonight?" she asked casually.

"Sleepover with *Maimeo* and *Daideo* while Dadai has his book club meeting," Noirin replied excitedly.

"That's grandmother and grandfather in Gaelic," Brendan interpreted.

She gave him a grateful look for the translation and said to Noirin, "That sounds like so much fun. What do you like to do when you stay with them?"

For the rest of the walk to school, Noirin chatted about what she liked best about staying with her grandparents.

After dropping Noirin off at her classroom, with goodbye hugs and kisses for both of them, they made their way back to Cups and Cakes. A few minutes into their walk, the heavens opened up. They quickly raised the large umbrellas.

"Let's go this way." Brendan pointed to a building

across the street. "I know where we can take cover for a few minutes while the worst of it falls."

She followed him across the street toward a bright yellow building. The sign read 'Lanigan's Pub.' They slipped under a nice-sized overhang which managed to keep them dry. He knocked on the door, and a few moments later, a man in his late forties appeared from the back.

"Brendan, hey, come on in and out of the rain," he said while stepping aside to let them through.

"Thank you, Declan. We were on our way back from the school when it started bucketing down out there. I knew you'd be here. Do you mind if we stay until the worst of it is over?"

"Of course not. Brianna and I are in the back preppin' for service. Make yourselves comfortable. Would you like some coffee? I have some fresh in the back."

"I'm fine. By the way, Declan, this is Lauren. She's our visitor from America, the one who's renting our flat," Brendan said.

"It's nice to meet you, Lauren. Brianna, my wife, is elbow deep in meatball mixture, but she'll come out when she can. Would you like coffee?"

"It's nice to meet you too and no thank you. I just had tea."

The pub owner nodded. "Well, make yerselves at home. I need to head back and prep. If you leave before I come back out, no need to lock up."

"Thank you, Declan. I'll have Cody bring along

some surprise goodies when he delivers your bread. On the house, of course."

Declan patted his slightly round stomach and said, "You're killin' me, Callery. How am I supposed to shed these extra pounds if you keep sendin' me Ellen's croissants? You know I can't resist them."

"No croissants then," Brendan said with a serious look.

Declan's face fell. "I changed my mind, I'll take the croissants," he added with a wink. "It was very nice to meet you, Lauren. Come back soon and try my Brianna's meatballs. You'll be amazed."

"I will and nice to meet you," she replied with a wave.

They took a seat at a table near the window.

"He's not jokin'. Brianna makes the best meatballs, ever. For years, my aunt has tried bribing her for the recipe, but she won't budge."

"That good, huh?"

Brendan nodded. "That good."

"I'm looking forward to trying them. I can't get over how friendly everyone is. Is this how it is all over Ireland?"

"Pretty much."

"In America, or at least in the neighborhood where I live, we barely know each other. We have rare conversations over the fence with the next-door neighbor, *if* we happen to be doing yard work at the same time. The people on the other side of us have a privacy fence, so we see even less of them. Maybe that's how it is in the city."

"Somewhat," Brendan agreed. "I lived in Dublin for a few years and there is less of this there. Were you born and raised in Tacoma?"

"No, I'm from Hammond Montana. Our closest neighbor was four miles away. We were good friends, but socializing always had to be planned around work. My parents are cattle ranchers. They own the cattle on a thousand hills."

"That's a lot of hills," he commented with a smile.

She returned the smile. "It's an expression, a reference from scripture."

"Yes, I know. Do you go to church?"

Lauren shook her head.

"Not a believer then?"

Her look hardened. "Oh, I believe. I'm just not on speaking terms with the Almighty right now." *Please don't ask me why*, she silently pleaded. Last night she'd realized even more that she needed the anonymity of her grief that this gracious country offered, a place where no one knew who she was, only what she chose to share. That anonymity would help her to get on with her life. For so long, her grief had defined her, and she'd gotten lost.

Brendan didn't ask her why. He simply said, "The Almighty will be there when you're ready to resume conversation." He paused for a moment to study her face. "I'm sorry if I upset you last night."

Lauren had been afraid that her abrupt departure from his flat would cause him to wonder. "You didn't upset me. I was sad to hear about Katelyn's death and seeing that painting, with Shane's incredible talent behind every brush stroke, it made me very emotional, that's all."

"He painted one for all of us, Aunt Shay and Uncle Quinn, Ellen and Mary, each one different. I'm sure you'll get a chance to see them all before you leave."

"I would really like that. How was it living in Dublin?" she asked, moving the conversation onto safer topics.

"I liked Dublin, but I missed home. I was a finance major and became a stock trader for the Irish equivalent of the New York Stock Exchange—much smaller of course. The goal was to become an expert investor, make a nice sum to invest in properties, continue to reinvest, and eventually move back to Tramore. Things just happened sooner than I had planned."

"Ellen told me about the new bakery in Dunmore East. I'm an accountant, so I have a head for business and numbers, but I'm also good with my hands. I can wield a paintbrush and lay tile. I told Ellen I would love to help her with the bakery, on a volunteer basis."

"You'd do that?" Brendan asked.

She shrugged. "I've been here less than a week, and already I'm realizing that I'm not good at playing the lady of leisure role." After Christopher died, she'd taken a leave of absence because she couldn't get up in the mornings, could barely breathe, much less put one foot in front of the other. Eventually, she went back to work, and then that's all she did—worked herself senseless, trying to numb the pain. Two weeks before leaving for Ireland, she'd handed in her notice.

Brendan leaned back in his chair. "That's awfully kind of you to offer your help. I'm buildin' the bakery from the ground up. Found a good-sized empty lot on the out-skirts of Dunmore East. I have a general contractor coor-dinating all the construction work, but we could use some help with settin' up the books and supply ordering system. Ellen's fabulous with her hands too, but not so good with the business side of things. I've given her free rein over the design because she's really talented in that area too. I'm sure she would love your help with pickin' out paint colors, fabrics, and wall art. We'll have a wall dedicated to quality prints of Shane's work, our artist in residence."

"That sounds great," Lauren replied. "Does Shane offer lessons to the public?"

Brendan chuckled. "He'd end up in prison for mur-der before he knew what hit him."

Lauren arched her eyebrows.

"Just kiddin," he added. "He has done a few lessons, but sparingly. He had a professorship at a university in Dublin. He didn't like it much. Artists are too sensitive; he's included himself in that stereotype."

"I think it's how artists are wired. Criticism is hard to take, for anyone, but I think it's harder for those who pour their heart and soul into their work, whether the work is good or not. Shane agreed to give me a lesson, when I begged for one."

Brendan's look had a touch of mirth to it. "Yes, I remember a lesson and dinner. He must really like you a lot. Do you paint?"

"Oh, no. I'm a colored pencil person. I just dabble but would like a lesson on painting. I've always wanted to learn. There is something really appealing about art and the desire to be an artist. I know I'm not talented enough, but it doesn't keep me from wanting to learn."

"It's good to expand your interests," Brendan commented.

"What do you like to do in your free time?"

"I'm a reader."

"That's right, the book club?"

"Yes, the book club," Brenden echoed. "Shane started it just after I left for Dublin. The year after Katelyn passed and things had settled down with me and Noirin, he forced me to attend, and worked it out with my folks to watch Noirin. I look forward to it. I wasn't always a big fan of the classics, but now I love them. Music is my other passion."

"Do you play?" she asked.

"I strum a little with the guitar, but I mostly just enjoy listening. I like all kinds, even opera."

"Even opera?" Lauren asked with a hint of surprise in her voice.

He nodded.

"I've never been able to develop an appreciation for it."

"That's okay. Not everyone has to like it all."

Lauren held his gaze for a moment. "I'm adopted."

He gave her a look of surprise, one that quickly changed to understanding. Brendan waited for her to continue.

"We have that in common. Orphaned or given away by our biological parents, me, you, and Noirin." She paused, and he could sense her hesitancy. "I'm falling in love with your daughter, Brendan. I hope that's okay?"

What did he say to that? It tied him up in knots with a combination of joy and apprehension. He'd lost so much, and he was afraid of losing more. Brendan knew it was only a matter of time before he'd fall in love with Lauren Ross, and in a year's time, his heart would be broken. She must've taken his thoughtful pause as a negative.

"I'm sorry. Maybe I shouldn't have said anything."

He leaned forward placing his forearms on the table. "I want my daughter to be loved by as many people who want to love her, but I do worry about what will happen when you leave."

Lauren nodded. "And that's why you're such a good father. I will keep in touch with her. We'll Skype regularly, and I'll visit."

Brendan gave her a look of acceptance. "Even if that never happens, even if you leave and forget, it wouldn't be the wrong thing for her. I can't protect her from pain. Noirin will eventually learn the value of people who come and go in our lives, and to appreciate the parts of them they leave behind." He was speaking to himself, encouraging himself not to push Lauren away, to embrace the time he would have with her. Yet the cost might be greater for him than for his daughter. It was a sobering thought. "I'm happy you're falling in love with Noirin, Lauren. She's obviously smitten with you."

Lauren smiled. Her shoulders relaxed. "I could never forget her or not want to be with her. Thank you, Brendan."

He smiled and then looked out of the window. "It looks like the rain has slowed. Shall we head back?"

Chapter Twelve

Ellen arrived at the bakery a half hour before the meeting. After work, she usually took a nap on book club nights because she had to be back so early the next morning. She'd forgotten to set her alarm and didn't have enough time to fix what she'd planned to make for her contribution to the meal. Deciding to go with her back-up dish, bruschetta, she realized she didn't have tomatoes. Knowing they had more than enough at the bakery, Ellen threw everything she needed into a bag and headed to Cups and Cakes.

While she chopped the tomatoes, her mind drifted to Donal, and she quickly pushed the thoughts of him away. Not too long ago, it was nothing to spend nearly every quiet moment daydreaming about him, spinning in her mind a fictitious love story. Ellen felt foolish when she thought about it now. Little girls daydreamed about that first kiss with the man of their dreams, their wedding day with said man. Little girls did those things, not grown women who were approaching their thirties.

She heard the bell chime on the front door. "Back here, Brendan," she called as she started on the onions.

"Hey, Ellen."

Her breath caught. It wasn't her cousin who had arrived but Donal. She stilled the knife she was using and looked up at him. "What are you doin' here?"

He looked a little taken aback. "Shane bribed me into comin', but I don't have to stay."

Ellen felt bad for being rude. She had been surprised, for Donal never came to the book club meeting. He didn't like fiction. "Don't be silly. You just surprised me. I thought you were Brendan. How did Shane bribe you?"

Donal sat the casserole dish he was holding down on the stainless-steel counter. "He promised to donate a painting for the charity auction in return for three months' worth of meetings."

Ellen finished chopping the onions and moved onto the basil. "You must be desperate for items to auction."

"Some. I just know Shane's paintings will bring in a lot of money for the food pantry, and it will be a big draw."

Ellen looked up from the chopping board and glanced at his casserole. "Do you need to warm that up?"

"Nah, I'll nuke it right before it's time to eat. It's still warm."

"What did you make?"

"Cheesy hash brown potatoes."

"You're killin' me, Donal. You know I can't resist your potatoes."

"I didn't think you needed to resist them."

"Well, I do."

The man could cook. Another one of her daydream scenarios, her and Donal in the kitchen together, cooking, stealing kisses while adding a pinch of this and a pinch of that to whatever they were making

"Can I help?" he offerred.

Ellen looked up from the chopping board. "No," she said a little too abruptly, not wanting to stir around anymore of her foolish dreams. She didn't want to have a real memory of him in the kitchen with her.

"All right then," he said, a puzzled look on his face.

She was saved from having to make an excuse for her abruptness by the sound of the door chime.

Donal left the kitchen to see who it was.

Ellen blew at the bangs that had fallen in front of her eyes. "I could murder you, Shane," she muttered to herself.

The rest of the group began to trickle in, making it easier to ignore Donal. She kissed her mother when she arrived and spoke with her friend Rachel and her husband Matthew. They were the only married couple who attended together. The rest of the group was made up of singles, a few widows and widowers, and college students. It was a diverse group of people with varied backgrounds and beliefs which made for interesting conversations.

And now there was Donal, for at least three months. Ellen felt frustrated and contemplated skipping out on the meetings until he'd paid off his debt. She took a bite of the cheesy potatoes and shot a pointed look at Shane, who happened to be looking her way.

What? he mouthed, a look of concern on his face. Julia, one of the college students, stole his attention before he could walk over and ask what was wrong. Relieved, because she had no quick excuse for the look she'd given him, Ellen stood to re-fill her cup. Donal followed her.

"What did you put in your bruschetta?" he asked while he waited for her to finish with the ice scoop so he could refill his own cup.

"Olive oil, lemon, basil, and garlic."

"May I have the recipe?"

"I didn't use one. Just eyeball it and taste as you go," she replied before turning to go back to her seat with Rachel and Matthew. She was being rude, and it made her feel worse, but she couldn't help it. Being around Donal wasn't good for her. No, this would be her last meeting until the fine young pastor was out of the picture or until she could find someone else to fall in love with, someone who would love her back.

"Is everything okay?" Rachel asked when she took her seat.

"Remember how I said I never wanted to go on a blind date and how I didn't want you settin' me up?"

"Yeah, you said you'd never talk to me again."

"Well, I've changed my mind." She looked at Matthew. "Were you the one tellin' me about that guy you work with who lives in Dunmore East, where the new bakery will be?"

He nodded. "James?"

"That sounds right. If he is still available and interested, set me up."

"Well, I know he is still single. I'll mention it to him tomorrow."

Before her friend Rachel could ask any questions, Shane began the book discussion.

Something was wrong with Ellen. Donal could feel it, had sensed it when he ran into her at the café the other day talking with the American. He finished wiping the last table. He'd stayed back after the meeting to help Brendan tidy up the bakery.

"Does Ellen seem okay to you?" he asked his friend who was sweeping the floor.

Brendan paused and leaned on the handle of his broom. "She seems fine to me. Did somethin' happen?"

Donal shrugged. "She seems off, not her usual chipper, talkative self. She's abrupt and has been missin' church because of the work at the new bakery."

Brendan raised his brows in puzzlement. "We're still under construction. Maybe she's spendin' her Sundays on the design and menu." Brendan hesitated for a moment. "This stays between us, clergyman-parishioner privileges, but I think what's wrong with Ellen is a guy."

"A guy?" Donal asked as he leaned against the counter. "Is she datin' someone?"

"She says no, but I can't figure out why she's here in Tramore. I even told her that the other day. She says she loves it here and there isn't a guy."

"Does she date?" he asked.

"Not often," Brendan replied.

Donal had only been in Tramore for a little over a year. It was his first pastorship out of seminary and a two-year missionary stint in Thailand. He'd never seen Ellen with another man. The thought of her dating someone did funny things to him. Ellen had always been a friend, related to his good friend. He enjoyed talking with her, seeing her bright face looking back at him from the congregation, listening to his message as if she couldn't get enough.

He also felt comfortable with her. Unlike the other single women in the church, Ellen never showed up at his office with a prepared meal and comments about how a busy, *single* pastor needed a home-cooked meal every once in a while. She'd never given him veiled pleading looks to be asked out. Ellen wasn't one to bat her eyelashes or make overtures at him. Yes, he definitely felt comfortable with her, and suddenly, he felt uncomfortable with the idea of her dating and being with someone else. It bothered him that he felt that way, something he'd have to think about.

He started to wipe down the counter, the last thing that needed to be done for the night. "How's the American?" Donal asked his friend, changing the subject.

When Brendan didn't answer right away, Donal glanced his way and found him staring toward the front door as if he were a million miles away. "Brendan," Donal called.

His friend blinked and then looked at him. "She's nice."

So, Brendan had heard him.

"She told me this morning that she's falling in love with Noirin."

"I gather, she's been spending some time with her. That's nice."

"Noirin can't seem to get enough of her. Last night, she invited Lauren up to look at her books. Lauren, by the way, treats my daughter like a normal person."

Donal knew the story of Eva. He and Brendan had become fast friends since his arrival in Tramore. Both of them were single, yet he noticed that women weren't bringing Brendan casseroles. They made a joke about it and how it was because Donal was much better looking. It was a joke, because while they were both attractive men, Brendan took the lead in the looks department. He had the height, and those Robert Downey Jr. looks. However, having a seven-year-old daughter with Down Syndrome didn't shine the spotlight of eligibility brightly onto Brendan's singlehood.

And for some reason, the idea of being a pastor's wife held some sort of appeal to the women who pursued him. Donal could only guess that they must have viewed the role as a position of status or importance. Though the opposite was true. His mentor had even warned him about the challenges a pastor's wife faces—the isolation, the difficulty in making true connections with other women in the church. It was one of the reasons Donal hadn't been interested in finding a wife at this point in his life. That and the fact that he hadn't met anyone who nudged him in that direction.

He looked up from the counter and asked Brendan. "How do you feel about Lauren fallin' in love with Noirin?"

His friend pulled out a chair and sat in it. Realizing he wanted to talk, Donal made his way to the table and took a seat across from him and waited for him to speak.

"I don't want Noirin to be hurt when Lauren leaves, but I also know it's part of life, the leavin'. If Lauren wants to love my daughter while she's here, then who am I to deny her that?"

"But?" Donal encouraged.

Brendan shot him a pointed look and narrowed his eyes. "How do you do that?"

"Do what?"

"Don't give me that 'I have no idea what you're talking about' look."

Donal leaned back in his chair and shrugged, "It's my super Spidey senses."

"Yeah, and I'm Iron Man."

"Well, you do look like him."

"No, I don't."

"Yes, you do."

It was Brendan's turn to shrug. "But seriously, how do you know there's a but in there?"

"Is there?" Donal grinned.

"You mean you don't know?"

"Not hundred percent, but I sensed one."

Brendan threw him an exasperated look. "Again, how do you do that?"

Donal leaned his elbows on the table. "You're serious? Well, maybe it's the minor in psychology I earned in undergrad or maybe it's because I'm called to do this.

Maybe it's because I know the number that Eva did on you, how much you loved her, how surprised you were that you didn't know that side of her. The part of her that could walk away so easily because life with you could become messy for a time. Or maybe it was the fact that she wasn't even willin' to give it a try. And now, you have this perfect stranger tellin' you she's fallin' in love with your daughter, but she's unavailable." He paused. "I noticed the wedding ring."

Brendan looked at him, his mouth agape. "Definitely not the minor in psychology but a gift," referring to his ability to read people. "Shane has spent some time with Lauren, and he's pretty sure her husband has passed away. But you're right, she's unavailable and only here for a year. I don't know if I'm willin' to risk gettin' hurt again. The more time I spend with her, the harder that will be."

"Yeah, that's a tough spot to be in."

"So, what do I do? Avoid her to protect myself? Deny Noirin a friend she'll always remember? Trust Lauren to have Noirin to herself and let them do things together without me?"

Donal looked thoughtful for a moment. "It's hard to say. Noirin *is* gettin' older. Maybe after spendin' a little bit more time with Lauren, just to be sure you can trust her to take Noirin to do things together, it might be safer to let them have time alone. Then take it from there."

Brendan nodded. "I already told her I would teach her how to drive a manual transmission. She bought a car to use while she's here."

"That will give you more time to get to know her." Donal paused. "Well, you know me. I like playin' things safe, so I'm probably not the best person to give people relationship advice."

Brendan gave him a knowing look. "It's better not to rush into things. Trust me."

"You didn't rush into things with Eva."

"Not at first. But it's funny how I didn't notice the little signs while we dated. She rarely asked what I'd like to do, where to eat, or what movie to see. We liked the same thing, so it never dawned on me that she suggested most everythin'. I just went along. When it came to her friends, I didn't realize how superficial things were. All they ever talked about was who did what on vacation, or their latest shopin' adventure. There was never any depth to our conversations, to their conversations. I loved her, but I know now it was a comfortable kind of love. It was missing that kind of love that grabs you by the heart and holds on until you can't see straight... makes you never want to see straight again."

It was Donal's turn to look thoughtful. "You're worried that you might feel that way with Lauren?"

Brendan wouldn't look at him while he spoke. "Last night, I left Lauren with Noirin, and while they talked books, I was in the kitchen doin' chores. A while later, when I walked into Noirin's room, I saw Lauren readin' to my little girl with her drawn to her side, and—it did a number on me. I wanted that, wanted what I saw to be my reality. Not just the picture they made but the woman herself."

Brendan shook his head as if to clear it. "I've only known her for a few days, and I'm already in trouble."

Donal reached over and patted his friend on his shoulder. "Well, no matter what happens, it will be an interestin' year. So, do you really think there's a guy in Ellen's life?"

"It's a feelin' that's all. Probably nothin'." He paused to look around the café. "I think we're done. I've got to get up early. Thanks for the help, man."

"Sure thing."

As they closed up the bakery, Donal continued to wonder about Ellen and the spark of interest that had sputtered to life.

Chapter Thirteen

"I'm never going to learn how to drive this thing," Lauren moaned as the Toyota Corolla jerked to a stop.

"Never is a really long time," Brendan commented patiently from the passenger side of the car.

"What if I can't figure this out?" Her voice was loaded with frustration.

"Then you'll sell the car to recover as much as you can, and you'll look for an automatic. But you'll get it. We've only been doin' this for fifteen minutes. What seems to be the hardest part?"

"The timing. I can't figure out how to release the clutch and press the gas without the car jerking."

That pretty much summed up the whole process. Brendan wanted to chuckle at the obvious but didn't. Since she was having a hard time articulating what was challenging her, he decided to take it back to the basics. "Okay, put the emergency brake on and don't start the engine. Practice pressin' and releasin' the clutch. Get a feel of how it moves." After a few minutes he asked, "How does it feel?"

"Okay, I guess."

"Press the clutch in and turn on the engine. I don't want you to worry about the gas right now. Go ahead and ease off the clutch, slowly. Do you feel that? How the engine is boggin' down. It wants to move. Slowly, release the clutch. Do you feel it movin'?"

"Yeah," she replied a little uncertainly.

"It's okay. We're movin' in first gear and you haven't pressed the gas. Go ahead and break. Now let's keep doin' that a few more times until you get used to releasin' the clutch."

They clutched and braked for about fifteen more times. "How does that feel?"

Lauren looked at him and smiled. "I think I'm getting the feel of it. I can tell when the engine is ready to engage."

"Good. Now let's try using the gas."

An hour later, Lauren was feeling so comfortable, she was ready to drive out of the parking lot. When she asked if she could, Brendan responded with, "How about we make that a part two. You still have to learn how to release the clutch on a hill, but I'd like some daylight for that."

Lauren's eyebrows knit together in worry. "Are hills hard?"

"Not terribly, but you do need to practice. Let's keep drivin' in the lot a bit more, until you're really comfortable with shiftin'."

A little while later, Brendan drove them back to their flats. There were hills on the way, and at each one, he stopped and had her listen to the way the engine sounded as he engaged the clutch. When he parked the car she said, "Thank you so much, Brendan. I really appreciate you teaching me."

RAIN ON A GOOD DAY

"Do you feel comfortable?"

"I do. I'm not stalling anymore, and the shifting is easier than I thought."

"Good. Just remember to listen to your engine. Before you know it, you'll be shiftin' without thinkin' about it. I still worry about you drivin' since you Americans drive on the wrong side of the road."

"Hey," she retorted with mock offense. "Besides, you've got that backwards. We drive on the right side; it's you Irish who drive on the wrong side."

Brendan chuckled while removing the key from the ignition and handing it to her. "We'll have to agree to disagree. Do you want to come up and say good night to Noirin?"

Her eyes lit up with pleasure. "I would love that."

As they climbed the stairs to his flat, Lauren said, "I hope it wasn't too weird letting you know how I feel about your daughter?"

He glanced at her. "I think it was nice."

She smiled a thank you. Noirin must've heard them in the stairwell, for she'd opened the door before they'd reached the landing.

"She's been watchin' out the window the last ten minutes," Mary said, as they entered the living room, Shadow barking out a happy greeting.

Noirin launched herself at Lauren, so happy to see her friend. "You came up!"

"I did. I came to say good night."

Noirin wrapped her arms around Lauren's neck then

128

rested her head on her shoulder. She smiled at her dad and Mary.

Brendan tousled her hair. "How would you like it if Lauren read you a bedtime story?"

"Both of you," the little girl said.

"I think that's a fine idea, Noirin," Mary added. "I'll leave you both to it."

"Thank you, Aunt Mary, for watchin' her," Brendan said before kissing her cheek.

"Of course. We'll do it again soon. How did it go, Lauren?"

"I didn't start off well, but I eventually got it."

"I knew you would. Well, I'll see you three later."

"Bye," Lauren said.

Noirin made a move toward Mary for a goodbye hug. "Bye, my love," Mary said as she hugged the little girl.

When Mary was gone, Brendan took his daughter into his arms. "Let's get you ready for bed, and Lauren can pick out a book."

A short while later, they sat on the couch together with Noirin nestled between them.

Brendan didn't look at the book while Lauren read but chose to focus his attention on her, studying her profile with her angled cheeks and the outline of her jaw. Her elegant neck was fully exposed due to the ponytail she wore. He'd realized it was her preferred style, easy and unpretentious. He focused on her full lips as they formed to make the sounds of the words she read. Her voice was animated to match the story, inflecting at the right moments and softening when the story called for it. He knew when the story was coming to an end. He'd read it many times before. He focused his attention on the book.

"I love that story," Noirin commented in a cheerful but sleepy voice.

Lauren closed the book and looked at her. "It is nice. I've never heard of it before. What was your favorite part?"

"When the baby turtle finds her mum. I miss my mum."

Lauren looked at Brendan who nodded for her to go ahead. He appreciated her consideration to have him address his daughter's comment first. She was considerate and good with people.

"I know you miss your mommy; you'll always miss her and that's okay. I heard she was wonderful. It makes you miss her even more, doesn't it?"

Noirin nodded and then yawned.

"You're knackered, sweetheart," Brendan commented. "Let's go to bed."

His daughter stood and reached for Lauren's hand signaling her to join them.

After the seven-year-old was settled in her bed with a round of good night hugs and kisses complete, Brendan and Lauren made their way to the living room.

"I'd like to make dinner for you both sometime next week, a thank you for your help with the driving lessons."

"That's very nice, but not necessary."

"I'd really like to," she encouraged.

He nodded. "That would be grand, thank you."

"You're welcome. See you in the morning."

He smiled. "Have a good night."

When she left, Brendan plopped down on his chair and leaned his head back. He closed his eyes and felt the tension building in the back of his neck. Separating himself from Lauren was going to be difficult. He thought about dinner at Shane's tomorrow evening, and now dinner next week, and realized he was just going to have to deal with it.

Shane took one more taste of his stew before replacing the lid. He opened a cabinet to retrieve bowls and then opened a drawer for napkins, choosing a deep shade of blue. He glanced at the clock as he headed for the table. He had an hour left before Lauren, Brendan, and Noirin were due to arrive, enough time to finish the clouds he was working on for the painting he'd used as collateral to get Donal to come to the book club meetings.

He smiled to himself as he picked up his palette and looked at his scene. He'd sketched in the clouds, the sea, and the dock from a village of his imagination. Most of his paintings were from his imagination. He'd preferred painting that way from the moment he first picked up a brush. He didn't have anything against artists who liked to replicate the world around them. He'd simply felt that the real thing had already been done justice. But something from his imagination, now, that was all his.

He looked away from his fictitious dock and glanced

at his beloved portrait, *Life in Shadows*, the picture Lauren had asked him about. The woman in the painting, with her bright blue eyes, stared back at him. She was his very own Mona Lisa, his crowning glory. It hung in his studio, his most sacred place.

He sighed and focused once more on the colors he had been using for the sky, and thought about his bargain with Donal. Shane had no idea if bribing his young friend to attend the book club meeting would spark the interest Shane sensed that Donal could have for Ellen. If only he'd pay attention for a moment. Ellen was in love with the young pastor, but for whatever reason she'd kept her feelings to herself. And then there was Brendan, falling for Lauren, afraid of losing again.

He lifted his brush to the canvas, happy with the colors he'd blended. Shane had never intended to play matchmaker with anyone. But the last time he'd dreamt of his Mona Lisa, he started sensing things—the way Brendan looked at Lauren, the pain embedded behind the young woman's gaze, a pain that mirrored his own. And recently, he'd noticed the longing in Ellen's eyes when she looked at Donal and thought no one was watching. The pointed look she'd given him at the book club meeting confirmed what he'd suspected. He may have mouthed *What* to her, but he'd known.

Love was all that mattered, and he'd given his nudges. It was all he would intentionally do. The rest would be up to the four of them.

Shane pulled back from the brushstrokes he'd made.

Happy with the results, he mixed a different shade of blue. He loved the light in his house perched on Old Waterford Road; it was slightly elevated with no buildings to block the light. His studio, of course, had the best light. He'd helped it along by replacing two of the walls with picture windows and adding skylights. In the corner, he had set up a second easel and a table for Lauren's lesson on Monday, the day they planned to get together to paint. She was really talented with colored pencils, and he was curious to see how she would do with the oils, especially since she'd never used them before.

Shane paused to look at the clock on the wall. They'd be here soon. He had a few more things to do before they arrived. He made good time of putting away his supplies and taking care of the last-minute details.

A short while later, the doorbell rang.

"Hello," Shane greeted the three of them, already looking like a family. They all smiled back at him before Noirin reached for him.

"*Pog*?" he requested before she happily obliged and kissed him. He hugged Lauren, then Brendan. "Did you walk?" he asked while showing them in.

"I drove," Lauren said proudly. "Brendan wanted me to practice going up hills."

"And how did you do?" Shane asked while leading them to the kitchen.

She looked at Brendan. "How did I do?"

"She did really well."

They gathered around the small kitchen island.

Brendan placed his breadboard on the counter and Lauren sat down a bowl. She'd asked what she could bring for the meal, and Shane had suggested a salad.

"What kind did you bring?" Shane asked

"A Greek salad. I put the hummus on the side."

"That sounds great."

"It smells so good," Lauren commented. "And your house is lovely. Brendan told me about Katelyn's paintings. He said you painted one for yourself. I'd love to see it."

"Of course," he said before turning to Noirin who was still perched on his hip. "Do you want to see your mom's painting?"

"Yes!" she agreed with enthusiasm.

He led them to the living room, to a writing desk in the corner. Above the double pedestal desk hung Katelyn's picture. It was a scene of a cottage by the sea. The young woman was holding her daughter's hand. The house over-looked the sea. Below was a dock so she could walk down and go sailing.

"A couple of homes had come on the market before she died. Katelyn had looked at them both and considered makin' an offer. This resembles one of them."

"It's beautiful, Shane," Lauren said as she took in all the details. "Is Noirin in all of the paintings that you did of Katelyn?"

"She is."

"Well, I can't wait to see the rest of them."

"Soon," Brendan added.

She scanned the room at his other paintings. "You'll

have to tell me more about your other pieces, when we have more time. Are they all yours?"

Shane shook his head. "Only two are mine; the others are ones I've collected over the years. I'll tell you more about them on Monday. Are you all hungry?" he added.

"Yes!" Noirin exclaimed.

Shane kissed her cheek and then led them to the kitchen. They all pitched in and made quick work of putting the meal on the table. Talk about the upcoming week's plans dominated the conversation while they dished up the food.

When Lauren took a bite of the stew, Shane asked, "So how is it? Have I proven the stereotype right or wrong?"

"Let me see," she said and lifted her spoon for another taste. When she was done savoring the chunks of beef and root vegetables in a thick rich sauce, she smiled. "I think this is the best stew I've ever had. Don't tell my mother, who by the way, will be here in May for a visit."

"Just your mom?" Brendan asked.

"Both of my parents. They've wanted to come to Ireland for a long time."

"What are your plans?" Shane asked in between bites.

"I'm not sure. But my mother did say she's not leaving without a wool sweater."

"Well then, you'll have to take her to Aran Islands," Brendan said. "The sweaters are authentic, the best. And speakin' of the best, have you tried the butter yet?" he asked while glancing down at the center of the table.

Lauren shook her head, and he passed her the butter tray.

"Wow, it's really good," she commented after slathering a pat on a slice of bread and taking a bite.

"We get it from farmer Dunne over in Carrigavantry. He's a dairy farmer. Sells most of his milk commercially, but he keeps enough to make his own butter and cheese. The best in the county for sure, probably in all of Ireland."

"We can take you there sometime," Shane offered. "Noirin loves to visit the farm. She enjoys the animals."

"That sounds wonderful. Would you like that, Noirin?"

"Yes, please."

Lauren smiled. "Such a polite girl. Would you like more bread, sweetheart?"

Shane couldn't keep from looking at Brendan to gauge his friend's reaction. They made eye contact, and Brendan gave him a knowing look. It was nice to see how natural mothering came to Lauren.

"There you are, Noirin," Lauren said as she handed her the buttered slice of bread.

"Thank you."

Lauren reached up and brushed a stray curl from the small girl's forehead and smiled. "I like animals and farms too." Lauren looked at Brendan and Shane. "Ellen offered the use of part of her parents' garden to grow some vegetables and herbs."

"That's great. Mary never uses all of the space."

"Ellen said the plot she uses for Cups and Cakes will be enough for the new bakery and then some."

Brendan nodded. "Ellen mentioned a dryin' space for the new bakery for the herbs she wants to bake with. She's been experimentin' with lavender biscotti. She'd also like to bottle the dried herbs and sell them with recipe cards."

Lauren wiped her mouth. "That's a really great idea. She could have pictures of the dishes on the cards."

"You could draw the pictures," Shane added.

Lauren looked surprised. "Me? No, I was thinking you could do that. I love your logo design of Cups and Cakes."

Shane looked at Brendan. "She's a very talented colored pencil artist. 'Colorful realism' is that what you called it?"

"Yes, but I'm not good enough."

"Well, let me and Ellen be the judge of that," Brendan said in between bites. "We'll be honest with you, and we trust Shane. If he didn't think you were talented enough, he would have never mentioned it."

"Brendan is right, and besides, I'm really busy with a number of projects."

"Yeah, like bribing Donal into comin' to the book club meetings."

Shane grinned. "So, he told you, did he?"

Brendan nodded and Shane filled Lauren in on the details.

"Donal needs to expand his horizons." Shane

sat back in his chair. Expanding the pastor's horizons included having him realize what a catch Ellen was. While he thought it, he'd never speak it out loud.

Brendan, who was done eating, leaned back in his chair too. "I don't think I could say the same about me. I don't enjoy readin' nonfiction, and Lauren doesn't enjoy opera."

Shane threw her a look of mock disapproval. "You're killin' me, Lauren. You don't like opera?"

She laughed, but before she could comment, Noirin said she was done eating.

"Okay, let's wash up and then we'll go get your bag of toys and you can play while we talk." She looked at Shane and Brendan. "We'll be right back. Which way to the bathroom?"

"Noirin knows the way."

When they left the dining room, Shane looked at Brendan. "She's a natural."

"Yeah, she is."

"Are you doin' all right?"

Brendan shrugged. "I've decided that I intend to enjoy getting to know Lauren, enjoy whatever time we have with her. We'll take her to the farm, invite her on our walks, help her with her garden. I'll introduce her to my folks, invite her to family dinner, and when she moves on, I'll move on, like I always have."

"It will be worth it," Shane said confidently.

"I hope you're right."

When Lauren and Noirin come back into the dining

room, they helped to clear the table and then helped Noirin set up a puzzle she'd brought along. While the seven-year-old worked to put the pieces together, the adults debated over the virtues of opera which ended with plans for the three of them to take a trip to Dublin to see one.

Over coffee and dessert, the conversation shifted to Shane's work and the second gallery he had recently opened. They talked about the new sculptor he would be interviewing in the next week. Brendan filled her in on the real estate investing he and his uncle did on the side, something his uncle planned to do full-time once he sold his accounting firm the following year.

The conversation drifted to some tentative plans to have Lauren help with the business and graphic side of the new bakery. When Brendan discussed pay, she insisted on volunteering. He refused and neither would budge. Shane stepped in to offer a solution. "Lauren, ask Ellen if she has a recipe she's decided on. Work on the first one for free. If Ellen and Brendan like your work, charge them half the goin' rate. The same with the accounting work for the tearoom. There, now, you've gone and met in the middle."

Brendan and Lauren stared at each other for a moment. It was Brendan who spoke first. "Let's sleep on it. I'm not comfortable with you doin' work and not being paid fairly."

"I understand, but what about a work visa? I can't be on your payroll while I'm in Ireland."

"I'll pay you as a contractor, and mail the checks to your home address in Tacoma."

Shane interrupted. "You don't have to decide now. Think about it."

"All right," Lauren agreed. "We probably should be heading home." She peered down at Noirin, whom she'd been holding in her lap for a little while.

"I think you're right," Brendan said.

"Thank you, Shane, for everything," Lauren said as she stood with Noirin. "Dinner was terrific. My turn next time."

"I like the sound of that. We'll start your lesson on Monday, after we walk Noirin to school."

"I'm looking forward to it."

After they had left, Shane went back into his studio and looked at his Mona Lisa, taking in the lines of her face and the light behind her blue eyes. "I feel it—hope for Brendan and Lauren," he said to her. "He's fallin' in love, and she'll feel the same for him." He paused. "I miss you. I'll always miss you."

Chapter Fourteen

Lauren adjusted the temperature of the bath water before leaning back and closing her eyes. The week had flown by for her, something that hadn't happened in a long time. In the last year, time had a way of dripping by like a slow leak into a large empty bucket. Pain had a way of doing that... but things were changing.

It was hard to believe she'd already been in Tramore for nearly two weeks. She'd spent every morning with Shane and then Noirin as they walked the little girl to school. On Monday, she'd had her first painting lesson. She was terrible with oils, but she had a good time.

Shane had quickly become a bright spot in your life. He was wise and kind, and his patience when teaching was commendable. "So, what do you think?" Lauren had asked. She'd stepped back from her canvas and had stared at what was supposed to be a tree.

Shane looked thoughtful for a moment. "Well, I think you'll have better success as a colored pencil artist."

And Shane was honest. She loved that about him, valued it.

Then there was Noirin, someone she'd felt like she'd known all her life. Most every afternoon, after Brendan picked her up from school, she and Noirin would spend time together, at the bakery or her apartment while he closed up. They had fun playing, reading, and singing together. Noirin especially loved helping Lauren make her after school snack, which almost always included peanut butter. The child was obsessed with the stuff.

She was grateful to Brendan when, on Monday, he suggested that she and Noirin hang out at Lauren's place, if she liked. He thought they might be more comfortable there. The fact that he trusted her with his little girl made her feel valued and appreciated again. This was something she'd missed feeling since Christopher had passed.

On Tuesday evening, she had made them dinner. She had it ready, so when Brendan arrived at her front door to pick up Noirin, they could easily enjoy dinner together. She took pleasure in talking with Brendan, someone else she felt like she'd known all of her life. He might not have enjoyed reading nonfiction, but he knew his history. Lauren had enjoyed learning about the recent history of Ireland and found it fascinating. She hadn't known much about the Irish War of Independence in 1919 and their struggles to establish themselves as an independent nation.

On Wednesday, she spent most of the day researching her mother-in-law's maiden name and was frustrated to discover there wasn't a Stacey Walsh who'd lived in Tramore within the last sixty years. At one point, she'd texted her father-in-law asking him if he was certain that she'd said she was from Tramore.

His response had been brief—*Not sure. It's been a while since she mentioned her hometown, let alone Ireland. Maybe I got it wrong.*

Lauren decided that the following week she'd go to the Waterford County seat and search the records there for a Stacey Walsh. She mentioned it to her father-in-law, and he thought it would be a good idea.

Toward the end of the week, Lauren attended her first book club meeting. At first, she'd been apprehensive about joining the group, not wanting to be the newcomer, afraid that people would ask her questions she wasn't ready to answer. But no one had, and it proved to be an enjoyable evening. She had missed seeing Ellen there.

On Friday afternoon, when they had gone to Ellen's parents' house to assess the garden space, she mentioned to Ellen that she'd attended the book club.

"Oh, I'm so sorry; I didn't realize you had decided to come to a meetin'."

"It was a spur of the moment thing. Yesterday, when Brendan came by to pick up Noirin, he talked me into it."

"How did you like it?"

"It was enjoyable. The conversation can be a little lively, thanks to Mrs. Gallagher."

Ellen chuckled. "Yeah, there's never a dull moment with that one, but she's good people and a bit lonely since Harold died."

There had been that moment of sadness at the thought of Mrs. Gallagher missing her husband, something Lauren knew all too well.

As they strolled through the garden, she asked Ellen why she didn't attend.

"Donal. Last week was his first time. Shane bribed

him into comin'. He's been tryin' to get Donal to come for ages. The good pastor doesn't like fiction. It's torture for him to read. He's obligated for three months. Shane promised him a paintin' for the charity auction. Until his commitment is over, I'm takin a break. It's too hard being around him. But I do have a date."

"With Donal?" Lauren looked confused.

"No, with James. He's a friend of Rachel and Matthew; you would have met them yesterday."

Lauren bent down to pluck a leaf of red lettuce, the only thing growing in the spring garden so early in the season with the cooler temperatures. Seedlings had been started at the tail end of winter and were nearly half their size. "I do remember them. Nice couple. So, why are you dating James if you're in love with Donal?"

"Because I need to get over him. He's obviously not interested in me, and I'm just pining away for him. I need to move on and thought the best way to do that would be to date—seriously."

Lauren sighed as she remembered her time with Ellen in the garden. She understood her new friend.

As she sunk lower into the bathtub, she remembered how it had been for her when she first started dating. Lauren had never been interested in asking a guy out. Call her old fashioned or a prude, but it wasn't in her nature to pursue men. If they were interested, they could make the first move. Like Christopher had. Even though she had dated a little in college, it was her husband who had stolen her heart, nearly from the start.

She swallowed back the tears. It hurt, but she was glad to have loved and been loved by him. Lauren knew it would be impossible to ever cherish someone else as much as she cherished Christopher. She was glad to know what it was like to be adored, even if only for a short time. The memories of him and their life together would light the years ahead. They wouldn't be lonely, just sad without him.

Lauren sighed once more, her breath scattering the bubbles in her bath. And now, she had new friends, Ellen, Shane, Noirin, and Brendan, people who had come to mean so much to her in such a short time. They gave her something to look forward to. In just a couple of weeks, she'd remembered what it was like to look forward to each new day, and what it would bring, what she would discover. She had her new friends to thank, and someday soon she would tell them about the love of her life, her pain, and the healing they had unknowingly brought to her.

Lauren dunked her head under the water so she could begin washing her hair. The water was cooling, and she needed to be in bed early. Tomorrow she was scheduled to go with Ellen and Brendan to Dublin for the weekend to meet with the tea supplier and test out some different blends for the new tearoom.

Lauren felt a rush of excitement. The emotion was unused and rusty, but it was a welcome feeling.

"Are you almost ready, Brendan?" Ellen hollered toward the office. "Lauren will be here any moment, and we need to hit the road." They had arrived together very early to get the baked goods prepped for the rest of the service. Their assistant bakers, Ilene and Martha, would get them baked in time and throughout the morning. Aine, John, and the other servers had the front of the house all under control.

She heard Brendan shifting into the kitchen.

"Lauren?" he asked, a puzzled look etching his brow.

"Yeah, didn't I tell you how I invited her to join us? It was mother's idea. She knew Lauren wanted to go to Dublin and didn't like the idea of her goin' off alone. She knew we were makin' the trip and told me to invite her along."

When Brendan didn't respond, Ellen's eyes widened in surprise. "I seriously thought I mentioned it to you. I hope it's fine?"

"Of course, I was just surprised. I guess she knows what time to be here."

"She's probably waitin' for us as we speak."

They worked quickly and gathered the rest of their things, while giving final instructions to their staff before heading to the front of the bakery.

Lauren was there with her overnight bag and a to-go cup. She raised it and said, "I'm addicted to this stuff. I'll go bankrupt before the year's out."

Ellen laughed. "Which flavor?"

"The *Fifth of November*."

Brendan held the door open for them. "It's one of my favorites too."

"And I have my daily offering." Lauren glanced at the pastry box she held in her other hand. "I still can't figure out who keeps leaving me pastries every morning. It's been two weeks and every day, without fail, there's a box waiting for me."

Brendan smiled inwardly. He was the one leaving her the boxes. It started that first morning of her arrival, after he'd seen Lauren crying the night before—a little something to cheer her up, and he hadn't wanted to stop. Every morning, after he arrived and finished the first bake, he picked a different treat, placed it in a box, and set it outside her door. Seeing how she smiled now in appreciation, it made him feel good. He wanted to keep the mystery going, and so he said nothing.

"She has an admirer," Ellen piped in as she placed her overnight bag in the trunk. "I'll sit in the back, Lauren. I can stretch out more."

"Are you sure. I don't mind the back."

"I'm sure."

Soon, Brendan was maneuvering his car onto the main road that would take them to Dublin.

He handed Lauren his cell phone. "You're our guest. You pick the play list."

She opened the appropriate app and scrolled through his playlists for a moment.

"I love *Snow Patrol*," she said before pressing play.

Chasing Cars played over the sound system, and it

made him feel good and happy because he was driving to his favorite city with Lauren by his side and his cousin in the back.

The two of them chatted about the garden plans for the new bakery, while Brendan settled into the drive and listened with interest to their conversation. They drew him in every now and again with a question or comment. Halfway to Dublin, the conversation changed to the schedule for the weekend.

"Lauren, while Brendan and I are at the tea supplier, I thought you might enjoy tourin' the *Book of Kells* exhibit at Trinity College. We will have plenty of time to drop you off before headin' up town?"

"Oh, I thought I'd be joining you at the supplier?"

"Is that what you'd like?" Brendan asked, taking his eyes off the road for a moment to look at her.

"I would love it," Lauren replied. "It sounds interesting... if you don't think I'll be in the way?"

"Of course, you won't," Ellen said with emphasis. "For the evenin', I thought we could take you to a restaurant called, *The Avenue*. What do you think about that, Brendan?"

"I think she would love it."

For the rest of the trip, they talked about their plans for the weekend. Brendan simply enjoyed the idea of being with Lauren, with no thought for the future and how hard he was destined to fall. His gaze swept the countryside, taking in the many sheep dotting the rolling green hills, a site that had become very familiar to him on his many trips back-and-forth between Tramore and Dublin. It had been as comforting then as it was now.

When they arrived at the supplier, they only waited in the lobby for a few minutes before Flynn Wilson came out to greet them.

"Brendan, how are you?"

"I'm good. Do you remember my cousin Ellen?"

"Of course, it's good to see you again," Flynn said.

"The same."

Flynn turned his gaze to Lauren.

"This is our friend, Lauren. Flynn is a tea master and the owner of the company. We met and became friends when I helped him with some investments."

Flynn and Lauren shook hands. "It's nice to meet you," she greeted.

"You're American."

"Yes. I'm in Ireland for the next year. Brendan and Ellen invited me to join them on their trip to Dublin."

"Well, welcome to Ireland." He turned his attention back to Brendan and Ellen. "Are we ready to blend some teas?"

They nodded.

As they walked to the tasting room, Flynn said, "So, tell me a little bit about the new tearoom. Is it casual, elegant, or something in between?"

Brendan looked at Ellen, signaling for her to respond.

"Somethin' in between for the décor. But the food will be high tea elegance. We're visitin' the Marble Falls tearoom tomorrow mornin' to sample their savory options for recipe ideas."

Flynn held open a heavy wood paneled door and motioned them inside. "Good choice of tearooms to visit. What will you serve the food on?"

"Laura Ashley table ware," Ellen replied.

"Another good choice. That helps with a general direction to go. Have a seat," he said while gesturing to a large table equipped with an electric tea kettle, taster mugs and spoons, tea holders, and bowls.

Flynn asked Ellen a few more questions about the variety of the menu. While she answered, he began blending a mixture of various teas and flavors from the large variety of glass jars sitting on the table. When he was done, he passed the cup around for them to smell.

"Is it a chai?" Brendan asked.

"The vanilla is reminiscent of a chai, but instead of cardamom, I've added blueberry to a black tea and threw in some lemon verbena."

"It smells lovely," Lauren said.

"Let's see how it tastes," Flynn said as he poured boiling water into the cup. "We'll let that steep. Here's another blend I thought might interest you. It's a chocolate coconut."

"That sounds interesting," Brendan commented. "What's in it?"

"It's a black tea base with cocoa beans, toasted coconut, honeybush, and chocolate flakes."

"What's honeybush?" Lauren asked. "I've never heard of it."

"It's a bush that grows in South Africa. The flowers smell like honey," Flynn replied.

"It won't turn bitter if steeped too long?" Brendan asked.

Flynn gave Brendan a look of appreciation. "You do know your tea." He looked at Lauren and Ellen. "It's similar to rooibos tea which can be a bit medicinal. I don't think you'll find that with this blend. Let's steep this. Are you ready to try the blueberry lemon?"

He poured the strained liquid into the small tasting cups and handed them each a spoon.

"Wow, that reminds me of my blueberry lemon cake," Ellen said after taking a sip.

Lauren took another taste. "It's really good."

"It has my vote," Brendan added.

And so did the cocoa coconut blend. Flynn served them four other blends—all a hit.

During the tasting session, Brendan enjoyed watching Lauren's reactions and appreciation of the experience. She was open and smart, interjecting relevant questions and comments throughout their time with Flynn.

What intrigued him the most was her interest in his family business. It was obvious from her chosen career that she had a head for enterprise... but this was more. She seemed to come alive when they talked about ideas for the new tearoom.

They hadn't discussed the monetary issue of her helping any further. He had been determined to pay her the full value of what she as worth and was completely against having her help for nothing. Watching and listening to her while in Flynn's tasting room, Brendan decided to move toward Shane's compromise, and pay her half of what the work was worth. He arrived at the decision because he hoped that in the process of helping to build a new endeavor and giving a part of herself to the new tearoom, she might never want to leave.

Chapter Fifteen

On the way to the hotel for an early check-in, the three of them brainstormed on some fun names for the new teas. Some they liked, most they didn't, and laughed at some of the crazier ones like Cocoa for Coconuts, a play on 'cuckoo for cocoa puffs,' a catchphrase used by the breakfast cereal's cuckoo bird character, Sunny. Brendan had given Lauren a bemused look when he informed her that no one in Ireland would make the connection because Sunny the cuckoo bird didn't exist here.

"I have to remember that I'm not in Kansas anymore," she said.

"Kansas?" both Brendan and Ellen questioned in unison, a touch of bewilderment behind the word.

"Yeah, you know Kansas, from the movie *The Wizard of Oz*?"

"I thought they were in Oz," Ellen said.

"They are, but the movie starts off in Kansas."

"But I thought you were from Tacoma and Montana?" Brendan added.

Lauren let out a playful sigh. "I really have to stop with the colloquialisms."

"The what?" Brendan said with a teasing grin.

When she realized he was giving her a hard time,

she rolled her eyes at him and the three of them burst into laughter.

She finished explaining her "I'm not in Kansas anymore" comment. Neither Brendan nor Ellen remembered it from the movie but appreciated the explanation.

"I like it," Ellen said. "I'll use it from now on."

They laughed again, and then after tossing around a few more name ideas for the teas, they settled on one for the blueberry lemon blend, *Blue Brew.* It sounded young and fresh.

For lunch, they made their way to the Hipster Triangle, formally known as Dublin's Creative Quarter, an area of the city that was full of new, up-and-coming, forward-thinking restaurants. They landed at Fiddle Faddle, Brendan's favorite place for fish and chips. It was a nondescript building with an equally nondescript interior, but the fish was amazing with very *forward-thinking* sauces like mayo and miso, and a chipotle raspberry.

They had a lively discussion about what it meant to be forward-thinking and then teased about the name of the restaurant Fiddle Faddle, which, by definition, meant nonsense.

"They can call this pace whatever they want as long as they keep making fish that tastes this good!" Lauren's comment was made with a dead-serious tone to her voice.

It caused both Brendan and Ellen to laugh boisterously.

"I'm serious. I feel like I've had a moment of enlightenment, like this is the first time I've ever tasted fried fish."

"We can tell ye'r serious," Brendan said with a wide grin, thickening his Irish brogue.

Lauren paused at the smile on his face. All morning and afternoon, when she'd catch one of them directed at her, she wondered at the warmth that filled her. She didn't know why she hadn't noticed his smile before. Thinking back on their previous conversations, they had mostly been serious and laced with sad history. Here in Dublin, there was a freeing sense, a release from all that they were, which created an openness between them. Like the fish they were eating. It was as if she were seeing his smile for the first time. And yet the look was oddly familiar, which puzzled her. The softening of his big brown eyes, and the way his lips parted slightly as they formed his smile, it relaxed and soothed and had a way of softening all the hard parts that had filled her this past year.

"Where did you say we were going for dinner?" Lauren asked.

Ellen, swallowing a bite, answered, "*The Avenue*."

"Can we come back here instead?" Lauren suggested.

Brendan chuckled and looked at Ellen. "We've created a monster."

Ellen nodded. "As much as I love this place too, we have to go to *The Avenue*. It's amazing. And besides, Flynn is lookin' forward to joinin' us."

"How about we stop by on our way home tomorrow?" Brendan offered.

Her eyes lit with pleasure. "Really? You don't mind?"

He wasn't smiling at her now but his look was tender

and full of something she couldn't quite read. It held a hint of something meaningful, something—wonderful. Lauren felt the warmth again and realized she liked it. She liked the way Brendan Callery looked at her, and the way it made her feel.

"I don't mind at all. Do you, Ellen?"

Her friend shook her head. "It's no great sacrifice for me, and I can take some to go for my parents. They would love some."

"That's a good idea. I'll get some for Noirin and my folks too."

After lunch, Brendan drove them to Jervis Street for a tour of the Leprechaun Museum, a place Brendan had visited before moving back to Tramore. It was a fun museum dedicated to Irish folklore and mythology and its appreciation of the country's tradition of storytelling. The history of the leprechaun was far more intricate and varied than the modern-day version of the solitary shoemaker who hordes gold in a pot at the end of a rainbow.

The earliest mention of leprechauns was in the thirteenth century tale known as the *Adventure of Fergus, Son of Leti*. Leti falls asleep and is awakened to the realization he has been captured by three leprechauns who are dragging him to the ocean. Leti manages to escape and becomes the abductor. The four strike a bargain. The leprechauns have the power to grant wishes, and they agree to each grant one wish to Leti in exchange for their release.

As they walked through the museum and learned the history of the leprechaun, both Ellen and Lauren were surprised to discover that leprechauns, unlike typical fairies and woodland sprites, were not always creatures of favorable opinion but were often portrayed as manipulative, mischievous, and rude drunkards. There were other variations of the leprechauns portrayed over the centuries, which the three of them found fascinating. They especially enjoyed the room with the larger furniture and objects that gave visitors the feeling of being a leprechaun.

After the tour of the museum, they had time to do a river boat tour of Dublin on the river Liffey, with great views of some of the city's monuments. It was a popular tourist attraction and the three of them barely made it on board. They found seats at the back of the boat, squeezing onto a padded bench.

When the boat took off, Lauren was glad she had brought a warmer jacket and had layered her clothing, something she'd learned to do since arriving in Ireland.

"Are you ladies warm enough?" Brendan asked.

"I'm good," Ellen replied.

"Me too."

The tour guide began talking about the history of Ireland starting with the arrival of the Vikings. At key parts of the city, the tour guide would briefly talk about a building or monument, interjecting bits of history and knowledge about the location.

The sun was beginning to set. Lauren took in the darkening skyline and the lights that began to flicker on in response to the setting sun. It felt good being on this boat, in this dynamic city, with two people she was comfortable calling her friends.

During the intermission, refreshments were served. When Ellen excused herself to grab a drink, Brendan asked Lauren, "How are you enjoyin' it?"

She looked at him and wondered how she could convey all that this moment meant to her. How it was rolled up into the past two weeks, and the change that his country and the people he loved had brought to her life. "It's incredible! All of it! Thank you for letting me come with you. I'm glad I didn't make my first trip to Dublin alone."

"I'm glad you didn't either." He looked away from her and focused on the skyline. "Tramore is my home, but I did enjoy livin' here. There is something about big city living. It has this appeal. How about you? You moved from a very rural area to a big city."

"I like living in Tacoma. It was intimidating at first, a lot to consider and to be mindful of. My father was a nervous wreck. He started drilling me about safety a year before I left for college. We didn't have anything close by that gave lessons on self-defense; otherwise, he would have enrolled me in a class. So, he taught me everything he could think of, which wasn't much."

"Hopefully, you didn't have to use any of it?"

She shook her head. "None of the physical stuff, but I did use the knowledge he poured into me—like always avoiding the no-go areas. Before I left home, Dad gave me a map of the Seattle-Tacoma area and had highlighted all the risky places. The research he'd done must have taken him hours."

"I think I'll like your dad when I meet him in May. Although, I probably won't have to worry too much about that with Noirin." He paused, still studying the skyline.

"And why's that?"

He looked at her then, and she noticed the traces of sadness behind his gaze, and she realized the answer to her own question. Lauren could have prevented her reaction if she'd had time to think about it, but she wouldn't have wanted to. She reached over and placed her hand on top of Brendan's. "I'm sorry. Sometimes I forget Noirin has Down Syndrome and that she won't be able to live a completely normal life."

Brendan held her gaze as he spoke. "Moving off to a big city to start a career like you and I had the opportunity to do won't be the same for Noirin. She would need support. How much support is uncertain at the moment. I won't know until she's older. And although it scares me to death to think about her livin' on her own, I want to do what I can to help make that happen for her."

Lauren squeezed his hand and then placed hers back in her lap. "I can only imagine how hard it is not to worry."

"Her appointment is on Tuesday."

Before she could respond, Ellen arrived with three bottles of water. "I thought you guys might like these."

"Thank you," Brendan said.

"Yes, thank you."

"Isn't this nice." Ellen commented as she took her

seat. "It's been so long since I've been on a boat tour. I forget how wonderful Dublin is."

The city was everything Lauren thought it would be and then some. She glanced over at Brendan who was watching the city scape glide by. This had been his life for several years. A place that suited him. But he loved something more: a home, a family, and most of all a little girl. And without a thought or a care to what he wanted, he gave it all up and accepted the challenges, the fears, and the uncertainty of raising the little girl he loved, the little girl Lauren loved too.

Yes, Lauren had realized today that she liked how Brendan's smile made her feel. But beyond the smiles, the person that was Brendan Callery elevated those feelings to a whole other level, feelings that were both welcoming and confusing.

Chapter Sixteen

They decided to take a cab to dinner as parking would be a challenge, especially if they decided to do some other things afterwards. The two ladies were quieter than normal. Brendan sat up front with the driver and talked about the weather, business, and various other things. Lauren seemed to be lost in her own thoughts, and Ellen was missing Donal.

It had hit her on the boat ride. For the last several weeks, Ellen had done a great job of pushing him out of her thoughts, avoiding him, and accepting how she would never have the relationship with Donal she'd been dreaming about for the last many months. There had been a sense of acceptance and finality to her efforts. She felt good about them. Ellen thought about her plans to have dinner with James on Tuesday. She didn't quite know how she felt about her date with a total stranger. Part of her was excited; the other part was apprehensive.

She'd checked James out on Facebook and assumed he had done the same. Neither of them had canceled, so it was safe to say they both liked what they'd seen. She had no objections to his appearance, but—he wasn't Donal.

Pushing Donal out of her life had left a vacancy, and her heart wouldn't allow it to remain empty. During the boat ride, the feelings had all came rushing back in—the longing, the joy of who Donal was, his decency, his faith, his commitment. She loved his sense of humor and that serious side of him. He was wise beyond his years when it came to life and spiritual matters. He was practical, and yet there was a spontaneity that could spark on any occasion and without provocation.

The week before Christmas, Brendan had planned a dinner party at the bakery with friends and family. After dessert was finished, they got onto the subject of figgy pudding from the song *We Wish You a Merry Christmas*, and Donal had enticed them all to go Christmas caroling, something none of them had done in years.

The stop at the first house ended with bursts of laughter after the homeowners had smiled, wished them a merry Christmas, and closed the door. They had been so off key. By the second home, they had done much better. The smiles of surprise and warmth that the homeowners bestowed upon them had been priceless.

Afterwards, when back at the bakery, they'd laughed and relished the moments of their adventure over hot chocolate and more desserts. The next morning, Donal had popped into the kitchen at Cups and Cakes. "Good mornin', fine bakers. I'd like to place an order for five figgy puddings, please."

Brendan had thrown a towel at Donal. As for Ellen, she'd laughed, appreciating the warmth and joy of his nature.

Her eyes followed the sites on Dublin's busy streets, and she sighed at the memory. It must have been an audible sigh. She heard Lauren asking her if she was okay.

Ellen gave her friend a smile. That's how she saw Lauren, as a friend. "I'm good," she said, but with her forefinger she drew the shape of a 'D' on the seat in between them.

Lauren gave her a knowing 'we'll talk more later' look.

The drive to *The Avenue* wasn't too long, even with traffic. Brendan paid the cab driver and then met them on the sidewalk. Flynn was waiting for them in the bar.

Ellen was happy to have him join them for dinner. The one and only time they'd met had been on a trip to Dublin to visit Brendan. Her first impression had been a favorable one. The tasting, earlier that afternoon, furthered her positive impression of him. He seemed to be a bit older than Brendan, who was three and a half years her senior, making Flynn about mid-thirties. He was a good conversationalist, something she appreciated in a person.

She noticed the way his eyes strayed toward Lauren. Ellen was picking up on a definite interest in her American friend. But she wore a ring. Ellen was pretty certain that something must have happened to her husband. She never mentioned him and there was a sadness that seemed to linger behind her gaze, especially at certain times. It was obvious Lauren didn't want to talk about it, and so none of them asked.

"What do you like best about this place, Ellen?" Lauren asked as menus were presented to them.

"Besides the trendy décor, the food is spectacular.

The halibut is my favorite. Have you ever been here before, Flynn?"

He nodded. "A couple of my suppliers have brought me here. It is a real treat. Thank you again for askin' me to join you."

"I'm glad you were free," Brendan added before looking at his menu again. "I used to bring investors here."

Flynn nodded. "I like being wined and dined. But I've always wondered what it would be like to have to be the one doin' the wining and dining with business partners."

Brendan closed his menu and placed it on his plate. It was obvious he knew what he wanted. "It wasn't my favorite thing to do. At first it seemed great—meals on the company's dime at really nice restaurants—but then it got old, especially when tryin' to make conversation."

"But you're so easy to talk to," Lauren interjected.

He smiled at her. "I'm outgoin' enough, but when I had to keep the conversation goin', I couldn't help but wonder if they were silently beggin' me to shut up."

They all laughed at the thought.

"I can't imagine that happenin'," Ellen remarked.

The waiter came by with glasses of water and took their drink orders.

"How long have you been in the tea business?" Lauren asked when the waiter had left.

"It's my family's business, fourth generation. For the longest time, we only supplied major tea buyers— *Twining's* and *P&G* in the U.K., *Bigelow* in the U.S., and *Barry's* here in Ireland."

"I love their tea. I've already sent my family and in... " Lauren was about to add something and then corrected herself before resuming, "... my family a few packages,"

"There are places in the U.S. where you can find Barry's. I can send you a list."

Lauren grinned. "I'm one step ahead of you. No one in Tacoma sells it, but there is a shop in Seattle, and a few other places with online ordering." She looked at Brendan and Ellen. "It's your *Fifth of November* tea that's going to cost me a small fortune in shipping costs."

"That is a good one," Flynn agreed. He looked at Brendan. "All of our blends are proprietary, so you'll only find that exact flavor profile at Cups and Cakes."

Brendan nodded. "Flynn's company just started workin' with small businesses a few years ago."

"I didn't realize that," Ellen commented. She looked at Lauren. "Aunt Shay never experimented with blends. She always carried the standards, *Earl Grey*, *Irish Breakfast*, and so on. When I finished culinary school and came back home to the bakery, Brendan introduced the blended teas."

"And I'm glad you did!" Lauren said with an appreciative smile.

The waiter arrived with their drinks and to take their food orders.

Over dinner, they told Flynn about their afternoon. He'd never been to the Leprechaun Museum and said he'd have to put it on his list of must-sees. The conversation turned to travel and places they'd been to. When Ellen mentioned to Flynn how Lauren planned to travel around

Ireland, he said, "That sounds adventurous. If you're here in Dublin again, give me a call, and we can get together. I'd be happy to show you around." He reached into his pocket for a business card, and handed it to her.

Ellen noticed some of the warmth leave Lauren's eyes, but she took the card and thanked Flynn. During the rest of dinner, her friend was quieter than normal. While they waited for their coffee to arrive, Ellen said she had to go to the restroom and asked Lauren if she'd like to join her.

Lauren stood with her.

As they walked toward the back of the restaurant, Ellen linked her arm through Lauren's. "Now it's my turn to ask if everythin' is all right with you?"

Lauren looked at her and she could see moisture gathering in her eyes.

"It will be," she replied and then quickly changed the subject. "You drew the letter 'D' on the seat. Something happened with you and Donal?"

Neither of them had to use the restroom. It had been an excuse to get a moment alone with Lauren. Accepting that she didn't want to talk about what was bothering her, she told Lauren about her moment on the boat.

"I'm like you, Ellen. I never pursued men. Right or wrong, I'm a little old-fashioned, but you and Donal are friends. Do you think you could say something to him, or at least invite him to dinner some time, just the two of you, and see where things take you?"

Ellen looked thoughtful for a moment. "He's good

friends with Brendan, and other members of my family and Shane. I don't want things to become awkward if it doesn't work out."

"But what if it does work out?"

It was Ellen's turn to tear up a bit. "I want so much to have that *somethin'* with him. I'm just scared it won't happen."

Lauren reached for Ellen and pulled her into a hug. "I understand."

They held each other for a few moments longer.

"We probably should get back, or they'll wonder," Ellen said.

"I think I have to use the bathroom, after all. I'll be right out."

"Okay. Oh... and Lauren," she paused to look at her friend. "I know it's not easy to share things, but I want you to know that I'm here for you."

Lauren gave her a grateful smile. "Soon, Ellen. Soon, I'll share with you. I just need more time."

Ellen nodded before leaving the bathroom.

A short while later, Lauren returned to the table. Ellen could tell she'd been crying. Her gut twisted in knots for her friend and for whatever it was that was hurting her. She cared for Lauren and didn't want to see her suffering. Yet she wouldn't speculate, and more importantly she wouldn't press her to talk.

After dinner, they said goodbye to Flynn, and Lauren seemed to brighten up a bit more. She even suggested that they take an after-dinner walk.

Brendan recommended a walk down Aston Quay to the Ha'Penny Bridge.

"It's fairly quiet at night, but the walk alongside the river is grand," he commented as they exited the cab. The driver had dropped them off a couple of blocks from the bridge. Most of the store fronts that lined Aston Quay were closed for the evening. The architecture was fun and interesting, a mix of neo-classical with Georgian influence, with other styles thrown into the mix.

They walked at a leisurely pace, and Brendan oriented them on their location. "To the north a few blocks is the Leprechaun Museum. And south, across the Ha'Penny Bridge, is the Pub Crawl. Let's head in that direction."

When they reached Anglesea Street, they decided to head into one of the pubs on the corner, *The Auld Dubliner*. Live music greeted them. They headed to the bar to order drinks and then found seats toward the back. It was crowded and lively, the music a mix of rock and blues. Too loud to talk, the three of them sat back and enjoyed the performance, and sipped their drinks.

An hour later, they decided to call it a night.

In the hotel lobby, they agreed on a time to meet for breakfast and entered the lift together.

They were on different floors and Brendan left first. When the doors closed, Lauren asked, "What are you going to do about Donal?"

Ellen shrugged. "I think I'll go on my date with James and see after that."

Lauren nodded and hesitated for a moment. "Ellen,

I'm not one to hand out advice, especially unsolicited, but I would like to encourage you not to wait too long. Life is too short."

The dinging of the lift signaled the arrival to her floor. Ellen gave Lauren a brief hug. "Thank you," she said before exiting. "I'll see you in the mornin'," she added with a wave goodbye.

Lauren smiled as the doors began to close.

Ellen sighed as she made her way to her hotel room. Lauren may not have been willing to share her story just yet, but Ellen was starting to put the pieces together and wouldn't be surprised if Lauren's husband had passed. Her new friend was right. Life was too short, and she should have a conversation with Donal. But *should* and *would* felt as far away from each other as Kansas and Oz.

Chapter Seventeen

Brendan couldn't sleep. Tired of tossing and turning, he slipped out of his shorts and into his jeans and t-shirt, and headed down to the lounge. It was open late and quieter than he thought it would be. Most people were probably out enjoying Dublin's nightlife.

Piano music played softly in the background while the bartender, a young man in his early twenties, dried stemware with a towel. Brendan ordered a pot of tea and made his way to a table near the door where he could peer out into the lobby and watch his fellow guests walk by.

He was a people watcher—had done it quite often when he lived in Dublin. He liked to imagine the lives of those who passed him by. The odd couple that didn't quite seem to match. The David and Victoria Beckham's of the world who seemed too perfect. The pinched face couple that looked as if they could barely tolerate each other. The older couple who still held hands as they shuffled along to wherever they were going, still heading in the same direction after all their years together.

They were his favorite, the older couples who still held hands. Life would have brought them challenges; what life is free of them? The fact that they were still together with hearts and hands linked, it never failed to bring a smile to Brendan's lips.

While dating Eva, when he saw an older couple still affectionate with one another, it always brought forth a surge of longing for the woman he loved. During those moments, if she'd been nearby, he would have reached for her hand to tug her toward him so he could softly kiss her. The times when Eva hadn't been with him, he would have pulled out his phone to text the words, *I love you.*

She'd never failed to reciprocate with tender kisses of her own and returned words of *I love you too.* Until the day he'd told her he was taking full custody of Noirin.

Three Years Ago

Brendan was exhausted. The emotional stress of the last two weeks was more than he could handle, or so it seemed. He was managing somehow, because he was back at his flat in Dublin, putting one foot in front of the other. Eva had left Tramore a few hours after Katelyn's funeral. She needed to get back to work the next day. He'd stayed a few more days to work out some details and to be there for his aunt and uncle. He'd also needed them too.

While Eva had been with him in Tramore, he hadn't had the time, or the nerve, to tell her about the decision he had made the evening before Katelyn's funeral. The decision was to raise Noirin. It made him uneasy to think about the 'what ifs,' but he was sure of Eva's love for him. He wouldn't have bought the ring the week before Katelyn went missing if he didn't believe she loved him too and was committed to them. They had talked about building a life together.

He looked at the clock over his fireplace. She would be here soon. She'd promised to stop by after work. Brendan unpacked his suitcase and tidied up his flat. He'd left in a bit of rush after receiving his uncle's call, but now, he gave his place the attention it needed.

A couple of hours later, when he heard the knock on the door, he nervously placed his hand over his pant pocket to make sure the ring was still there. He took a deep breath and opened the door. Eva greeted him with a grief-filled smile. "Brendan," she said softly as she wrapped her arms around his waist and laid her cheek against his chest.

They held each other for a few moments until she pulled away to look up at him. "How is everyone?"

"Not good," he said as he led her to the couch and pulled her down next to him.

They didn't say anything at first, just sat there holding each other.

He was working up the courage to tell her about his decision.

Finally, he pulled away so he could look at her.

Brendan held her gaze and tucked a stray strand of her hair behind her ear. "You know how much I love Noirin, don't you?"

The wary look that replaced the soft loving one she'd been openly gazing at him with caused him to pause. He knew. Before she even uttered a word, Brendan knew things would not go the way he had hoped.

"Brendan," Eva said, her voice wavering. She fingered her necklace. "I..." she paused. "I was worried about this."

He'd seen the signs, but he still wasn't prepared for the raw pain, sharp and cutting.

Eva reached for his hand. "Please, will you reconsider? Why can't your aunt and uncle raise her? They're her grandparents."

Brendan stared at her, his mouth open at a loss for words. Mingled with the piercing pain that took his breath away came the confusion. Did she not know him? Did she not pay attention to his parents' circumstances, the people who had given him everything or how he adored Noirin?

He stood and walked to the window overlooking the street in front of his building. She stayed where she sat.

Brendan didn't know how long it took for him to form a response. Time seemed to stand still. Finally, he found his voice. "I love you, Eva, and I want to spend the rest of my life with you. That life will include Noirin being loved and raised by me."

He didn't turn back to look at her, but continued to look out into the darkening sky, with the sun setting behind Dublin. His hand was in his pocket fingering the diamond he'd bought for Eva. Brendan wouldn't beg or plead.

She never came to him, but quietly left his apartment. The sound of the door closing brought forth the tears he was holding back. They blurred his vision, but he could see her walking down the front steps of his building. He couldn't see her clearly, only the shadow of her form.

Sometime later, after sorting through the contents of their relationship, he realized that she'd always been that way. *They* had always been that way—real but never in focus and never sharp enough to know where the lines began and where they ended.

Brendan may not have known where the lines with him and Eva began and ended, but he knew where they were drawn with Lauren.

Earlier that afternoon, while on the boat, she'd reached for his hand. In a moment of shared vulnerability, she had touched him to give him comfort. It was the touch of a friend, nothing more, nothing less.

Later, at dinner, the lines with Lauren became even clearer and more sharply focused.

He'd noticed the change in her the moment Flynn had offered to show her around Dublin the next time she was in town. Engaged and talkative the whole day, even with Flynn, it had been as if a light switch had been turned off. After his colleague's invitation, she hadn't become totally withdrawn; but it was obvious that something had changed. And when Lauren had returned from the rest-room without Ellen, he could tell she'd been crying.

Brendan had felt the sharpness of this new discovery as keenly as the day Eva had walked out of his life. And with Lauren's own discovery, the dots had been connected in her heart with those same precise, focused lines.

Her husband *was* gone, but she still loved him and longed for him. Sitting in the restaurant at a table clothed in white linen and cut crystal, with Flynn's offer hanging before her, Brendan was certain it had been the first time anyone had given her a reason to think beyond her husband and toward the possibility of a life without him.

Brendan imagined the sharp piercing pain that had resurfaced in her heart—no, not resurfaced, it was always there. Day in and day out, he could see it in her eyes, behind the smiles and the wit she showed the world. Tonight, that pain had spun out of its normal orbit and onto another path, one she wasn't ready to take, one she may never be ready to take.

He'd known people like her, people very close to him who had found that one great love and then lost it, never to recover.

While on the boat, when Lauren had placed her hand on his, the contact had pushed him toward taking a risk. The warmth and the comfort of her touch had held a world of promise for him. While walking into The Avenue, he'd ushered her through the door with his hand at the small of her back. Wanting to guide and to protect her, he'd dared to imagine that Lauren could be his great love, casting what he had with Eva into deep contrasting shadows.

But then he'd seen the drawn lines and had felt numbed by them. There would be no moving toward taking a risk with Lauren.

"Brendan?"

He looked up from the teacup he'd been staring at and saw Lauren standing in front of him.

He sat up straighter and couldn't find any words.

She looked surprised to see him. "I couldn't sleep and thought I'd come down here and draw. Ellen is going to do the lavender biscotti for the new tearoom. I had an idea for the recipe card." Her voice held a tinge of uncertainty.

He could tell she had been crying again. The pain of his discovery washed over him anew.

"The same with me," he managed to say. "I mean, I couldn't sleep either."

"May I?"

"Of course. Can I get you some tea?"

"That would be really nice, thank you."

He walked up to the bar and ordered tea, *Barry's Irish Breakfast*, because he knew she enjoyed it. And for as long as he lived, he would remember that she loved *Barry's* and the *Fifth of November*.

When he returned to the table, he noticed she had taken out her sketch book and pencils. She'd finally shown him her work the night she'd made him dinner. She was very talented and had that artistic flare. She reminded him too much of Shane; same circumstances, same hearts, eternally broken and adrift.

"I'm sorry you couldn't sleep," she offered while stirring her tea. "Were you thinking about Noirin?"

She was remembering their conversation on the boat.

"Yes." It wasn't a total lie, but she'd never know the truth about where his thoughts had taken him.

"Her appointment is on Tuesday." She was holding a pencil, rocking it back and forth between her thumb and forefinger.

"Yes, that's right." He didn't want to think about the 'what ifs' with his daughter. He hurt too much as it was. "I'm glad you're enjoyin' Dublin." He needed to change the subject.

"I am enjoying it. Do you mind if I draw while we talk?" She paused the rocking of her pencil between her fingers and looked at him. "Am I interrupting? Would you rather I go?"

Yes, he thought to himself, but then he would feel even more lost and empty without her.

"You're not interruptin'," he assured. "What is your idea for the biscotti?"

She described it to him—the colors, the placement. Lauren did this while she worked out on paper what she envisioned.

"Do you miss Dublin?" She didn't look up from her drawing when she asked the question but continued to sketch out her design.

"Sometimes. It's nice to be within drivin' distance. I make the trip with Shane as often as I can. Noirin and I've attended his gallery shows, especially when he's featurin' a new artist he can't stop talkin' about. His gallery is top notch. You'll enjoy seein' it tomorrow."

They had made plans to stop in after visiting the tearoom.

"Was it hard leaving your career in Dublin and going back to your family business?" It was then she looked up, her eyes curious.

"Being a stock trader was a means to an end. I don't miss the stress and the pressure. But if I'm being honest, I never envisioned goin' back to the bakery full time. I've worked there since I was a teenager. I liked it well enough, but I had big plans and dreams. I was determined to make my fortune in real estate. My uncle and I shared that dream. When Aunt Shay became sick, I wanted more than ever to make it a reality. But when Katelyn passed, everythin' changed." He paused. "My folks didn't want me to have full custody of Noirin. They were adamantly opposed to it."

Lauren's eyes widened. "I never would have guessed."

"They wanted the best for me. I was young with a promisin' career." And he had a woman who loved him. When he'd told his parents about Eva's wordless retreat, they hadn't been surprised. It was one of the reasons they'd insisted upon keeping Noirin with them.

"What changed their mind?"

He looked down at his cup. "I reminded them how much I loved her and that they had done the same for me. Sacrificed. They were newlyweds, just startin' out in life, tryin' to make ends meet, but they never hesitated to make me their own." He gave her a wan smile. He knew it never reached his eyes. "My Aunt Mary, she likes to tell me the story."

"What happened to your parents?"

"I don't know who my father is. My birth mother's name is Glenna. She was a drug addict. It was a miracle she stopped using when she found out she was pregnant. My Aunt Shay and Uncle Quinn offered to help her, and she accepted. She lived with them during her entire pregnancy. They took care of her and things seemed to be better for Glenna. A week after I was born, she took off. Said she had to run to the store... and never came back. My aunts searched for her everywhere. They kept track of her PPS number."

When she gave him a confused look, he added, "Sorry, that stands for personal public service number; it's our equivalent of your social security number, I think."

Lauren nodded.

"Her number's never been used. My folks think she probably overdosed with no identification and is buried in an unmarked grave, somewhere.

"Because Glenna had been reported missing, my parents received a few calls from the police that first year, calls about nameless women who'd been found dead. They matched her description, and my parents were asked to take a look at the bodies. When the third call came, they told the police they couldn't handle another viewin'. If Glenna was alive, she didn't want to be found, and there was nothin' more they could do." He shrugged. "Every year, on her birthday, they still ran a search on her PPS number and nothin'. That stopped after Katelyn died."

Lauren offered him a deep sigh. Her expression was slightly slack, but she didn't say anything.

Knowing she was adopted too, he asked, "Did you ever find out who your birth parents were?"

Lauren cradled her teacup in her hands, her drawing forgotten. "I've never wanted to look. It's hard knowing that you weren't wanted by the person who brought you into this world, that you weren't wanted enough to make whatever sacrifices were necessary to stay together." She sighed. "That's not fair. I don't know the circumstances of the woman who gave birth to me. Maybe I would have died had she tried to make it work, and she knew it. I'm sure, like most mothers in that situation, she thought she was doing what was best."

"I can't believe that about my mother."

"Why is that?"

"She had help and support—people who loved her and were there for her. My aunts have never excused my mother's actions, but they do remind me how the three of them had a terrible childhood, how Glenna had turned to drugs, and how much of a game changer that was."

He pushed his teacup forward so he could fold his arms on the table. "When I was a teenager and old enough to understand things, I played the scenarios in my head. My mother wouldn't have lasted long strung out on drugs. So, she's either dead, like my aunts believe, or she got clean and never came back for me, never came back to the people who have always loved her. Either way, it's tragic."

Lauren leaned her arm on the table, while holding his gaze. She propped her head onto her hand and studied him for a moment. "It is very tragic. *The Lord gives and the Lord takes away.*"

She blinked back the tears that filled her eyes. He could see her swallowing back the knot that formed in her throat.

"Is that why you're not speaking to Him?"

Lauren looked away and picked up her pencil. She started to draw as if she intended to ignore the question. At one point she used her free hand to swipe at her eyes before refocusing on her drawing. It made him think of blurred lines and the shadow of Eva's figure the day she'd walked out of his life.

She didn't look at him when she said, "I'll tell you one day."

Brendan stood and moved to stand by her side. He placed a hand on her shoulder and gave it a gentle squeeze before turning to leave.

He too had to rub his eyes to see the buttons on the lift. With five little words, "*I'll tell you one day,*" and before she could ever belong to him, Lauren Ross had become his greatest loss.

Chapter Eighteen

Donal's gut twisted itself into knots when he didn't see Ellen from the pulpit. All through the song service, he'd looked for her hoping she was running late. She hadn't attended last Sunday either, and he was worried.

He managed to get his thoughts under control and focused on his sermon.

After the doxology, instead of making his way to the back to wish his parishioners farewell, he made a bee-line to Mary and Jack O'Leary. "Would you mind waitin' around until I've said my goodbyes? I want to talk with you both for a minute."

"Sure," Jack agreed.

After everyone had left, Donal made his way to where the O'Learys sat waiting for him.

"Thank you for stayin'. I am worried about Ellen."

Jack raised his eyebrows in question but let him continue.

"A couple of weeks ago, I asked Ellen if everythin' was okay. I had noticed she wasn't comin' to church regularly. She told me she was really busy with the new bakery, but that she would be back the followin' Sunday. She never made it, and she's not here today."

Donal couldn't help but notice the uncomfortable look that flickered across Mary's face. But then she quickly recovered. "She's in Dublin this weekend with Brendan. They had a meetin' with the tea supplier."

He felt a bit relieved by the news but couldn't shake the feeling that something wasn't right. "Does Ellen seem okay to you?"

Jack responded first. "She seems normal; very excited about the new bakery. It's all she talks about. On Friday, I met the American, Lauren. She came by the house to look at the garden. She'll be using some of the space and helpin' out with the bakery's plot. She and Ellen were quite excited and spent a good deal of time talkin' about their plans."

Donal's shoulders relaxed a bit.

Mary spoke next. "I agree with Jack. I haven't noticed anythin' unusual."

He knew how close Ellen was to her parents, especially her mother. If something was wrong, Mary would surely know. But then why had she looked uncomfortable when he'd mentioned Ellen's absence the last several weeks? He wouldn't press the issue.

"Well, thank you for reassuring me."

When the O'Learys left, he moved to the pulpit to retrieve his bible and notes. He stood there for a moment thinking about Ellen and the concerns he had about her behavior of late. He didn't mention to her parents that Ellen also hadn't attended the book club meeting this past Thursday. Mary hadn't been there either, but then Shane had mentioned that she'd had some real estate showings that evening. It wasn't unusual for Mary to miss, depending on her client's schedules. But no one knew why Ellen hadn't showed.

The last time he'd spoken to her, she been abrupt and distant, and when he started attending the book club meetings, she didn't show. He had a nagging feeling that whatever was wrong with Ellen had to do with him. The thought caused his stomach to tighten. Had he done something to offend her? He thought through every interaction with her over the past couple of months, and he couldn't think of a single thing he might have said to upset her.

He sat down in one of the choir chairs and stared across the empty church. He missed Ellen. He missed her very much and couldn't seem to pinpoint the exact moment when she had become so important to him. For the last year, she had always been around. Now she was gone, and it panicked him.

He'd been praying about the turn his feelings had taken but couldn't find peace. It eluded him—just like Ellen.

As his gaze moved toward the direction where she normally sat, his eyes caught the shine of aluminum in the front row.

Donal sighed in frustration at the sight of the casserole that Fiona Hughes had made for him. If another single woman brought him a casserole, he was bound to lose it. He sighed. Donal would never really lose his cool, but he wanted to. He'd want to in a really bad way, and then maybe the single women in his church would get the message.

Getting married would fix that problem. Donal straightened up in the chair. *Now where in the world had that thought come from* ? His mind immediately flew to Ellen. Donal looked up toward the ceiling of the church and narrowed his eyes. He said out loud, "Really?"

Lauren was determined not to cry. Brendan had dropped her and Ellen off at the bakery before driving to his parents' house to pick up Noirin.

After depositing her bags into her bedroom, she plopped down on the couch and willed away the tears. She was so tired of crying, so exhausted from the sorrow. The last two weeks, Lauren had been given a reprieve, a respite from her pain. And then on Saturday, it had all changed.

At first, she'd been stunned by Flynn's offer, and then she just hurt. She'd seen the interest in his eyes, and it was the first time, since losing Christopher, that she'd been confronted with the reality that she was still here and would be expected to move on with her life.

In the year since Christopher's death, this new reality, this new perspective had never presented itself. Everyone in her circle of influence was either married, or they knew the depth of her loss and that she was off limits.

Lauren lay down on the couch and lifted her arm over her eyes, frustrated by the fresh new prick of tears. Christopher had been her soul mate, the one person she was destined to be with. She believed in true love and that everyone had someone. She had found her someone and then lost him. Lauren knew he felt the same; he had told her on their second anniversary, on the yacht. She relived that night in her mind, remembering as many of the details as she could manage—the food, the feel of the boat on the water, the way Christopher had touched and caressed her under the stars.

Lauren felt the ache grow in her belly, the need that oftentimes stirred when she thought about him. She missed his touch. She missed touching him, her sweet, sensitive lover, always giving more than he took.

She had teased him once, several months after they were married. "I'm waiting for the real Christopher Ross to show up." He'd been holding her in his arms, trailing his forefinger up and down the length of her forearm when she'd spoken.

"Oh yeah?" His voice had been sleepy and content.

"We're always told in movies and books, and even by people we know, that at some point the honeymoon will be over. That not too long after, we'll find ourselves staring at the *real* Mr. and Mrs. So-and-So."

"You mean, you're not real?" He slid his hand down the length of her. "You sure feel real to me."

She laughed. "No joking. I'm trying to have a serious conversation with you."

"What happened to pillow talk filled with sweet nothings?" he murmured.

"This *is* pillow talk. Serious pillow talk."

That must have gotten his attention because he

pulled away to look at her. "Are you really expecting some other version of me to walk into the house in the next week, month, or year?"

She shrugged. "When people date, they put their best foot forward, and then they begin to relax and show their true selves."

"Well, first of all, you ruined that for yourself by spilling your coffee all over me. There was no putting your best foot forward that day."

Lauren laughed at the memory. "I guess I did kind of break the ice, a little bit, didn't I?"

He kissed her. "A little bit. But do you really believe that we'll wake up one day different?" When she didn't say anything, he asked, "Are you the same person I dated and was engaged to? Have you changed?"

"I don't know. I don't think so, but shouldn't you be answering that question?"

"All right then, my answer is you're the same. You're the same woman I met at our coffee shop, the same woman I'm lying here with now. Am I the same to you?"

"Every bit."

"Then what's the problem?"

"If it doesn't happen, then why do people say it does?"

He looked thoughtful for moment. "I can't speak for everyone else. But we did a lot of things right, Lauren. We spent a chunk of money on pre-marital counseling. It helped us to work through the land mines before we ever stepped on them. It helped us to see how we would react in different situations. It showed us that we have the same values and perspective on life. Those things are important. When I was dating you, I never pretended to be someone I wasn't."

"You're a little more anal about being tidy than I thought you would be."

"And that's a bad thing because...?"

"When I get busy, I don't keep up the house as well as I'd like."

"Have I ever told you that it bothers me?"

"Well, no, but one day you're going to tell me. You're just being nice."

"Because we're still in that honeymoon phase." He lifted his arm as if he were checking his watch. "When exactly does that end, so I can be prepared to tell you what I really think about your housekeeping skills."

Her eyes widened and her brows furrowed. "Christopher, I'm serious."

"And so am I. If it bothered me, why would I wait to tell you? Have I ever done that before? Have you done that to me? Are there things you want to tell me but haven't?"

He had turned the tables on her, and she wanted to be angry with him. But because he was right, she knew she couldn't.

Her facial expression softened, and she felt the first rush of remorse. "I'm borrowing from trouble, aren't I?"

In response, Christopher reached for her, drew her hard against his body, and kissed her senseless. When he finally pulled away, he said, "And that is why I love you, so much. Our honeymoon lasted ten days. It was glorious. But you know what? I love this part better. I love seeing you bothered by something, but in your goodness, you can see through to the truth. That is the woman I fell in love with, the woman I love more today than I did five minutes ago."

And Lauren had loved Christopher more each and every day that she'd known him. Her love for him was so complete, so all-encompassing that even when he'd passed away, there was nothing left for anyone else, no room in her heart for another.

How blessed she'd been to be loved by him!

She thought of Ellen and Donal and what love could do for them, if they were meant to be together.

And then she thought of Brendan. Her chest ached from the memory of their moment in the hotel lounge. The way he'd looked at her, the soft squeeze he had given to her shoulder before leaving her alone, because he knew it was what she'd needed.

Had he ever loved anyone the way she loved Christopher? He too had lost so much. Was he as afraid to move on as she had been before coming to Tramore? He was as guarded as she was. She sensed it, felt it like a tangible thing, and it bothered her.

But he never pressed her for the answers to the questions he surely had.

She lifted her arm from her eyes and looked at the diamond on her ring finger, the sparkling solitaire that she'd been overjoyed to receive. It was the symbol of her everlasting love to a man so unchanging. To all the

Flynns out there, she'd never take it off, and soon, those who had come to mean a great deal to her would know the reason why. Lauren would give them the answers to their questions. And then she would continue on with her life—without a man, save the one who had already given her true love and a trove of sweet memories, enough to last her a lifetime!

"Sweetheart, it's late and Lauren's had a long weekend."

"But I want to see her. I missed her," Noirin whined, something she didn't do very often.

He was trying to herd her up the stairs and away from Lauren's door so she wouldn't hear them. If he didn't have two bags with him, he would have hauled her into his arms and rushed her up to his flat.

His daughter wouldn't budge. "Please, I want to see her."

Brendan was having a taste of how things would be a year from now, after Lauren returned to the States. It worried him. His worry turned to frustration, and he was about to take on a not-so-nice tone with his daughter when the door to Lauren's flat opened.

"Hi, sweetie," she greeted Noirin as she lowered herself and opened her arms.

His daughter ran to her and held onto her like it'd been years since they'd last seen each other.

Lauren held onto her just as tight and closed her eyes, savoring every moment. "I missed you so much, Noirin."

She pulled away to look at his little girl, her hands cupping the sides of her face. "I can't wait to tell you all about our adventures."

"Mine too. I had fun with Daideo and Maimeo."

"Aw, I'm so glad. I love you. Do you know that?"

Noirin's curls bounced with the nod of her head. "I love you too."

Lauren kissed her and then pulled her into her arms once more. "I'll see you in the morning for your walk to school, okay?"

"Okay. Tomorrow,"

Lauren stood to her feet acknowledging Brendan for the first time. "Hi," she said.

"Hi."

They stared at each other for a minute, unsure of what to say.

"I hope we weren't disturbin' you?" he offered first.

"I was hoping I'd hear you." She glanced down at Noirin who'd moved to Lauren's side, her hand caressing his daughter's hair.

On the way back from Dublin, Brendan had thought many times about how he could put some distance between the three of them.

Noirin's actions, a moment ago, confirmed to him that it was too late. It might be too late for his daughter, but not for him. Lauren loved Noirin, and she would keep her safe. Brendan wouldn't deny his daughter time with

Lauren, but she would do it on her own, as much as he could get away with.

He looked at Noirin. "Say good night. It's time to get to bed."

Lauren bent down and gave her another kiss and a hug. "Goodnight," she said to them both, before entering her flat and closing the door.

I wish you'd never come to Ireland, Lauren Ross. It was a lie, but he wanted to believe it so badly.

Chapter Nineteen

Stacey loved her daughter-in-law. Lauren was the daughter she never had. As good as their relationship was, Stacey loved Lauren most of all because of how she had loved her son. It was a mother's gift to see the child one had raised being loved and cherished, so well taken care of by another. While some mothers might feel threatened by the woman who would take that central place in their son's life, she hadn't. All Stacey ever wanted was the best for Christopher. He'd had that in Lauren.

Stacey remembered the first time Lauren had called her "Mom." The weekend after they had returned from their honeymoon, the newlyweds had come to the house for dinner. Lauren had walked through the door ahead of Christopher saying, "Mom, Dad, we're home!"

Hearing those words had brought tears to Stacey's eyes. The salad she had been tossing, had been blurred by the emotion. She'd quickly dried her eyes and rushed to greet the two of them, kissing them both on the cheeks.

She'd reached for Lauren's hands. "I love you like a daughter," she said, her Irish brogue thicker than normal with emotion. It was something she'd wanted to tell Lauren on her wedding day but hadn't because it was a day for her new daughter and her own mother. As it should be, just as it had been a day for her and her son. Placing his boutonniere on the lapel of his tux, she had looked at him with all the love she felt shining brightly in her eyes. "Have I told you lately how proud I am of you?"

He'd smiled at her, that sweet smile of his. "You know it's impossible for me to count the number of times I've heard it. But do you know what's even better?"

She'd shaken her head, her eyes filled with tears.

"More than your words, you've shown me how proud you are of me, how valued and loved I am. Thank you, Mom."

It had been a tender moment. And now, the thought of her son gone and no longer alive for any of them to love still brought her to her knees with grief.

She sat on the couch and stared at the envelope with her name on it. Losing her son had not only turned her world upside down, it had shaken loose the cobwebs that held her past exactly where it belonged: in Ireland.

Stacey may have been born in Ireland, but her life began in New York when Fred had saved her. She hadn't known what truly living meant until her husband had shown her what it really looked like. He had shown her the promise of true love, faith, and purpose and how it could cast the darkest of lives into brilliant sunlight.

She stood from the couch, the letter from her daughter-in-law on the sofa untouched, and walked to the window. It was a gray cloudy morning, and the sky looked as if it would unload any minute. Stacey looked upwards and felt the uneasiness she'd felt ever since Lauren had announced she would be taking a tour of Ireland.

It had been an out-of-the-blue decision made two weeks before she'd left. They hadn't expected her at the house that evening and were surprised when she showed up.

She'd looked as sad as she always had.

"Hi, Mom," she greeted Stacey with a kiss to her cheek. "Is Dad here? I was hoping to talk to you both."

They walked to the family room where Fred was reading, and Stacey tried not to feel anxious about what Lauren had to share.

When they were all seated, she said, "You know I've been meeting with a counselor."

They both nodded but waited for her to continue.

"Dr. Moore suggested that I consider taking a trip somewhere. She feels like it will help me to deal with the grief."

Stacey felt relieved. "Well, I think that's a grand idea, Lauren."

Her daughter-in-law gave her a wistful smile, as if she wasn't quite convinced that the doctor's advice would really help.

"Where are you planning to go?" Fred asked.

"Ireland."

The room could have been loud and noisy but she would have heard Lauren's words. They reverberated in her mind while her heart began to race.

Lauren kept looking at Fred when she made the announcement.

"I'm planning on being there for a year, traveling."

195

Stacey didn't know what to say, but managed to ask, "Why so long?"

"Because I don't even know if after a year I'll be any closer to being okay. And Christopher and I always wanted to go to Ireland. We used to dream about doing an extended tour and had started saving for it. He'd always told me that if the opportunity ever came for him to find a temporary job there, he'd seriously have to consider it.

"I was reluctant to do this, but I've thought long and hard about Dr. Moore's advice and about Christopher's love for Ireland, and I think it's the best thing for me to do. I want you to visit. Mother and Father are coming to stay with me for a week in May, wherever I might be at the time."

Stacey's heart was still racing and her head was pounding when she asked, "So you won't be staying in one place?"

"I'm not planning to at the moment. I want to travel the country and also go to Paris."

Tears welled up in Lauren's eyes. Her daughter-in-law had been remembering her and Christopher's honeymoon, their wedding gift to their son and their new daughter.

It would be impossible for her to visit Lauren in Ireland, but she didn't say anything. Fred spoke instead. "We'll talk it over. I'm glad you're going, Lauren. I think this will be a good thing for you. When do you leave?"

The rest of the conversation had been a blur as

Stacey felt the weight and uneasiness about Lauren's decision settling in around her.

Now, seeing the letter her daughter had written to her brought to the surface the pain she had conscientiously buried away all these years.

Stacey walked back to the couch and picked up the letter. She looked at the stamp from her homeland, no return address, just Lauren's name in the familiar writing of her daughter-in-law's hand. Stacey wouldn't read the letter. She couldn't.

She walked to her bedroom and opened her dresser drawer and placed the letter underneath her nightgowns. That night while Fred slept soundly, she stared at the dresser drawer and tried not to think about what the letter said.

Donal struggled to catch his breath as he stared across the street toward Lanigan's pub. He watched Ellen as she leaned her elbows attentively on a table and spoke to another man, someone he didn't recognize.

The surprise of seeing her with someone else caused his heart rate to increase and a knot to form in his stomach. He'd known it was a possibility. Brendan had indicated as much the night he expressed his concerns about Ellen. This must be the man keeping her in Tramore.

He stood there and watched her while contemplating what to do. He had walked from the rectory to the pub to put in an order of Brianna's meatballs, but suddenly he no longer had an appetite. He hadn't stopped thinking about Ellen since Sunday when she hadn't shown up for church, and he'd begun to wonder if she was upset with him about something.

Donal heard her laugh at something the man said, and his stomach twisted even tighter. He should turn around and head back home, open up a can of something from his cupboard, and forget about the meatballs. Even as he decided to do exactly that, he found himself crossing the street and walking toward their table in the outdoor patio area.

Once he stepped onto the pavement and was close enough for her to hear him, he called out to her, "Ellen?"

She looked away from the man she was with. When their eyes connected, he could see the wariness behind her look—only for a moment—but she quickly covered it up and smiled at him. Her initial look confirmed his suspicions: she was upset with him. "Donal, what are you doin' here?"

"I decided to have some of Brianna's meatballs," he replied and then looked at the man seated across from her.

"Oh, James, this is the pastor of my church. His name is Donal Kavanagh."

Not friend, just her pastor. The realization of her words cut quicker than seeing her with another man. Was that all he was to her? "It's nice to meet you, James," he managed to say.

The other man smiled. "The same here. You're more than welcome to join us, if you'd like."

Donal was surprised by the man's offer, but declined. "Thank you, but I don't want to intrude." He turned his attention to Ellen. "Well, I better get my order in before all the meatballs are gone. It was good to see you, Ellen, and again, nice meetin' you, James."

The couple smiled and bid their goodbyes while Donal made his way inside Lanigan's. He decided to get the meatballs to go rather than take a table like he usually did. Before he could approach the bar, he heard his name and realized that Aine from the bakery was trying to get his attention. She was with her husband.

He walked over to their table.

"Hi, Donal. Are you here for dinner?"

He nodded. "I was planning to grab something to go."

"You should join us," her husband Peter offered. They were a nice couple who attended Holy Cross, so it wasn't often he had the chance to talk with them. But he had always enjoyed their company when he had been invited to Cups and Cakes' employee events.

"That would be great," Donal said and took a seat.

"We just got here and are still waitin' to put in our order, so perfect timin'," Aine said. "Did you see Ellen on your way in?"

"I did. She introduced me to her friend. Have you ever met him before?"

Peter shook his head, and Aine said, "I thought he might be someone from your church. She's never mentioned him at work before."

The waitress came by to take their orders, and Donal was even more curious about the man Ellen was with. He was glad they were seated in the patio area; seeing her smile at the stranger and laughing at his comments would have pushed him further over the edge of these feelings he couldn't seem to control. Suddenly, he realized that those feelings had a name—'jealousy,' and the realization didn't sit well with Donal. He forced himself to focus his thoughts on the couple who had invited him to join them, and after placing his order, he asked them how they had been doing. They had a lively conversation about their work, football, and the upcoming charity auction for the food pantry.

Donal didn't realize how much time had passed, and it was time to leave. They left the restaurant together, and to his relief, Ellen and James had already left.

If it weren't for the fact that Ellen lived with her parents, Donal would have marched over to her house and confronted her with his concerns. But he didn't want to cause her parents to wonder. Instead, he made his way down Main Street and headed back to his house.

The streets of Tramore were quiet as dusk settled on the small town with only a few faint streaks of light on the horizon. He enjoyed walking the town at night, with lights glowing from store-front windows and apartments overhead. Sometimes he would catch glimpses of people inside their homes settling in for the night, and it would make him feel good about being a part of a community that was so welcoming.

Donal's thoughts turned back to Ellen. He was alone now and able to process the feelings he'd finally recognized. They were new to him. He'd never cared enough for another woman to feel that sharp prick of jealousy followed by the dread that settled deep inside. He didn't like it. And worse, he didn't know what to do about his growing feelings for her. The suddenness and the surprise of them slightly terrified him. Was he ready to do something about them? And if he did, what if she rejected him? How would he cope? The possibility that she might reject him mattered to him. It mattered a great deal, more than he cared to think about.

Donal made the turn down Market Street and knew what he would do.

Chapter Twenty

The next morning, Donal left his house much earlier than normal. Today, he had a longer walk to make than the short walk next door to the church office. When he entered the bakery, the smell of freshly baked goods made him smile with pleasure. He'd smelled that scent more times than he could count, but today was different. The sweet yeasty fragrance was because the woman he cared about had created the tantalizing aromas with her own hands.

An image of her baking in his kitchen and coming home from the office after a long day came to mind. He imagined coming up to her and greeting her with a kiss and asking her how her day had been. The moment filled him with a yearning he'd never felt before.

He greeted John, who was at the front counter, with a nod and a hello before he made his way to the kitchen.

Ellen was busy rolling out some dough alongside her two other bakers.

"Good morning," he called out.

All three of them looked up from their work. Ilene and Martha smiled at him, but Ellen did not. The happy feeling that he'd felt when he walked into the bakery dissipated.

"How are you, Donal?" Ilene greeted him first.

"Fine. It sure smells good in here."

Both ladies smiled at him in response.

He turned his attention to Ellen who had gone back to rolling her dough. "Ellen, I know you're busy, but I was hoping to talk to you for a minute?"

She looked up at him. "I'm ready for a break." She looked at the two bakers. "I'll be back in a few minutes." Ellen reached for the towel around her waist and wiped her hands before turning toward the office.

She led him in and he closed the door. "How was your date last night?" he asked.

Ellen smiled. "It was fine. How were your meatballs?"

She made no move to have a seat at the desk, and he stood close to the door.

"Brianna's meatballs are always good."

Donal was stunned for a moment by how beautiful Ellen looked. He'd always found her attractive in a platonic sort of way. He'd never cared for tall willowy women, but had always preferred petite women like Ellen. He wasn't an overly tall guy, and she complemented his five-foot ten frame perfectly. Seeing her now, in light of the feelings that had been pulling at him for the last two weeks, it filled him with desire, a punch in the gut kind of desire.

He swallowed hard and held her gaze. "I've been worried about you, Ellen."

The look in her eyes grew guarded. She shrugged. "I can't imagine why you would be worried about me."

"Have I done something to offend you?" Donal couldn't stand wondering any longer.

Her eyes widened and then relaxed a bit. "Why would you ever think such a thing?"

"Are you goin' to the book club meeting tonight?"

Her eyes widened again, but this time didn't relax as quickly. "I uh... I have work to do."

"That's why I think somethin' is wrong. You haven't been comin' to church, and when I started attendin' the book club, you stopped. What am I supposed to think? Look, I'm sorry if I've said or done anythin' to offend you. I wish you would just tell me what I did."

She looked away from him. "You've done nothin', Donal."

He wasn't convinced and neither was he ready to let it go. "Then why stop comin' to church?"

"I don't want to talk about it." Her voice rose an octave.

"That's not good enough, Ellen. I'm your pastor, and I'm worried."

Her eyes narrowed. "I said I don't want to talk about it."

"Ellen, please!" The frustration in his voice was evident.

She placed her hands on her hips. "Fine, do you really want to know what's goin' on, Donal?"

He nodded, his gut tightening in apprehension.

"I'm lookin' for another church to attend."

The pain in his chest almost had him sitting in a chair. "But why?"

"I need a change, and I need to get back to work," she added as she made her way toward the door.

Donal's words stopped her. "You know, Ellen, more than your pastor, I thought we were friends."

She looked at him then, and he noticed the tears gathering in her eyes. "And you know what, Donal, that's the problem." She didn't elaborate.

He badly wanted her to, but he wouldn't ask, so he let her open the door and walk away.

He sat in the closest chair, his mind and heart reeling from all she had said and everything she hadn't formed into words. He'd fallen for her, but she clearly wanted nothing to do with him. For the first time in his life, Donal Kavanagh didn't know what to do.

"Ellen!"

She looked up from the counter and saw Brendan standing on the opposite side staring at her with concern in his eyes.

"You're ruinin' the dough. How long have you been whackin' it to death?"

Ellen stared down at her hands, which were now resting on the blob of flour. She honestly didn't know how long she'd been at it, but she felt how badly her fingers ached and realized it must have been a while. She looked around the kitchen and realized that Martha and Ilene were gone and remembered they had left for their lunch break.

She wiped the back of her hand against her brow, and

willed for the tears not to come. She had let Donal's poking and prodding get the best of her, and she'd poked back at him, unkindly. What made her feel worse was that he thought he'd done something wrong, something to offend her. He was such a good a man, and the only thing wrong she'd ever known him to do was not love her. And that couldn't even be considered wrong, for you can't help whom you love.

The tears refused to be held back and spilled down her cheeks. Brendan went quickly to her side, holding her. She leaned into him, her face pressed against his chest, and allowed herself to cry and to be comforted by her cousin. He didn't push for answers, just soothed her ragged emotions.

"I love him so much," she finally said and followed it with a sob. "I've tried to stop and to forget about him, but I can't."

She looked up at him and asked, "Have you ever wanted someone so badly that you felt like you would do anythin' to have them—I mean anythin'?" Ellen shook her head as if to clear it. "I would never compromise my values, but sometimes I feel so desperate for him to love me that I think maybe I could."

There was a look of understanding in Brendan's eyes and she remembered Eva. "But you do know what that's like. I should have talked to you about this a long time ago."

Brendan gave her one more hug before dropping his hands to his sides. "How long have you been in love with James?"

"James?" she asked baffled by the question.

"Aine told me she met him last night. I knew there was someone keeping you here in Tramore. Why have you kept it a secret?" Brendan looked a little hurt.

Ellen chuckled at the timing and irony of her confession and her blind date with James. "Last night was the first time I'd met James. I'm not in love with him: I'm in love with Donal!"

Her cousin's eyes grew round and his mouth opened as if trying to form words he couldn't quite let go of. Eventually he managed to say, "Donal, pastor Donal, our friend?"

She turned to the counter and picked up the ruined dough. "It's the only Donal I know," she replied as she threw it in the trash can.

"Ellen, stop fidgeting and look at me."

She obeyed.

"You're in love with Donal?" He was still surprised but smiling.

"That's what I said."

"That's terrific. Why didn't I ever see it before? You two would be perfect for each other."

She crossed her arms over her chest and gave him a pointed look. "Yeah, grand in theory, but he's so not interested. He has gorgeous women throwin' themselves at him—or rather their casseroles—and then there's me. To Donal, I'm just someone who attends his church, a member of his flock, someone he's obligated to look after." Except he said he was also her friend. The tears burned the back of her eyes again.

Brendan's look softened. "Ellen, you're a beautiful woman, and I'm not just sayin' that because you're my cousin. Where did these image issues come from? I know your parents and can't imagine they would have ever said anythin' to make you feel less about yerself."

She shrugged. "Maybe I watched the tellie too much while growin' up and subscribed to too many fashion magazines. But I don't look like those women. And then there's Julia; she's drop-dead gorgeous and practically drools every time she sees Donal."

"Yeah, and Donal has never once asked her out, nor any of the other women who hound him with their casseroles. And if you think he's determined to marry someone who looks like Taylor Swift, then you don't know him as well as you think."

Ellen looked down at her hands. "I know he's not shallow. It's why I love him, but he's never noticed me in that way, and being around him is drivin' me crazy." She paused. "I hurt him?"

"What do you mean?" Brendan asked.

She looked up at him and told him about his visit earlier that morning.

Brendan sighed. "I'm goin' to go talk to him."

"No!" Ellen said a little more sharply than she intended. "So, help me, Brendan Callery, if you dare say anythin' about my feelin's to Donal, I'll never speak to you again. I mean it. If there's ever a chance that he's interested in me, he'll have to figure that out on his own and make a move. You better promise me."

Brendan hesitated. "I promise. But why can't you ask him out, Ellen? As a friend to start with and see where it goes?"

"Funny, that's what Lauren said."

His eyebrows lifted in surprise. "Lauren knows how you feel about Donal?"

She gave him a sheepish look, knowing the turn the conversation was taking. "I didn't plan to say anythin'; she figured it out and asked me. I didn't want to lie."

He seemed to accept her answer. "And see, that's why I think you need to ask him to a friendly dinner. Men can be very obtuse. We don't read between the lines well and sometimes we're even more scared to make the move than we realize."

"Has he ever said anythin' about me to you?"

Her cousin looked thoughtful. "He didn't say I couldn't mention it, but sort of. A few weeks ago, after the first book club meetin' he attended, he stayed back to help me clean up. We started talkin', and he said he was worried about you. I told him I thought your problem was a guy." Brendan laughed. "Boy was I right about that one!"

She punched his arm lightly, but grinned. "What did he say?"

"I didn't think too much of it at the time, but now, lookin' back, I think it kind of bothered him a bit."

She felt a small stirring of hope rise up in her chest. Was it possible he could feel something for her, more than just friendship?

"That's why I think you need to do somethin'.

Instead of invitin' him to dinner, bake him somethin' and take it to him. Your apology for how things went down this mornin'."

"Yeah, like all the other women who proffer their casseroles to him? I don't think so."

"You're right, he doesn't like it when they do that. Really, what he doesn't like are the expectations that come with the dishes. But you're not like that, Ellen, and he knows that. Just bake him somethin' simple and take it as a peace offerin'."

"But what if he can never love me the way I love him?"

He gave her a sympathetic look. "You'll find a way to deal with it. I'll help you. And eventually you'll find someone who will make you just as happy, even more so."

Brendan reached for her and pulled her into a hug. "Promise me you'll make him somethin'?"

"I'll think about it."

"Good enough."

Chapter Twenty-One

Lauren was confused and slightly hurt. It had been two weeks since the trip to Dublin, and something had changed between her and Brendan. Gone was the ease of the friendship they had been slipping into. He was always pleasant when she saw him, but he seemed distant. Things had changed between them the night in the hotel lounge. Had she shared too much or had she not shared enough?

She remembered the promise she had made to tell him everything, the same promise she had made to Ellen. And still, she hadn't followed through.

Or had their conversation opened doors that hadn't been opened in a while? They had spoken about his mother and how she had abandoned him. She remembered how she had felt hearing about his mother's choice to turn from her son, only to run back into the arms of her addiction. Above all, Lauren had felt angry at the woman who hadn't the foresight to see what a gift she'd had.

Ever since hearing about Brendan's abandonment, Lauren had played every scenario in her mind. Never having been an addict, she couldn't begin to imagine what drove a person to make the kind of choice his mother had made; but neither could she find an excuse for it. Even so, her sole comfort had been in knowing the outcome.

Brendan had been given the gift of a loving family, and he'd thrived in spite of it all.

And today, for the first time, she would be meeting the woman who had raised him. She'd already met Quinn at the bakery. He had been the one to extend the invitation to dinner. They were eager to meet the woman their granddaughter couldn't stop talking about.

It stung a bit that the invitation had come from them rather than Brendan. Once again, her mind wandered to the fact that things were undeniably different between the two of them. It not only hurt, but it worried her. Having only known each other for a short while, Lauren was uncomfortable asking what had changed.

She would give it time and continue to push onward with her friendship with Brendan. She would tell him about Christopher and hope that their relationship would turn back from where it had started... before Dublin.

Lauren put the car in park. The Callerys didn't live too far from the bakery, but she'd brought a salad, and the bowl was heavy and too awkward to walk with.

After receiving the invitation, she'd learned from Brendan how they always had family dinner on Sundays. Shane would be there as well as Ellen's family. It was a tradition that the two sisters had started soon after Mary had married. Mary was the youngest of the Stewart sisters and had married her husband Jack a couple of years after Shay and Quinn had become a family.

It was Ellen who had greeted her at the red door of the cute yellow house with black shutters. The entry way was as inviting, and the smells that greeted her reminded her of home.

"I'm so glad you're here!" Ellen exclaimed while giving her a hug.

The two of them had spent a lot of time together since their trip to Dublin. Lauren had been eager to help with the new bakery and the garden. After completing the drawing of the lavender biscotti for the recipe card, Ellen and Brendan had finalized an offer for her. All three of them had finally agreed on Shane's compromise, half the going rate for anything Lauren did with the business.

She hadn't wanted the money, but in the end, she knew it was important to Brendan to pay her, and so she acquiesced. Today, she brought with her a new drawing for a second recipe card. Ellen had decided to add an Irish rarebit recipe, toast topped with a leek and cheese sauce. Lauren had enjoyed drawing the leek and had decided that with all of the recipe cards she would draw not only the dish but also the main ingredient as a background element to the picture.

"Did you bring the recipe card for the rarebit?" Ellen asked.

"I finished it this morning."

"Ooh, I can't wait to see it. Did I tell you how much I loved the biscotti drawing?"

"You did, but I love eating your biscotti more."

Ellen laughed and took the salad bowl from Lauren. "Here let me help you with this. Your hands will be full in a minute. Noirin hasn't stopped asking when you'd be here. I'm surprised she's not storming the gates as we speak."

When they entered the spacious family room, the little girl, whom she loved, squealed with delight and ran to her. Lauren scooped her up in her arms and kissed her on the lips. "Hello, sweetheart, how are you doing?"

Noirin placed her small hands alongside her face and grinned at her. "You're finally here."

"I am," Lauren replied before turning to the other people in the room. All eyes were on her, all familiar except for one. "Hello, Mrs. Callery," she said to Brendan's Aunt Shay. "It's nice to finally meet you."

"Likewise. Come, so I may have a better look at you." His aunt was sitting in a comfortable chair near the stone fireplace. It wasn't lit, due to the sunny weather, but she imagined her sitting there in the colder months warmed by its heat and its charm.

Lauren walked over to the woman who had loved Brendan as her own and shook her hand. "We're so glad you came," Shay greeted. "I've heard so much about you, and I can't wait to get to know you better. Our little magpie here can't stop talkin' about you."

Noirin knew she was being talked about and reached toward her grandmother indicating she wanted to be held by her. Lauren released her into the older woman's arms who placed her on her lap.

Shane was beside her and reached out to give her a welcoming hug. "Ellen showed us the first recipe card." He looked around the room. "I told you she was talented."

Mary came up to her to give her hug. "It's lovely! I can't wait to see the whole series. They will be a big seller.

Last night, Ellen picked out the recipe box that she'll sell in the tearoom. Did she show you?"

Lauren nodded. "She texted a picture. I love the floral design. Were you able to find matching tea canisters?" she asked her friend.

"Unfortunately, not. I'll have to go with a complementary style instead."

After acknowledging Jack and Quinn, she turned to Brendan who was seated in a chair near the entrance to the dining room. She waved at him and he gave her a smile. "Glad you could make it," he said but with a hint of that distance that had wedged itself between them.

After a few moments of chatting with each other, they moved into the dining room to have dinner. Lauren watched as Quinn helped Shay from her chair and led her to the table. They looked good together, affection for one another evident in their eyes. She also noticed the way Quinn touched his wife and the way Shay held onto her husband.

Lauren held back for a moment along with Brendan. As they followed his parents into the other room, she whispered to him, "They look really good together."

He smiled at her compliment and she saw something in his look, something that looked a little like longing. She felt it too, and for a moment, the warmth of the picture of the older couple caused her to feel sad because she would never have that again with Christopher. She'd never have that with anyone. The errant thought pricked at her. Did she want that with someone else, someone other than the man she had loved completely but had then lost?

215

Lauren didn't have time to ponder too much on the thought. She was immediately drawn into the conversation that had begun around the table, as Mary and Ellen were bringing in the dishes and setting them in the center.

Extended family was something she could never experience enough of. Her parents' siblings had all moved away, and they only saw each other once a year. Stacey had been tightlipped about her family in Ireland. Her father-in-law's only brother had never married. Instead, he traveled the world with his work for an international company. There had never been regularly scheduled family dinners with cousins and aunts, something she would have enjoyed very much.

During the meal, they talked about many things. There was much laughter and some lively debating between Jack and Quinn, who Lauren realized were very good friends.

She appreciated seeing Brendan interacting with his parents. He sat next to Shay, and at one point, he laughed at something she said and then kissed her on the cheek. She could tell it was something he did often.

Being around his family, she'd noticed that his smile was back, that achingly, oddly familiar smile that she'd discovered in Dublin. The smile that warmed her every time he'd directed one at her, but hadn't done so since. She wanted it back, and Lauren decided she would do what was necessary to win it back. She knew what that would be and realized it was time.

Over dessert, Brendan chose that moment to tell his family the good news. "I received Noirin's test results back, and all is well!"

"What a relief!" Shay exclaimed as she pressed her hand to her chest.

Everyone else joined in with words of relief.

It was good news. Brendan had found out on Friday but held onto it until their family dinner. The reassurance he felt had been elating. For another year, he could breathe a little more easily. It was hard knowing that this is the way it would always be, this cycle of build-up to worry and then the knee-weakening relief. But if it meant having Noirin as his child, he'd do it every time.

Ellen, who was seated on his other side, reached for his hand and gave it a squeeze. He smiled at his cousin, though his joy ebbed a bit at knowing Ellen's struggle with Donal. It had been nearly two weeks since she'd told him about her love for his friend, and she still hadn't made a move. He understood her decision not to pursue him—respected it even—but he couldn't help but feel that if she made the first move, she'd be very happy with the outcome.

Donal had been somber and out of sorts himself. He'd attended the last two book club meetings, but it was obvious he was there because of the promise he made to Shane, not because he wanted to be there. When Brendan had tried talking to his friend, he said everything was fine. Brendan knew Donal wasn't okay. Not one to meddle in another person's business, he'd let it go, and hoped for the best between two great people who deserved love and happiness.

Sunday dinner usually ended with the men watching football during the season and the women talking. Cork City was playing Waterford, his favorite team. They were always a fun match to watch, but his mind wasn't into it.

Earlier, while they had finished dessert, Lauren had mentioned her trip to Waterford and then on to Mourne Mountains in Northern Ireland. Shane and Brendan's parents seemed surprised she was going alone. He wouldn't allow himself to worry. She wasn't his to worry about, and honestly, he was looking forward to a break from Lauren. Several days of not seeing her would do him some good.

When the evening ended, his parents hugged Lauren and told her to stop by anytime; their door was always open. She told them she would visit after she returned from her trip. They exchanged numbers, and Brendan felt even more frustrated that there was another layer of his life where she had become entrenched.

Lauren left first, followed by Ellen and her folks. On the way to his car, Shane asked, "Is everythin' okay with you and Lauren?" *So, he'd noticed.* Brendan wasn't surprised. His friend was very intuitive.

Brendan nodded in response to the question. "Somethin' happened in Dublin. Let me put Noirin in her car seat."

A few moments later, he said to his daughter, "I'll be back in a minute, sweetheart. I need to talk to Uncle Shane." He kissed her forehead before closing the door.

He told Shane about the incident with Flynn at *The Avenue.*

218

CHAPTER TWENTY-ONE

"So, why has that come between you and Lauren?"

"She'll never be free of her husband, Shane. It was obvious, and I've realized I need to put some distance between us, just when I had begun to hope and had decided to enjoy being with her no matter how long I had. There was a part of me that thought she might stay, but I know she never will."

"It could still happen. She needs time that's all."

"Like you needed time, Shane?"

His friend looked a little taken aback by the comment, but he didn't say anything.

"She's just like you," Brendan continued. "Your one grand love lost to you forever and you've never recovered. Have you ever tried to move on—to love someone else?"

Shane didn't answer but simply stared at him. There was nothing for his friend to say because Brendan already knew the answer. He was right, and they both knew it.

"I'm sorry, Shane. That was your choice to make, and I've never held it against you."

"Until now?" Shane interjected.

"No, not even now. It's just that I see that same loss in Lauren, and I'm convinced that she'll never be able to let go. It bothers me to think about it; but I have to accept it. And in the meantime, I have to protect myself. I've lost so much as it is. I'm not interested in losing more—if I can help it."

The two of them stared at each other for a long moment.

"I'm sorry," Brendan said again. "I shouldn't have said anything."

"No, you're right about my struggle. And maybe you're right about Lauren. But what if you're wrong? Consider what you'll lose if you are, Brendan."

He thought about what Shane said but didn't know how he could gamble risking it all. Because that's what he'd be doing, risking it *all*. In the month that he'd known Lauren, she'd grown to mean more to him than Eva ever had. It seemed impossible, but it was true.

Brendan looked at Shane. "Has she talked to you about him?"

The older man shook his head. "How about you?"

"No, but she told me in Dublin she would."

"Well, that's good. Maybe after she tells you, you can go from there."

"I'm not holdin' my breath. Why does this always happen to me?" Frustration laced his words while he raked his fingers through his hair. "I told her about my birth mom. I've relived Eva all over again these past couple of weeks. It makes me angry, and then it just hurts."

"Don't give up, Brendan. The right woman is out there for you. You'll find her."

Brendan looked in the back seat. Noirin was asleep. "I need to get her home."

They shook hands and left his parents' house.

As he merged onto the street that would take them home, he thought about the coming week and how Lauren would be gone. He exhaled a sigh of relief.

Chapter Twenty-Two

Lauren had made it in good time to Waterford. Waiting until after she and Shane had walked Noirin to school had helped to avoid the traffic. Shane hadn't hidden the fact that he was worried about her taking off for Northern Ireland alone. On the way back to the bakery, he'd given her a laundry list of dos and don'ts and made her promise she would call if she needed anything. She'd promised before hugging him goodbye.

She was excited about her solo adventure, but realized she would miss them all. She felt a little silly and slightly overdramatic over the emotions. But they were real, and they were hers, feelings that were so very different from what she'd felt the past year. Because of that, she welcomed them.

Her thoughts drifted to Brendan. She would tell him about Christopher when she returned from her trip. Lauren had made the decision last night after leaving the Callery's home. It was time. These were her friends. They would understand her pain and still allow her to be who she was. No, not who she was, but who she was becoming. She was a different person. Her loss had made her different, and she was discovering who that new person was. Lauren smiled as she followed the signs to downtown Waterford. She had to admit she liked that new person.

An hour later, Lauren was hopeful, but overwhelmed. Her search for a Stacey Walsh had yielded thirty results in the surrounding area. Now she had the arduous task of determining which one might be her mother-in-law. For the first time since starting her search, she felt apprehensive. Stacey Ross hadn't wanted her family to know about her life in Ireland. There was a reason she kept her past tightly under wraps, even from Fred. What if Lauren uncovered something that could never be undone? It was something to think about. Lauren wouldn't do anything with the list of names until she returned from her trip.

It had taken Lauren over four hours to make the drive north to Mourne Mountains, which included a stop for lunch in Dublin at Fiddle Faddle, of course. She couldn't resist it. Lauren hadn't stopped thinking about their fish and chips since their visit and knew she would never be able to resist stopping in if she were ever in Dublin. And for the remainder of her stay in Ireland, she would make the drive as often as she could just for a taste. She tried not to think about how much she would miss their food when she returned to the States.

She took a selfie in front of the restaurant's sign and texted the picture to Ellen and Brendan. *Couldn't resist stopping. I wish you were both here.* She received an immediate reply from Ellen. *I'm so jealous and miss you already!* Lauren hadn't received a response from Brendan.

Pulling into the driveway of the bed and breakfast in Kilkeel, Lauren put her car in neutral. She let off the clutch and checked her phone. Over two hours later and still no response from Brendan. Somehow Lauren knew she wouldn't get one. If he didn't respond, she'd know that her suspicions were correct and that something was wrong between them. She sighed and turned off the car and set the emergency break. Lauren didn't want to think about it right now. She'd worry about her relationship with Brendan later.

After gathering her bags, she made her way through the front door of the bed and breakfast, admiring the lobby of the place she would call home for the next several days. When she was done checking in and storing her bags in her room, she left to go explore.

It was getting too late to venture out toward the mountain range, so she made her way to Newcastle Road and walked around Kilkeel. After a while of exploring, she made her way to a small café that was still open.

She pulled out her tablet and a notebook and started planning the things she would do while in the area. Lauren had known she would come to Mourne Mountains. It was a place she and Christopher had planned to visit on their trip.

A year before he'd passed away, they had spent an evening at their coffee shop with their laptops and had mapped out all the places they would visit. He'd been the one to discover the beautiful mountain range. Their love of the outdoors made this an obvious choice, and Lauren had written the destination down in her notebook.

She brought the notebook with her to Ireland. While she was here, she wanted to visit all the places she and Christopher had planned to visit together. Some of them she'd do with her parents when they arrived in a couple of weeks, like the Cliffs of Moher. She'd already visited Dublin with Ellen and Brendan. And now she was here at Mourne Mountains.

Lauren looked at the notebook and placed a check mark next to the words. What would she do when she was done marking off the last place? There was a purpose in making this year- long trip to Ireland. It had started off as a way for her to heal and to deal with the pain of her loss. But it had turned into something more. She realized now what that more was. It was an opportunity to con-nect with Christopher once more, to do something they had both planned to do together. And when the final place was marked off her list, she didn't know what she would do. Surprisingly, she was okay with that. She'd learned over the last few weeks the value of taking things one day at a time.

She looked at her phone. There was still no response from Brendan. Lauren started a new text, with just his name on it and typed, *I miss you and Noirin. Please tell her I said hello.* Her finger hovered over the send button. She was afraid to send the text, and she hated the way it made her feel—like she'd lost someone else who was impor-tant to her. She'd make things right when she returned to Tramore. She had to.

Lauren pressed the send button and to her relief a

few seconds later she received a response from Brendan. *Noirin misses you too.* Lauren felt the sting of his reply. Noirin missed her but he didn't. It was obvious to Brendan that their relationship centered around her feelings for his daughter, nothing more. She had thought it was more. She wanted his friendship—needed it—needed it even more than she needed Ellen's or Shane's. Her brows furrowed at the thought because she couldn't understand why. What was it about Brendan that made her feel that way? Was it because they had a shared connection of abandonment and loss? She realized that must be the reason and it made her more determined than ever to repair whatever had been damaged between them.

Donal was depressed. He recognized the symptoms. The last time he'd felt this way was when he was in Thailand working as a missionary. He'd been assigned to a remote village and had been terribly homesick. It had taken him weeks to muddle his way back to normal.

Lying face down on his bed, he knew this was worse. It was so bad he had to leave the office after a counseling session with one of his parishioners. He'd told the woman it was okay to divorce her cheating husband without first seeing what could be done to salvage their marriage.

Marriage was forever and forgiveness should always be advised first. Realizing his mistake, he'd quickly retracted the statement and then apologized to her because he wasn't feeling well. He righted the session, and after it was over, he told his secretary, Shona, he wasn't feeling well and asked her to reschedule the rest of his appointments.

When he arrived at his house, he removed his shoes and flung himself face down on his bed. He tried not to think of Ellen and how much he wanted her. It killed him to think she didn't want to have anything more to do with him. How ironic! The minute he'd realized how much she'd come to mean to him, she was wiping her hands clean of him. And for what reason, he still didn't know.

He'd been tempted to ask Brendan if he knew anything, but had decided against it. He and Ellen were family and Donal didn't want to drag his friend into a mess he had no idea how he'd made.

Not knowing what he'd done wrong made him feel like such a failure. It had been nearly three weeks since his last conversation with Ellen, and he still didn't know what to do. He'd tried asking her, but she'd refused to say. What more could he do?

Worse was the terrible feelings of loss. He'd never been in love before, but somehow, Donal knew this was probably what it was like—unable to sleep at night, unable to think of anything else, unable to focus. When the love wasn't reciprocated, it had way of making a person feel as if they'd been cheated out of something wonderful.

What would it be like to kiss her, to hold her hand, and to feel the softness of her in his arms? He groaned into his pillow. Donal was torturing himself and he knew he had to stop.

At some point he must have fallen asleep because he woke with a start when he heard the doorbell ringing, insistently. He stood up from the bed, groggy, his mind muddled, and made his way to the door.

Shona was on the other side holding a plate with a card on top. It made him angry because he knew it was from one of the single women from the church.

"I'm sorry to bother you, pastor, but Ellen was insistent that I bring this to you. She was worried when I told her that you weren't feelin' well."

Ellen! His mind raced with the name that had filled nearly every free thought these last few weeks.

"Thank you," he said as he took the plate from her.

"Can I bring you anythin'?" his secretary asked, her brows furrowed with concern.

"I'm okay, but thank you. I'll talk to you in the mornin'."

She nodded before turning to leave.

Donal sat on his couch, the plate on his lap, covered with clear wrap. He could see that she had made him langues de chat, a classic French butter cookie dipped in mint chocolate ganache. They were his favorite. He remembered the first time he'd tasted them at a Christmas party and had fallen in love with them. He'd told Ellen then how much he'd enjoyed them. *She remembered.*

He felt hopeful and crazy all at the same time. He

stared at the card, afraid to open it, concerned over what it might say. Donal reached for the envelope and tore it open.

I'm sorry, Donal, for upsetting you. You have to believe me when I say that you have done nothing wrong. I remembered how much you loved these. I put them on one of my plates instead of a bakery box, so you could return it to me.

It was signed simply, *Ellen.*

Donal set the plate down and looked at the time. He knew Ellen would be on her way home and that her parents would still be working. He freshened up and then transferred most of the cookies to a container, leaving a few of them on the plate.

It didn't take long for him to reach her parents' house. He saw her in the garden. She'd seen him pulling up, was standing there watching him, her eyes solemn and wary. He felt the hope he'd been holding onto slip away, but he forced himself out of the car and grabbed the plate.

When he entered through the gate, he stood there and looked at her, taking her in. She was wearing pink wellies, jeans, and a light blue sweater to complement the blue of her eyes. Gloves covered her small hands.

"Thank you," he said as he lifted the plate of cookies.

She gave him a small smile. "Shona said you weren't feeling well."

CHAPTER TWENTY-TWO

He nodded. "I haven't been feeling well for a few weeks now."

A flash of regret filled her eyes. "Do you want to have a seat?" she asked nodding toward the bench at the far end of the garden.

It was a bit chilly. The sky was overcast, but rain wasn't in the forecast until the evening.

"Are you warm enough?" she asked. "We could go inside. Mum and Dad are at work," she offered as they took a seat on the bench. He sat the plate of cookies down on the grass beside him.

He had rushed out of the house without a jacket but had on a long-sleeved shirt.

"I'll be fine. Besides, it's really nice out here. I've always enjoyed your parents' property. The views are grand."

She looked straight ahead and didn't say anything. It was as if she was waiting for him to begin the conversation.

"I read your note, Ellen. I'm still havin' a hard time believin' that I've done nothin' wrong."

"And I'm sorry for that, Donal. The truth is you've done everythin' right."

She was looking at him now.

He was confused. "But I don't understand. Your words and your actions say somethin' completely opposite."

She nodded. "I can't talk about it, Donal."

His gut clenched in knots. They were back to where they'd started, both of them afraid to say what they really wanted to say. Well, he wouldn't be afraid anymore. If he didn't tell her how he felt, he knew he'd regret it.

"I've always liked you, Ellen. You're fun to be around. You are kind and generous, and the way you love your family, it makes me speechless sometimes." He held her gaze. "In the last few weeks, I've come to realize somethin' else."

Her eyes widened in anticipation. Did she feel it too?

"I've realized I have feelings for you. That I want to explore the possibility of being more than friends." When she didn't say anything, he quickly added, "I understand that you're probably into that James guy. Brendan told me he thought there was a guy keepin' you here in Tramore, but..."

He didn't get a chance to finish because Ellen abruptly stood to her feet and began walking to the fence. He followed her. She stopped when she reached the barrier, her back to him.

"Ellen, I had to tell you how I feel. When you gave me the plate of cookies, I had hoped there might be a chance. Would you say somethin', please?"

When she turned to him, there were tears in her eyes. "No one is keepin' me here in Tramore but myself. I'll tell you the same thing I told Brendan that day. I love it here. This is my home. I don't need to be in some big city, workin' at a fancy restaurant to find satisfaction in what I do. And that James guy, that was the first time I had met him."

Donal felt elated. "So, you're not seein' James?"

"He was very nice and asked me out again. I said yes."

His brows furrowed. "I understand. I'd like to ask you to dinner too, if I may?"

She smiled at him, that full breathtaking smile, a smile that he'd taken for granted for so many months. It shocked him to think how he'd simply just enjoyed it, never realizing until now how stunning it was and how he wanted to see that smile every day for the rest of his life.

"I would like to have dinner with you, Donal," he heard her say.

He smiled back. "I'm glad to hear it. How does Friday evening sound?"

"That works great."

Donal looked over toward the plate of cookies sitting by the bench. "Care to share a cookie with me?"

She laughed. "Did you have one yet?"

He shook his head. "My stomach was too twisted up in knots to eat anythin'." He gave her a sideways glance as they walked to the bench. "Do you promise I haven't done anythin' wrong?"

They sat down, and he reached for the plate of cookies and removed the plastic wrap.

"You just listed a few of my virtues, Donal. You can add honesty to that list," she answered before taking a bite of one of the langues de chats. "And don't ask me anymore whys. I'll tell you everythin' soon enough."

He accepted her answer and took a bite of one of the cookies. "Wow, these are amazin'!"

He draped his arm over the bench and scooted a little closer to her. "Have I told you how much I love to hear you speak French? What are these called again?"

"Langues de chat."

"That sounds as good as they taste." He held her gaze and fought the urge to kiss her. He wouldn't... not yet. He wanted to savor every new moment, every new experience with Ellen. Sitting with her on a bench, in the chilled spring air was the first of those moments, and he'd unwrap it slowly, with great anticipation, and then dream about how it all felt.

They talked for a while, until the sun started to lower in the sky.

When it was time to leave, she walked him to his car.

"I'm glad you came by, Donal. I'll see you tomorrow at the book club meetin'?"

His eyes lit up with pleasure. "You'll be there?"

She nodded. "Do you want to come to the bakery a little early, and I'll show you how to make bruschetta?"

He couldn't help it but he reached for her to hug her. She wrapped her arms around him, and they stayed that way for a while. "Thank you for not pushin' me away, Ellen." He wouldn't tell her how much he needed her, not yet. But soon.

She stood on the driveway and waved as he pulled away. When he looked in his review mirror, she was still standing there watching his car drive off into the dimming light of evening.

For the first time in weeks, Donal felt the peace that had been eluding him. He smiled and uttered a prayer of gratitude.

Chapter Twenty-Three

When are you coming home? Ellen texted Lauren. Her friend must have been on her phone, for she received an immediate reply. *Saturday.*

Good. I'll be able to tell you all about my date with... guess who?

Who? Lauren texted back.

Donal!

Donal?

Yes, I can't wait to tell you everything. Hurry back!

I'll call you when I get to my place. Come over! I want to hear every last detail!

You got it.

"What are you grinning from ear to ear about?"

Ellen jumped at the sound of her mother's voice. She hadn't heard her come in. She got up from the kitchen stool and ran to her mother and gave her a hug.

"What's this all about, sweetheart?"

She reached for her mother's hand and dragged her to the living room. "Sit. I need to tell you somethin'."

"Okay. If you weren't so happy, I would be a little terrified right now at the sound of those words."

Ellen couldn't stop grinning.

"I'm in love, mother!"

Her mother looked confused and then surprised. "Are you in love with that guy, James. Isn't it too soon?"

Ellen giggled. "I went out with the guy one time and everyone thinks I'm in love with him, even Donal."

"Donal? What does he have to do with all of this?"

"You have to promise me that you won't be upset with me. Do you promise?"

"You know I can't promise that without knowing what it is you have to say. So, no I won't promise not to be upset, but I will promise to try and understand. Now will you just tell me?"

"I've been in love with Donal for a while now."

Mary's eyes widened. "That's why you've been lookin' for another church?"

Ellen nodded, and then she told her mother about her growing feelings, her insecurities over his lack of interest in her, and how she stacked up to the other women throwing themselves at him."

"Oh, sweetheart," Mary said when she was done. She tucked a strand of Ellen's hair behind her ear and said, "I know I'm your mother, so I'm supposed to say you're beautiful, but you really are, darlin'."

"Thank you, Mum. It's been hard to think it when Donal hasn't paid me a lick of attention this past year. I knew I needed to move on, but I hurt him in the process."

Ellen told her mother about how she'd been distancing herself from Donal and the conversation they'd had the morning he came to the bakery.

"I apologized with a plate of cookies and he returned

them to me this afternoon." She paused, and feelings she didn't have words for pooled inside her like melted wax. He'd been so sweet, and she could tell by the look in his eyes how much he really did care for her, more than as her pastor and her friend. There was something wonderful in that look.

"He asked me out to dinner."

Mary looked thoughtful. "I really like him, Ellen. He's a good man, and I think the two of you will be very good together."

"So, you're not mad that I never said anythin'?"

"I would like to have known. I always felt like we could share things with one another, but then I also know this was a little different. He isn't just someone we know. He's the pastor of our church, and he's good friends with Brendan."

Ellen looked relieved. "Thank you for understandin'. He texted me when he got home. He's taking me to Waterford, to a nice French restaurant. I'm so excited and a little nervous. I want so much for this to work out, and I don't want things to be awkward now that he realizes he has feelings for me." She thought back to the moment on the bench, when he'd draped his arm over the back and had told her how he loved to hear her speak French. And the way he had hugged her when she offered to teach him to make bruschetta. There had been nothing awkward about those moments.

"Just be yerself and everythin' will be fine," her mother admonished. "Do you know what you're plannin' to wear yet?"

"No, I was hoping you could help me pick out somethin'."

"Did you even have to ask?"

They laughed. Ellen loved her mother so much. She'd always been close to both of her parents, but being a woman, her mother understood her, and she was truly grateful.

Ellen heard the door to the bakery open and knew it was Donal. She started to feel a little nervous about seeing him again. Would things be different? Perhaps he'd changed his mind about wanting to date her?

She left the kitchen to meet him. When she saw him, she stopped and took a moment to appreciate him. His brown hair was combed to the side, stylish and neat. She loved the cleft in his square chin and adored the one dimple that appeared when he smiled. His hazel eyes held hers, and everything inside of her melted.

"Hi," she managed to say.

He walked up to her and lifted the back of his hand to stroke the side of her cheek. "Hi," he replied, his gaze never leaving hers. She saw the longing in his eyes and felt it in his touch. She closed her eyes. "So, I wasn't dreamin' after all?" When she opened them, he was smiling at her.

"Funny, I was thinkin' the same thing. Yesterday was... it was wonderful, and I was worried I'd imagined it all."

She shook her head. If only he knew how many times she'd dreamt of this moment. She wouldn't tell him. It was too soon. And all that mattered was he was finally looking at her—really looking at her.

"We've been friends for a while," she said. "I don't want that to change. I don't want things to be strange between us."

He looked puzzled for a moment. "Do you feel they are?"

"No, just different. But for me, it's a good different. How about you?"

He gave her a wide grin, that dimple of his deepening even more. "Oh, you have no idea, Ellen. And I'm leavin' it at that. Walk me into that kitchen and show me how to make bruschetta before I change my mind."

His words caused a knot of desire to swell in her belly, causing her knees to weaken, slightly. She did as he asked and showed him how to make bruschetta. When they were done, he spooned a bit onto a piece of crusty bread and held it up for her to taste.

"How did I do?" he asked.

She chewed and swallowed. "It's wonderful, but then I've always known that you can cook. What did you bring tonight?"

"Take out. I didn't have time to make anythin'. Was plannin' to at lunch time, but I had plans with your dad?"

"My Dad?" Her eyes grew round with surprise.

"Mmm. I wanted to ask him for permission to date you."

Appreciation poured through her, and she was speechless.

"I hope you don't think I'm too old fashioned, but he is your dad, and he's also one of my parishioners. Besides, if I had a daughter, that's what I would want."

When she didn't say anything, he looked a little concerned. "Ellen?"

She shook her head as if to clear it. "Sorry, I'm just savoring what you said. That is awfully sweet of you, Donal."

He grinned, and she wanted so badly to kiss that dimple of his. How many times had she imagined doing that very thing?

They heard the front door open. A moment later, Brendan walked into the kitchen. He looked surprised to see them standing there.

"When I noticed that the door was unlocked, I got worried. I didn't know you were comin' to the book club meetin', Ellen."

"Sorry, I forgot to mention it today." She'd forgotten because she'd been walking on cloud nine all day and hadn't had a chance to tell Brendan about Donal.

Donal cleared his throat, and said, "I just want you to know that I asked Ellen out to dinner on Friday. I hope you're okay with that?"

Brendan grinned at both of them. "I thought you two were lookin' a little cozy when I walked in."

She and Donal looked at each other and smiled.

"Of course, I'm good with it," Brendan added. "So, where are you goin' on your first date?"

They told him while they finished getting the bruschetta ready for the book club meeting.

It was Shane who stayed back, this time, to help Brendan clean up afterwards. He was worried about Brendan. But more than that, he hadn't stopped thinking about the conversation they had outside of his parents' house. It had bothered him, not because it had been said, but because it was true.

They were done with everything, and Brendan asked, "Did you notice anythin' different tonight?"

Shane grinned from ear to ear. "Why do you think I bribed Donal into comin' to the book club meetin'."

"Seriously?" Brendan said, a look of disbelief on his face.

"Ellen may have thought she was hiding her feelin's for Donal, but I could tell. I caught her lookin' at him a little too long a few too many times, and I started to wonder."

Bendan dropped the washcloth on the table he'd been cleaning. "I am so obtuse. I never once suspected. She finally told me a few of weeks ago when I walked in on her while she was upset. She told me everythin'."

"You're not the only one who's obtuse. I was very close to givin' Donal a bit more of a nudge, but I told myself not to interfere—and I didn't."

When Shane noticed the guarded look on Brendan's face, he said, "And I'll promise you the same thing. I'm not plannin' to interfere with you and Lauren. I'm not a matchmaker. And don't tell Donal that the book club bribe was just a ruse. I'll tell him myself—on his weddin' day!"

"Yeah, I think you're right about the weddin' day. He's a goner."

Shane's grin softened. "Do you have a minute, Brendan?"

"Sure," he said and took a seat at one of the tables. Shane sat across from him.

"I want to thank you."

"Oh, yeah? For what?"

"I've been thinkin' a lot about what you said to me the other day—and you are right."

"I've felt bad about that, Shane. I wasn't tryin' to take out my frustrations on you, and I know what I said sounded rather accusing. It wasn't meant to be that way."

Shane nodded. "I know. But I want you to know that I needed to hear it. I've never told you or anyone this, but I met a woman a few years ago. She came into my gallery, and we started talkin'. She was easy to talk to, kind and intelligent, a widow. For the next six months she came to every showin' I had, bought some of my pieces, and some of my client's work. I always enjoyed visitin' with her." He paused. "I knew why she kept comin' back. She wanted somethin' more, but I couldn't give it to her. Because, you were right. I had my great love. Then I lost her, and I've never been able to see anyone else in her place.

"After hearin' you, I realized somethin'. I've been cheatin' myself all of this time by denyin' myself the joy of givin' love to another. And I want to change that. I know you're comin' to the showin' on Saturday afternoon, and I'd like for you to meet Morrigan. I called her and invited her to the gallery and to dinner afterwards. She said yes."

Brendan smiled. "That's really good to hear, Shane. I'm proud of you. But what you also need to remember is that you deserve to be loved too."

They stood and bear-hugged each other.

When they pulled away, Shane said, "I don't want you to give up on Lauren."

"I have to, Shane. The closer I get to her, the harder it will be for me."

Shane understood. He wouldn't press the point with Brendan.

Instead of heading home to his quiet empty house, Brendan took a walk to the Lower Strand. The view and the sound of the ocean always calmed him. He wasn't an envious person but he had to admit, it was hard not to feel the emotion when he thought about Donal and Ellen—and now Shane and Morrigan. There had always been his Aunt Shay and Uncle Quinn, and even Mary and Jack, two couples he'd always admired and respected because they loved each other and were committed to that love, no matter what. He'd always believed that one day he would have the same thing.

He'd been so close to having the same with Eva.

Brendan removed his phone from his pocket and looked at the picture he'd saved of Lauren in front of Fiddle Faddle. He smiled as he looked at her beautiful face, her brown eyes smiling at him. It was a picture for him and Ellen, so the smile was really theirs, but it didn't matter because she had at least thought of him when she'd taken the picture.

He couldn't bring himself to reply back to her text, but he couldn't delete the picture either. So, he saved it to his phone and knew he'd continue to look at the picture long after she was gone.

No, he hated feeling envious, and so he put the self-pity back on the shelf where it belonged. He was happy for his cousin and friend, and for Shane. And Brendan would continue to celebrate with them.

He looked again at Lauren's picture. For a long moment, he simply stared at her before he pressed the delete button. It was hard to do but he knew he needed to. When she was finally gone, he didn't want any pictures of her around to remind him of her. When the picture flashed away, he sighed and felt the heaviness of losing her settle deep inside of him.

Chapter Twenty-Four

Donal had arrived a few minutes early so he could step inside and say hello to Mary and Jack. He'd felt relieved when he'd told Jack over lunch that he'd like to date Ellen. Her father had grinned with approval.

Ellen opened the door and smiled at him. He couldn't take his eyes off her. She wore a light blue sleeveless dress with a flared skirt and crème-colored heels that showed off her pretty legs. Her blonde hair was swept up, exposing the long line of her neck. Her makeup was subtle, her lips a rosy pink. She took his breath away, and for a moment, he couldn't speak.

Instead, he reached for her hand and continued to admire her from head to toe. "You look amazin'," he finally managed to say.

"Thank you," she said as she took in his attire—blue sports coat, beige dress pants, and brown leather shoes. "You look really good yerself." He could see the gleam of appreciation in her eyes and it made him feel incredibly special.

"I'd like to say hi to your parents before we leave."

"Sure, they wanted to say hello too."

Mary and Jack were in the living room and stood when they heard them approaching.

Ellen's mother hugged him, and he shook hands

with Jack, who said, "I've taken Mary to Maison Blanche before. I think Ellen will enjoy it."

Donal nodded. "I've never been but heard good things about it. I'm glad you enjoyed it."

"You'll have a nice time," Mary said with a twinkle in her eye.

When they were in the car and headed toward Waterford, Ellen asked, "Do you think it's weird that I still live with my parents? When I came back from Le Cordon Bleu, I had every intention of findin' my own place. But when Brendan suggested I run the new bakery, I decided to wait, and was undecided about where to live. I'd thought about lookin' for a place in Dunmore East."

Donal took his eyes off the road for a minute to look at her. "I think it's sweet that you like your parents enough to continue to stay with them." It was true. He'd thought that many times over the past year, especially when he'd seen Ellen interacting with her parents. But he didn't like the idea of her moving to Dunmore East. It wasn't that far away, but it was further away from the parsonage than her parents' house. "Are you still considering movin' to Dunmore East?"

"I was plannin' to look at apartments next week, but there's no rush. The bakery won't be done until the end of August."

"Will you let me know before you do anythin'?"

"Sure. I can do that."

He smiled at her and then turned his attention back to the road.

They talked about her plans for the bakery all the way to Waterford. Donal had the car valet parked. When he stepped onto the sidewalk at the entrance of Maison Blanche, he took another opportunity to admire her appearance. "You really do look wonderful."

Ellen looped her arm through his and said, "Thank you. You make me feel wonderful."

When they were seated and decided on their choices for food and drinks, she asked, "I know you have a brother. Are the two of you close?"

"For the most part. Garrett is four years older than me. He's married and lives in London. We see each other a few times a year and talk on the phone almost every week."

"Is his wife from London?"

"No, he married an Irish girl. Work took him to the U.K. And you? You were an only child. How was that?"

"I didn't feel like an only child. Growin' up with Brendan and Katelynn was as good as havin' siblings. We were always together, even for holidays and vacations. I miss Katelynn a lot. You would have liked her."

He reached over to squeeze her hand. "I'm sure I would have. You're a good judge of people—you know that?"

She smiled at him and turned her hand over so she could wrap her fingers around his. The sensation of her touch felt incredibly good. "Of course, I am. I'm here with you, aren't I?" she said.

He laughed. "If I agree, then I'm arrogant."

"Go ahead and agree. I won't hold it against you," she teased.

The waiter arrived with their drinks and appetizer, and he reluctantly released her hand.

"What can I get you," he asked referring to the appetizer sampler they'd agreed on.

"How about one of everythin'."

He dished up a plate and handed it to her.

"You have such good manners. Who do I have to thank for them?"

"My father," he replied.

"Really?" she said with surprise in her voice.

"We haven't always been close. He worked a lot. We're better now, but he did teach me what it meant to be a gentleman. How are the three cheese gougères?" he asked glancing at the cheese puff on her plate. "I just butchered that. How do you say it, again?"

"Goo-zhair," she pronounced slowly.

He tried to repeat it but his tongue got tangled up, and they both laughed.

"These are really good. All of it is good, so far," she said.

"Did you know French before you moved to Paris?"

She nodded. "I studied it in school. When I knew I wanted to go to Le Cordon Bleu, I started learning on my own with one of those language software programs. It worked out great. I had learned more than I realized. While I lived there, I worked really hard on my pronunciation. It makes an impression on the French."

"Well, you can practice on me any time you'd like. I could listen to you speak it all day."

"*Je vous remercie. J'aime parler français, spécialement pour vous*," she replied.

He smiled. "I wish you could feel my pulse racing. I don't even care what it means. It just sounds so tender."

"Let me see your hand," she said.

Donal reached across the small table and rested his hand in front of her. Holding his gaze, she turned his hand over and placed her finger over the area of his pulse. "I feel it," she said before running her finger down the length of his hand to his fingertip.

His heart *was* racing, and her eyes never left his. It was an intoxicating moment, something he'd never experienced before.

"Why haven't you ever dated any of the women who are always cookin' things for you?" Ellen asked, her hand now resting in his, her thumb stroking the side of his hand.

"So, you noticed?"

"How could I not? They're so obvious."

"Yes, they are. When Shona showed up at my door with your plate of cookies, I thought it was one of them, and I got angry."

"I almost didn't make them for you, for that reason."

"I'm glad you did, Ellen, or we might not be here together. You're different. I don't see you that way. You've never thrown yerself at me." He paused for a moment. "When is your second date with James?"

Before she could answer, their entrées arrived. She

let go of his hand, and waited until they had been served before answering, "I'm meetin' him tomorrow."

He didn't want her going out with James, but he wouldn't demand her not to see him. Donal and Ellen were friends who were exploring the possibility of more. And even though he knew his heart would soon be lost to her, he didn't know fully how she felt about him. So, he accepted that she might date James, or other men, and he would have to be okay with it, for now.

"We're meetin' at the bookstore for coffee," she added. "I didn't want to tell him over the phone or through a text that I had met someone else. I want to tell him in person that I won't be able to see him anymore." She looked down at her plate, but he'd caught a flash of uncertainty in her eyes before she looked away. She continued, "I don't want to be presumptuous, but it doesn't feel right to keep seeing him."

Ellen looked up at him then. Forget that he would soon be lost to her—he already was! He lifted her hand and placed a kiss on the back of it, his eyes closed. His lips lingered there for a moment before he looked at her. He could tell by the look in her eyes that she was headed down the same road as he was. "Thank you, Ellen."

What she wanted to tell Donal was that she would do anything for him.

She swallowed the lump in her throat and squeezed his hand. "*Tu es un homme si bon,*" she whispered before translating. "You're such a good man."

He kissed her hand again and held it for a moment

longer before reluctantly letting it go. "You're magnificent," he said softly.

She died a little by those words—the good kind of dying, the kind that makes you want to hold onto a moment forever, rather than move on.

Later that night, when he walked her to her door, he held her hand, their fingers entwined. When they reached the porch, he grabbed her other hand and faced her.

"Thank you," she said. "I had a wonderful time, Donal." It was better than anything she had ever imagined all these months of secretly loving him.

"I did too, Ellen. Will you call me tomorrow after you meet with James?"

She smiled at him, remembering his reaction in the restaurant. She was exhilarated to know he hadn't wanted her to see James but was understanding enough not to pressure her.

"I'll call you," she agreed. He let go of her hands... and she didn't like it. She wasn't ready for the evening to end. "Will you kiss me goodnight, Donal?"

He reached for hands again. "Do you know how badly, I want to?"

She shook her head, unable to find the words.

"I want to—so badly. But more than that, I want to savor every step we take together, Ellen. I won't be able to resist you for long, but I will for tonight. And when I finally do kiss you, I'm certain I will feel like I've died and gone to heaven."

He did kiss the back of both her hands before letting them go.

"I'll talk to you tomorrow," he said with a sigh.

She nodded, still speechless. Ellen leaned against the porch railing for support as she watched him climb into his car. The joy that filled her was an incredibly heady feeling. When she could no longer see the taillights of Donal's car, Ellen looked up at the night sky. It was a cloudy evening with no stars in sight. But she could see the moon through a break in the clouds, and she sighed at the beauty of it. "Thank you," she said, her heart filled with gratitude to the Giver of all good things.

Chapter Twenty-Five

It was hard for Fred to fall asleep. He'd tried everything from reading in bed to sleeping aids, to homeopathic remedies, and none of it helped.

His issue with nodding off hadn't always been a problem. It had started after Christopher's death.

He looked up at the dark ceiling and swallowed back the knot of pain that never failed to form in his throat when he thought about his beloved son, whom he missed terribly.

They had been blessed to have such a fine son, who rarely gave him or Stacey reason to worry. There had been one year, after Christopher had turned fifteen, that had finally given them pause when he started hanging out with some questionable kids from school. Fred and Stacey had spoken openly to their son about their concerns and counseled him about making good choices, including the people he chose to hang out with. A few months later, he came home one day to say he would no longer be friends with those boys.

When they asked why, Christopher had said they were pressuring him to do things that weren't right, and so he'd made the choice to end things.

They had been so proud of him. Then to see him grow into a fine young man, who worked hard, and who had married the woman who was perfect for him, Fred and Stacey had felt as if all the pieces of their hopes and prayers over the years had come together.

And then suddenly, Christopher was gone.

He turned on his side and looked at his sleeping wife's face. How they both ached from their loss, and how they had clung to one another! He was grateful they had and that the death of their son hadn't torn them apart.

Fred loved Stacey more than he'd ever loved another soul. Looking at her now, her face, soft and slightly lined with age, was a very different picture from when he'd first met the broken and fragile wisp of a woman who'd stolen his heart with her desperation.

It had been impossible to turn away from her, and he was glad he hadn't. She'd made his life better, and she'd given him a son, a precious child, whom he had the privilege of loving. He'd always told her that she never had to give him another gift because she'd already given him the greatest possible one.

Leaning over, ever so gently, he placed a soft kiss on her forehead before laying his head back down on his pillow. He continued to look at her and to admire her features, features he knew and recognized better than his own.

Fred was worried about her and was beginning to think that encouraging Lauren and Christopher to save for a trip to Ireland, with hopes of finding out more about Stacey's past had been a mistake. Ever since Lauren had shown up at the house announcing her year-long trip, his wife hadn't been the same.

He didn't know much about her past life in Ireland other than that it wasn't worth talking about, too tragic and too difficult for her to even think about. Because he loved her, he accepted her need to keep her past dead and buried... until Christopher had begun to wonder about his heritage and where he'd come from.

Fred's side of the family was as American as apple pie. He was certain his descendants had come over on the Mayflower. He joked about it, not really knowing for sure, but as far back as he was able to trace his ancestry they had all been born in the U.S.

From early adolescence, Christopher had been intrigued by the fact that he was half Irish. His book reports, essays and various other school projects had been, as much as possible, about the Irish. Unfortunately, his son had learned early on never to talk to his mother about his passion for all things Irish. Once, when he'd probed Stacey about where she'd come from, her name, and her tartan colors, she had snapped at him angrily in a maddening sort of way, and had told him to never speak of it to her. Fred had been shocked at her reaction; it was something so out of character for the loving and patient mother she had always been.

When she'd realized what she'd done, his wife stooped to her son's height and pulled him to her, apologizing for her reaction.

"My life is here, Christopher, with you and your father. The most glorious life ever. My life back then, in Ireland, it makes me so sad to think about. I'm sorry I can't tell you more, but you have to promise mommy that you won't ask it of me."

Their son had nodded his head with quivering lips and had never again spoken of Ireland to his mother.

As Christopher grew older, his intrigue never wavered, but instead of discussing it with Stacey, he discussed it with his dad, secretly.

His son had been determined to make the trip, but had hesitated because part of him was afraid of hurting his mother. Realizing that his curiosity was never going to abate, he and Lauren had made the decision to save and make the extended trip... and then Christopher had died.

Fred didn't like seeing his wife this way, upset and hurting, knowing that Lauren was in a place Stacey desperately wanted to forget. But he was glad that his daughter-in-law had gone. Christopher would have wanted her to go, and he was certain it would bring healing to her.

He couldn't resist kissing Stacey's forehead again, and when he pulled away, he was surprised to see her eyes flutter open. There was a dazed look in her eyes as she tried to make sense of the time.

"I'm sorry, baby. I didn't mean to wake you up."

She edged closer to him. "Having a hard time falling asleep?"

"Yeah," he said as he reached for her.

They were quiet for a moment, just simply holding onto one another.

"I love you, Stacey."

She pulled away to look at him, trying to read his

expression in the dark. "Oh, honey, I love you too. It's so hard, I know." She raised her hand to touch his cheek and then kissed him on the lips. "It's so hard."

"It is hard," he said past the knot of emotion welling up in his throat. "She'll be home soon."

"You knew I was thinking about her?" Surprise filled his wife's voice.

He pulled back to look at her and nodded. "She'll always love us, Stacey. Christopher will always be a part of her."

Fred saw his wife's tears in the dark and then he felt them, wiping them away with his thumb, and then kissing her wet cheeks where they'd fallen.

"I can't lose her too," she cried.

"We won't, baby, we won't."

Fred was confident of it. He didn't know how: he just knew.

Brendan was happy to be in Dublin with Shane. It had been a while since he'd been able to make a show at the gallery, and he'd needed the distraction. His Aunt Shay had been feeling very well lately and asked if they could have Noirin for the weekend. Brendan always enjoyed making the trip with his daughter, but he was glad to have her spend time with his parents doing things she would enjoy more than dressing up for a gallery show.

Brendan was the one who really enjoyed dressing

up. Working at a bakery didn't afford him a lot of opportunities to wear a suit and tie, something he'd done every working day of his career as a stock trader. As for church, it was casual, and he always felt silly if he wore anything more than dress shirts and slacks.

As much as he enjoyed gallery shows and looking at the art, what he enjoyed most was having the opportunity to wear more than just jeans and a T-shirt or a polo. For his trip to Dublin, he splurged on a new suit, a gray, two-button-closure jacket with a vest. He chose a blue, green, and gray tartan tie to go with the suit.

He looked at himself in the mirror as he donned the jacket. He and Shane had arrived Friday evening and had worked all morning setting up for the show. Brendan checked his watch. It was half an hour before the doors would open and everything was in place.

"New suit?" Shane asked as he entered the office.

"Picked it up in Waterford last weekend."

"It's very smart."

Brendan was adjusting his tie and happened to glance at his friend through the mirror. His hand paused. "Now, that's a suit!" he exclaimed as he turned to look at Shane.

"Do you like it?"

"Armani?"

"Shh, don't say anythin'."

"I won't have to. It screams *expensive* ! You must really be interested in Morrigan? In the past, I've had to practically drag you to Dunnes just to buy a shirt and tie. And now look at you! I'll start confusing you for a Dubliner."

"That's not happenin'. Once a *culchie* always a *culchie*."

Brendan chuckled at Shane's affectionate term for someone from rural Ireland.

They heard a tap on the open door to the office and turned toward the sound.

Lauren was standing in the doorway smiling at the two of them. "If I didn't know you two better, I would have thought you were calling each other mean names."

"Lauren!" Shane exclaimed as he walked excitedly toward her. She reached for him and gave him a hug and a kiss on the cheek. "What on earth are you doin' here?"

"There was a pop up on Messenger last night about your event. I was leaving Northern Ireland this morning and decided to stop in at the gallery on my way back to Tramore."

Brendan was shocked to see her. It had never crossed his mind that she would be here at the gallery. He'd wanted a reprieve. He'd wanted this event to take his mind off of her for just a little while longer; yet here she was. It frustrated him. The fact that she was wearing a stunning black cocktail dress, with her hair twisted in a fashionable knot, accentuating her Asian features, didn't help the annoyance that crept in. It had been a good relaxing mood until she'd tapped on the door.

"Hi, Lauren," he heard himself say. "I hope you had

a good trip. If you'll excuse me, I need to check with the bartender before the show begins."

He wanted to kick something, but instead, he walked out of the gallery and onto the sidewalk, pacing in front of the storefront to calm himself. He raked his fingers through his hair and took a deep long breath. After a few more moments of pacing, he went back inside and made his way to the bar. It hadn't been a lie; he did need to speak with the bartender, but it had only taken a minute.

To his relief, the featured artist walked through the door. She was early, and he was glad for the distraction. Sarah Burke had been at the gallery most of the morning working alongside Shane and Brendan, preparing for the show but had left to get ready before the doors opened.

"Sarah," he greeted. "I'm glad you're here. The guests will begin arrivin' soon. How are you doin'?" It was the oil painter's first break. Shane had seen one of her paintings hanging on a wall in a coffee shop. Impressed, he'd managed to track her down. After seeing her portfolio, Shane had offered to do a showing of her work.

"I'm so nervous," Sarah replied.

Brendan welcomed the distraction of encouraging the artist, and refused to think about Lauren and her intrusion on his reprieve.

"I'm really glad you're here, Lauren," Shane said as he reached for her hands.

"I shouldn't have come." It was obvious Brendan hadn't wanted her there. His less than enthusiastic response to her arrival had been obvious to her. Coupled with the distance she'd felt from him the last few weeks, Lauren was confused.

"I thought Brendan and I were friends," she said, rejection punctuating her words.

"Brendan *is* your friend. He's just strugglin' right now. In time, all will be made clear."

She was even more confused by Shane's veiled words, but now wasn't the time to press the issue. He had a show to put on, and she didn't want to get in the way. "Maybe I should just go?"

"Nonsense. I have someone I want you to meet, a friend of mine. Her name is Morrigan. We have plans for dinner afterwards, and I insist that you join us. I won't take anythin' but a yes."

She smiled, appreciating her friend who reminded her so much of her own father. "I accept. Where is the ladies' room?"

Lauren entered the restroom and was glad to see a bench she could sit on. It always seemed like she took one step forward and two steps back. Her time at Mourne Mountains had been all that she'd hoped it would be.

When she'd started planning the trip, she'd been afraid that seeing one of the places she and Christopher had planned to visit together would open up the wounds. That it would hurt worse than it already did. But to her surprise, it hadn't been that way at all. There had been moments of sadness, but Lauren had also been joyful.

Keeping to the path the guide had pointed out to her, she'd followed it until it opened up to a breathtaking valley. She had cried at the beauty of it. "Oh, Christopher, I wish you could see this!" she had said out loud. And then she found herself talking to him as if he were sitting right beside her, something she'd never done before.

Having that one-sided conversation with her late husband had done something to her. It had shifted the pain of losing him, just like Dr. Moore said it would. He *was* gone, and he would never come back. But because she knew him and loved him, she could still share things with him and know what he would say or how he would feel about what she was experiencing. It caused her to realize that her husband would always be a part of her. There was both joy and sorrow in that discovery. But this time, more joy than sorrow.

The drive south, back toward Tramore had been good as she thought about the step forward, she had taken. Then, seeing Brendan's reaction and remembering his distance, she had felt as if she'd stumbled backwards further than she'd come.

She sighed. Lauren knew she couldn't fault Brendan, for she'd held a part of herself back from him. She'd held back from all of them, and in some ways it hadn't been fair. All she could hope for was that when she shared this very important part of herself, it would help to bridge the gap that had wedged itself between Brendan and herself.

Chapter Twenty-Six

Shane found Brendan standing by the door of the gallery. The guests would be arriving soon, but he needed to speak with his friend first.

He was disappointed in Brendan's reaction at seeing Lauren. He understood what the young man was going through, but he knew Brendan well enough to know he would feel bad knowing that he'd hurt Lauren's feelings. And he needed to know he had.

Before Shane could say a word, Brendan looked at him and said, "I was a real *eejit*, I know."

"And why were you? I've never seen you like that before."

Brendan sighed. "I wasn't expecting her. I was glad she went to Mourne. Seein' her everyday wears on me. I want this year to be over with, and fast."

His friend was in way deep. Shane realized that now and truly felt sorry for him, but more than feeling sorry for him, he felt helpless to make it better. Brendan was like the son he'd never had; it was natural for him to want to fix things. And saying what he was about to say next wouldn't make it better. But the young man needed to hear it.

"Lauren knows somethin' is wrong. Said she thought you two were friends. She was plannin' to leave,

261

but I talked her into stayin'. She's in the bathroom right now tryin' to pull herself together."

There was a pained expression on Brendan's face. "I'll go talk to her. I'll make it right."

"Brendan, you need to do more than that. You need to continue to be her friend. But more than that, you need to stop being afraid to fall in love with her, and let yerself go. And when the time is right, you need to ask her out."

"Like Flynn did? You didn't see the look on her face or see the way she closed herself off." Brendan's voice rose in frustration.

"You're not Flynn. She cares about *you*."

"And what if she breaks my heart?"

"Then I'll be here to help you pick up the pieces. We all will. The young man I'm lookin' at isn't a coward. He's dealt with many losses, and he did the bravest, most selfless thing I've seen. He took a special needs child and put her cares and concerns above his own. He gave up everythin' to call her his daughter. That's who you are Brendan. Not this fearful man, closin' himself off from the most wonderful person he'll probably ever meet."

"The problem with all of it, Shane, is that I'm already in love with her." The flash of pain he saw in Brendan's eyes was hard to take. Before he had a chance to say anything, his friend walked away.

Shane let him go and wondered why the most wonderful experience in life, love, also had to be the most painful.

When she walked out of the bathroom, she hadn't expected to see Brendan standing there, waiting for her. She stopped and held his gaze.

Remorse reflected in his eyes. "How was your trip to Mourne?" he asked.

He wouldn't admit he hadn't been happy to see her, but by the look of regret in his eyes, she knew she'd been right, and it worried her. The fact that he was dancing around the issue increased her concern.

"It was a good trip," she replied. "A place I needed to go. How is Noirin?"

"Missin' you," he said with a smile. "Aunt Shay was feelin' really well and wanted to have her stay the weekend with them."

"Are you going home tonight or staying in Dublin?"

"I had plans to go home. How about you?"

"The same. Shane invited me to dinner after the showing. Would you rather I not go?"

His expression looked pained. Brendan reached for her hand and tucked it in the crook of his arm, so he could lead her away from the bathroom door. "I would love for you to join us. I'll feel less like a third wheel havin' dinner with him and Morrigan."

She smiled at him before her expression sobered. "I know it will be late, but do you think we could talk afterwards, or will you be picking up Noirin?"

"No, she's stayin' with my parents tonight. Talkin'

will be fine." He stopped in front of a painting. They could hear guests coming in and milling around, the din of voices filling the early afternoon air. "Come look at the artist's paintings. Her name is Sarah Burke. I'll introduce you in a bit."

As Brendan walked with her to view the paintings, she noticed he was wearing a suit, something she'd never seen him wear before. She admired the way he looked, his tall frame, his striking features. She'd never noticed him in this way before, and she took a moment to take in his appearance. He caught her gaze, and he looked back and smiled. It was back—that oddly familiar smile that filled her with warmth. It had been missing these past few weeks; she'd been missing it.

"What?" he asked still smiling.

"Oh, just realizing that I've never seen you in a suit before. You look really nice."

"I miss wearin' a suit."

She nodded in understanding. As a businessman he would have worn a suit to work every day.

"It suits you," she said with a wink at her play on words.

He laughed, and it felt so good to hear the sound.

The rest of the show was a blur of faces and conversations as they mingled with others, drank champagne, and nibbled on hors d'oeuvres; canapes with salmon, melon and prosciutto, and stuffed cremini mushrooms.

They met and entertained Morrigan when Shane

and Sarah were busy talking to the guests about her work and the gallery.

Lauren liked the older woman who had a varied knowledge of art. When Morrigan discovered that Lauren drew with colored pencils, she let her know that she was a collector of colored pencil art. Morrigan offered to show Lauren her collection the next time she was in Dublin.

She looked at Brendan, then asked, "Would you like to come with me? We could make a trip of it. Bring Noirin with us?"

"I'd like that."

And he'd meant it. All afternoon he'd been thinking about what Shane had said. He wasn't a coward, but he'd acted like one since their last trip to Dublin. But was he ready to toss his cares to the wind? He wasn't so sure. Lauren wanted to talk to him, probably to ask him why he was being so distant toward her. What in the world would he tell her? He might be considering tossing his cares to the wind and following his heart, but he wasn't so reckless to tell Lauren the truth about why he'd pushed her away. He'd evade that topic as best he could.

The four of them rode to the restaurant together, after they'd closed the gallery. It was only late afternoon, so they were seated quickly and chatted about the showing while they perused the menu.

"The steak is really good," Brendan pointed out to Lauren. Both Shane and Morrigan had been to Ace, a trendy restaurant in the Hipster Triangle, and not too far from the gallery.

"Steak sounds good. Is that what you're having?" Lauren asked.

"I was thinking about it or the swordfish. Do you like swordfish? We could share?"

"That sounds good."

Shane looked at Morrigan. "Do you want to order different things and share too?"

She smiled at him. "That sounds lovely."

"How long have you two known each other?" Lauren asked before taking a sip of her water.

"About three years," Morrigan replied.

"We met at the gallery. Morrigan was a guest to a show," Shane offered.

"Are you from Dublin?" Brendan asked.

"Born and raised. I grew up in Portobello."

"That's a charming area. Shane, didn't you live near there while you taught at Lansdowne college?"

"Yeah, Morrigan and I realized that her childhood home was only a stone's through away from the flat I rented."

"Do you still live in Portobello?" Lauren asked Morrigan.

"No, I live on Grafton Street."

They talked about Dublin neighborhoods while they waited for their food. When dinner arrived, the topic of conversation switched to Brendan's new bakery and Shane's second gallery.

When Brendan told Morrigan about Ellen's idea of selling recipe cards of some of the dishes that the tearoom would make, he pulled out his phone and showed her the picture Lauren had created of the lavender biscotti.

The older woman looked at her. "You understated your talent, dear. You're really quite good."

"She's exceptional," Brendan said but didn't look in her direction. He was afraid the look in his eyes would reveal too much.

"How many different ones did you and Ellen decide on?" Shane asked.

"Four to start with. We might do another series. She's thinking she'd like to do recipes that the tearoom won't offer. She doesn't want to give away too many of her secrets."

They laughed. "Ellen is Brendan's cousin. You've heard me talk about her before," Shane explained.

Morrigan nodded. "Your family sounds wonderful, Brendan."

"They are. You'll have to visit Tramore soon."

"I would like that."

"Do you hear that?" Shane asked.

A piano had started.

The four of them looked over to the far corner of the restaurant to the black baby grand and the man sitting behind it.

"There's a dance floor. We should dance." Before anyone could object, Shane stood and held out his hand to Morrigan. "Shall we?"

She smiled as she left her chair and placed her hand in his.

Brendan followed suit and was pleased to see Lauren take the hand he offered, without hesitation.

When they reached the dance floor, he slipped his hand around her waist and raised the hand he was holding to his chest but kept their bodies at a discreet distance. She looked at him and smiled. He smiled back losing himself in the feel of her under his hand and the look of ease in her big brown eyes, so unlike her reaction to Flynn's simple offer to show her around Dublin. Hope sparked somewhere in the recesses of his fear.

"It's been a wonderful afternoon," she said softly as they began to sway slowly to the music. "A lovely way to end my week." She looked over at Shane and Morrigan who were dancing much closer together than he and Lauren.

"They look good together," she offered before turning her eyes back to his.

"They do."

"He's never mentioned her before."

"I just learned about her myself."

Lauren's brows lifted in question.

"It's not my story to tell." He gave her an apologetic look.

"I love that about all of you. How you let the stories remain where they are until they're ready to be told. Ellen, Shane, and you." She sighed. "I'm so glad I came to Ireland. And have I told you lately, thank you for letting me love Noirin?"

Brendan couldn't find the words. He felt ashamed for how he'd treated Lauren, a woman hurting so badly, needing to be healed. She'd come here to find a way to be whole again, had started to mend, and then he'd hurt her. Feelings of guilt and shame washed over him, and they made him feel small.

"Brendan, what's the matter?"

He'd shown too much. No, not too much, but enough. "I'm, sorry, Lauren. Your friendship is important to me, and I just want you to know that."

Her smile was gracious as she accepted his apology. "Thank you."

In one day, he'd come full circle in his struggle with Lauren. He would spend this year with her, loving her and savoring every moment she offered him. He'd no longer push her away. And if at the end of it all, she couldn't find a way to love him back, he would pick up the pieces and move on. Just as he'd always done!

Chapter Twenty-Seven

James just left. I'm still at the bookstore. Do you want to meet me here?

Donal had been waiting for Ellen's call. He quickly texted back; *I'm on my way.*

Can't wait. Bring 'Jane Eyre' with you, and I'll have a peppermint mocha waiting for you.

He texted her a smiley face and a thumbs up.

Normally, he'd walk, but he was too eager to see Ellen, so he hopped in his car and did his best to observe the speed limit.

When he saw her at the back corner of the bookstore café, he smiled at her and took the seat across from her. "How did you know that peppermint mocha is my favorite?" he asked, while reaching for her hand and stroking the top of it with his thumb.

Her eyes rounded in surprise at the question. "Uh, I just know. Women are very observant you know."

"Unlike men?" he asked with raised eyebrows.

"Uhm, well, you said it, not me."

He laughed. "Why do I have *Jane Eyre* with me?"

"Because we need to finish the assigned chapters and I thought we could do that together."

"I'd rather look at you than a book and hold your hand instead of turnin' scratchy pages."

Her eyes glowed in response. "What's a girl to say to that?"

And what was a guy to do when the woman he was falling in love with looked at him like that?

"But, you're right. We do need to read the chapters and it's better to do it together than alone. So..." Donal stood and scooted his chair so he was sitting beside Ellen, their shoulders and legs touching. "So," he repeated, "if we're plannin' to do this together, we'll do this right. Much better don't you think?"

Ellen linked her arm through his, placed her hand in his, and simply gazed at him adoringly.

"I learned somethin' about Jane Eyre," he said taking in the fullness of her look and the desire it stirred in him.

"Oh, yeah, what's that?" she replied softly.

"She was a strong woman, a woman of character. There is a depth to her that one should aspire to, male or female. I love this part of the book." Donal thumbed through to an ear-marked page and read:

> *I remembered that the real world was wide and that a varied field of hopes and fears, of sensations and excitements, awaited those who had the courage to go forth into its expanse, to seek real knowledge of life amidst its perils.*

When he finished reading, he looked at Ellen. "It may not be one of the more famous lines from *Jane Eyre*, but it sums up nicely who she was, a woman fiercer than her more tragic circumstances and determined to do what was right, no matter the cost."

He paused and held Ellen's gaze. "She reminds me of you."

"But how? I've had a wonderful life, far easier than Jane Eyre's."

"Maybe so, but we shouldn't be defined by our tragedies. Jane wasn't defined by hers. She was who she was, no matter what. That's what I see in you, Ellen. You're real and without pretenses. You weren't afraid to pursue your dreams, and when you lost Katelyn, you remembered to love her and weren't afraid to miss her."

Ellen pressed her lips to his cheek before resting her head on his shoulder.

They sat there like that, each lost in their own thoughts. It wasn't a time for words. It was a time for emotions to settle, to root themselves deeply. Donal loved Ellen. He knew it as surely as he was breathing. He wouldn't take long to tell her because he sensed she loved him too.

After a while, he opened his book and started reading the love story that had begun to define his own. His and Ellen's lives were polar opposites of Jane and Rochester's. Rochester, a man of questionable morals, was now transformed by the power of love, and Jane, who had been dealt a tragic hand at life, eventually gained the only thing she'd ever truly desired: to love and to be loved.

It had been the surprising gift of love that had

transformed Jane and Rochester, and it was the surprise of love he had for Ellen that had taken purchase and bound him to her forever. Yes, he *would* love Ellen—forever.

Donal understood now the draw of literature and the prose that centered on love. If there was more fiction like this to be found, then he would enjoy discovering it for as long as he lived.

Finished with their reading, their lattes consumed, Ellen wasn't ready for the evening to be over. "How about I make you dinner?" she offered.

"We'd have to go to your house."

"Oh." She had thought they could have some alone time at his place.

When Donal read her thoughts, he gave her a look of regret. "We can't go to my place unless we invite someone over."

He was right. It wouldn't look good for him if he'd brought a woman over, alone.

"We'll go to the bakery then."

He grinned. "What did you have in mind to make? Can I help?"

"You better believe you're gonna help. I've dreamt about cookin' with you for so long."

Ellen realized her mistake as soon as the words left her mouth and knew Donal would connect the dots.

His grin grew wider. He leaned over and kissed her

forehead before standing to his feet and drawing her up with him.

He grabbed their books and their cups. As they made their way to the trash can, he asked, "Do we need to stop at the store?"

Donal was giving her a pass, one of the many reasons she loved him.

They decided to make boxty. The potato pancake was apparently Donal's specialty and his mother's recipe. Ellen had insisted they make something he could teach her, and that's what they had landed on.

They talked about anything and everything while she shredded the potatoes for the pancake and he prepped the fish.

"I can't believe you're squeamish about cleanin' fish," he teased.

"Hey, I'm a baker, not a cook. I don't do dead things well—except eat them."

He nudged her side with his hip and laughed.

Ellen was dying for him to kiss her, but she wouldn't push. She thought it was incredibly sweet how he wanted to take things slow. The few men that she'd dated had been that way too. She'd never been into fast guys, but with Donal everything was different. She felt like she would crawl out of her skin if she didn't touch him, if she wasn't near him.

While he fried the potato pancakes, she whipped up some soda bread.

"Is that Cups and Cakes' recipe?" he asked.

"It's been in Uncle Quinn's family for generations. I wouldn't even think to alter it."

Donal had finished the last of the pancakes and was watching as she rolled out the dough. "Do you need some more flour on the counter?"

"Yes, please."

When the loaf was formed and placed onto a greased baking sheet, she handed him the paring knife. "Do you want to put the cross on top?"

"To let the fairies out?"

She laughed and appreciated his knowledge of Irish lore and how it carried over into food. "To let the fairies out," she replied with a wink.

After he made the cross, he lifted the pan and placed it in the oven.

They waited until the last minute to cook the fish, and when it was all done, they took the food to a table in the dining room and sat down to enjoy it.

"Wow, this is really good, Donal! I love the shellfish cream. So, your mum is a good cook?"

"Really good. Garrett and I liked cookin' with her. She insisted that we learn, but it wasn't hard to want to do it. She's fun."

"Do you miss home?" Ellen knew he was from Limerick and how he went home fairly often.

"I used to, especially when I was in Thailand for my mission work. But I like it here more. I enjoy our church. Speakin' of church, you'll be there tomorrow, right?"

275

She felt tension rising in her for the first time since they had started down this path. "It'll be strange, Donal?"

He sat his fork down. "What do you mean?"

"How am I supposed to show up tomorrow and pretend like nothin's happened?"

He looked genuinely puzzled. "I don't understand?"

"People will know somethin' is goin' on between us. They'll talk."

"Come here," he said while holding out his hand to her.

She stood from her chair and walked over to him. He pulled her down onto his lap and wrapped his arms around her waist. "Tomorrow, when you show up for church, I'm meetin' you out front. After givin' you a big hug, I plan to take your hand in mine, and we're goin' to walk into church together, just like that—if that's okay with you?"

Her eyes grew wide with pleasure. "Are you sure?"

"I already met with the deacons this mornin'. I told them about us. And besides, if another woman brings me a casserole, I think I'll lose it."

She draped her arms around his neck. "You really don't like that do you?"

"I really don't like it. It makes me feel obligated to somethin' I'm not interested in."

"I'm sorry," she said and held his gaze.

"What are you doin' next weekend?" he asked, his eyes flickering to her lips and then back to her eyes again. She could tell it was getting harder for him to resist. Ellen liked knowing he wanted to kiss her as much as she wanted to be kissed by him.

"I'm all yours." She hadn't meant the double entendre and saw the effect it had on Donal when he swallowed hard.

"Good, I'll pick you up at eight. We'll be gone most of the day."

"Do I get to know where we're goin'?"

"Nope," he said his voice tight with emotion. "It's a surprise," he managed to say. "And now, I think we need to get back to our dinner."

Oh, how she was tempted, tempted to take this where she wanted so badly for it to go. But she loved him and valued his sense of doing things right.

She stood up from his lap, then bent down to kiss the dimple on his cheek. She could at least take pleasure in that.

Before they'd finished their meal, the front door opened and in walked Lauren and Brendan.

"Oh my gosh, what are you two doin' here?" Ellen asked as she jumped up and went to give them a hug.

"We saw you through the window and thought we'd step in and say hi," Brendan replied.

"How was the showin'?"

Lauren had texted her that morning, letting her know she would be stopping in Dublin for the gallery show and that they'd have to catch up tomorrow.

"It was really nice—my first," Lauren replied.

"Doesn't Shane do a good job?" Ellen remarked.

"He does."

"Have you guys eaten dinner?" Donal asked. "We have plenty left."

It was Lauren who answered. "We had an early dinner, but we wouldn't want to intrude."

"Stay," Ellen said.

Brendan looked at Lauren. She nodded. "Well, if, you're sure?"

"We're sure. Sit," Donal encouraged.

"Mmm, you made boxty," Brendan said to Donal. "My favorite."

"What is boxty?" Lauren asked as she dished up a plate.

Brendan explained the dish to Lauren. "Donal makes a really good one."

"Do you want me to warm it up for you?" Ellen asked.

Lauren shook head. "No, this is fine." She took a taste. "It's really good."

Donal grinned his appreciation.

"And I'm happy for you both," Lauren added between bites.

Ellen gave Donal a pleased look, which he returned, and the two of them gazed at each other for a moment longer.

Brendan turned to Lauren. "Maybe we need to give them time alone, after all. We can take our plates and make a run for it."

Lauren giggled at the thought which caused Donal and Ellen to laugh.

"No, seriously, I'm happy for you too. And, Donal, you're lucky you're my best friend and I know you. Otherwise, I'd be givin' you an earful right now."

"I'd expect no less."

The conversation drifted to Lauren's trip to Mourne Mountains. They'd all been there before and shared their thoughts about that region of Northern Ireland. When they were done eating and talking for a while, Brendan offered to help clean up, but Ellen shooed them out the door. "Donal and I made the mess; we'll clean it up. Besides, you both had a busy day. Out you go!"

Ellen gave Lauren a hug. "I'll give you a call tomorrow?"

"That sounds good."

When her cousin and friend left, she reached for Donal and hugged him. "Thank you for a wonderful dinner and for those wonderful things you said about me at the bookstore."

He hugged her back. "I meant every word."

And she knew he did.

Chapter Twenty-Eight

Brendan helped Lauren with her bags. After dropping them off at her flat, he led her up to his place so they could talk, still worried she would ask him why he'd been so distant the past few weeks. When he closed the door behind her, he offered to make coffee.

She pressed her hands against her jeans. They'd both changed out of their formal attire before leaving Dublin. He had followed her in his car wanting to be behind her in case she made a wrong turn or had car trouble.

Brendan could tell she was nervous, and she declined the coffee while taking a seat on the couch. He sat beside her. And waited for her to begin.

She started to tear up and drew a deep breath. Lauren looked down at her ring. It was a beautiful solitaire. She stared at it for a moment longer. "His name is Christopher." Her voice trembled.

Brendan was surprised she wanted to talk about her husband. He was relieved but also anxious.

"We were married for seven years. I lost him a little over a year ago." She sucked in another breath. "I'm sorry; this is harder than I thought it would be." The tears welled up in her eyes.

He reached out and touched her hand. "It's all right, Lauren. Take your time."

She turned her hand over to clasp his and held on tight as if she were holding onto a life line.

"We had been saving for an extended trip to Ireland, but he died. I came here because I needed to get away from everything that was familiar and everything that reminded me of him. I needed to go someplace where no one knew who I was or what I'd gone through. I needed to try and find myself again." She was crying now and didn't try to stop the tears from flowing down her cheeks.

"Then I met you—all of you—and I started to come alive again. I felt things I haven't felt in over a year. I was afraid that if I told you about my pain, it would change things. I didn't want that. I'm sorry I withheld this from you."

"You don't have to apologize, Lauren. You've done nothin' wrong. I've suspected that somethin' happened to your husband and knew you would tell me in your own time." He stood to grab a box of tissues and handed it to Lauren before he sat back down.

"Thank you."

He nodded. "Was he good to you, Lauren?"

She nodded. "He is the best man I've ever known. The way he loved me..." She paused, her voice cracking with the pain she felt. "Words are inadequate. He was everything to me."

"I'm glad. You deserve to be loved."

She looked at him, her expression sobering. "You deserve the same, Brendan. Have you ever been in love?"

He nodded. A knot of emotion formed in his throat.

"Her name was Eva. I wanted to spend the rest of my life with her." He looked away and focused on the painting of Katelyn and Noirin in the field of poppies. "Eva wanted a life with me, but not one with me and Noirin. What hurt the most was that she wasn't even willing to try. I loved Noirin more, and so I let Eva go."

Lauren reached out for his hand this time. "How could anyone not want her?"

He smiled at her. It was one of the reasons he'd fallen in love with Lauren. Seeing how she adored his daughter, did something to him. Her open heart and unconditional love: it was a gift.

"Tell me about Christopher." He wanted to know all about the man who had loved Lauren so well.

She told him how they'd met, and they laughed about the coffee and his stained shirt. Lauren told Brendan about their house in the suburbs, the garden she loved, the way Christopher enjoyed sitting outside while she piddled with her plants. She told him about their hammock and the countless hours they'd spent there lounging in it together, reading and talking. And then she shared with him their dreams of having a family.

Lauren began to cry, again. "You know, besides wishing he were still alive, I wish that I'd had his child. I wish that he'd left a piece of himself behind for me to love and to hold onto."

Brendan reached for her then, and soothed her as she let the pain that consumed her run its course. In between sobs, she said, "Christopher fell asleep at the wheel. He'd been on a business trip in Portland and drove home. Oh God, why?" she cried as she clung to Brendan. All he could do was hold her, wanting desperately to take her pain away, to take it upon himself. But he knew he couldn't, so he just held her, leaning into the couch and cradling her as she cried.

At some point, they both fell asleep. Brendan opened his sleepy eyes and saw the clock above the mantle. It was early morning. He looked down at Lauren who was fast asleep. He carefully slipped out from underneath her and placed a cushion under her head. He then reached for the throw on the back of the couch and covered her with it.

Brendan looked down at her sleeping form for a moment longer. He knew what it was like to lose someone you loved, but not the way Lauren had experienced it. When you'd given your life, your body, and your heart to someone, the relationship was different. Losing that could be devastating. He sensed that depth of pain churning below the surface, and now, it had a name and a personality. But Brendan wouldn't give up hope. He had come too far and had too much of his own emotions vested in this lovely woman sleeping peacefully on his couch.

When Lauren opened her eyes, she was a little startled at first, unsure of where she was. Then she recognized the living room and remembered the night before, and relaxed. She noticed Brendan asleep in a chair across from her, his feet propped up on an ottoman, his head cocked to one side.

It had felt so good to be held by him. It had been so long since Christopher had held her, she'd almost forgotten what it felt like.

Surprisingly, it had also felt good to share with Brendan about her husband. There was an unburdening of the load she had been carrying around with her since arriving in Tramore.

Lauren continued to study his sleeping face. His big brown eyes were closed, but she appreciated the shape of them, the outline of his dark eyebrows, while he slept. His lips were slightly parted, and the curve of his chin was so appealing.

He was good-looking, and she was fairly certain that with his looks and personality he had no trouble attracting women. Her mind shifted to the woman who had broken his heart. Eva was her name. Brendan hadn't said much about her, but she could see the pain behind the look in his eyes. He loved her enough to want to make a life with her, but she'd refused that love. Not one to judge too quickly someone she didn't know, Lauren made an exception of Eva. The woman was a fool.

Brendan, who was loving and gracious, had this amazing ability to look past the surface of a person and the circumstances of life, and find the treasure seated within. How could anyone refuse someone who had the ability to see life and people the way he did and to make the kinds of sacrifices that took courage and strength.

She sat up. And how fortunate she was to have him

as her friend, to have him in her life. She stood and walked over to the chair. Lauren knelt before him and reached for one of his hands, cupping it in both of hers.

He stirred at the contact, and after a moment, his eyes fluttered open. She smiled at him, and he sat up quickly, rubbing his eyes with his free hand.

"How are you?" he asked, his brows furrowed in concern.

Lauren let go of his hand and perched on the edge of the ottoman. "I'm good. Thank you for listening to me. I'm glad I told you."

Brendan drew his feet off the ottoman and placed them on the ground beside the chair so he could sit up straighter. "It's obvious that your husband was a wonderful man. I'd like to know more about Christopher. You know you can talk to me about him anytime?"

She nodded.

"Your planned trip to Paris—you both went there together."

Lauren was surprised he'd remembered. "We went there for our honeymoon."

"I think it's a really good idea for you to make that trip. When were you married?"

"August 8 is our anniversary."

"Then that's when you should go." The look in his eyes was tender and caring.

She smiled at him. "That *would* be a good time."

They gazed at each other for a moment, before Lauren spoke. "Will you do me a favor, Brendan?"

"Of course."

"Will you tell Ellen and Shane about Christopher for me—the details? I feel like I can talk about him now, but the details..." her voice tapered off.

"I will tell them for you."

She nodded and stood. "Thank you, for everything."

He made a move to stand too.

"I know I haven't shown it lately, but I will always be here for you, Lauren."

Her eyes teared up. "Will you hold me, please?"

He didn't even hesitate. His arms were gentle but firm around her as she laid her cheek against his chest and wrapped her arms around his waist. "I've forgotten how good it felt to be held," she murmured.

The gentle strokes along her back were response enough. They both savored the contact. When they finally pulled away, they smiled at each other.

"I'll make you breakfast," he offered.

"I can help."

He gave her a wide grin, the smile she loved.

A while later, when they were seated across from each other enjoying French toast and eggs, he asked, "Will you come to church with me?"

Her face fell, and she looked down at her plate, moving her eggs around.

Brendan reached for her hand. "It's okay to be angry with Him, but not forever."

Lauren looked up and held his gaze. He was right, and she knew it. Her progress hadn't been just about finding herself and dealing with Christopher's death. It had also been about her anger with God. She just wasn't there yet.

"Ask me again, next Sunday."

He smiled. "I can do that. After church, I'll speak to Shane and Ellen. Will you come to dinner tonight at my parents?"

"I'd love that. I can't wait to see Noirin. I've missed her."

"We'll stop by to say hi after we get home, and we'll ride together to dinner. It looks like it's planning to rain all day today."

She looked out the window and saw the gray overcast sky. Rainy days no longer matched her mood. Beams of sunshine had found their way back into her life. Lauren looked at Brendan and felt as if he were the brightest of them all.

Chapter Twenty-Nine

"I miss you so much, Mom. I'm glad you received my letter. Snail mail is fun." Lauren had written a letter to her mother-in-law about her time in Tramore. She took care to omit the name of the city, but couldn't help but mention the people she'd gotten to know. The letter had caused her to miss Stacey even more. It wasn't just proximity and not being able to see her whenever she wanted. Lauren missed *Stacey,* the woman she loved and admired as a mother, who had grown slightly reserved since she'd left Tacoma.

"Oh, darlin', I miss you too." But there was a catch in her mother-in-law's voice.

"What's the matter, Mom? I'm worried about you."

There was a long pause. When Stacey spoke, it was with a tear-filled voice. "I'm afraid of losin' you, Lauren."

She sighed. This was one of the things she valued about Stacey—always open with her feelings. She never expected others to read her mind. She never manipulated emotionally. It was something she'd passed onto her son, and it had made their relationships much easier.

"I need you to listen to me, Mom, really hear me, please. I will always love you and Dad, and will be there for you both, no matter what. Losing Christopher hasn't changed that and it never will. You're too important to me."

"Thank you, darlin'. You are such a gift. I wish we'd Skyped instead, so I could see your beautiful face."

Lauren smiled. "I know. I was just thinking about you. I'm actually working in a garden."

"You're gardening, again?" Stacey asked.

Lauren frowned. "Yeah, remember I mentioned my friend's garden in the letter?"

"Oh, that's right."

Her features relaxed. "Anyhow, I was thinking about you and wanted to hear your voice. But we'll set up a time tomorrow evening, so I can talk to both you and Dad. We'll Skype then. Mom told me you both were going to the ranch for a visit in June."

"We are. You know I love visiting your parents."

Lauren was truly blessed. Her parents had become good friends with them over the years and genuinely enjoyed spending time with each other. It made celebrating holidays and even vacations so much easier, because all six of them had spent most of them together.

She chatted with her mother-in-law for a little while longer. When she was done, she immediately phoned her father-in-law who would still be at work and hoped he was able to answer.

"Hi, Lauren," she heard him say after the first ring.

"Hi, Dad. Is this a good time?"

"Always for you, sweetie. How are you?"

"I'm doing well. Just got off the phone with Mom. The three of us have a Skype session tomorrow evening."

"I'm glad; you know I always look forward to them."

"I'm worried about her."

Her father-in-law paused for a long moment.

Lauren added, "You're worried about her too, aren't you?"

"I am. Ever since you left, things have been different. She's sadder and a little withdrawn. She's never been withdrawn before, not even after Christopher died."

Lauren closed her eyes and pinched the bridge of her nose. "Did I do the right thing coming to Ireland?" Even as she asked the question, she thought of the people who had become so important to her, here in this small town off the southwest coast of this rugged country, and she knew she had made the right decision. The thought of never having met them caused a twinge of sadness.

"You did the right thing making that trip. I don't want you to worry about anything. Just get better. You already sound better."

She smiled. "I am. Oh, before I forget, I went to Waterford and confirmed there weren't any Stacey Walshes born in Tramore. There were about thirty registered in the surrounding area. But," she paused, "I have a funny feeling about all of this, and I think I should just let it go. If she doesn't want us to know about where she's from it's probably better that way."

"I think you're right, Lauren. Better to let sleeping dogs lie."

Lauren couldn't have prevented the upward tugging of her lips if she'd tried. She loved her father-in-law's use of idioms. He had a good repertoire of them, and when he used them, Stacey and Christopher liked to roll their eyes in jest because they'd heard them for so long. But they all enjoyed them, and he knew it.

"Well, I'm glad you agree, Dad. I will let it go. I don't want to keep asking her to come visit, so I'll let that go too, even though she's not from Tramore. I'll plan to come home for a bit, mid-summer to see you both. Mom and Dad will be here next week."

"Yes, I know. I've been talking to your dad about dates for our annual visit to the ranch."

"My mom told me. I'm so glad you're going."

"Me too."

"Well, I'll let you get back to work so you can get home, and I'll talk to you tomorrow. Love you."

"Love you, too."

Lauren put her phone back in her pocket and bent down to get the trowel she'd been using before making the calls to her in-laws. It was early morning and the sun wouldn't hold out much longer before the rain came. She had lettuce and leeks to harvest. She'd told Ellen she would deliver the lettuce to the bakery and how she would prep the leeks and vacuum seal them to be frozen.

She'd also planned to deliver some to Brendan's parents. Shay was looking forward to seeing her.

She made good time of the harvesting and loaded the produce in her trunk, setting aside a basket for the Callerys.

When she arrived a short while later, she let herself in as Shay had instructed, so she wouldn't have to get up.

"Shay?"

"In here, darlin'."

Lauren smiled as she made her way toward the living room. Shay was propped up in a chair, a book on her lap. She could hear Bach playing quietly on the stereo.

"How are you doing?" Lauren asked as she bent to kiss her cheek. How easy it was to fall in love with these people. Lauren had come to dinner again the Sunday after Shane's gallery showing, and on Wednesday, she came with Brendan and Noirin for the first time. When Lauren had invited Brendan and Noirin to dinner, she realized they had standing dinner plans every Wednesday with his parents.

Every night that week, the three of them had spent them together. After walking with Brendan to pick up Noirin from school, she would take the little girl back to her place to play and read. While Noirin worked on her homework, Lauren prepared dinner and helped her with questions in between seasoning and stirring. By the time Brendan came to pick up Noirin, dinner would be ready, and he always agreed to stay.

One night, shortly after they'd started this routine, he thanked her for all she was doing, especially the homework.

"You have no idea what a timesaver it is for me, Lauren," he'd said as they sat together on the couch and watched as Noirin played with her toys. She had purchased some toys and art supplies to keep at her place, so Noirin wouldn't have to carry things back and forth between their flats. They'd had fun shopping for them. The purchase included a miniature kitchenette set with cooking utensils and plastic food. Noirin couldn't seem to get enough of it.

Each night, before they left for their flat, not only did Noirin hug her, so did Brendan. Gone was the awkward distance, and in its place was something better than before. There was an intimacy, a connection that hadn't been there. Since sharing with Brendan about Christopher, everything had changed—for the better.

"I'm doin' very well actually," Shay said, replying to Lauren's question. "Some days are better than others. Today is better."

"I'm glad." Lauren lifted the basket she held in her hand. "I brought you lettuce and leeks from the garden. How about I wash them up for you and put them in the fridge?"

"That sounds grand. I'll follow you in and have a seat at the dining room table so we can talk."

As they slowly made their way to the kitchen, they talked about the garden, how it was coming along, and the next recipe card Lauren was working on—a tomato pie. Ellen had brought a couple of them to Sunday dinner, and everyone had loved the dish and agreed it would be a good choice for the tearoom.

"I'm so thrilled for Ellen and Donal. He's a good man and pastor. They make a fine couple," Shay commented as she watched Lauren prep the vegetables.

Lauren turned to give Brendan's aunt a smile. "I think it's wonderful too. She told me Donal has a surprise for her on Saturday."

"Oh," Shay said with a knowing look. "I wonder what that's all about."

"I don't know, but he isn't telling her where or what, just what to wear and what to bring with her."

"What has he told her?"

"To dress in layers."

"Of course—a must in Ireland."

"So, it sounds like it will be outdoors."

"Hmm, I have no idea what he could have in mind. There are so many options. Well, Ellen will have fun givin' us an account of the day when she returns."

Lauren nodded and focused on rinsing the leeks.

They were quiet for a moment before Shay spoke up. "Brendan told me and Quinn about your husband. I'm sorry you had to go through that."

Lauren turned to the older woman with an appreciative smile. "It's been really hard, but this place has made me better. No, not this place but the people: all of you. I didn't know if I was doing the right thing by coming, especially for a year, but I know now it was the best I could do to help myself."

Lauren paused the rinsing she was doing and placed the washed leeks in a bowl. She dried her hands and went to sit across from Shay. "My mother-in-law is afraid of losing me. I love her and my father-in-law very much. They're like second parents to me. I don't know how else to reassure her that nothing will ever change between us."

Shay gave her an understanding look. "I imagine the daughter-in-law and the mother-in-law dance is a tricky one. I had wondered how things would be between Eva and myself." Shay paused. "Brendan said he told you about her. It killed me to see his heart broken, but I can't say that I'm not somewhat glad."

"Why is that?" Lauren's curiosity was peaked.

"Eva was a nice girl, but I couldn't help but wonder how deep things flowed with her. She was good to Brendan. None of the emotional drama that women can sometimes bring to a relationship. We didn't have much interaction, but the few times she came to Tramore, we failed to connect. Yet, when he told us he wanted to raise Noirin, we had refused him."

"Brendan mentioned that."

Shay nodded. "Somehow, I knew Eva would never be okay with raising a child that wasn't hers, let alone one with Downs. We had hoped that by refusing Brendan guardianship he would give up and marry Eva. We knew how much he loved her and didn't want to see him in pain."

"And how do you feel about things now?"

Shay gave her a knowing, happy look. "I'm glad she walked out of his life. The way he loves Noirin, the way he took to being a father, it was a beautiful thing to behold. And most important of all, I want him to know that crazy, all-in, all-consuming love, like what you experienced with your husband. Brendan told us how good he was with you and how much you loved each other."

Shay continued. "When two people connect in such a life-changin' way, you don't move on easily from that.

I want that kind of love for my son. Mary and I have that, and we can't help but want the same for our children."

Lauren was quiet for a moment, taking in all Shay had said. She didn't know Eva, but she too was glad Brendan made the choice he'd made. She also wanted him to experience that same earth-shattering kind of love. "I want that for Brendan and Ellen too," she finally said.

"Now," Shay said. "That doesn't help you with your mother-in-law. Have you told her that nothin' will change?"

"I have."

"Good, just keep tellin' and showin' her."

"Yeah, I guess that's all I can do."

They chatted for a bit longer about the relationship between a daughter-in-law and mother-in-law before Lauren went back to work.

She made it to the bakery in time to walk with Brendan to Noirin's school.

"How was your afternoon?" he asked as they headed up Main Street.

She told him about her conversation with her in-laws and her mother-in-law's worries.

Brendan suspected that her mother-in-law was worried that she would find someone else to love and the change it would cause to their relationship. He wanted to ask Lauren if she thought that might be the issue, but he was afraid of what she would say. He imagined it would be something like how she could never love anyone like she loved Christopher, so there was no need for concern. It wasn't something he wanted to hear.

He was too happy with the way things were since their conversation about Christopher. He was at peace with his decision to love Lauren and to enjoy her company as much as possible, as much as she was willing to give. Since then, she'd given him so much—every evening together, their afternoon walks picking up Noirin. They even had plans to visit farmer Dunne's place on Saturday to see the animals and to buy fresh butter.

Brendan forced himself not to think about the future but to simply live in the moment.

Tonight, they would go to the book club meeting together. Tuesday night, she had come up with them to their flat, and after putting Noirin to bed, they had read *Jane Eyre* together. When she left, she hugged him. They always hugged now, and he loved every moment, the way she felt in his arms, no matter how brief the contact.

After Brendan reassured Lauren that she was doing the right thing with her mother-in-law, she said, "Shay and I also talked about Eva."

He looked at her. "Oh yeah, do I need to be worried?"

Lauren laughed. "No. Shay just mentioned how she was relieved that things didn't work out."

He was quiet for a moment.

Lauren must have misunderstood his quietness. She reached for his forearm to stop them in their tracks. They stood there looking at one another. "Did we overstep?" she asked.

He shook his head. "I'm glad things didn't work out either. I realized after the fact that lovin' Eva was merely comfortable. I'm glad I found out before it was too late that she wasn't in love with me enough to make the kind of commitment required to be with me and Noirin. I'm convinced that if we had married under normal circumstances, like I had planned, the first sign of serious trouble, she would have bailed."

"I'm not sure if Shay ever told you, but that's exactly what she thought."

Brendan was thoughtful for a moment. "You know, I never really asked my parents what they truly thought about Eva. I thought their comments about her being nice were enough. I never invited them to tell me if there were any true concerns." He resumed their walk. "I'll never make that mistake again."

They drew quiet as they continued their walk to Noirin's school. Eventually, it was Lauren who spoke. "The hardest thing that Christopher and I had to face was infertility."

Brendan looked at her, but she continued to look straight ahead. He sensed she didn't want to meet his gaze.

"We'd tried for a year and nothing. We had an appointment with a fertility specialist the Friday after he would have returned from Oregon."

Brendan felt his chest tighten with concern. They had never made the appointment because of Christopher's death. He didn't know what to say. Words seemed inadequate. So, they continued to walk.

Again, Lauren broke the silence. "When we started researching fertility costs, our insurance didn't cover treatments. We were overwhelmed." She paused. "He was so sweet. He said he'd sell everything we didn't need in order to pay for the treatments. He also said he'd work a part-time job. It never came to that, but I know he would have done it. Christopher was a cleaver not a leaver."

Brendan turned to look at her. "Eva is a leaver—at least with me she was. She proved it."

Lauren held his gaze for a moment, her expression a little bleak. "Her loss. I'll never know the reason we couldn't conceive—if it was me or if it was Christopher, but it no longer matters."

Her words were like a knife to his chest. She'd confirmed what he'd suspected from the moment Flynn had made his offer in Dublin. But instead of running like he wanted to, as he'd done that night, Brendan felt a determination rise up in him. He wouldn't accept that as her final answer. Brendan had ten months to convince Lauren she couldn't live without him. He would never succeed by pushing her away.

Chapter Thirty

Ellen breathed in the fresh air and took in the sight before her. "It's wonderful, Donal," she said as her gaze rested on the small white cottage-shed enclosed by a white picket fence. Two birch trees towered over the shed, offering shade and a place to hang a hammock. Rows of tilled earth contained sprouted seedlings that would bear a variety of crops in the upcoming months.

She turned to him. "Who owns this?"

"My parents. We've had this plot for as long as I can remember. The same with most of the neighboring plots. The Maguires are to the left and the Browns to the right. Growing up, we came here most weekends. On the other side of the ridge is a large creek that all the kids loved to play in. We'll take a walk down there later."

He reached for her hand and said, "Let's go take a look inside the shed."

"It's charming," she commented as they walked toward the structure. "I love the classic lines and the French doors."

"There's only enough room to sleep two. Garrett and I slept in a tent that we pitched right over there." He pointed to a grassy patch of earth right next to a door on the side of the shed. "On rainless nights, Garrett and I would fight over who got to sleep in the hammock first. Mum made sure we took turns."

Ellen took in the details of the cottage. The walls and floors were white. A beige sisal carpet anchored the full-size bed and small sofa that sat in the corner. Near the door was a counter with a sink and storage above and below. The ceilings were vaulted with a fan centered in the space.

"There is an outdoor storage closet on the back of the shed, where we put the fold-up table and chairs. I'll get those and set them up on the patio, and then I'll build a fire."

"Donal, this is really nice. Thank you."

He smiled at her. "I'm glad you like it. I was hopin' you would."

Ellen helped him set up the fire in the round stone pit that sat in the center of the paved patio area. Donal had also brought blankets to lay over the hammock because of the slight chill in the air.

The large ice chest he pulled out of the back of his car indicated he had brought food and drinks along. Of course he had—he'd thought of everything!

When all was in place, she took a moment to appreciate the romantic setting he had created for her—for them.

He reached for her hand. "I know it's not some grand escape, but I hope you enjoy being here as much I did growin' up."

"It's a little slice of heaven here on earth. I couldn't be happier."

Donal smiled at her reassurance. "Do you want to see what my parents have planted?"

"Sure."

They walked along the rows and tried to identify the various plants. Ellen was impressed with how many Donal knew. She hadn't known him to be much of a gardener.

"I dabble," he said. "Mostly container gardening. I have tomato plants and herbs in the backyard at the parish. It's not because I don't want to garden, but I'm only one person. Last year, your parents and other members of the congregation plied me with their spoils. I never wanted to refuse anyone, but I couldn't eat it all, so I did a lot of canning. Did you know I can my own vegetables?"

Her eyes rounded in surprise. "I did not. Canning is good. Things don't go to waste that way."

"Exactly. Are you hungry? Do you want somethin' to drink?"

"No, I'm good. I'm ready to explore."

"Okay, let me grab my backpack. We'll head toward the forest and see if we can find some rhubarb. There are stalks of it that come up every year along the edge of the forest where we'll enter."

After they had gathered enough rhubarb to fill the plastic container Donal had in his backpack, he asked, "Do you think this is enough to make something with?"

"Are we cooking on the fire?" she asked.

He nodded. "Mum has cast iron skillets in the shed and other cookin' utensils, bowls, spoons etc. And I brought everythin' you need for bakin'."

"Includin' butter?"

"Yup," he said, proud of himself.

She grinned. "A man after my heart."

When she'd said the words, she held his gaze to gauge his reaction. There was a knowing gleam in his eyes. He kissed her forehead before placing the lid on the container. When it was stowed away in his backpack, he grabbed her hand and headed into the forest.

It was incredible. The trunks of the trees were covered in moss, the moisture thick and pervasive giving off a pleasant, earthy smell.

Very little light penetrated the thick canopy. Fallen logs became a challenge. Half the time Ellen found herself being hoisted over trunks by Donal.

"I don't want you fallin' and twistin' anythin'," he'd said after the first time he lifted her over a log, quite unexpectedly.

She couldn't help but wonder if it was just an excuse for him to touch her, for she wasn't in real danger of twisting an ankle. Ellen didn't care if it was an excuse. She loved having his hands on her.

On the way back to the cottage, Donal asked her if she liked to fish.

"I've only ever fished with a net over the side of a boat, the way Shane taught me, so I'm not sure."

"Want to give it a try?"

"I'd love to."

"Good, and let's hope we catch somethin' or all we'll have is vegetables for lunch."

"And rhubarb crumble."

"Is that what you're plannin' to make?"

She nodded.

"A woman after my heart," he said with a grin.

Ellen Sighed. *How she loved him!*

It was her turn to do the kissing, so she kissed the dimple on his cheek.

It was the best morning ever, foraging for their food and cooking it over an open fire.

Stuffed from their lunch of trout and sautéed vegetables with a side of buttered new potatoes, Donal and Ellen sat side by side in the Adirondack chairs on the patio.

"I can't even think about eatin' that crumble right now," Ellen said, eyeing the cast iron pan she'd removed from the fire.

"Yeah, I'm in no rush. But I am goin' to clean up our dishes."

"I'll help," she said and began to stand to her feet.

Donal placed a hand on her shoulder. "Let me take care of it. It's no trouble. Relax and enjoy the view."

She didn't argue with him and watched him as he walked into the cottage with an armful of dishes. The doors were wide open, and she could see him through the window over the sink.

If Ellen were any happier, she'd think she'd died and gone to heaven. All week she'd been reminding herself that this was real, that Donal had asked her out and had made his affections for her known to the world. In private, he had sent random texts telling her how he was thinking about her, how he wished she was with him. They'd seen each other every day over the past week.

She'd never been in love before, and for so long she had loved Donal from a distance only dreaming of what it could be like with him. Now that she knew, she was over-whelmed at times.

Ellen understood that new love's first run of emotions could be very heady, and after things settled down, they would change. But she also knew that the change was even better than the first blush of love, for those emotions were staying and powerful, because they were deeply rooted. Her parents were proof.

Ellen had lost count of the number of times, over the years, she'd heard her mother tell her father how he still made her heart flutter. As exciting as these feelings of new love were, she looked forward to the intimacy and the depth of a settled love and how it sustained and built up a couple. She would have that with Donal, she was certain.

"What are you thinkin' about?" Donal asked as he reached for her hand.

She hadn't heard him approach and was happy he was near.

Before she could answer, he pulled her to her feet and led her to the hammock. He stretched out first on top of the warm blankets and then motioned for her to join him.

When she was lying beside him, snuggled close with her hand laying across his chest, she felt like she could cry.

The way he felt, the way they felt together, it whispered promises of what was to come.

They lay quietly for a while, the hammock swaying slightly in the cool air. She could have easily nodded off if her whole body hadn't been singing with awareness.

"Ellen," she heard Donal say.

She lifted her head to look at him.

He drew her up until her face was lying next to his, their eyes locked. "I've known you for a little over a year now."

She nodded unsure of what to say, not sure if she could say anything.

"I'm sorry it took me so long to get here."

Her eyes filled with tears. *He knew.* He'd connected the dots, after all. Donal knew she had secretly loved him for a while.

"Don't cry, sweetheart," he said as he brushed at a tear that managed to escape. "I wanted this day to be special. Do you know why?"

She swallowed the lump of emotion that had formed and shook her head, still unable to speak.

"Because I want you to always remember this day, the day I told you how much I love you."

She closed her eyes at the words and then quickly opened them. Finally, she spoke. "I'll never forget. I love you too, Donal."

Her eyes never left his as he shifted to his side and sought her lips with his own. When she felt the warm brush of his mouth, she finally closed her eyes and died a little inside.

It was a tender kiss, achingly sweet and full of promise. It had been worth waiting for.

When he pulled away, she looked into his eyes and saw the first glimmers of that sustaining and powerful love.

It was hard to pack everything up and head back home. Donal wished they could stay at the garden cottage forever, but it was getting late, and they had over a two-hour drive back to Tramore.

When everything was in its place, the cottage tightly locked up, and the fire put out, he reached for Ellen and drew her to him one last time before they left. His arms were draped around her waist pressing her to him. The feel of her body against his felt right, like she'd always belonged to him.

Donal lowered his mouth to hers and kissed her in the descending twilight. She tasted wonderful. Her lips were soft and inviting. He moved his lips to trail kisses along her jaw line before moving to nuzzle and taste the delicate skin of her neck.

He heard her moan and looked at her. Ellen's eyes were glazed over, and her breath was coming in faster than normal. She was intoxicating. "I don't want to leave," she whispered before pressing her forehead to his chest. "And I want you somethin' fierce, Donal."

He lifted her chin so she could look at him. "I know, *ma moitié*."

Her eyes grew big at the term of endearment, which meant "my other half" in French. "Oh, Donal. Do you mean it?"

He pressed her harder against him, desire lighting a fire in his belly. His voice was shaky with the intensity of what he felt. "I love you so much, Ellen, and I know as sure as I am breathin' and holdin' you in my arms that you were made for me." He kissed her but only for a moment before he pulled away to look at her. "I want to spend the rest of my life with you, grow old with you. 'I want your joy to be as bright as the mornin' and your sorrows to merely be shadows that fade in the sunlight of my love'." It was a blessing he used at weddings, and for the first time, he understood the fullness of its meaning.

She smiled in contentment. There was no need for her to answer with words. Her answer was in her eyes, but she gave it anyhow. "I feel like I've loved you for so long, Donal. The lines of when it began are blurred. I can't remember the exact moment I knew, but I'll always remember this moment, when I accepted your invitation for a life together. *Je suis à vous*," she added and then translated, "I am yours."

He would do well belonging to her, safe in her capable and loving hands. He kissed her one last time before reluctantly letting her go. Hand in hand, they walked to the car. "I want us to pick out your ring together. I'll take you to Dublin, and we'll celebrate at a nice restaurant."

She stopped and looked at him. "Is this really happening?

Donal bent down and kissed her lightly. "This is really happening, sweetheart."

Chapter Thirty-One

"If you smile any wider, your face will crack."

Donal looked up from his desk and over to where Brendan was standing in the doorway. He was holding a white paper sack.

"I'm gettin' married; what do you expect me to do?"

"Exactly that," Brendan answered as he closed the door to Donal's office and took one of the seats in front of his friend's desk. "You haven't had any time for me lately, so I thought I'd bring lunch to you. Shona said you were free."

"Perfect timin'. What'd you bring?"

"Brianna's meatballs."

Donal grinned even wider. "You know me, man."

"I do, but I have ulterior motives."

Donal leaned back in his chair, his face sobering. "Is everythin' all right?"

Brendan shrugged and then opened the bag so he could give Donal his to-go container. "Eat first and tell me when, where, and how. Ellen didn't give me details. She's crazy over the moon happy, you know."

Donal's wide grin was back, along with a contented look. While they tackled their lunch, he told Brendan about their day and how he'd figured out the week before the reason Ellen had been avoiding him, why she'd been looking for a new church: she was in love with him.

"How did you know?" Brendan asked after swallowing his last bite.

"The night we ended up at the bakery to cook dinner, she slipped and told me that she'd dreamt for a long time about cookin' with me. It all started to make sense."

Finished with his meatball sandwich, Brendan sat back in his chair and asked, "Have you guys settled on a date?"

"As soon as we're done with pre-marital counseling. I can't wait too long. She drives me crazy." Donal didn't have to say anymore, and Brendan didn't want him to elaborate. He could read between the lines. "Ellen talked to her mother, and they're confident they can pull off a fabulous weddin' in no time. We're goin' to Limerick tomorrow to meet my parents." He paused. "Man, I can't believe it's been nearly a week since I asked her to marry me." He shook his head as if to clear it. "Anyhow, Ellen and Mary already have the venue lined up, *The Acres* in Waterford, and invitations go out early next week."

"That's a grand place to get married."

He nodded. "It will have to be indoors; not enough time to plan for an outdoor weddin' and a backup plan. So, enough about me and Ellen. What's on your mind?"

"I'm invoking pastor-parishioner privileges, which means you can't say anythin' to Ellen. I just need to talk to someone. I'm in love with Lauren, and it's killin' me."

Donal's expression softened in understanding. "I suspected as much, and she's not over her husband."

"She'll probably never be over him."

"Has she told you that?"

"Yeah." Brendan told Donal about the conversation they had regarding the infertility she and Christopher struggled with. "But I'm determined to make it really difficult for her to walk away from me ten months from now."

Donal was done with his sandwich too and closed the lid to the container. "Well, I think you're off to a good start. The two of you have been spendin' a lot of time together."

"More than a lot, and she's initiated most of it. Do you realize we have dinner every night together? She makes me dinner. I leave the bakery and stop by to pick up Noirin, and she has dinner made for us. Most nights she walks up with me to help tuck Noirin into bed. I think she'd do it every night, but she's sensitive about infringing on my time with Noirin. She's amazin' that way. On those nights, she usually stays and we talk about anythin' and everythin'...

"Then there's the family. You started comin' to family dinners on Sunday about the same time she did, and now she's comin' to dinner on Wednesdays with me and my folks. She stops by to see Aunt Shay at least twice a week. They adore her, by the way. Never said that about Eva."

"That all sounds grand, Brendan. Not to mention how she absolutely loves Noirin. There's no issue there of wantin' to be a part of raising a child with Downs. But you want more. You want to show—to tell her how much you love her."

Brendan gave him an appraising look. "You really are good at this. And yes, that's exactly the problem. The minute I move in that direction, she'll bolt like a frightened colt. I saw it happen." He told Donal about Flynn and how Brendan had distanced himself from her afterwards.

"What did she do when you pulled away?"

"She told me about Christopher."

Donal gave him a knowing look. "I don't think you'll have anythin' to worry about."

Brendan felt hopeful. "Enlighten me."

He leaned his elbows on his desk. "She's drawn to you. When you distanced yerself, it affected her, and she pursued you because, whether she realizes it or not, she wants you in her life."

"As a friend."

"For now. The closer the two of you get, the more she'll realize that she's made to love and to be loved. She's hurtin' over the loss of her husband, but she'll want that kind of love again."

"Shane never did."

Donal nodded. "Ellen mentioned that. She was surprised to hear that he'd met someone and invited her to dinner. He's the same way, made to love and be loved; it just took him longer. It won't take that long for Lauren."

"So, do I just keep doin' what I'm doin'?"

"Yeah, and hopefully she'll take the lead. If she doesn't, I think when it's time to leave, it'll hit her, and she won't be able to do it."

Brendan felt better than he had in weeks. The

possibility of loving Lauren completely and for her to love him back buoyed his spirits in a way that hadn't happened since meeting her.

"She really does love Noirin," Brendan said a little wistfully.

"I have to ask you, Brendan. You mentioned how she and her husband had issues with fertility. Have you thought about what that might mean?"

"Yeah, a lot actually. If, one day, I'm fortunate to call her my wife and we're unable to have children on our own, I'll sacrifice whatever is necessary to help make it happen medically. And if that doesn't work, we'll adopt. I don't need a biological child to feel the fullness of being a father. Noirin is proof of that. All three of our lives are proof of that. We've all been orphaned but have known incredible love."

"Yes, you have," Donal agreed.

"I can't believe you're here!" Lauren called out in delight as she ran toward her parents who were exiting security.

She hugged her father first. "Hi, baby girl. I've missed you," he greeted while giving her a kiss on the cheek.

She kissed him back. "I've missed you too. Mom," she said next as she reached for her mother, "can you believe you're here?"

Angie shook her head. "You know I've always wanted to come to Ireland."

"I can't wait for you to meet everyone. Brendan and Noirin are here. Let me introduce you." The night before they left, she'd told her parents they would be joining her. They were excited to meet the father and daughter she hadn't been able to stop talking about.

Brendan was holding Noirin and both smiled at her parents when they approached.

"Brendan and Noirin, these are my parents, Angie and William Fellows."

Brendan extended his hand to William first and then to Angie. "It's so nice to finally meet you. This is my daughter, Noirin."

"Hi, Noirin," Angie said first while placing a gentle hand on the girl's arm.

"Hi, Lauren's Mom and Dad—that sounds funny," she said and looked at Brendan.

He chuckled and looked at the Fellows. "Noirin normally uses the Gaelic version for mom and dad. Lauren's been teachin' her the American version."

"Can you tell us the Gaelic version, Noirin?" her dad encouraged.

When she told them, they both smiled. William said, "I like the way your version sounds better."

"Yes, it's very lyrical," Angie agreed.

"What's lyrical mean?" Noirin asked.

"It means like a song," Brendan explained.

Noirin's eyes grew bigger with pleasure. "Lyrical," she repeated.

"Shall we get your bags?" Lauren suggested.

315

They were a happy group talking and getting to know one another while they waited for the bags to arrive and then loaded them in the car.

They had picked up her parents at the airport in Shannon, the same one Lauren had flown into two months ago.

When they arrived at her flat, Brendan helped bring in their bags. After showing them to their room, he said goodbye.

Lauren, who was holding Noirin, followed him to the front door.

"I thought you might stay? I have a roast in the slow cooker."

"You're sweet to offer, Lauren, but I'm sure your parents want to spend some time with you alone. We'll meet up another night for dinner. Actually, I almost forgot. If it works with your schedules, my parents would like to have them for dinner on Wednesday. On Sunday, I know you'll be with them on Aran Islands; otherwise, they'd have an invitation for that night too."

"We should be able to make Wednesday. Do you want me to bring up a plate for the two of you later?"

"I promised Noirin pizza."

"I love pizza!" she said exuberantly to Lauren who was still holding her.

"I know you do, sweetheart. I love it too. But I love you more," she said before giving a tummy tickle to her favorite little girl, who laughed boisterously in response.

She looked at Brendan. "You two enjoy your dinner.

CHAPTER THIRTY-ONE

We'll see you in the morning at the bakery before we leave for Aran Islands."

He smiled at her. "I really like your parents."

The grin she gave him was bright. "We are both very fortunate to have such great parents."

Chapter Thirty-Two

They arrived at the bakery around seven, and her parents met Shane and Ellen for the first time. A few minutes after they arrived, Brendan and Noirin walked into the store. They all sat and talked for about half an hour and then it was time to make the drive to Aran Islands.

As they headed for the door, Lauren pulled Ellen aside and asked her about the plans for picking out the rings. She had met Donal's parents the previous weekend.

"The Saturday after the auction for the food pantry. It was the soonest we could both get away."

The auction was scheduled a week away. That same morning, she planned to drop her parents off at the airport for their nine o'clock flight and then arrive in time to begin helping with the set-up for the evening event.

"I'm so happy for you, Ellen." Lauren smiled and felt a little wistful. She remembered being engaged—all the milestones. It had been a wonderful time in her life.

"Oh, I almost forgot," she added as she reached into her bag and pulled out a folder. "Here is the drawing of the tomato pie? What do you think?"

Ellen held the drawing and studied it carefully. "It's terrific, just like all the others."

"This one was a little tougher and that's why it took me longer. I'll have the rhubarb crumble picture ready by next week." She gave Ellen a knowing smile. "I think it's great that you added it to the menu. What a story to tell your customers and your grandkids!"

"Grandkids!" There was a dreamy look in Ellen's eyes. "Is this really happenin'?"

Lauren hugged her. "It's happening! Got to go; my parents are waiting for me in the car. I'll call you when we get back."

"Be safe."

Brendan and Noirin were talking to her parents by the car. Her mother had Noirin in her arms. Lauren smiled at the realization that their little girl had already stolen someone else's heart. *Their little girl*? The thought both stunned and alarmed Lauren. When had she started thinking about Noirin as her little girl? Not too long after she'd met her, actually. The connection had been nearly instantaneous. It didn't trouble her, but she couldn't help but think about how in a few months it would be time to go home. Lauren shook off the thought and the ache that began to form in the middle of her chest.

"Are we ready?" her father asked.

"Ready," Lauren said as she reached for Noirin to give her a hug. "I'll miss you, sweetheart."

"Miss you too," the little girl said before giving Lauren a kiss on the lips. She held Noirin close to her for a moment longer before handing her to Brendan.

"Please be careful, and call me if you have any issues," Brendan requested.

"I will. We'll be back Tuesday afternoon."

He nodded.

She turned to enter the back seat of the car. Her parents were already inside, sitting up front.

"They're wonderful people, Lauren," her mother said.

"Yes, they are." They were more than wonderful: they were a part of her. The thought of not seeing Brendan and Noirin for the next few days caused a heaviness to weigh on her.

The whole week of her parents' visit, she'd only seen Brendan and Noirin in passing, except for Wednesday dinner. During the day she'd been too busy to miss them, but at night, the longing she felt settled on her like a fog.

On their way to Aran Islands, they had stopped at Limerick and Ennis. They arrived first at Limerick, stayed the night, and then went to Ennis in the morning and spent the day there. They took a full day to explore Aran Islands, and to buy sweaters. On the return trip, they walked the cliffs of Moher before making their way to Dingle.

It had been a whirlwind four-day trip, but it was time spent with her parents that she would always remember.

On Wednesday, they explored Waterford and Tramore until dinner time when they met up at the Callerys. It had been a really warm evening and both of the older couples hit it off well, just as she expected.

At one point, the four of them abandoned Lauren,

Brendan, and Noirin, to look at pictures of a trip to Iceland the Callerys had taken a few years ago. Iceland was a place that her mother and father had dreamt of going for a long time.

Lauren and Brendan were sitting at the dining room table talking while Noirin sat comfortably on her lap and slept. It was getting late.

"Is she gettin' too heavy for you?" Brendan asked as he made a move toward his daughter.

"Touch her and you'll get your hands slapped," she said with a wide grin.

Brendan chuckled. "I guess that means you're fine."

"More than fine. Mom and Dad are pretty beat; do you mind if I come up with you to tuck her in?" Lauren pressed her lips to the top of Noirin's curls. "I've missed her so much." She looked up at Brendan. "And I've missed you."

At that, something flickered in his eyes, something she couldn't quite read but it comforted her to see it.

"And we've missed you," he said.

"So, you'll come for dinner tomorrow night?"

"Nope," he said with a shake of his head and a determined look.

"But I want you to. My parents would love to have you join us."

"You won't change my mind, Lauren. They really are terrific people, and I've enjoyed the time we've spent getting to know them, but they came here to spend time with their daughter. So, no dinner tomorrow or Friday.

But if you want, I'll go with you to the airport on Saturday. Noirin will be stayin' with my folks."

She was disappointed, but she would take what she could get. "All right then, I won't bug you anymore."

"Good, because I can be pretty stubborn when I want."

"I've noticed," she said, giving him a cheeky, knowing look.

It didn't take Lauren long to join them upstairs.

After tucking Noirin in, he said, "Have some tea with me."

His emotions were racing, and he didn't want her to go too soon. Hearing Lauren tell him earlier that she'd missed him, had been unsettling—in a good way. Wanting him and Noirin to come to dinner the following evening had pushed those feelings to another level. He felt the change in her—in them. And for the first time, he was beginning to believe she could once day love him as a man.

"Make it coffee and you've got a deal," she replied.

"Coffee it is."

She walked toward the kitchen and put the kettle on. He loved how she made herself at home. It told him she was comfortable with him, with them. It was something she'd done more of lately.

Lauren paused as she turned the knob to the stove. "You're really making me suffer, you know."

He raised his eyebrows at her while pulling down some cups. "And how am I makin' you suffer?"

"I really want you to come to dinner."

"You said you wouldn't bug anymore."

"I know but I can't help it."

"Look, Lauren, I think it's grand that you want us there." It was terrific, actually. "But you have to trust me on this. If I had trekked half-way around the world to see Noirin, and she wanted her friend and his daughter hanging out with us all the time, I'd be a bit put off, no matter how much I liked the guy."

She gave him a resigned look.

"How about some lavender biscotti to cheer you up?" he offered, to soften his persistent no. When she didn't respond right away, he asked, "Are you poutin'?"

The scowl she gave him, was answer enough. She was adorable. He didn't mind her pouting for the right reasons and this was definitely on the acceptable list of reasons. He was about to bribe her again with biscotti, when she suddenly wrapped her arms around his waist and pressed her cheek against his chest.

Brendan quickly reciprocated the hug and closed his eyes. He hadn't held her since the morning after she'd told him about Christopher, and it had left him feeling empty.

"I just need to be held for a minute. And then I'll stop pouting."

"I've started the timer."

She pulled away to look at him and smiled when

she saw the teasing look in his eyes. She rested her head against him once more and sighed.

His voice was tight when he said, "Take as long as you'd like."

And she did, until the whistle on the kettle began to blow.

Reluctantly they both pulled away. "I'll take that biscotti," she said as she turned off the stove. "You owe me."

Brendan smiled inwardly. He'd give her so much more—all of him and all that he owned—if she wanted it.

Angie pulled back the sheets and sighed.

William looked at her as he removed his watch and placed it on the nightstand. "Everything okay?"

She sat cross-legged on the bed in Lauren's guest bedroom. "You know she's never coming back home."

He sat down on the other side, facing her. "It's pretty obvious she adores Noirin. I always knew she would be a terrific mother, but seeing her with that little girl, it makes me a little teary eyed. But you're not thinking of Noirin, are you?"

"No, she's falling in love with Brendan, even if she doesn't know it."

"How does that make you feel?"

"Happy and sad. She loved Christopher so much. But she needs to move on. She needs to find love again and to have the chance to be a mother." Angie paused. "Stacey won't take it well. We've already spoken over the phone, and she's so afraid of losing Lauren. And now with her living half-way across the world, it will make it even harder. I don't know, myself, how I'm going to handle being so far away from her."

William reached for her hand, "What do you think about retiring here?"

Her eyes grew wide with surprise. "Is that even possible?"

"People do it all the time. We might be living in a tiny one-bedroom flat, eating beans and potatoes every night, but I'd be okay with that."

"Wow, to live here! It would be amazing."

William smiled. "Yeah, it's an amazing place. We'll start looking into things when we get back home, and we'll wait to say anything to Lauren."

"I think that's a good idea. I don't think she realizes the direction she's headed, and if we say anything, it might spook her. Christopher was her life."

"That was really easy you know," William said with a grin.

"What?"

"A couple of weeks after Lauren left, I started thinking about the idea of retiring here. I didn't think you'd want to make such a big move so late in life."

She leaned over to kiss him on the lips. "I'd follow you anywhere."

He smiled, "Same here."

Chapter Thirty-Three

It was hard to see her parents leave. The only downside to their visit was Brendan's refusal to have dinner with them. She had spent the last few wonderful days seeing her parents enjoy Ireland. They spent Thursday in Dublin and drove back that same night. Her parents wanted to relax a bit before their long flight on Saturday.

On Friday, they had lunch at Lanigan's Pub and went crazy over Brianna's meatballs, exclaiming how the pub owner could make a fortune selling them retail. And now, her mom and dad were leaving. Part of her wanted to follow them, but the other part of her wanted—needed to stay.

She and Brendan remained in the screening area and watched them until they made it through the checkpoint and were no longer in sight.

"You have really terrific parents, Lauren."

She smiled at him. "Yours are pretty amazing too."

Brendan looked at his watch. "How about we take a detour?"

"Do we have time—with the auction this evening?"

"Hold on a second," he said as he fished his phone out of his pocket. He pressed a button and held it to his ear. After a moment, he said, "Hey, Donal, how did you do on volunteers for today?"

Brendan looked at Lauren while he carried on his conversation. "I'm at the airport with Lauren and thought we'd take a little detour."

He paused while Donal replied and then said, "Of course we'll make it in time for the auction." He paused once more, still looking at Lauren. "Are you sure? Okay. Thanks, man. We'll see you later."

He ended the call and placed his phone back in his pocket. "Donal said they had more volunteers than they needed. Father O'Farrell—he's the priest at the Catholic church halfway between Tramore and Dunmore East—rounded up a number of volunteers from a sister parish in Waterford. They don't need us until the auction starts. So, what do you think?"

"Sure, where to?"

"A town called Adare. It's not really much of a detour—mostly on the way back home—but we have to veer a bit south." He was leading her out of the airport terminal as he spoke. "I think you'll enjoy stoppin', and the next time your parents come to visit, you can take them there and stay longer."

"It sounds great," Lauren replied, happy to be spending time with Brendan.

The drive took a little over half an hour. Soon stone walls began lining the way into Adare. To the left, on the main street, was a school that looked like a castle. Only in Ireland did children go to school in what looked like castles.

As they drew closer to the center of town, colorful buildings with thatched roofs began to appear. It was like stepping into the shire where the Hobbits lived in Tolkien's *Lord of the Rings*.

"It's fascinating!" Lauren remarked, her face practically pressed to the glass.

"I'll drive through the town for a pre-tour, and then we'll settle on a place to park."

A while later, they found a place to park along what appeared to be the main shopping district of Adare. It was a picturesque town with a romantic feel, and busy.

"It's a really popular place, isn't it?" Lauren commented as they strolled down the street at a leisurely pace.

"The weekends are always the busiest. When we have a chance, we'll have to come back on a weekday."

She liked the sound of that, of them coming back here together. "This is great. I'm glad we came today."

Lauren loved strolling through the shops and looking at the wares and odds and ends, each store unique in its offerings. It was amazing how similar things were in the U.S. but also very different. At one shop, she found the cutest little knitted hat with rabbit ears. "Noirin would look so adorable in this. Don't you think?"

Brendan was gazing at her, a look of contentment on his face. "She would look grand in it."

"You're enjoying yourself, right?" she asked. "You don't mind shopping?"

"I do enjoy shoppin'. I can always find somethin' interestin' to look at. And I love to people watch. See that older couple over there." Lauren followed his gaze. "They look good together, happy, even after however many years of being together."

"Maybe they're newlyweds."

He chuckled. "Well, I've never thought of that before. But I don't think so; they're too familiar with each other to be newlyweds. They fit and move while lookin' at one another like they've been together for a long time. See..." he said a little quieter, not wanting the couple to overhear him talking about them, "see how he reached for her purse as it slid down her shoulder, like it happens all the time and he was expectin' it. Puttin' it back on her shoulder was an involuntary gesture. He probably didn't even realize he was doin' it."

"Hmm, I see what you're saying, and you might be right."

At that moment, the older couple made eye contact with them. Because they were staring blatantly at them, the only thing Lauren and Brendan could do was smile and wave. When the couple smiled back and then walked away, they chuckled quietly, amused that they'd been caught.

Lauren directed her gaze at another couple in the check-out line. "What about them?"

"Newlyweds, definitely newlyweds."

"Okay, so how can you be so sure?"

"He keeps checkin' out his wife like he'll devour her any minute and right on the spot. I wouldn't be surprised if they're honeymooning here in Adare. Got married here even."

Lauren's face flushed at the thought. She looked at

RAIN ON A GOOD DAY

Brendan and felt the temperature rise even more. The way he was looking at her was not too dissimilar from the way that man had been looking at his wife. It surprised her. Was she imagining it because he'd simply created the context for such a thought, or was he really looking at her as if longing and desire were actually coursing through his veins? The thought both stunned her and caused her body to tingle with awareness. Why all of a sudden was she seeing Brendan in this light, and why wasn't it causing her to run for the hills? The way she'd done with Flynn over a simple invitation?

The look in his eyes became hooded and was quickly masked with humor. She hadn't imagined it, and it caused her to wonder about what had just happened.

Brendan didn't give her a chance to dwell on it for too long. He was holding up a pair of knitted socks with a felted wool fox appliqué on the cuff. "My aunt Mary would love these. She is always complaining about her feet being cold, even in the summertime. I'll get these for her."

"And I'll get this hat for Noirin."

As they stood in line to make their purchase, Lauren couldn't stop thinking about how insightful Brendan was, the way he saw things and people.

"What are you thinkin' about? You wandered off for a minute," he asked.

There were four people in front of them. It was a busy store. "I was thinking about how insightful you are, how well you read people."

He seemed genuinely surprised by the compliment.

"Not me. That's Donal's gift. If you are right about me being that way, I would have seen the real Eva a mile off. Would have saved myself a lot of heartache."

He turned away to look at the line ahead of him. Had he said too much? Lauren wondered what he was thinking. He wasn't normally a guarded person, but he hadn't been overly talkative about the woman he'd loved and lost.

She didn't know what to say to that. She couldn't relate; neither did she have some pat explanation. So, instead, she slipped her arm through his and just stood next to him while they waited in line.

All the shopping they had done worked up their appetites and they settled on a cozy French style café, with the dining room flanked by two stone fireplaces. It was a nice spot to sit by in the colder months.

They ordered and then found a quiet table in the back corner. They'd beat the lunch rush and were pleased to find that the restaurant wasn't overly busy.

"Thank you for the detour," she said while taking a sip of her water with lemon. "I know why this town is so popular. Did you ever come here with Eva?"

He leaned his forearms on the table. "No, she didn't care too much for leavin' Dublin. We dated for six months, and she only came to Tramore a couple of times. She was a city girl through and through."

"But she knew how much you loved Tramore?"

Brendan nodded. He looked down at the table but didn't have a chance to say anything because the food had arrived.

When the server left, they commented on their choices and ate quietly for a bit.

"You don't talk much about Eva. Would you rather I not bring her up?"

He wiped his mouth with his napkin and shrugged. "Not necessarily... but why do you want to know?"

"Because she's a part of you. She's one of those key people who came into your life and helped shape you."

"But not all people are meant to stay," he interjected, a touch of sadness in his voice.

"No, they're not all meant to stay. Just like Christopher," she added quietly. She'd finally formed the words that had wound themselves up so tight in her mind and spirit that they couldn't be expressed... until now. She was never meant to have Christopher for very long; only for a season. She still struggled to accept it, but the revelation didn't turn her into a quivering mass of pain and anger, like it would have done nearly three months ago.

She did her best to describe to Brendan what she'd just realized.

When she was done, he gave her an understanding look. "Does it make it easier to understand your loss?" he asked.

Lauren looked thoughtful for a moment. "In some ways. It doesn't ease the pain of missing him and wondering how I'll go on without him."

But truth be told, she was managing to do just that. But did she want to? At least all the way? It was too much for her to think of at the moment. She was simply glad she had taken a step forward.

Brendan leaned back in his chair and held her gaze. "Christopher will always be a part of you, as he should. And if I know you, he will be celebrated. He'll remain with you in the best kind of way. I can't say that about Eva." He looked away. "I purchased a ring a few weeks before Katelyn died. I was waitin' for the right moment. After we buried my cousin, and I knew I would raise Noirin, I was certain that Eva loved me enough to give it a try."

He reached up and rubbed his brow. "I had the ring in my pocket the day I told her about my guardianship plans." Brendan swallowed hard. "She asked me to change my mind, and when I wouldn't, she walked out of my front door. I never had the chance to even show her the ring."

Lauren felt for him. "And the fact that she was in your life, and even the part about her leaving—it did help shape you." They were words to bring him comfort.

He finally looked at her. "How?"

"It showed you what you're made of, your loyalty, and the deep and abiding love that you have for those who matter. You were willing to do what was right by a little girl, by your parents, all at the expense of a great loss. You may have realized some things about Eva that you didn't see until after it was all said and done, but don't minimize the loss that cut very deep and the mark it left on your life. You're too good for that."

He looked down and picked at non-existent lint on

his pant leg for a moment. "I think I have some accepting to do when it comes to Eva."

Lauren gave him a smile of approval. "Ask me to come to church with you tomorrow." He'd asked her every Sunday since she'd told him about Christopher, but she hadn't been ready, until now.

Brendan looked up at her, and his eyes widened in surprise. "Will you come to church with me tomorrow?"

"I would love to," she replied, feeling a little freer than she had the day, the week, the month before.

Chapter Thirty-Four

"Do you have time to stop by my house?" Shane asked as they left the school building.

"Sure. I wanted to stop by the garden for a while, but I have time. I've noticed that Morrigan has been coming to Tramore quite a bit." She threw Shane a knowing glance.

He grinned. He was in love with Morrigan, very much in love with her, and she with him. "Yeah, she says she likes it here."

"I think it's the people she likes—or maybe a particular person."

He laughed. Shortly after the gallery showing on one of their walks to and from school, he'd told Lauren more about how he'd met Morrigan. But he'd not gone into much more other than they had lost touch and then had reconnected again recently.

While they walked to his house, they talked about Morrigan and her life before meeting Shane. She'd been married for close to thirty years. Her husband hadn't been the most attentive partner; he'd worked a lot and had been more interested in making money than spending time with his wife.

They were childless, and when her husband died, she'd been sad but not for the normal reasons. Morrigan's sorrow had been over the choices her husband had made, the choice to make other things the priority instead of the person who had stood in the shadows, faithful and supportive throughout his life.

"That is sad, Shane," Lauren commented.

He opened the front door to his house and stood to the side so she could enter first.

"It is sad, but I admire her. She made a commitment to him and she never wavered. This way," he said as he nodded toward his studio. "I want to show you somethin'."

Lauren gave him an eager smile. He knew she loved his work and had bid way too much at the auction on Saturday for his painting of the cottage by the sea.

"It wasn't too much," she had said that night, after making the purchase. "And I'll treasure it forever."

When they entered the studio, he let her look at his current project, *The Cliffs of Moher*. "I mostly paint from my imagination, but I was inspired by your parents' excitement over seein' the cliffs. Morrigan and I are plannin' to make a trip when I get closer to putting the finishin' touches on it. We'll rent a boat so I can see it from the view I'm paintin' it."

"It's going to be magnificent when you're done." Lauren continued to study the picture.

"I actually brought you in here because of her." He nodded to the corner of the room where his prized painting, *Life in Shadows*, sat on an easel. Shane reached for it. "Come," he said and led her from the studio into the living room.

"I told you I would tell you about her one day. Have

a seat," he offered, while he leaned the painting against the chair opposite the sofa. Shane sat down next to her and looked at the painting. "She was my wife, the love of my life."

Lauren's eyes grew soft with sympathy. It was a pain she knew too well. She placed her hand on top of his and left it there as he continued to talk. "We had six years together, one less than you and Christopher. We also had a child, but she miscarried." It was harder than he thought it would be to relive those moments.

"Oh, Shane, I'm so sorry." There were tears in his friend's eyes.

He nodded. "I was too, for so long. Our last two years together, she battled leukemia and lost. I remember feelin' so helpless. It's the worst feelin' ever to see someone you love more than your own life dying, knowin' there is absolutely nothin' you can do.

"Most of those last two years were good. Shortly after her diagnosis, she made a list of all the things she wanted to do and see before she died. We were always hopeful she'd be cured, but she didn't want to take any chances. So, we did as many of them as we could."

Shane stood from the couch and walked over to the painting of his wife. "I painted this picture of her years later. I created her with age, character, and beauty. I didn't want to create an image of her at the age of her death, I wanted to paint a picture of what she would look like had she lived." He continued to look at the painting as he spoke, his wife's blue eyes looking back at him glowing with love.

"To grow old with her was the only thing I desired in life. I would have given up my art, and everythin' I owned, just to have this one dream."

He turned to look at Lauren. "This paintin' held all of my hopes and dreams. They were wrapped up in Stacey, who she was and what she was to me.

"Before she died, she made me promise I would love again." His voice cracked, and he pinched the bridge of his nose for a moment.

Lauren stood and stepped toward him, waiting for him to continue.

He finally looked at her. "I couldn't make that promise, Lauren. I loved her more than I could ever imagine lovin' another person. It made Stacey sad, but she didn't pressure me. And for all of these years, I've never let myself love anyone in that way."

He reached for her hands. "Someone recently told me somethin' that made me realize how wrong I was to make that choice." Lauren was crying now, the tears, rolling down her cheeks... and he let her. He wanted them to fall, to help cleanse the wounds that were still tender.

"Lauren, it was a conscious choice. I could have found someone else to love, but I didn't. And I've recently realized how selfish it was for me to make such a decision, how selfish it was to deny someone the pleasure of being loved and cared for by me. And my friend reminded me that I deserve to be loved and cared for too."

Her head was bent and her shoulders were shaking. He drew her into his arms and held her while she cried, while she dealt with the understanding in her own life that had come with the telling of his story.

When she was finished weeping, he told her the full story about Morrigan and how he had pushed her away. He told Lauren about his second chance with this incredible woman and how second chances come around rarely in life. He shared with her how he planned to ask Morrigan to spend the rest of whatever days they had left together.

Brendan grew alarmed when Lauren wasn't at the bakery to meet him for their usual walk to the school to pick up Noirin. She was always there waiting for him. He grew even more concerned when Shane entered through the front door, a somber look on his face.

"Lauren's fine," his older friend said when he was close enough. "She asked me to tell you not to worry, but she left for Paris for a few days."

The tension he was feeling eased up a bit, but his brows knit together in worry. "Why would she go so suddenly? I thought she was goin' to Paris on her and Christopher's anniversary?"

Shane placed a hand on Brendan's shoulder. "I promised you I wouldn't meddle, but I had to tell her about Stacey. I showed her the paintin' and told her everythin'. But mostly, I told her how wrong I'd been to push love away all of these years. It's all I told her.

"She's away, wrestling with everythin'. It's a good

thing, Brendan. She suddenly wanted to go to Paris, and I have a feeling she wanted to go there so she could reconcile her love for her husband and the possibility of havin' a future with someone else. She doesn't want anyone to call her. I also need to tell Ellen."

Brendan nodded and Shane turned to walk toward the back of the bakery to talk to his cousin.

To say Brendan was shocked was an understatement. He was stunned, confused, and perhaps a little hopeful. But reconciling the possibility of loving someone else didn't mean it would be him whom Lauren chose to love.

He took a step toward the front door and paused. But the last few days with her had told him it was possible. The way she had looked at him at the shop in Adare, with that wide-eyed intensity, her cheeks filled with color at the comment he made about the newlyweds. The look on her face had told him something: that she felt something for him. He hadn't meant for the moment to become sexually charged— it had just happened. He'd stated the truth about what he observed, and for a moment, he let down his guard, let it slip before quickly covering it up. The amazing thing was seeing how Lauren hadn't shut down like she'd done with Flynn.

On the way home from Adare, he told her more about Eva. Lauren had helped him to see even more clearly the truth about Eva and his relationship with her, and how it had a part in shaping who he was today. She had thanked him for talking openly with her about the woman he once loved.

On Sunday, she went to church with him, as promised, and it had felt good having her next to him while they listened to Donal's sermon. Afterwards, as they had walked home, she said, "I'm not angry anymore, Brendan." She'd looped her arm around his and they had carried on in silence while Noirin skipped ahead of them. It had been a simple statement, but it had held a world of meaning. Most importantly, he was glad she had reconciled herself to the One who had created her.

Brendan drew closer to Noirin's school. He wasn't completely sure Lauren was in love with him, but in the short walk to pick up his daughter, he decided that when Lauren returned from Paris, he would tell her how he felt. At that point, he would be all in, and she would either become the greatest love of his life, or she would refuse him. Either way, she'd know.

Chapter Thirty-Five

Fred was exhausted. He'd had several long weeks at work, and things weren't much better with Stacey. When he walked into the house, it was unusually silent.

None of the usual smells of a home-cooked meal greeted him.

Stacey was a part-time dietician. For years, she had been a stay-at-home mother, until Christopher had started middle school. She decided then to attend college and became a dietician working for a medical practice on a part-time basis.

It had been a great opportunity for her, giving her something to do in the morning but still having time for her family. When Christopher graduated from high school, she continued to work part-time because of how much she also loved caring for Fred. It made him feel wonderful knowing she loved him enough to want to take care of him.

Fred grew even more concerned when he noticed that the only light on was in the mudroom.

"Stacey," he called as he sat down his work bag and laptop and placed his keys on the ceramic tray on the bench. When she didn't answer, he realized she must be out. His brows drew together in puzzlement. Normally they made a habit of telling each other if they had plans or were running late. He started to feel a rise of panic in his chest. His thoughts turned to Christopher and his car accident, and Fred couldn't help but imagine the worst.

He went to the garage to make sure her car was gone, and it was.

He reached for his phone and dialed her number. No answer. He looked at his watch. It was too late to call her work; it was after hours, and no one would be there to answer.

Dialing her number again, he checked the basement to see if she was down there and hadn't heard him. Maybe her car was in the shop.

Nothing downstairs and still no answer. Fred was now in full-blown panic mode. *Where could she be?* He had some of her friends' phone numbers in his contact list, for he was friends with their husbands, and started making call after call.

No one had seen her or heard from her.

Fred began checking every room in the house. When he came to their bedroom, he didn't notice the piece of paper on the bed, but he noticed a number of her clothes missing from the closet and drawers.

Stunned and unable to stand, he perched down on the bed and sat on the paper without realizing it. That was when he heard the crunching sound. He reached under him and pulled out a note... in her writing. It was sitting on top of an envelope. Fred read the note.

You betrayed me, Fred! How could you! Don't call me; I won't answer.

He was certain that his heart would stop. He looked

at the envelope with a postmark from Ireland. It was a letter from Lauren.

He quickly read the contents, and when he was done, Fred realized that his wife was from Tramore, after all.

"What have you done, Fred?" he cried out, his voice filled with an overwhelming grief. It was a grief not unlike what he had felt losing his son. He was certain he'd lost his wife, forever.

Lauren couldn't believe they had the same room available. She had called the bed and breakfast at the airport, while waiting for her flight, and had been disappointed to discover they were full.

When she left the Charles de Gaulle Airport, she found herself directing the cab driver to Rue de Rivoli in the heart of the Tour Saint Jacques Square in Paris. Standing on the curb in front of the row house, Lauren peered up at the short set of stairs that led to the candy apple red door. On a pure whim she entered.

The receptionist at the front desk informed her that they'd had a cancelation just a couple of hours ago and they would be happy to accommodate her. When Lauren mentioned how grateful she was for a room because it was the place where she and her husband had spent their honeymoon, the Vue du Jardin room, the woman said, "Hold on a moment, Miss."

Lauren watched as the receptionist clicked the

mouse and looked at the screen. "There! I have moved the couple checking in tonight and have placed you into the Vue du Jardin." She looked up from the screen with a pleased smile on her face. "They'll never know."

Lauren gave her a grateful smile. "This means so much to me. My husband passed away last year. I came here to remember."

Moisture brimmed in the woman's eyes. "I'm glad you're here, Miss."

And so was she.

After Lauren had deposited her overnight bag near the wardrobe, she sat down in the chair in the lounge area and surveyed the room. Everything was the same. She remembered it so clearly—the warm yellow walls with white crown molding and chair rail. Lace curtains, probably from Belgium, graced both windows topped by matching valances.

"It's so elegant!" Lauren had said to Christopher, all those years ago, as she walked into the room taking in all the details. "The desk looks to be an antique, or a good reproduction—late nineteenth century maybe. And the paintings, are they real?"

She turned to her husband who was standing quietly watching her. "I'm so gauche, aren't I?" she said feeling a little embarrassed.

Christopher shook his head and walked over to her. "You're wonderful, Lauren. You're perfect. I love every-thing about you."

She draped her arms around his neck and nuzzled

his nose with hers in response. "You're pretty incredible yourself, you know that?"

He smiled. "I'm really going to enjoy being married to you."

Lauren smiled at the memory and allowed the tears to fall. This is what she'd come here for. She was here to remember and to say goodbye. Not goodbye to Christopher because she could never live a day without thinking of him, loving him, missing him. She was here to say goodbye to the idea that she could never love anyone else, because she'd already fallin in love with that someone. Two people actually, a man, a really wonderful man, and the daughter he loved so selflessly.

She would spend the next two days in Paris doing all the non-touristy things she and Christopher had done. She would walk along the Seine at sunset, and stand on the Pont Alexandre III Bridge, looking out over the vast city lit up like a bright starry night. She would remember how they had stood there amazed that they were in Paris, but more amazed they were there together.

She would go to the café next door to the bed and breakfast, the place they liked to go for their croissants. Where they lingered over coffee and pastries, relaxed and enjoying the pleasure of each other's company,

Lauren would also visit Le Bernardin, the glorious French restaurant that had cost them a small fortune to dine at. She would have dinner there and remember that night, a night they had enjoyed so well. She would recall how after sitting down, she'd looked at the menu, then quickly lowered it, her mouth hanging open in shock. Christopher had looked at her with the same stunned expression. Lauren would remember how they had laughed their hearts out and how the other patrons had given them surreptitious glances.

She would reminisce about the moment the waiter came by to take their drink order, and how Christopher ordered a two-hundred-dollar bottle of wine. She'd nearly choked on her water. When the waiter left, he gave her his 'come what may' look and said, "We have a credit card, and if I have to, I'll work at *our* coffee shop as a barista until I've paid off this dinner." This caused another eruption of laughter.

Before she left Paris, she would sit in that same restaurant and enjoy the food and think back to how wonderful their meal had tasted. How they had shared and fed each other—like two people in love and in Paris ought to. She would savor the truth that the experience was worth every extravagant dollar.

Then Lauren would remember the nights they had spent making love, learning how to please one another, all the exploration and sometimes the laughter that came with the learning.

And when she had remembered everything about their time in Paris, she would leave and return to Tramore to ask the man she now loved if he would like to share a life with her.

"Stacey, you have to talk to him!"

"No, I can't." She was adamant and determined.

"But you love him."

Stacey began to cry. Angie reached for her and held her while she released the pain that had gripped her since she had caved and read Lauren's letter. She did love Fred, more than anything, but he'd betrayed her. It was the only explanation as to how her daughter-in-law had ended up in Tramore.

After she settled down, she reached for a tissue from the box Angie had given her. She looked at her friend. "Thank you for letting me stay here until I figure this all out. I didn't know where else to go."

Stacey had fled Tacoma in a blind, heartbroken kind of fury and had driven to Montana to Angie and William's ranch. She hadn't even called—just showed up on their doorstep the following day.

Angie smiled at her. "You're welcome here any-time." She brushed a strand of hair away from Stacey's face, and added, "I'm glad you know that." She patted her hand. "Stay as long as you like, but eventually you will have to talk to him, and I won't take no for an answer."

Stacey nodded. How did she unburden the pain of her past, a past she had kept hidden from the man who meant everything to her, the man who had given her a second chance at a life worth living? She'd been prepared to go to her grave never telling him about all the things she'd done—all those horrible things.

But after reading that letter, everything changed.

Brendan was partly thrilled and partly terrified. He was on his way to Dublin at Lauren's request. She had texted him the night before asking if he could meet her there. He arranged for Noirin's care through Shane and his folks, and Ellen had the bakery covered.

She'd asked if he would meet her outside of Fiddle Faddle at eleven.

I miss you so much, he'd texted back, regretting that he hadn't told her those words when she'd travelled to Mourne Mountains, after she'd expressed them to him first.

Oh, Brendan, I miss you! she replied.

I'll be waiting.

It took him a little bit to find parking, but he'd anticipated it and still managed to arrive five minutes early.

He didn't have to wait. Brendan stopped when he saw her standing in front of the restaurant. She watched him coming and stood there looking at him. There was longing in her eyes. She didn't make a move toward him, and it took everything he had to walk calmly to her rather than run and scoop her into his arms.

"Hi," he said when he was standing a few inches in front of her. He reached up to touch her hair, sweeping it to the side with his fingertips. "How was your trip?"

She closed her eyes for a moment and then opened them. "There is a park just around the corner. Can we go there and talk?"

She sounded serious, and his chest tightened at her words. She seemed happy to see him, but he could tell that what she had to say was weighing on her.

When he nodded, she reached for his hand, and they walked silently toward the park.

It was a square of green space with a tiered, basin fountain in the center. Four stone paths led to the fountain and large oak trees stood like sentinels in each corner of the square. Flowers lined the walkways.

Lauren led them to a bench.

When they sat down, she said, "My trip to Paris was hard but necessary." She paused. "I asked you to meet me here in Dublin, because, while in Paris, I realized this was the place I first felt the change in how I saw you. At the time, I hadn't realized what that meant.

"It was your smile that had me thinking differently about you. It was as if I'd seen it for the first time. Yet it looked familiar to me and brought me comfort. Your smile has a way of softening all the hard parts that took root inside of me this past year."

Lauren took a deep steadying breath. "I'll always love Christopher, and he will always be a part of me in a way that no one else can ever share. When I met him, I had never loved another man."

Brendan felt the weight pressing heavier on him, but he didn't speak.

"Shane told me he mentioned our conversation to you."

Brendan nodded.

"I had to go to Paris to remember Christopher. There was another reason. I had to say goodbye, not to him but to this idea I had since our first trip to Dublin, that he was the only man I could ever love, with no space for another."

Joy and hope replaced all of the heaviness and worry. Brendan reached for her hand, expectancy filling him.

Lauren smiled at the contact and held his gaze. "I've found someone else to love. I didn't go looking for him. I didn't even ask for it to happen. But it did. The love I have for this man is different, but no less abiding and no less wonderful or thrilling. I love this man because I am different. He helped to shape me into a better person than the one that came here. He molded me, and over the past several weeks, I've come to realize he fits me perfectly."

She shook her head as if to clear it. "It's impossible for me to understand how I could fit so wonderfully with one man and then just as perfectly with another. I can't explain it, but all I know is that it's possible. I love you, Brendan."

Brendan looked down at her hand as he tried to rein in the emotions that left him speechless. He noticed she was no longer wearing her ring. He looked back up at her and hoped she saw the understanding and the fullness of the love he felt for her reflecting in his features.

He lifted Lauren's hand and kissed the finger where her ring used to be.

"It's the shaping," he said. "That's how it's possible, Lauren. You taught me that. The shape of you and Christopher allowed you to fit together. When you lost him, it changed you and formed you into someone different. It's the reason I can fit so perfectly with you now, and I'm glad I do, because I love you too. I have for some time." He searched her eyes. "I pushed you away after Dublin because I was convinced that you'd never be able to love anyone else. I had lost so much and was afraid of being hurt again."

She lifted her hand to caress the side of his face. "How could I not fall in love with you, Brendan? You're wonderful, and the love you give comes with a beautiful little girl. I want her as much as I want you." She paused. "I'm sorry that Eva hurt you. But I am really glad she failed to see what a gift you *both* are."

Brendan's response was to kiss her. There was an intensity to their first kiss, not one of passion and desire, but something more substantial, like the solidarity of commitment, steadfastness, and honesty. It was the undercurrent that would charge their growing love and future, and they both felt it.

After a moment, Brendan's kiss was gentler as he savored every sensation, the taste of her, the feel of her under his hands that pressed her close to him. When they parted, he pressed his forehead against hers. "You're the gift, Lauren, a sweet wonderful gift!" He looked at her. "I want to spend the rest of my life unwrappin' who you are."

Her eyes looked dazed from the effects of his touch, but she smiled at him. "I was hoping you would make an offer, because if you weren't, I would. Living without you and Noirin isn't an option for me."

Brendan kissed her again, this time with great passion and desire. All the feelings that had been building up to this point since the moment he saw her weeping at her dining room table came flooding into every crack and crevice of his past and all that he'd lost.

With Eva, the lines had never been in focus, but had always been blurred and slightly unreadable. With Lauren, they had quickly come into focus, sharp and precise. And before she ever belonged to him, she had become his greatest loss. Today, with her heart and her words, she extended those clear, brilliant lines and had become his greatest love.

Chapter Thirty-Six

"Mmm. I could stay here and do this all day," Lauren murmured against his lips. He felt and tasted so good. Somehow, she knew he would.

Brendan lifted his head to look at her. She could see the love and desire behind the look; it both thrilled and comforted her.

"But we need to be headin' home," he said.

"I like the sound of that," she said softly.

"Do you?" he asked, his eyes searching hers.

"Wherever you and Noirin are is where I want to be."

He sat back and held her hand. "Funny, I was thinkin' the same thing."

Her eyes widened in surprise. "You would leave Ireland for me?"

"Without question," he answered before leaning in for another kiss, his lips lingering for a moment longer.

When they parted, there were tears in her eyes. "I truly love you!"

When he swooped in for another kiss, she placed her fingers to his lips to tell him, "I don't want to leave Ireland. My family will want to murder me for saying it, but this is my home now, my new life. I fell in love not only with the people, but with this place."

Brendan reached for her hand, with its fingers

still resting against his lips, and kissed it. His eyes were glowing and filled with slight disbelief. "You're serious, aren't you? You're not just sayin' that because you're in the moment."

She shook her head. "I'll work things out with both of my families." She paused. "I love Christopher's parents like my own."

Brendan did swoop in to kiss her, quite successfully this time, before she could halt his progress. When he pulled away, he said, "I will fall in love with his parents too. And I want to know everythin' about him, Lauren. We would have been friends, wouldn't we?"

She nodded. "The best. The two of you are so much alike, yet so different." She looked away for a moment. "I'm new at this, Brendan. I've never come into a relationship having loved someone else. You have to promise me that if I overstep, consciously or unconsciously, you'll tell me. I don't want to bring expectations into the middle of us. You are your own person and not Christopher, and I don't expect you to be like him. I love you for who you are."

"I know, *a chuisle*, *a chroí*," he said sweetly, the Gaelic words rolling off his tongue in their lyrical way.

She smiled. "What does that mean?"

"'My pulse, my heart.'"

It was her turn to kiss him. "I love it. And what Gaelic term of endearment shall I use for you?" she asked when she pulled away.

He looked thoughtful. "I know the perfect one, *dia diaga*."

"*Dia Diaga*. Am I saying it right?"

"*Dia Diaga*," he enunciated again.

She tried again.

"Perfect," he said with a grin and a flash of something else.

It was a suspicious look. "And what does that mean, exactly?"

"Oh, it's a very popular term of endearment." His eyes were gleaming with mischief. She saw it now.

"Is that so? I do have Google Translate at my fingertips, you know."

He laughed rather boisterously because he knew he'd been had. "It means 'god divine.'"

She pulled away from him. "I am shocked, Brendan Callery. You were going to continue to let me call you that, weren't you?"

"I would have fessed up—eventually."

"Oh, that's grand, eventually," she said with mock disapproval.

"Grand, aye? And she's already speakin' the way of the Irish. Gone are the 'We're not in Kansas anymore' phrases." He started tickling her and she giggled.

When they were both breathless from their laughter, she looked at him. "How is this so easy?"

"Because we fit together, Lauren. I never told you this, but that first night that you arrived in Tramore, I was comin' home from the bookstore, and I happened to be walkin' by your flat. I saw you cryin' at your table. Seein' you cry that way, it did somethin' to me." He held her hand in his and fingered the tan line along her ring finger. "I'm the one who's been leavin' the bakery box by your door every mornin'."

"You!" She couldn't believe it. "And you kept giving me one, even when you were mad at me?"

"Not mad, frustrated and heartbroken."

Her eyes softened. "I'm sorry, Brendan. I had no idea."

"How could you? You have nothin' to be sorry for. Tellin' me about Christopher, it changed everythin'. I was determined to love you, no matter the cost, and to make it impossible for you to leave me when the year was over. I'm really happy it never came to that."

"So am I."

They kissed one last time.

"We probably should go," he said.

"Fiddle Faddle first please. I'm starving," she requested.

"I've created a monster. One thing first." He pulled out his phone and she watched as he typed up a text message.

When he was done and had put away the phone, she asked, "Work?"

"No, you'll see."

The drive home flew by and they arrived in Tramore early evening. Instead of heading to his parents' house to pick up Noirin, he drove to the bakery.

He put the car in park. "I need to stop here first. Come inside with me."

"Brendan what is everyone doing here?"

He could see them through the windows, the lights were on, and their people were milling around.

"You'll see." He leaned over to kiss her before exiting the car, and leading her into the bakery.

"You're here!" Ellen called out above the din. The sound of her voice announcing their arrival caused all eyes to turn to them.

Noirin noticed them too and ran straight for both of them, wrapping her arms around their waists.

"*Pog*," Brendan said to her as he lifted her into his arms. After she complied, she leaned over to give Lauren a kiss too.

All the people they loved were standing there in Cups and Cakes, an air of expectancy surrounding them. Shay was leaning on Quinn's arm. Mary and Jack stood side by side, his arm around her shoulder. Shane and Morrigan held hands, and Ellen had her arm looped around Donal's.

"Shane called us all here and said you had some news." Jack was the first to speak.

Lauren looked at Brendan, a happy smile on her face. He knew she would appreciate the gesture of bringing their loved ones together to share their news.

"And he told us all to bring somethin' to eat. What's goin' on?" Mary added, a bright smile on her face.

Brendan cleared his throat. "Lauren has decided

that she's not returnin' home after her lease is up. She's stayin' in Tramore."

The room erupted into a burst of happiness, everyone exclaiming how glad they were to hear it.

"Lauren, what a thrillin' bit of news!" Shay exclaimed, her face beaming.

Ellen was crying. "I can't believe you're stayin', Lauren." She reached for her friend and gave her a hug. When she pulled away to look at Lauren, she said, "I have dibs on being your BFF."

Everyone laughed.

"Well, actually, Brendan has dibs on that one," she beamed up at him and Brendan knew everyone would know by that look how they felt about each other. With the exception of Shane and Donal, no one else had known about the budding love between them.

Brendan looked at Lauren and nodded for her to continue, wanting her to tell the others. She looked at all the faces she'd come to know and love. "I came here broken and needing to find myself." Her eyes moved to Shane, for he'd known from the beginning the reason she'd come to Ireland. "I'd lost so much, never expecting to gain..." she paused and her voice quivered as she continued, "never expecting to gain all of you." She looked at Noirin, who seemed to be taking it all in. "I fell in love with you first, sweetheart, and then I fell in love with your father. We want to make a life together with you—if you'll have me."

Noirin wasn't prone to tears, but upon speaking her proposal, the little girl with the mop of curly brown hair, who was loved so selflessly and unconditionally, shed a few. "Yes," she said, her bottom lip quivering slightly. "I love you, Lauren."

She grabbed her little girl from Brendan's arms and held onto her as if she would never let her go. When they finally pulled apart, they looked at each other. "I promise to always love you and care for you, just like your dad. He's done a great job, hasn't he?"

Noirin beamed, "The best!"

Their group, small in number but mighty in spirit, came alive with congratulations and hugs. There were some tears too, happy tears. After all the 'hows' and the 'how come we never knews' were over, they began to set out the food they had all brought.

She saw Shane, who was bringing out a dish. He stopped and smiled at her before placing it on the table. Lauren reached for him and hugged him. When she looked at him, she said, "I haven't thanked you yet, and I have so much to be thankful for."

He reached for her hands. "Are you kiddin' me, darlin? I should be thankin' you. You came here to find yerself, but because of you I found myself again. If you had never come, I'd still be livin' my life—what's left of it—with blinders on." He paused with a thoughtful look on his face. "Do you remember what I said to you when you told me why you were here?"

That day seemed like a lifetime ago, but she remembered. "You said that when I find her, I might be surprised not by her, but how I *would* find her."

CHAPTER THIRTY-SIX

He grinned. "Sharp as a tack you are. And were you surprised?"

"Unbelievably so."

"What are you two talkin' about?" Morrigan asked as she sidled up to Shane and slipped her arm around his. He let go of Lauren's hands and placed his in Morrigan's. "We were talking about how thankful we are. Have I told you lately how thankful I am for you?"

She beamed a brilliant smile at Shane.

Lauren leaned over to kiss both of them on their cheek and then left them alone to find Brendan.

He was at a table with his parents. Quinn was keeping Shay company while the rest of their family, including Noirin, buzzed around readying the meal.

"That was beautiful, Lauren," Shay said as she reached for her hand. She had taken a seat next to her.

"I meant every word of it." She glanced at Brendan. "He's just a bonus. It's always been about Noirin."

They laughed and Brendan kissed her cheek.

"Do you remember our conversation a while ago about the mother-in-law and daughter-in-law dance?" Shay asked.

Lauren nodded, her eyes bright with emotion.

"I have a really good feeling, darlin, that we're goin' to move very well together."

Lauren leaned over and kissed Shay's cheek. When she leaned back in her chair, she said, "Oh, I couldn't agree with you more."

"I'm happy for you, Son," Quinn said as he patted

Brendan on the shoulder. "I'm not one to get too emotional, but I feel like I could cry a whole bucket right about now. And before, I embarrass myself, I'll excuse myself." He stood and looked at his son. "I am so proud of you, Brendan. You are my joy." He turned to Lauren and bent down to kiss her on the cheek. "Welcome to the family, sweetheart. You belong to all of us now."

"Thank you, Quinn."

When he walked away, she added, "I think I could cry a bucket too."

"Well, that makes three of us," Brendan said as he stood to his feet. "Hear that? Someone's playing some music—let's dance, and we'll cry that bucket together."

It was a mid-tempo song but Lauren and Brendan danced as if it were a slow one. She leaned her head against his chest while they swayed to the music and let the tears fall. They were happy tears, so unlike the sad and mournful ones she'd cried for the last year.

She didn't live her life with rose-colored glasses perched on her nose and think that because she'd found all of this her life would be trouble-free from now on. Loving someone so completely, as she had Christopher, and then losing him had taught her that lesson, very well.

But in the learning, she'd also come to realize what was most important: the living. And oh, how she'd begun to live again!

Chapter Thirty-Seven

When Lauren returned from the school, she stopped into the kitchen to say hello. Brendan was rolling croissants. His head was bent down. The music his staff loved to play in the background was low, and she could barely make out the words.

"Hi," she said as she made her way to his side.

He looked up and a smile filled his face.

She kissed him. "Where is everyone?"

"Ilene called in sick. Martha had to do an emergency run to the store for more cream." He gave her a sheepish look. "I've been a little distracted lately and missed it on the last supply order." The sheepish look turned into a gleam.

"Is that so? Well, I wonder who's to blame for the distraction?"

He kissed her. "For the life of me, I can't figure it out. Just some American who happened to show up here in our fair little town."

She laughed.

"And Ellen is makin' a phone call in the office," he added with a nod in the general direction.

"I'm sorry that Ilene is sick and for being such a distraction."

"I'm not. My hands are all greasy because of the buttery dough, otherwise I'd kiss you proper."

"Excuse accepted; you're also short staffed and probably have a lot to do. How can I help?"

His eyes widened. "Ugh, I'm a little more than featherbrained right now. How could I forget to tell you that your father-in-law showed up?"

"Fred?" she exclaimed and panicked. "Did he seem okay? Where is he?"

"He's fine, *mo chroi*. He told me he'd rented a room over at the Cottage on the Strand. I talked him into stayin' with me and Noirin. I didn't want to volunteer your place. He's upstairs in my flat."

"No, that's fine. He'll stay with me. I need to go talk to him. I'll stop by when I can."

"Bye," she heard him call out as she rushed out of the kitchen and up the back stairs to Brendan's flat.

The door was unlocked and she walked right in. "Fred," she called.

There was shuffling in the hallway, and she saw him coming out of the guest bedroom.

Lauren rushed to him "Dad, what's the matter? What are you doing here?" She could see by the look on his face he wasn't here for pleasure. His eyes were sallow with dark smudges beneath them. "What's happened to Mom?" she cried, tears rolling down her cheeks because she knew something terrible had happened.

He reached for her which made her cry even harder. "She's fine—at least I think she's fine."

Lauren pulled away to look at him and wiped her eyes. "I don't understand."

"She's left me, Lauren."

"What! That can't be right. Mom loves you! It has to be some mistake."

"It's not a mistake," he said and then began to cry.

She reached for him and held onto him.

After a few moments, she said, "Here, sit and tell me what happened."

When they were seated at the dining room table, he just sat there for a long moment staring out of the window. "It was all a mistake. I should never have told you and Christopher about Tramore. But he wanted desperately to know where his mother was from, to learn more about her heritage and the place she was born and raised. I should have done what she'd asked and left it alone."

Then Lauren wouldn't be here and the thought felt selfish. Here she was happy again and at what expense? A marriage ruined.

"Why did she leave, Dad?"

"I'm not entirely sure. I came home from work, and she wasn't home. I found the letter you had written on the bed with a note attached saying I had betrayed her and that I wasn't to contact her."

Lauren shook her head. "I don't understand. I wrote that letter a few weeks ago. I never told her I was in Tramore and only mentioned all the wonderful people I'd met since I arrived."

"She must be from here. Otherwise, why would she tell me I'd betrayed her?"

"I'll try to call. I spoke with her a few days ago and told her I was going to Paris. She seemed fine... well, I did sense that something was not right, but we chatted for a while like we normally do."

Fred hung his head. "That was before I found her gone."

Lauren pulled her phone out of her pocket and dialed her mother-in-law's number. It rang and rang and went straight to voicemail. "Mom, it's me. Please call me as soon as you get this message."

"Where could she have gone?" she asked her father-in-law.

"I already checked at the cabin. She wasn't there. I've called every single one of her friends."

"Did you call my mom?"

"No, I didn't think about it. I only called her friends in Tacoma."

Lauren quickly called her mother. "Mom!"

"Lauren, how are you?"

"Mom, something has happened with Stacey. Fred is here in Ireland and said she's left him. Have you heard from her?"

There was a bit of a pause before her mother answered. "Lauren, she's here with me. I'm sorry; I assumed that she'd at least let him know where she was. She's working things out, but she's fine."

Lauren exhaled, the tension leaving her body at the knowledge that her mother-in-law was okay—at least physically. "Can I talk to her?"

CHAPTER THIRTY-SEVEN

Fred's eyebrows rose in relief as he realized that his wife was in Montana.

"I'm sorry, sweetie, but she doesn't want to talk to anyone right now. She just needs time, and I'm trying to help her. Let me talk to Fred."

She handed her father-in-law the phone and listened to his side of the conversation.

"I understand," she heard him say.

"Okay, thank you, Angie. I'll be in touch."

He hung up and handed the phone back to Lauren. He rested his back against the chair and looked like he was going to cry again.

"Your mother asked me not to come to the ranch. She said Stacey needs time and asked that I give it to her." He paused, "At least I know she's safe."

"I still don't understand what brought all of this on. I never mentioned Tramore. There isn't a Stacey Walsh who was from here."

"Then she must know some of the people from here, people in your letter. I read the letter and you're right. All you did was talk about the people you met. So, someone in your letter is the key to all of this."

She couldn't think about it right now. She was more concerned for Fred. "Everything is going to be all right. I know Mom, and she's not going to walk away from over thirty years of marriage and the man she loves—all because you told us she might be from Tramore."

"She's hiding something; I have no idea what."

"Let's not think about it right now. You're exhausted."

"I had plans to stay at one of the B&Bs here in town, but your friend Brendan insisted I stay with him until we figure something out."

"You're staying with me. Let's get your things, and we'll go downstairs. My flat is on the first floor."

He sighed heavily. "I'm sorry to drag you into this, Lauren, but I didn't know what else to do. I didn't know who else to turn to."

"I'm glad you turned to me. That's what I'm here for, Dad. Now let's get you some rest."

After Fred was settled in the guest bedroom and lying down for a nap, she went to the bakery to see if Brendan was available.

She found him in the office.

"Hi," he said when she walked in. Realizing something was wrong, he quickly stood to his feet. "What's happened?"

Lauren told him everything after he led her to one of the chairs and took the one beside her.

"This is really bad, Brendan. I've never known Stacey to do anything like this. She loves Fred."

"I think your father-in-law is right, and she probably knows someone you mentioned in your letter. Was it just us—me and my family?"

"And Shane." Her brows furrowed in concentration. "When Shane was telling me about his wife and mentioned her name, I vaguely remember thinking how she had the same first name as my mother-in-law. I didn't think about it again—until now. I'm sure it's just a coincidence."

"It has to be. Do you think your mother-in-law may have known Shane's wife?"

Lauren frowned. "I don't know, but I'd like to see if he's available so I can ask him."

"Let me check with the team, and if they can manage without me, I'll go with you."

A short while later they were sitting at Shane's kitchen table.

"I can't think of another Stacey that my Stacey knew."

"Did she have any siblings?"

"A brother. He lives in France, but we don't get to see each other very often."

"Hmm," Lauren murmured.

"What is your mother-in-law's maiden name?" Shane asked.

"Walsh," she replied.

"What?" Brendan said.

"That's impossible!" Shane exclaimed almost at the same time.

Lauren gave them a confused look.

Shane was the first to speak. "Are you sure that's her maiden name?"

"I'm fairly certain. Christopher had it written down in the notebook with our travel plans. That and the city of Tramore. Fred had given him the information a while ago when we were planning our trip." Lauren explained to them how curious her husband had always been about his Irish heritage and how tightlipped Stacey was about her past life.

Brendan and Shane looked at each other for a moment before Shane spoke slowly: "Walsh was my wife's maiden name."

Lauren couldn't believe it. "Then there has to be some kind of mistake. Where was your wife from? I searched the records in Tramore and there isn't a Stacey Walsh that has been from here in over sixty years."

"She's from Waterford."

"Maybe my father-in-law misunderstood. I think we need to talk to him." She lifted her arm to look at her watch. He'd been sleeping for at least a couple of hours and only wanted a nap so he could adjust better to the time. 'Let's go see if he's awake.'

Fred was awake when they entered her flat.

"Hi Dad, I want to introduce you to Shane."

The two men greeted one another, and Lauren asked them if they could sit at the table. "I'll get some tea going."

While the water was boiling, she asked, "Did you get some rest?"

"No, I couldn't sleep."

She gave him a sympathetic look. "Earlier you had mentioned that if Mom is not from Tramore, then she must know people here. It could be someone I wrote about in my letter to her. I went to Shane's house to see if his wife knew a Stacey Walsh." She paused. "Dad, Shane's wife's name is Stacey Walsh."

Fred looked just as confused as she had. "I don't understand. Are you saying my Stacey might be your wife?"

Shane shook his head. "No, my wife died many years ago. We just find it odd that they have the exact same name."

Fred sat back in the chair, a baffled look on his face. The tea kettle started to whistle.

They continued to talk while Lauren served the tea. "Dad, are you sure her maiden name was Walsh?"

"Yes, it's the name that's on our marriage certificate and the one on her passport."

Lauren brought the tray to the table and took a seat. Suddenly she wasn't in the mood for tea and no one else seemed all that interested either.

"The only one who's going to solve this is Stacey, and until she's talking to me again, it won't do us any good to speculate."

"You're right, Fred," Shane agreed. "It is odd for them to have the same name, but there's always an explanation. I'll stew things over and see if anythin' comes to mind. And on that note, I do need to be goin'. I have some gallery business to attend to. Fred, it was very nice to meet you. We'll have to get together before you leave Ireland."

Her father-in-law shook Shane's hand. "Happy to meet you too. I wish I were here under better circumstances, but getting together will be good."

"I should be goin' too," Brendan said. "I called over at the Cottage on the Strand and canceled your reservation.

There was no charge. They were understandin', and I'll be takin' over a box of pastries to them in the mornin'."

"Thank you, Brendan."

He smiled at Fred.

"I'll walk you out," Lauren said as she followed him to the front door. She closed it behind her so they could talk privately. "I'd like to wait a bit to tell Dad about us. He's not in a good place."

He bent down to kiss her softly on the lips. "I understand. He's the priority right now. I love you."

She returned the kiss. "I love you too."

Chapter Thirty-Eight

After lunch, Lauren encouraged Fred to take a walk with her. They walked up to the Holy Cross church to take a turn through the garden. "It's so peaceful out here," Fred remarked. "And Brendan and Shane are very kind, just like in your letter."

"They are pretty wonderful. I can't wait for you to meet Noirin. Would you like to walk with me to her school to pick her up? This is her last week before summer break."

"Yeah, I'd like that. It was pretty obvious in your letter that you love her."

She took her eyes off the pebble path and looked at her father-in-law. "I am very much in love with her. I don't think I've met a sweeter child in all of my life."

"I'm happy for you, Lauren. It was the right thing for you to do, coming here."

She reached for his hand to halt their steps. "I'm glad I came here too. But at what cost? I can't stand the idea that my coming here could tear you and Mom apart."

"It won't, Lauren. I love her too much, and I know she loves me. We're going to figure this out. I just needed to adjust and get my bearings. I'm not going to mope around worrying about everything ending between us. She's mine. I loved her from the moment I first laid eyes on her."

Fred took a deep steadying breath. "There is so

much more to our story—to her story. We've told you and Christopher only what we, mainly Stacey, wanted you to know. I may have messed up by encouraging you and Christopher to come to Tramore, but I won't make the same mistake twice. She'll have to tell you if she chooses. But I'm convinced that in the middle of that story is the answer. I'll give Stacey the time she needs, and then I'm going to fight for her."

Lauren reached up and hugged him, relief filling her. Fred was always such a strong person, and to see him like she had this morning troubled her more than she cared. This confident, can-do man, standing before her now, this was her father-in-law, the man her husband admired and respected more than any other man.

When Lauren pulled away, she smiled at him. "You were Christopher's hero."

He nodded because his son had never failed to be open about his feelings. Tears gathered in Fred's eyes. "I miss him so much, Lauren."

"I miss him too, Dad. I will always miss him. He was such an amazing man, the best of men. And I have you to thank for that. You were everything a father should be to their son." She paused. "And you're right. Stacey will never let you go. You're too precious to her—to all of us."

He wiped his eyes and kissed her cheek. She took his arm and resumed their walk.

They were quiet and thoughtful for a while. Fred was the first to speak. "You're in love with him, aren't you?"

"I was waiting for the right time to tell you. I do

love Brendan. I was convinced I could never love anyone besides Christopher. I felt so fulfilled in my love for him I thought I could live the rest of my life satisfied with what I had. While that may have been true, I recently learned I have a lot of love to give and how there is something wonderful about giving that to another, freely and without conditions. And to have that love reciprocated, it's hard to live without."

Fred was quiet for a moment. "I'm really glad to hear it, Lauren." It was his turn to stop their walk and turn to her. "I made a promise to Christopher."

Her eyes grew wide with anticipation.

"It was after that anniversary he surprised you with the yachting trip."

"Our second."

Fred nodded. "He'd asked me to dinner one night, shortly after you returned, and he made me promise that if anything happened to him, I wouldn't allow you to remain stuck in your grief. He wanted me to promise I would do everything possible to make sure that you loved again."

Lauren was stunned. She remembered their time on the yacht and how terribly she had reacted to his gift— the emotional outburst she'd had at the thought of losing him. "Yes, I told him I didn't know how I could live without him."

Fred nodded. "I know. Christopher told me about the gift and how you had reacted. He was worried about you. So, I agreed." He paused to search her eyes. "No matter how things turn out, you were meant to be here,

Lauren. And I don't want you to question that for a minute. Christopher would be very happy to see you living your life fully—and loving again."

She reached up to touch the face of the man who was so much like his son, kind and compassionate, generous of heart. Both he and Christopher had given her a gift today. Since discovering her love for Brendan, she'd never once felt any kind of guilt, but hearing her husband's request to his father did something. It brought everything full circle and made this new direction in her life complete.

She took her father-in-law to Lanigan's that night. While they waited for their order, he said, "I'm returning home in a couple of days. I need to get back to work. I'll check in with Angie. I have to—no, I *will* believe that everything will be okay. I'll keep you posted. And then at some point I hope to come back here and explore your new home."

So, he knew she was planning on staying. "When Brendan asked me to build a life with him, he was ready to do it in Tacoma. He was going to leave all of this behind, just to be with me."

"You sound surprised."

She shrugged. "It's never easy leaving all that you've known behind."

"And yet you're willing to do it."

She nodded. "I'm a different person now than when I

left Tacoma. This place is a part of the person I've become, and I can't leave it behind." Her eyes teared up. "But it's hard to think about leaving you and Mom, not being able to see you when I want to. I won't ever stop loving you, and I'll come home as often as I can." She looked thoughtful for a moment. "When I told Brendan I loved you and Mom like a second set of parents and that you were an important part of my life and always would be, do you know what he said?"

Fred shook his head.

"He told me he would fall in love with the both of you too."

Her father-in-law swallowed hard apparently moved. "That was kind of him to say."

Fred continued, "No one knows what the future holds, Lauren. The past year, the past week, is proof of that. You know Stacey and I don't have to worry about money, and anytime you want to come home, all you have to do is say the word."

She reached out to squeeze his hand. "Thank you, but I am hoping that you and Mom will use that money to come visit me, too. Anything is possible if you're determined."

Fred chuckled, and his face softened. She was happy to see the light coming back in his eyes.

"I am determined. Have you told your parents about you and Brendan?"

"Not yet. I was waiting. Well, actually I was procrastinating. I knew it would be hard for all of you to take. But I do need to tell my mother soon. Then she can break the news to Stacey. I'll call her in the morning."

"Noirin, it's time to brush your teeth." Brendan dried off the last of the dishes and put the plate in the cabinet.

"Okay," he heard his daughter say.

He heard the front door open. It was Lauren. Brendan smiled as he made his way to the living room.

"Hi," he said before giving her kiss. "I didn't think you'd come up tonight."

"And miss tucking in our little girl? Fred turned in early."

"How's he doin'?" he asked, as he reached for her and drew her to him.

"Much better now. I think knowing Stacey is safe helps, but he's determined to make things right. They love each other very much. Fred's a hard man to walk away from, and my mother-in-law knows it." She smiled sweetly at him. "I told him about us. Or rather he guessed."

Before she could elaborate, Noirin came running into the room. "Lauren!" she exclaimed as she hugged her.

"Hi, sweet girl. How was your day? I'm sorry I couldn't pick you up from school. I have a visitor, my father-in-law, and he's looking forward to meeting you."

"Where is he?"

"He's downstairs sleeping right now—which you should be doing too. Are you ready for your story?"

How easily they'd fallen into this ritual of bed-time stories. Brendan remembered the first time he'd seen Lauren sitting in bed with his daughter reading to her. It had stunned him. It was a vision of something he'd dreamed of for himself. When he'd first seen them together, as they were now, he never expected it would become his reality. The realization caused a slow ache to bloom deep inside of him, a welcoming sort of ache.

A short while later, he and Lauren were sitting on the couch together. She was tucked under his arm with her head against his chest and her arm around his waist. She was telling him about the conversation she'd had with Fred. "I had no idea that Christopher had spoken to him, how he'd made him promise that he would help me find someone else to love again. It was another reminder of how much he loved me."

Brendan kissed the top of her head. She was not a hard woman to love. "You make it incredibly easy."

She wrapped her arm tighter around him in response. "I'm trying not to worry."

"I know."

"I've been thinking about something."

"Hmm?" he said.

"Our house, mine and Christopher's, is paid for. I was thinking I needed to go home and put it on the market. But what if I turned it into an Airbnb instead? I could manage it remotely, hire a service for the housekeeping and property management. All of the revenue, less expenses, would be pure profit. When we go to visit Fred and Stacey, we could even stay there."

"I think that's a grand idea. And if you did that, it would allow us to extend our stays in Tacoma so you could be with your family more."

She raised her head from his chest so she could look at him. "What do you mean?"

"I've been thinking a lot about things. I want Cups and Cakes to stay in the family for generations to come, but I want to follow my dream of real estate investing. Uncle Quinn wants the same. He's plannin' to sell the accounting firm, and then he'll have more time to help me. We already have four properties under our belts, and as a team, we can accomplish more.

"I'd like to make Ellen a business partner. She'll run the tearoom, and we'll find someone to manage Cups and Cakes full time. Aine might be interested. We can continue to work around her kid's school schedules."

Lauren nodded in approval. "I could help on the business end of things, keeping the books, hiring, and marketing. Ellen and I work great together, don't you think?"

"I think so. By the way, she's determined to usurp my BFF position. She told me as much the night we came back from Dublin, when we met everyone at the bakery."

Lauren laughed. "That sounds like Ellen. She's a very close second, and I already told her that."

"I'm confident this could work," Brendan explained. "And if you keep your house, then during the summers we could go to Tacoma. I can work from anywhere. You too, if you're handling the business end of the bakeries. I don't know how big your house is, but we could have our family visit with us."

"It's not a huge house—three good-sized bedrooms

and a finished basement. Christopher did a great job finishing it out, and there would be plenty of room."

He felt excitement stirring inside of him. "I think this could work."

She smiled. "It *will* work. We just have to figure out these living arrangements—and fast. It's getting harder and harder to leave you at night."

Brendan felt the slow burn of desire he always felt when they were like this. "It won't be long, *mo chroi.*"

"You have something up your sleeve, don't you?" she asked searching his eyes, a knowing smile on her lips.

"How can you be so sure?"

"Because you love me, and you want to spend the rest of your life with me."

He kissed her, then shifted so he could take her fully into his arms. He deepened the kiss sending their pulses racing. When he pulled away, they were both breathless.

"I do love you and want to spend the rest of my life with you."

It was hard to see Fred go, but she knew he needed to get back. She kept in touch with her mother about her mother-in-law. Still no progress. Her mother did tell her that Stacey was spending a lot of time alone on walks and in her room. Her mother was convinced that everything would work out. It brought some peace to Lauren.

She looked down at the drawing she was working on

for the table menus for Ellen's wedding. She'd sketched out a ring of flowers at the top; a table number would be entered in the center and the menu listed below. Each of the nine by five menus would be placed on an easel next to each centerpiece. Guests would be able to pick up the menus and pass them around.

Lauren looked up from her drawing and stared out the French doors that led to the patio. Her flowers were growing like weeds, and the colorful pots she had planted, shortly after she had arrived in Tramore, were bursting with even more color. They had been the inspiration for Ellen's table menu design.

She thought about her own future. She and Brendan had begun to make some plans for a wedding, had even set a date for early September. Elegant and small was the goal. They kept their thoughts to themselves because of the ring. He still hadn't given her one and hadn't explained why. Lauren didn't ask. It didn't concern her, for there was no question it would happen. She suspected he was up to something. Lauren smiled at the thought.

Lauren had broken the news to her parents about her and Brendan, over a Skype session. They were ecstatic but not surprised. "I told your father during our visit that you were in love with him," said Angie. "You just didn't know it yet. And because of our insightfulness, we have some news of our own." Her mother looked at her father signaling for him to tell the news.

William cleared his throat. "I told your mother we shouldn't say anything yet, but she insisted, so don't get your hopes up too soon. That master's degree in animal husbandry, well, it might have paid off. I submitted an application for a teaching position at a small agricultural college outside of Dublin in the direction of Tramore."

"Are you serious?" Lauren nearly shouted.

"Yes, I started doing research on how to make the move to Ireland when we retired, and I stumbled across the position. Regardless of the job situation, we would like to retire there."

"That is fantastic, Mom and Dad! I've got to let you go. I need to tell Brendan. Love you, bye."

She raced from her house and ran to the bakery.

"Hi Aine, is Brendan in the back?"

"No, he went to his parents' house for a minute."

"Is everything all right?" she asked feeling a touch of concern.

"Yes, everythin' is fine. He made them some soda bread."

The door to the kitchen opened and Ellen walked out. "Lauren, you're here. I was comin' over to see you for a minute."

"Oh, my word, Ellen, you're never going to believe this!" Lauren exclaimed and ran to her friend and hugged her. "My parents are planning on retiring here. My dad may have a shot at a job outside of Dublin. Can you believe it?"

"Seriously?" Ellen exclaimed. She reached for Lauren's hands and they began jumping up and down in excitement while customers looked on in amusement.

With ecstatic grins on their faces, they disappeared to the back.

It thrilled her to think of her parents being so close by. For years she'd lived so far away and all of that would change. If her father got the job, they would only be about an hour and forty minutes away.

Glancing down at the table menu, her thoughts drifted to her mother-in-law. She prayed that everything would work out. If only Stacey could find it in her to visit Ireland and talk about whatever was bothering her, then her decision to make a life in Ireland would be complete.

Lauren looked at the time. She had about half an hour before the book club meeting. Brendan and Mary wouldn't be joining them this evening. They had a potential property in Waterford to look at. This evening was the only time the seller could show it for the next few days.

Her phone rang. It was Brendan. "Hi," she answered with a smile.

"Hi, sweetheart, I hate to ask this of you, but I think I may have left the oven on. Would you mind runnin' up to my place and turnin' it off for me?"

"Of course, I'll head up, right now."

"Thank you. If I'm back in time, I'll stop by the meetin'. And if not, would you like for me to stop by your place, if it's not too late?"

"Even if it's too late, stop by. I want to see you."

"I will. I love you."

"I love you too."

As she walked up the stairs to Brendan's flat, she

smelled food and thought it was odd. She wondered if Brendan had not only left the oven on but had something in it.

When she unlocked his door, the oven wasn't the only thing on. The living room was lit with candles. They were artistically placed around the room, and the mantle looked especially gorgeous with a flower arrangement in the center.

"What's going on?" she asked when she saw Brendan standing near the dining room entrance looking smart in a plaid button down and khakis.

He walked to her and pulled her into his arms. "Are you surprised?" he asked softly, while holding her gaze.

Lauren felt the joy of this warm romantic setting. "I had no idea."

He kissed her and then took her hand so he could lead her to the dining room. A spring bouquet graced the center of the table, which was dressed in white and set with bone china and crystal glassware. Candlelight illuminated the space.

She noticed the music playing quietly in the background, Chopin or Mozart.

"I made you dinner."

Lauren wrapped her arms around him. "Thank you for this. I guess that means no book club tonight?"

"No book club tonight. Do you want to help me put the food on the table?"

"Absolutely. I didn't realize how hungry I was until I smelled the food as I was coming up."

When dinner was ready, he poured them a drink and then explained the menu.

"I grilled steaks the way you like it, I hope, and I made a chimichurri sauce to go with it."

"I've never had chimichurri."

Brendan took a spoon and dipped it into the sauce to scoop out a taste. He lifted the spoon to her lips.

"Mmm, that's really good. What's in it?"

"Mainly parsley and garlic, but there's also olive oil, oregano, and red wine vinegar."

She smiled. "What is oregano?"

"You know—oregano."

"It sounds like your saying Oregon with an o at the end of it, like the state in the U.S. And I don't know what that is."

"Here," he replied as he stood from his chair and then came back to the table with a spice jar. "This stuff is oregano."

"Oh, I see. You mean ore-*gan*-o," she replied while enunciating the herb the American way.

"You say it funny," he said with a smile.

She laughed. "So do you. Well, however it's pronounced, this sauce is really good. What else did you make?"

"Asparagus. I know it's your favorite, and I have a French baguette with farmer Dunne's butter. For dessert I have crème brûlée. That you can thank Ellen for."

They began plating their food. "It all sounds really good. And what's the special occasion?" she asked with a knowing look.

He leaned in to kiss her. "What if I told you it's a 'just because I love you' occasion?"

"Uh huh, you're going to make me wait, aren't you?" She knew this was the day, the engagement ring moment.

He shrugged. "If you're good, I might not wait until the last minute."

Her eyes softened and gone was the playfulness. "I would be happy to wait till the last minute. I have what I want: you."

Brendan placed his hand at the back of her neck and drew her to him slowly. When his mouth found hers, she tasted the tart, remnants of the chimichurri sauce on his lips and deepened the kiss. After several long, wonderful moments, he pulled away, his eyes glazed over with desire. "I hope you like it, *mo chroi*."

She kissed him again. "I will treasure anything you give me."

Brendan's gaze turned serious. "I know." After a moment, he nodded at her plate. "Did I get the temperature right on your steak?"

"It's great."

They talked about summer break and the plans they had made. Lauren would care for Noirin. Brendan had happily notified the day care that she would only be there on occasion. They had already taken the sailboat out, but it would be a regular thing for them over the summer months, something he and Noirin did more of as the season grew warmer.

The summer solstice was fast approaching, and

Brendan always enjoyed going to the festival in Lough Gur. It was geared toward families with children and included a fairy ball, arts and crafts for Noirin, as well as good food, drinks, and merchant vendors. His family usually brought a picnic lunch and took advantage of the beautiful lake front.

When dinner was done, she helped him wash the fine bone china, impressed that he owned such an elegant set. When he told her the dishes belonged to his parents and how they had let him borrow some pieces for the occasion, she smiled at his thoughtfulness.

It took them longer than normal to get the dishes done and the food put away because of all the stolen kisses in between.

"Finally," Brendan said as he led Lauren to the sofa as shadows danced around the room from the candlelight.

After they sat down, he leaned over to the coffee table and picked up a small blue box that was sitting next to the flowers.

Her eyes glowed in anticipation.

Brendan draped his arm over the couch and held her gaze. "It took me so long because I had the ring custom made. The gemstone has been in my uncle's family for two generations. It was his grandmother's. As the oldest child, he was gifted the stone by his mother. Uncle Quinn gave it to me the night we made our announcement." He paused and held her gaze. "I think it's interestin' how he never offered it before."

He was referring to when he was going to propose to Eva. Surely, he'd have mentioned his plans to his parents.

Lauren liked knowing that Quinn had felt she was worthy of such a gift. "It's because I fell in love with his grand-daughter first."

Brendan laughed. "You're probably right. Seriously, though, I think it's because he knew there was someone else who would love me better, someone I would love and cherish, like I'd never felt for another." He opened the box and presented her the ring.

Lauren stared at the round cut emerald, her eyes wide with surprise. "Oh, Brendan, it's exquisite! I've never seen anything like it before."

He lifted the ring out of the box and held it out to Lauren for her to take a better look.

"The four-point petals are called a halo." They were accentuated with diamonds.

"Are those pearls?" she asked. At the base of each petal was a small round pearl.

"They are."

She looked up at him, appreciation bright in her eyes. "You had this made for me?"

He nodded. "I worked with a designer in Waterford."

"Will you put it on my finger?"

He took the ring from her hand and placed it on her finger. He smiled as he watched her staring down at the bright emerald, enjoying his gift to her.

"I love you, Lauren. I feel it so strongly that some-times words feel inadequate. I wish I were a poet and could write or recite beautiful words to convey how I feel. Because that's what you deserve."

She placed her hand along his cheek, her thumb caressing the contours of his face. "I don't need poems; just knowing how much you love me is enough. How quickly you've become everything to me. That night when we told your family about our plans, I was joking about you being a bonus. I may have fallen in love with Noirin first, but you are my heart, *mo chroi*, and you always will be."

Brendan lifted her hand to kiss the ring that now adorned her finger. "You have no idea how glad I am to hear it." He kissed the ring one more time before continuing, "I'm sorry for your loss, sweetheart. I will always ache for the pain that you feel at havin' lost Christopher, but I promise you that I will love you in the best possible way, and that we will celebrate his life together."

Her eyes brimmed with tears, happy and grateful tears. Lost for words, she kissed him and showed him how thankful she was to have him.

Chapter Thirty-Nine

Donal looked at his watch as he knocked on the O'Leary's front door. He was arriving much later than he'd planned.

Lauren answered. "Hi, Donal," she greeted before opening the door wider. "Ellen's in the kitchen with her hands full."

He followed her in and closed the door. "How are you doin'?"

"Couldn't be better. How are *you* ? Just one month before the wedding—lots to do."

"You have no idea," he commented with a grin.

Lauren led him into the kitchen.

"Hi," Ellen said with a happy smile when she saw him. She was at the table with a glue gun in her hand. "We're almost done with the favor boxes. Here, have a look."

Ilene and Martha were planning to make French macarons for the wedding favors, their gift to Ellen and Donal. Ellen and Lauren had spent the afternoon putting together the boxes, adding the cover, and gluing a sage green ribbon on top. He had planned to help, but an emergency with a church member had pulled him away.

He looked up at Lauren who had designed the cover of the box. "It's beautiful, Lauren." She had drawn two love birds sitting on a branch in the color scheme of their wedding, cream and sage with touches of peach.

"Thank you. It was fun. But I must run. Brendan and I are taking Noirin to the Leisure Park."

Ellen stood from her chair and hugged her friend. "Thank you so much for all your help.

Lauren kissed her cheek. "I'm glad to. You two have fun. We'll see you later."

Donal reached for Ellen. "You look knackered."

"A little. It's been a lot to do in a short amount of time; but worth it." Her eyes were glowing and happy, matching his.

She kissed his check before taking her seat.

"What can I do to help?"

"Ever use a glue gun before?"

"Nope."

"It's easy, but you have to be careful not to get any glue on your hand or you'll be hurtin'." She scooted one of the completed boxes over to him. "Take one of the covers and turn it over. Put a dot of glue on each corner and then place it on top of the box. When you're done, take one of these bows and glue it in the center. Pretty easy."

"I think I can manage."

"How is Mrs. Wilson?" Ellen asked.

"Not doin' well. They confirmed it was a massive stroke. They gave her the anti-stroke meds and now it's a waitin' game to see how she does. She's been out of it almost since arrivin' at the hospital. Glen is distressed. Their children are makin' their way home. I left when his oldest son arrived... How is that?" he asked after gluing on the first cover.

"Perfect. We only have about twenty more to do. Mum said she was bringin' home dinner. Are you hungry?"

"I'm famished." He reached over and placed his hand on Ellen's forearm. "I know we've talked about this durin' our counseling sessions, but will you be okay with what happened today?"

"You mean the plans we had to work on the favor boxes and the emergency call you received from Mr. Wilson?"

He nodded.

Ellen put down the glue gun. "I'd be lyin' if I said it would never bother me. But I'm also goin' into this with my eyes wide open. What you do is important, and I'm proud of you for it. Being there for your congregation is the most important thing you'll do as a pastor, and we'll make it work. As long as you're not plannin' to tend to emergencies on our honeymoon or when our children are born, I think I can manage all the other times."

"That's why we have deacons, to help when I'm not available. Our children, aye? Already thinkin' about that, are ya?"

She smiled at him.

"Have you changed your mind about how soon?" he asked.

"No, I still want to wait. I want you all to myself for a while. Besides, I have to get the bakery off the ground and runnin'."

"I think it's pretty amazin' that Brendan and Uncle Quinn made you a business partner."

Her smile grew wider. "I'm still in shock, and the fact that I will have Lauren's help. She's smart as a whip when it comes to business matters. I'll need her to keep me on track. I don't do well with the numbers."

"But you sure can bake, like nobody I've ever known. And you kiss really nice."

"Is that so," she asked as she stood from her chair and walked to him.

She bent down and kissed him sweetly on the mouth.

Donal pulled her down onto his lap. "And you smell nice." He deepened the kiss. "And you feel really nice," he added in between kisses, while caressing her bare arms.

Being with Ellen was everything Donal had hoped for and more. While he hadn't thought a lot about marriage before realizing he was in love with her, the times he had, he'd wondered what it would be like, loving someone in that all-consuming way.

Having her in his arms, he'd never anticipated that grab-you-by-the-throat desire that had a way of turning into a deep fiery ache, spreading like wildfire across his entire being. The feelings were so intense that sometimes it frightened him. The fear he felt wasn't about being harmed or about loss; it was a fear of the vastness of those emotions and their limitlessness. With Ellen, he felt like he could love her for a hundred lifetimes and it still wouldn't be enough.

When he finally pulled away from her long enough to catch his breath, he told her how he felt.

Ellen cupped his face in her hands, her thumbs

caressing first his mouth, then his chin, all the while never taking her eyes off him. He could see the effect of his words on her as she gazed back at him. "Is it crazy to think we could both feel this way about each other in such a short time?"

He shook his head. "Not when it's right. You feel it don't you, sweetheart, that sense of rightness?"

"Oh, I feel it, Donal Kavanagh. I tried so hard to run from those feelin's. I'm glad you sense it too. There will be grand passion in our marriage, won't there?"

He closed his eyes for a moment and then opened them before answering. "I have no question about that, but it's what we do with that passion that matters most. Like putting each other's needs and desires before our own. Even before we take our vows three weeks from now, I promise to do my best in that respect."

The look in her eyes was soft and intense. "I promise you the same, Donal. We're goin' to be good together, aren't we?"

"Better than good, we'll be amazin' together. I look around at the people in our lives and I know it's possible."

Ellen laid her head on his shoulder and Donal simply enjoyed the moment of just being. In three short weeks he would be marrying this woman who meant everything to him, yet she already held all of his promises in the palm of her hands. They were hers to keep for however long they both lived.

Fred felt so lost without Stacey. He ached to hear her voice, and he longed to touch her, to know she was real, and that she still belonged to him. He truly was torn, wishing over and over that he'd never encouraged Christopher about Ireland or had given him the name of the city his wife had mentioned so many years ago. But then Lauren wouldn't be there—healing, falling in love, and building a new life for herself.

He was genuinely happy for her and satisfied that he'd managed to fulfill a long ago promise he'd made to his son. Christopher would be relieved and so was Fred. As he grappled with the new reality of how Lauren would fit into his life since she'd accepted Brendan's proposal, he conceded that he might be making regular trips to Tramore—alone.

It had been really nice to hear about their plans to keep the home she and Christopher had built, to turn it into an Airbnb rental, and the plans she and Brendan had made to spend summers in Tacoma. Stacey would at least have that time with her daughter-in-law.

He wasn't a man prone to tears. He felt a great deal—always had—but tears didn't come naturally to him, until Christopher had died and now since Stacey had left. Lately, he felt like he'd cried a river. He felt like shedding them now as he turned onto his street toward his cold, empty house.

Respecting his wife's wishes, he'd left her alone up in Montana. It was hard. A day's drive or a quick flight and he could have been on the Fellows' doorstep, begging and pleading for his wife's forgiveness and for her to come home to him so they could work things out. But he honored her wishes, though it took just about everything in him to do so.

With his thoughts in Montana, he didn't notice the lights on in the house when he pulled into the driveway. It wasn't until he'd parked the car in the garage, opened his door, and smelled food coming from the house that he realized something was different. Fred practically ran to the door that led into the mudroom and through to the kitchen.

Stacey was standing there. She didn't look well; she appeared to have lost some weight and there were dark circles under her eyes. She was wearing an apron, and her hands were clasped tightly in front of her.

It was everything he could do not to grab a hold of her and never let go. Instead, he stood where he was, uncertain, tentative. Words wouldn't come. All he could do was stare at her and wonder if he was dreaming.

"I made some lasagna, your favorite." Her eyes began to water. "I have so much to tell you, Fred, and I'm afraid that when I do, you'll be the one running away from me."

He moved toward her then, scooping her in his arms. Fred looked at her, and with all the intensity of the love he felt for her, he said, "I'll never leave you, no matter what you tell me. You're my life, Stacey. I'll always love you, and nothing will ever change that. Do you understand?" He hadn't intended the last part to come out so demanding, but it was the only thing he could do to convince the woman he treasured more than life to believe what he said.

She wiped the tears streaming down his cheek. "The first thing I need to tell you is that my name isn't Stacey."

Chapter Forty

"Shay?" Lauren called out as she entered the Callerys' home.

"I'm in the kitchen, darlin'," the older woman replied.

"Well, hello," Lauren said with a smile as she hefted onto the counter a basket of produce she'd picked from the garden.

"Hello, how are you? Did you have a good time in the garden this mornin'?" Shay was sitting at the dining room table with a notebook and pen.

"Always," Lauren replied before bending down to kiss Shay's cheek.

"What did you bring?"

"I have radishes today."

"Oh, that's grand; I love them in my salad."

"Me too. I also have some strawberries. I snatched a couple of scones from the bakery and thought the straw-berries would go nicely with them. How about I put the kettle on?"

"Thank you," Shay said. "So, how did it go with the venue? Were you able to get September 7 th?"

"Unfortunately, not. I had to go with plan B."

"Well, that's okay; the Dunraven is just as nice."

Lauren turned the knob on the stove. "It will be fine. Frankly, I could marry Brendan anywhere just as long as

I'm marrying him. But I know how important it is for you and Quinn to have this." Lauren gave her a compassionate look as she pulled down two teacups from the cupboard.

It wasn't necessary for the older woman to tell her how much it pained her not to be planning her daughter's wedding and to see Katelyn walk down the aisle. And so, Lauren had been determined to give her that with her only other child.

They'd already made a trip into Waterford to look at dresses. It was bittersweet not having her mother there, but her mother had understood and reminded her that she'd already had the pleasure of helping her with her wedding to Christopher.

As if reading her thoughts, Shay said, "I can imagine how hard it is to do this again. I know how much you love and miss Christopher."

Lauren brought the tea tray to the table and sat down. "It's funny, I was just thinking about when I tried on dresses with my mom and mother-in-law, and it made me sad for a moment. I can't help but remember. Part of me wishes I could keep my past and my present from co-mingling..."

"But why?" Shay interjected.

Lauren shrugged her shoulders. "Because there is a touch of sadness with the remembering. And I'm so happy right now. This experience with Brendan feels a little short changed."

"Have you talked to Brendan about it?"

She had, and as expected, he'd been completely

understanding, asking her about the moment she was remembering, wanting to know the details, holding her afterwards. "Brendan has been amazing," she said.

"And I suspect if the roles were reversed you would be too."

Lauren smiled. "I hope I would. It doesn't bother me when he talks about Eva. I know he loved her, and I'm okay with that. That love helped to make him who he is today."

"Oh, he may have loved Eva, but it doesn't hold a candle to what he feels for you. I see it all over him. The way he looks at you, the way he is when you're around, it's nothin' like I've ever seen." Shay looked thoughtful. "Thank you for includin' me in the plannin'. Seein' you in that dress was a special moment for me."

Lauren reached for Shay's hand. "I know how much you would have enjoyed having these moments with Katelyn. I would like to have known her."

There was a brightness in Shay's eyes. "She would have loved you. Thank you for lovin' Noirin the way you do. I know it's somethin' she would want to say to you. She loved that little girl more than anythin'—such a terrific mother! I was always impressed with how she handled being a single mother, never resentin' how she had to do it alone, and more importantly, never resenting Noirin's disability. She was proud to be her mother and I was proud to have her as a daughter."

The kettle started whistling.

Lauren stood to attend to the tea. "It's obvious that Katelyn was incredible with Noirin. She talks about her often. We've watched some of the home videos together. It's nice getting to know her in that way."

When she returned to the table, Shay reached for an album sitting beside her. "I have Brendan's baby book. I thought you might enjoy lookin' through it."

Lauren's eyes lit up. "I would love to."

She opened the album with its baby blue cover. "Oh my, what an adorable baby he was! Look at those curls!"

"He was a beautiful baby. I was angry with Glenna for so long. I couldn't understand how she could leave such a wonderful child behind. But then I'd remember how he now belongs to me and Quinn and how fortunate we felt to have him in our life. Knowin' he was safe and loved, I stopped being angry with her."

Lauren looked up from the pages. "His biological mom is the one topic of conversation where I feel like I have to tread lightly. He's only talked about her once." She remembered the night in Dublin when he'd shared about his mother, and she could sense the anger and the resentment. "I'm hesitant to bring it up."

"We don't often either. Here," Shay added as she flipped to the back of the album, "it's the only picture of his mother we keep in this book; the rest are tucked away. He didn't want it in here, but I insisted... Lauren, what's the matter?" Shay asked, concern in her voice when she saw the look on her face.

Lauren looked up at Shay. "I can't believe this!" She looked down at the picture of a woman in a chair holding her son, her face tilted downward as she looked fondly at the child in her arms. "Are you sure this is Brendan's mother?"

Shay looked confused. "I'm very certain. I took it myself. What's the matter, Lauren?"

Her hands were shaking. "Do you have any other pictures of your sister?"

"They're in a closet in my bedroom. If you help me up and to my room, I can show you which box."

Lauren's hands were still shaking as she led the older woman to the room.

"Are you plannin' to tell me what's goin' on?" Shay asked.

"I will, but I need to see the pictures first."

When Shay pointed out the box, Lauren reached up to retrieve it from the bottom shelf. She brought it to the bed where Shay sat.

Shay opened the box and pulled out the loose photos. She began sifting through them and started handing the ones that contained photos of her sister to Lauren.

Lauren was stunned and speechless. She at once recognized the photo in Brendan's baby album; she'd seen it countless times over the last several years.

She looked at Shay who was staring at her expectantly. "My mother-in-law—her name is Stacey and her maiden name is Walsh."

"I know, Shane had mentioned how ironic it was that his wife and your mother-in-law shared the same name. What does that have to do with Glenna?"

"Did Glenna know Shane's wife?"

"Stacey and Shane were a little older than us. We didn't hang out at the time; just saw each other in passin', but knew of them. Glenna idolized Stacey, who was beautiful and kind."

It wasn't necessary for Lauren to understand the connection between the two women to confirm what was dawning on her. The pictures in her hand were all the proof she needed. She reached for Shay's hand. "Stacey Walsh now Ross, my mother-in-law. She is your sister."

Shay's eyes grew wide with shock. A hint of pain lingered in the background as she began to process what was happening. "How is that possible?"

Lauren closed her eyes as the enormity of what was happening began to take hold of her too.

"Lauren, how is this possible?" the older woman repeated, worry and panic in her voice.

She opened her eyes. "The picture in the album, the one of Glenna holding Brendan, I've seen that picture many times. My mother-in-law has it framed on the mantle along with a number of other photos. I had always assumed it was a photo of Christopher and Stacey. Seeing these pictures of Glenna—she was so much younger, but she still looks the same."

Shay looked like she was going to faint. Lauren reached her for hand.

"How is this possible?" Shay asked once again, then began to cry uncontrollably. Lauren held her. "How could she just leave us? How could she leave her son, never to be heard from again? Were we that horrible that she didn't

404

want to have anythin' to do with us? Left us and moved all the way to America to start a new family while we agonized over her whereabouts and then grieved for her." The anguish and bitterness was heavy.

Lauren cradled this strong woman, who even in her illness seemed larger than life, and her heart broke for her—and for Mary, and for Brendan. *Oh, Brendan!* she immediately thought. *What will this do to him?*

After a long while of crying and asking why over and over, Shay finally said, "I need to tell Mary. I need Quinn."

"Of course. Here, lie down on your bed. I'll call them."

When Shay was settled, with a box of tissue in reach, she called both Mary and Quinn and told them to come immediately.

"Do you want me to call Brendan too?" Lauren asked

Shay reached for her hand that was holding the cell phone. "No, not yet. Please don't say anythin' to him yet. We need to talk. I'll call you." Shay began crying again, and Lauren placed a comforting hand on her back as she wept and waited for Mary and Quinn to arrive.

Mary came first and found them in the bedroom. There was panic in her eyes.

Lauren stood from the bed. "Shay is physically fine, but something has happened that she needs to tell you about."

Mary sat beside her on the bed. "Shay?"

"When Quinn gets here," Shay said without opening her eyes, a damp tissue clenched in her hand.

Lauren placed a hand on Mary's shoulder. "I need to go. This is a time for you and your sister and Quinn."

At the mention of his name, they heard the front door open.

"Shay!" he called.

"Back, here," Mary responded.

Lauren met him in the hallway. "She's fine. I'm leaving you guys alone to talk. I'll see you soon." She reached up and patted his shoulder, then left.

She didn't know how long she sat in the car staring out of her windshield too stunned to do anything. How would she be able to look at Brendan knowing what she knew? How would he take it when he learned that her mother-in-law was actually his mother, and that Christopher, the man she had loved completely, was Brendan's brother?

It was Lauren's turn to cry, to weep at all the questions and the grief that accompanied them. She was struggling to reconcile the woman she had grown to love over the years with the woman who had abandoned her whole family, without even a backward glance, so it seemed.

Lauren gripped the steering wheel in anger and frustration, her knuckles turning white. The Tramore skies began to open up, and the rain fell hard on the windshield. Her grandmother's comments about rain on a good day mocked her. It may have started out as a good day, a really good day, but it had turned into a terrible one, a tragic one. And it was all her fault.

She thought back to that first rainy day when she

had arrived in Tramore. How far she had come! But at what cost? Two families in turmoil; Fred and Stacey separated, and another family feeling abandoned and left believing they weren't good enough. And soon, the man she deeply loved would be grappling with the same pain. All at her hand.

When she thought about Brendan and the love she had for him, she knew it would have been better to never have come here. It would have meant sparing him and the others she'd come to love from the pain they were going through and would continue to suffer. The thought of never having met Brendan crushed her with the same kind of grief she felt at losing Christopher. Yet, Lauren would have sacrificed her own peace of mind and her own longings if it meant saving him from all of this.

But it was too late.

Her phone startled her. She half expected it to be Mary or Shay. But it was Brendan.

She hesitated. The moment he heard her voice, he'd know something was wrong, but if she let it ring, he'd worry and call his parents thinking she was at the house.

"Hi," he said when she finally clicked the answer button.

"Hi."

"Are you still with my Mum?"

"No, just heading back to the bakery."

"Were the radishes ready, like you'd hoped?"

She tried to keep the tears that were streaming down her face from being heard in her voice. She closed her eyes.

The pain he would face; Lauren had done this to the man she loved, but somehow, she'd make it right.

She took in a breath and answered his question about the radishes. "They were perfect. I'll be there soon."

"Okay," he hesitated before adding. "I love you."

"I love you too. See you soon," she replied her voice slightly breaking toward the end.

She clicked the phone off and wiped her eyes. *How could you do this, to him, to them, Stacey?*

Lauren held tightly to the steering wheel and then checked her watch to calculate the time difference between Tramore and Tacoma. It was early morning. Decisively, she reached for her phone and dialed Fred's number. He answered after the second ring.

"Hi, Lauren."

He sounded good, better than he had the last time she'd spoken to him. "I know why Mom was so upset when she read my letter."

She heard her father-in-law sigh. "I know too. How'd you figure it out?"

"I was looking through Brendan's baby album. His aunt kept the one and only picture of her sister and her son in that book. I recognized the picture. It's the one on the mantle with Mom sitting in a chair and looking down at the child she's holding. I always thought it was a picture of her and Christopher."

Fred gave an even heavier sigh. "I had no idea. I thought it was one of them too. Shortly after Christopher was born, it appeared. I just assumed that one of her friends had taken the photo. She came back, Lauren. She told me everything."

Lauren was crying again. "How could she do it, Dad?"

"It's hard to understand, I know. But she's trying to figure things out, how to make things right. Give her some time."

Lauren couldn't speak. She didn't know what to say.

Fred sighed again. "Lauren, I want you to enjoy this time with Brendan. It's a special time. You're getting married in a couple of months. Focus on starting this new life with him. Be there for him as he deals with all of this."

"He'll be devastated, Dad," she cried. "I don't know how to make this better for him. It's because of me that he's going to suffer. I never should have come."

"Don't say that, Lauren. Going to Tramore was the best thing that could have happened. Stacey feels the same way. She knows it now and realizes that this was meant to be. Thanks to your mother, she recognizes that this wasn't a coincidence but part of God's plan. You have to believe that things will work out."

She took a deep breath and wiped away the tears. "I'm trying... my mother knows?"

"Stacey finally told your mother what really happened. Your mother encouraged her to come back home and to start making things right."

Lauren reached for a tissue and blew her nose. "It has to be okay." She said the words more for herself.

"It will be okay, sweetheart. I'll be in touch, okay."

"Okay."

When they hung up, she texted Brendan and told him she wouldn't be back in time to pick up Noirin, and that she would stop by the bakery later that afternoon. She muted her phone and drove toward the shore. She needed to clear her head.

After finding a place to park, she pulled out her umbrella and walked toward the shoreline. The sky was calm, even in the rain. It wasn't an angry rain, just a steady one with gray clouds filling the sky. The waves seemed to be rolling in to shore in their normal cadence.

She didn't focus on the tragedy that had reared its ugly head today, but she chose to focus on the beautiful moments in her life. The points along her journey that had bloomed into something fiercely wonderful, the memories that were her greatest joy, Lauren would draw strength from them. Then she would march forward and face this new bend in the road, and hope that all would be well on the other side.

Chapter Forty-One

On her way home, Lauren saw she had a missed call from Mary. It was a message asking her to tell Brendan what she had discovered. She, her sister, and Quinn had all discussed things and felt she would be the best person to let him know.

She would head to the bakery and act as normal as possible. Then, after Noirin was put to bed, she would tell Brendan what she'd discovered.

When she arrived, she said hello to the employees before she made her way to the kitchen. Noirin was being entertained by Ilene and Martha who had given her a ball of dough to play with. They were making shapes and laughing.

"Lauren, look what I made!" Noirin exclaimed when she spotted her. She held in her small hands what looked to be a horse.

"Is that a horse?"

The little girl nodded exuberantly.

Lauren smiled at Ilene and Martha in greeting. "It looks like we have a Michael Angelo on our hands."

"That we do. How are you?" It was Martha who spoke.

"Good," she replied while bending down to kiss the top of Noirin's head. "Is Brendan in the office?"

"No, he asked us to mind Noirin for a bit. Said he would be right back."

"Okay. I'll give him a call. Thank you for entertaining her."

"You know we love havin' her," Ilene said.

She smiled her gratitude and then told Noirin it was time to go. With dough in hand, she said her goodbyes, and they walked to her flat.

When they entered the hallway that led to her apartment, Brendan was knocking on her door. His eyes were wide with relief when he saw her. "You didn't answer my calls, and I was worried. What's happened, Lauren? Aunt Mary didn't sound too good when I called her."

"You called Mary?"

"She picked up Mom's phone when I called, and I was worried when I got your text and you didn't answer my calls."

She opened the door and ushered Noirin in. "Honey, why don't you go into the kitchen and start working on your homework. I'll be there in a minute."

When she turned back to Brendan she said, "I'm sorry. I took a walk on the beach."

"In the rain? What's the matter, Lauren?"

She gave him a forced smile. "We'll talk. I promise, after we put Noirin to bed." She wrapped her arms around his waist and laid her head against his chest wanting to draw from the comfort of feeling him in her arms.

He held her, his body tight with concern.

After a few moments, she pulled away to look at him. "I'm going to attempt boxty for dinner tonight. Donal gave me his recipe."

He nodded and didn't seem reassured by her attempt at normalcy. "I'll see you soon," he said before kissing her forehead and turning toward the bakery.

She watched him exit through the hall door, and began to cry, with a prayer forming on her lips.

Brendan was more than worried: he was anxious. He looked at Ellen who was putting together her blueberry lemon cake. "Ellen, can you do me a favor?"

"Sure," she said while still focusing on adding a layer of sponge cake to the stack she'd been working on.

"I need you to mind Noirin for me. Somethin is wrong, and I can't wait until Noirin goes to bed for Lauren to tell me."

Ellen looked up from her cake, her brows furrowed. "What's goin' on?"

"I don't know. Lauren left my parents' house early this afternoon, texted and said she wouldn't be able to go with me to pick up Noirin and then didn't answer when I called her. I called my parents' house to see if she was there and your mother answered the phone. She said everythin' was fine, but she didn't sound fine. I'm useless right now and need to talk to Lauren."

"Well, now I'm worried. I'll run over and get Noirin and bring her back to the kitchen so I can finish up the cake, and then I'll take her for ice cream. Take as long as you need."

"Thank you. You can tell Lauren why I sent you and that I'll be over as soon as I'm done measuring this batch of ingredients."

Ellen nodded.

Brendan concentrated on what he was doing and worked as quickly as he could.

A short while later, he passed Ellen in the hall and gave Noirin a quick hug goodbye as he made his way to Lauren's flat.

He tapped before entering. Lauren was standing by the French doors. She turned when she heard him enter.

"It's stopped raining," she said. "Let's go for a walk."

He nodded and waited for her to grab her jacket, helping her into it. She reached for his hand and together they left the building, making their way toward Lower Strand.

They were silent for a long while, the worry eating away at Brendan. He was imagining everything possible: she'd changed her mind about living in Ireland; she didn't want to spend the rest of her life with him, after all. None of it resonated. Everything she had said and done up until this moment told him otherwise. Lauren loved him; she loved him very much. He was convinced of it. But then he'd thought the same about Eva.

Brendan didn't pressure her to speak but simply held her hand, their fingers intertwined.

As they rounded the bend that would take them to Lower Strand, she spoke. "Christopher always wanted a brother."

CHAPTER FORTY-ONE

He looked at her, but she kept her eyes trained forward.

"Not a sister, but a brother. I remember how we had laughed when we heard Fred recounting the story of Christopher's request when he was five years old. He'd asked his parents for a sibling. It had to be a boy, and if it turned out to be a girl, they'd have to give her back to God." Lauren paused. "I remember that retelling, but what I remember the most was how my mother-in-law hadn't laughed. I thought it was because she was sad that she couldn't have another child."

They reached the shore. Lauren led him closer to the water's edge and stopped when she reached the furling waves. She stared out over the expanse of water made dull without the sunshine. Brendan saw she was crying.

He couldn't stand it any longer. He needed to know what was wrong. He reached for her shoulders and gently turned her to him. There was pain in her eyes and something else—regret.

"Lauren, what is the matter? This is killin' me. What's wrong?"

"I should never have come here, Brendan. I'm so sorry."

"What?" He didn't know if he'd shouted the word, but he felt like he'd been stabbed in the chest with a knife. "Why would you say that, Lauren?" He wanted to grip her shoulders and shake some sense into her. Instead, he pulled her into his arms and held onto her, afraid that if he let go, she would be gone. "Don't say things like that, Lauren. Why would you say such a thing?" He pulled her away so he could look into her eyes. "Don't you love me anymore?"

She nodded her head vigorously but the tears continued to flow. "More than anything... but my coming here has hurt the people I care about both at home and here. What I have to tell you, Brendan, will hurt you, and I'm so sorry."

"Just tell me, Lauren." He felt like his chest would explode.

"I've learned why my mother-in-law was so upset when she read my letter, why she left Fred. I now know why she was so quiet that day Fred told us the story about Christopher wanting a brother." She wiped her eyes and took a deep breath. "Christopher actually had a brother and never knew it."

Brendan was so confused and couldn't understand what all of this had to do with him—with them.

"My mother-in-law had a child a few years before she had Christopher. She never told anyone, not even Fred. She'd left her son behind in Ireland. Brendan, my mother-in-law's real name isn't Stacey Walsh: it's Glenna Stewart."

"No!" He stood there wide-eyed and reeling from what he was hearing. *It wasn't possible. How was it possible?* "It's not true," he said aloud shaking his head in disbelief.

"It *is* true, Brendan." Lauren told him about the picture.

He dropped his hands to his side and clenched his fists. "I can't believe this. She left us, went all the way to America without even a word to me, to her family! My aunts lived all these years agonizing over what had happened to her!"

Brendan was beyond angry. He turned away from Lauren and walked back toward the street, too furious to think straight. How was he expected to process this? He wanted to punch something, to kick at the stone wall along the street. He wanted to find the woman who could so easily abandon them all and tell her what he thought about her.

As he stormed off, with no destination in mind, what he wanted was to never think of Glenna Stewart again. She wasn't worth another second of his thoughts.

Noirin was playing quietly in the living room, while Ellen and Lauren were in the dining room. "It'll all work out, Lauren," said Ellen, her arm wrapped comfortingly around her friend's shoulders.

She had told Ellen everything.

"He was so angry. It didn't seem like him to be so mad."

"No, that doesn't sound like Brendan but then it's hard to imagine how someone would react when they've discovered somethin' so shocking. My mother and Aunt Shay are a right mess." Ellen sighed. "But you have to get it out of your head that you should never have come. You are the best thing that has ever happened to Brendan. He would go through what he's goin' through a thousand times over if it meant havin' you."

Lauren shook her head. She wasn't so sure. "But what about your mother and Shay? They don't deserve this. It was better for them to think she was dead, unable to return than to know the truth."

Ellen was quiet because she couldn't deny it. "What I can say, Lauren, is that none of this was a coincidence. I don't believe in coincidences, and somehow, I don't think you do either."

Lauren didn't know what she believed anymore. All she knew was that she loved Brendan more than she loved herself, and she couldn't imagine a life without him. Where all of this left them, she didn't know, and it scared her.

Somehow, she managed to get through the rest of the evening, in spite of the fear and the worry. Brendan still hadn't returned and it was time for Noirin to go to bed. She took her upstairs to ready her for bed and then laid down with her, holding her, thankful that her little girl was oblivious to the trauma that seemed to be splintering her family.

It didn't take long for Lauren to fall asleep before she was awakened by gentle strokes to the side of her face. When she opened her eyes, she saw Brendan kneeling down beside the bed, his gaze gentle but intense.

"I'm sorry, Lauren," he said quietly, remorse softening his features. The nightlight in Noirin's room cast a warm glow over his features.

She turned to look at Noirin who was sleeping deeply

and then climbed out of the bed. Brendan pulled her into his arms. He buried his face into the side of her neck, and held onto her tightly. "I'm so sorry, *mo chroi*."

She pulled away and led him from the room. After closing the door, she cupped his face with her hands. "There is nothing for you to apologize."

Brendan scooped her up into his arms and took her to the couch. He laid her down and drew himself alongside of her taking her mouth with his and kissing her as if it had been years since he'd last seen or touched her. "I need you," he said breathlessly as he laid gentle kisses along her jaw line. "I've never needed anyone like I need you, sweetheart. You are everything to me." He moved his mouth to her neckline, and she ran her free hand in his hair, her breaths coming in short gasps. She moved her hand to his back to slip it under his shirt wanting to touch and feel him.

He reached around for her hand and drew it to his lips, his breathing more ragged than hers. Brendan closed his eyes as he lay beside her trying to calm himself. "More than needin' you, Lauren, I *want* you. I'll always want you, no matter what it costs me." He looked at her then, his eyes intense. "Please don't ever doubt that, and never ever tell me again that you should never have come here." Tears gathered in his eyes. "The thought of never havin' known you, or never havin' the privilege of lovin' you kills me to think it."

He swept her hair away from her face, his breathing more normal. "I've had a glimpse of what you've gone through losin' Christopher." He squeezed his eyes shut and drew her closer to him. "Oh God, I had a brother! She denied me that too!"

Brendan wept and all Lauren could do was hold him and weep with him. Earlier, while going through the motions of caring for and entertaining Noirin, she had put it all together. She'd finally realized why Brendan's smile looked so familiar: it was Christopher's smile. The realization had caused a fresh wave of grief to roll through her.

She sifted her fingers through his hair. "You have his smile," she said when she felt Brendan's hold relaxing a little.

He looked at her.

Lauren nodded. "I couldn't figure out why I was so drawn to it when I first noticed it in Dublin. It gave me comfort, and I loved it. Now I know why. I'm sorry she did this to you, Brendan."

He simply looked at her, his hand stroking her back. "I can't spend the summers in Tacoma. I can't be in the same city with her. It's hard enough knowin' we occupy the same planet. I'm sorry. I know I promised you I would fall in love with Christopher's parents too, but I can't."

She remembered the comment she had made to Brendan when she first told him she loved him and how Christopher's parents were like a second set of parents to her. The irony of it all would be almost humorous if it weren't so tragic.

Stacey's fears of losing her as a daughter-in-law were even more tragically ironic. She was angry with her mother-in-law and devastated to know she could do what she'd done. But Lauren would hear what she had to say, when she was ready to talk. Somehow, she sensed Brendan wouldn't be as willing.

Lauren stroked the side of his face. "It's okay, baby, I understand. You're my life now, and I belong to you."

He kissed her tenderly and then pulled away. "I won't ask you not to see her. She didn't do this to you; she did this to me, to my family. I know you love the woman she's been to you. I won't deny you that, but I just can't do it."

How she loved him, this undemanding, sensitive man, whom she knew would do anything for her! "I am so fortunate to be loved by you." She paused and added, "I told Christopher that too, and I'm telling you as well, because it's true. I will spend my life showing you how true it is. A day will not go by that you won't know how loved you are by me, no matter what."

She kissed him—an exclamation point to the words and the promise she felt so deeply.

Chapter Forty-Two

"What was she like?" Shay asked.

It was the following day, and Lauren had gone to see her first thing in the morning.

They were sitting in the living room in the chairs that flanked the fireplace.

Shay was staring at the painting of her daughter and Noirin that hung over the mantle. Shane had painted Katelyn pushing Noirin on a swing suspended from a large oak in a small clearing in the forest. It was the most stunning of the Katelyn-Noirin series. The way Shane had captured the light as it fell on the moss-covered tree trunks was so realistic, and the joy on both Katelyn and Noirin's faces was captivating.

When Lauren didn't answer Shay right away, the older woman reached out to touch her hand. "I want to know, Lauren."

She nodded. "Stacey is a wonderful woman. Christopher adored her. She was always there for him, and stayed home with him until he started middle school. She became a nutritionist and worked part-time at a practice so she could take him to school and pick him up each day.

"She and Fred are the ideal couple. It's obvious they love each other deeply, like you and Quinn and Mary and Jack. She is fun to be around, smart, and devoted.

"You talked about the mother-in-law and daughter-in-law dance well, Stacey knew the moves perfectly. I love her like a second mother. My parents and Christopher's parents became really good friends."

Lauren told Shay about Stacey's aversion to Ireland. This contrasted with Fred's encouragement to Christopher to learn more about his heritage, leading to their plans to visit Ireland—the now fateful trip to Tramore that had turned their world upside down.

"A couple of weeks after I moved here, I wrote my mother-in-law a letter telling her all about the people I'd met and how wonderful everyone was. I never told her where I was. I mentioned Brendan and his aunt and uncle who had raised him and how good they were to him. I also mentioned how hard it was to see his aunt suffering from MS. I told her about the friend I had made in Ellen and her mother Mary who helped me find a place to rent.

"I thought she'd read the letter after she received it, but I realized after Fred showed up here a few weeks ago that she hadn't read it all. Until then. That's when she left my father-in-law. He'd found the letter I'd written on the bed with a note stating why she was gone."

"What else did the note say?"

Lauren paused not wanting to tell Shay.

"It's okay, Lauren, please tell me."

"She told Fred he had betrayed her."

Lauren could see the hurt in the older woman's eyes.

Shay sighed heavily. "She was planning to go to her grave with her secret."

Lauren didn't need to confirm the obvious.

"What do you think she'll do now?" Shay asked.

"I called my father-in-law yesterday, after I realized who she was." She paused. "He knows. Stacey went home and told Fred everything. He said she was trying to figure out what to do. What do you want her to do, Shay?"

The tears began to roll down the older woman's cheek.

Lauren's heart ached for her. She knelt down in front of the woman she already loved and reached up to wipe away her tears.

Shay clasped her hands and held them tightly for comfort. "I don't know, Lauren. I don't know what I want her to do. I'm hurt and angry."

She nodded in understanding. "I'm so sorry I caused all of this."

It was her turn to be comforted as Shay gave her a tender smile. "Brendan told me last night, when he stopped by, what you'd said. None of this is your fault, darlin'. I couldn't have asked for a better person for my Brendan, no matter what it cost me. Mary feels the same. We'll get through this. We've had to deal with much worse."

Lauren couldn't help but glance at the painting of Katelyn before returning her gaze back to Shay, her hands still held tenderly in the older woman's grasp. Shay gave her a beseeching look. "I hope one day you'll be able to call me Mom too."

What grace, what openness, and what love she had been shown by this family—her family!

"I would be honored to call you Mom," she replied before placing a kiss on her cheek.

The following two weeks were a blur of activity in preparation for Ellen and Donal's wedding. It had helped to keep everyone's mind occupied and looking forward to the happy occasion, a reprieve from the trauma that buried secrets had brought upon the family.

Brendan, one of Donal's groomsmen, was having a hard time focusing on the ceremony. He found himself stealing glances at Lauren who was standing a few feet away as one of Ellen's bridesmaids. He was thinking about his own wedding to her in two months.

No, today wasn't a day to be thinking about the pain of knowing his mother was alive. No, he corrected himself: Glenna wasn't his mother. She was merely the woman who had given birth to him. Brendan put away the thoughts of all that had happened, and chose to focus on the day at hand. It was a time to celebrate the gift of love for his friend and cousin as well as his own happiness.

Lauren looked incredible in the sleeveless-silk-wrap dress she wore, flawlessly, the soft peach color complementing her pale skin tone and raven black hair. Her heavy tresses were swept up in a chignon supported with crystal studded combs with tendrils hanging down the sides to frame her oval-shaped face. He yearned to remove the combs and to run his fingers through the silky softness.

Would she wear her hair the same way when she walked down the aisle to him? Or would she wear it down with big curls framing her lovely face?

He forced himself to listen to the vows Ellen and Donal shared with each other. He smiled inwardly at how happy he was that they had found one another, his best friend and his cousin whom he thought of more as a sibling. They would be happy together because he knew them. Brendan appreciated their vows filled with promises of compassion, understanding, and unconditional love for one another.

When Donal and Ellen walked down the aisle as man and wife, all Brendan could think of was the woman standing across from him and the life they had started building together.

"You look incredible," Brendan whispered to Lauren as she slipped her arm through his when it was their turn to walk down the aisle to exit the sanctuary.

"Me?" she replied. "You look divine."

He led her to a corner in the vestibule as the newlyweds and their families formed the receiving line, and slipped her hand in his. Together they watched as the guests made their way out of the sanctuary.

"Can you believe that will be us in a couple of months?" he asked.

Her eyes were bright with happiness as she looked up at him. "I can't wait."

Brendan bent down to give her a chaste kiss on the mouth and was glad they were both in the wedding party so they could enjoy every moment together. Soon it would be time for pictures while the guests enjoyed a cocktail hour, and afterward, during dinner and dancing, she would be all his to enjoy. He looked forward mostly to the dancing. Brendan couldn't get enough of Lauren.

Noirin would be joining them soon. As one of the flower girls, she and the other children in the wedding party were currently being fed a snack by one of the wedding coordinators, hopefully to help them be more cooperative with the pictures before they headed to the reception at The Acres.

Everything progressed in a timely and orderly manner.

Lauren and Brendan held onto to Noirin in between pictures and she rode with them to the reception, chatting away about how exciting it was to be a flower girl.

"You look wonderful, sweetheart," Lauren complimented her as Brendan maneuvered onto the highway that would take them to Waterford and The Acres.

Noirin had giggled a thanks.

When they arrived at the reception, Noirin sat with her grandparents. The bridesmaids and groomsmen were expected to sit at the head table with the bride and groom to enjoy the dinner, which had been delicious.

When the music started, Brendan stood and walked over to Ellen. He bent down to kiss her cheek. "I'm so happy for you, Ellen."

She reached up to hug him. "I love you, Brendan."

After giving Donal a congratulatory handshake and a hug, he went to Lauren and offered her his hand.

She accepted with a smile and followed him onto the dance floor.

"I've been dyin' to get my hands on you all night," he said, their bodies close.

"Do you remember when we danced in Dublin, that night of the gallery show?" she asked.

"How could I forget! I was so in love with you and so frustrated at the same time; but then you danced with me. Do you remember tellin' me how thankful you were for lettin' you love Noirin and how happy you were that you came to Ireland?"

Lauren nodded.

"I felt so ashamed about pushin' you away. You'd come all the way here to find healin', and because of my fear, I distanced myself."

She looked thoughtful. "I remember. You had a look I didn't understand at the time, and then you apologized. Still no regrets that I came here?"

He knew why she was asking the question. It was the only dark spot on the day, a very small one. But he understood her need to ask and how she needed to be reassured of his well-being. He placed his forehead against hers, closed his eyes, and drew her closer to him. "How could I ever regret you, or this!" He opened his eyes so he could look at her and run his hands across her lower back. "No matter what happens in the weeks to come, nothin' will change how I feel. I'm sorry I pushed you away the day you told me about Glenna." He had apologized before, but like the night they had first danced together, he felt the need to say it again. "I don't make a habit of doin' that. I was so shocked and angry."

It was her turn to pull him closer to her as she looked into his eyes. "I know," she said before resting her cheek against his chest.

He raised his hand to stroke the side of her neck. "Will you wear your hair up like this on our weddin' day?"

Lauren looked up at him with smile, while his thumb stroked the soft creaminess of her skin. "As long as you promise to look as handsome as you do tonight."

He didn't care who might be watching them, Brendan bent down to kiss her softly on the lips lingering longer than he should. He knew he'd die a little every day until she was officially his.

Chapter Forty-Three

Stacey was shaking like a leaf as the driver entered the town of Tramore, the place that had been her home for the first sixteen years of her life. No, not a home, but the place she happened to live. There were no fond memories of this place for her, only of her two sisters and the very rare moments of happiness that she'd experienced with them growing up. She could count on two hands those moments. One immediately came to mind, the time when she, Shay, and Mary had stood outside of Cups and Cake Bakery with their noses pressed against the glass imagining what it would be like to have one of the delicious baked goods behind the tall-glass cases.

Disappointed that they would never know, they had turned away. They dreaded the moment they would walk through their front door knowing what awaited them, hard labor with a few drunken slaps thrown into the mix.

As they walked down the sidewalk, they heard someone calling out to them. "Hey," a little boy, close to their age, shouted. He ran to them and handed them a pretty pink pastry box with a gold seal used to hold the lid in place.

He smiled at them as he made his offering.

Shay, the oldest, seemed reluctant to take it. Both she and Mary eyed their sister silently pleading she would, their mouths already watering at the thought of what lay nestled under the lid of the pink box.

They didn't recognize the boy, which meant he went to the private school in town.

"Please take it," the little boy said as he continued to hold out the box to Shay.

Finally, she accepted his gift and said, "Thank you. We can pay you back."

It was an impossible offer but one that their big sister felt compelled to make.

"No, it's a gift," the little boy replied and then ran off.

The three of them stood there looking at the box and then slowly made their way home, careful not to drop the treasure that had been gifted to them by a stranger.

When they reached the pasture that bordered their land, they sat under one of the trees that ran along the fence line and looked at one another. They knew that if they were going to enjoy such a wonderful treat, it would have to be now and quickly before they arrived home too late and had to face even more of their parents' wrath.

When they lifted the box, they saw two different types of pastries, three of each so they wouldn't have to share. Rather than devour the treats, they savored them knowing they would suffer their parents' anger for being late, but how it would be worth it. They smiled at one another as they enjoyed each delicious bite.

Years later, they would discover that the little boy was Quinn. He'd seen the three sisters looking longingly at the pastries, and without even asking, he'd thrown the box together and gave it to them. Stacey hadn't discovered the fact until she'd returned to Tramore, pregnant and hopeless.

At the age of sixteen, she'd run away from home with a boy she thought she'd spend the rest of her life with, and instead, ended up strung out on drugs and turning tricks to support her desperate habit. She was nineteen when she had returned. By then, Shay had been newly married and her sister Mary was engaged.

After her return, Stacey learned that as soon as Shay could find work, she had removed herself and Mary from their parents' home and had reported their abuse. Word had spread around town. Outraged and embarrassed that their family's dirty laundry had been aired out for all of Tramore to learn, they had sold everything and fled.

Shay and Quinn welcomed her into their home and helped her during her pregnancy. To her surprise, Stacey had a healthy baby boy. A week later, she'd fled, desperate to numb the pain and to give her son a better chance at life than she could give him.

It was early afternoon when the driver pulled up to a pretty yellow house with black shutters and a red door. Stacey sat trembling in the car.

"Isn't this your stop, Ms.?" the driver asked, his eyebrows raised.

She nodded, and he stepped out to retrieve her luggage.

She had been too cowardly to call her older sister and had decided to simply show up—less chance of Shay telling her to leave her alone.

Fred, her dear Fred, had wanted to come with her, but Stacey had insisted she needed to do this alone. She'd made the mess and needed to right the ship herself—if it were possible. Stacey was convinced it wasn't but knew she had to try.

When the driver left, she stood on the porch for a very long time, trying to find the courage to knock. Finally, she pressed the doorbell and waited. It took a little bit for it to open. Stacey knew her sister was struggling with MS. And when she saw Shay at the door with a walker, she understood the delay. Her heart was in her throat and for a while she couldn't speak.

Shay looked the same, behind her frailness. Even with the signs of age lining her face, she was still lovely.

"Glenna!" Shay stammered as her face fell from the shock.

Stacey had half expected her sister to close the door in her face, but she didn't. She stood there as speechless as she was.

"I'm sorry I didn't call," Stacey managed to choke out.

"Why are you here?" Shay asked. It wasn't asked unkindly but it was edged with accusation. "You never intended to come back. Your husband told Lauren about the letter you had left him."

At the mention of her daughter-in-law's name,

tears sprang to Stacey's eyes. "I don't deserve to be heard, but I wanted to explain."

"I'm having a hard time with all of this, but I don't have the energy to stand here at the door talkin' to you."

Shay turned around and began shuffling further into the house. She hadn't closed the door and Stacey took that as an indication it was okay to come inside. And so, she did.

She tried so hard to hold back the tears as she followed slowly behind her sister.

When Shay was seated in a chair, she spoke. "You left without a word, never to be heard from again. We thought you were dead, Glenna, surely the only explanation for the silence." The words were heavy with accusation and Stacey blinked in confusion.

"But... but I did come back. I left you and Mary letters."

Shay gave her a look of incredulity. "When? We never received a letter."

She hadn't been invited to take a seat, but Stacey collapsed in the nearest one half in shock and half in weariness.

"Three years after I left, I came back. I saw the three of you, Quinn, you, and Brendan. You were holding a baby." Stacey paused and tried to fight the tears, but her voice quivered from the strain. "You looked so happy."

Her older sister's lips trembled. "We were happy, Glenna, but you left without a word. We thought you were dead. We were called to the police station to identify the bodies of nameless women who matched your description." Her sister was crying, and Stacey could no longer hold back the tears.

"I left letters with your names on them at the bakery. They explained everythin'."

Shay shook her head. "We never received the letters."

Stacey stood from her chair and wiped her eyes. She walked over to the window confused and even more afraid. She had explained everything in those letters, two of the hardest ones she'd ever written. But they didn't know. They'd never known.

Her shoulders shook from the pain of it all. Her past and all of her tragic mistakes came hurtling back at her. Stacey didn't want to relive it all again; she'd already done so with Fred. But she knew she had to. She had to make them understand. If there ever was a chance for things to be made right, she would have to tell them.

Stacey tried her best to rein in her emotions before turning to Shay who was watching her with tears still streaming down her cheek.

"I left those letters at the bakery. They explained everythin'. I was worried that if I mailed them, I'd never know for sure if you'd received them. I was certain that givin' them to the person at the front counter would ensure that you got them. I came here to say how sorry I am. And now, I need to explain everythin'—if you'll let me."

Shay sat there and looked at Stacey for a moment, an indecisive look on her face. Eventually she nodded, and Stacey added, "I'd like for Mary to be here too."

A short while later, Mary sat next to Shay, a stoic

look on her face. Stacey explained about the letters she had written and how she'd left them at the bakery, and why she was back in Tramore.

She rubbed her hands on the dark denim of her jeans and took a deep breath. "When I came back home, after findin' out I was pregnant, you both knew I had been using. What I never told you was the boy I ran off with, he was a scout. That's a person who travels around findin' young women without family or from broken homes, and he plays them, tricks them into fallin' in love with him. He promises them a new life free from their current troubles, all with the intent of trafficking them.

"By the time I had met Owen, I had already started drinkin' and had turned to pot, and he knew it. I was an easy target. I found out later he was actually much older than he looked and portrayed himself to be. As soon as I ran off with him to Dublin, I had my first hit of heroin. Once I was hooked, the only way I could get more was to pay for it—with my body." Stacey felt herself begin to tremble and her voice began to shake. She forced herself to continue. "I was given clothes, a decent place to live, and a steady supply of drugs, as long as I *paid* it all back. I needed the hits, and so I did. I sold myself for drugs."

She took a deep steadying breath. "One night, while walkin' the streets, I was solicited." Stacey began to cry; it was so hard to think about. "I recognized the man and told him I was already busy. He said he'd wait. I told him I'd be busy after that. Before I knew what was happening, he'd dragged me into an alley and... he raped me."

Stacey looked up at her sisters, and through her own tears, she could see that they were crying too. How she hated sharing this with them! But she had to help them understand.

"We were always careful. We were taught to never turn tricks without a condom and we were all on birth control. I had been sick and had forgotten to take my pills. The man who raped me never used a condom."

Stacey could see the sorrow in her sister's eyes, but she pressed on. "That man..." she paused... "I recognized him. It was Uncle Nevan."

Mary gasped and Shay raised her hand to her mouth.

Stacey closed her eyes and sucked in air trying to control her breathing, but it wouldn't come fast enough.

She bent forward and began to sob. She felt a hand on her back and another around her shoulders while tissues were placed in her hands. She pressed them to her face and began to cry like a wounded animal. "He knew who I was," she cried sobbing even harder. "Said he'd always wondered what it would be like."

The arms around her tightened and all three sisters cried for the tragedy that was the Stewart family.

"I tried, Shay. I tried so hard to be okay, to be better after I came back to you for help. But the pain, it was so bad. Seein' my son but not being able to forget, it was too much for me to bear. All I could think about was numbing the pain... and so, I left.

"I knew you would be a wonderful mom. I saw you with him those first few days after he was born, so lovin', so kind. You had started buildin' a beautiful life for yerself with Quinn, sweet Quinn, who gave us pastries that day."

They were all sobbing and crying, the release of their pain like a letting of their blood, poisoned by the evil of others.

They sat that way for a while. Mary eventually broke the tearful silence. "What happened after you left, Glenna?"

"I went back to the drugs, like a dog who returns to his own vomit. I was sold to a crime ring in New York. We were given new identities, fake U.S. passports and social security numbers, high dollar escorts this time. We were able to choose our own names. I chose Stacey Walsh's. I always thought she was so pretty and kind.

"I wasn't in New York for very long before they had me workin'. I was at a cocktail party with a lot of businessmen, a hotel ball room at the Ritz. The man who paid for my services for the evenin' was stayin' at the same hotel. Shortly after I arrived, he was ready to go up to his room.

"When the door closed, the man removed his jacket and asked me to have a seat. I was prepared to do whatever—nothing mattered to me. All I cared about was my next hit, counting down the minutes." She began to cry again. "I'll never forget what happened next. He took my hands gently in his and told me I didn't have to live this way anymore.

"At first, I was angry. I felt judged and condemned. But there was somethin' in his eyes—kindness and sincerity. It did somethin' to me and, for some reason, I was no longer angry. I began to cry. I told the man how I didn't want to live this way anymore; but the drugs, I couldn't live without them. He asked me if I trusted him, and for the life of me I couldn't explain it but I did.

"He told me to wait and he would be back. I remember sittin' there in his hotel room thinking I should just leave. I had a few more hours before my next hit. That's how they kept up the illusion of freedom. They always knew you'd come back for the next hit.

"But I didn't go back that night. The man had gone to a local drug store to purchase all the things he needed to help me when I began to withdraw. He nursed me through the agony—five days in that hotel room.

"When the worst of it was over, he booked me on a flight in a seat next to his and took me to Washington State, where he lived. He checked me into a ministry for recovering drug addicts and checked on me once a week via phone.

"He never said much, just asked how I was and how the program was goin'. During those conversations, he always shared with me a little about his faith. Through his words, combined with what I'd learned from the ministry, I finally understood how people like him could exist and how people like me could have a new life.

"Six months later, a week before I was scheduled to be released, with a job lined up, a place to live, and a sponsor, he showed up at the ministry. He had a bouquet of flowers and an invitation to dinner the Friday after my release. We weren't allowed to date while in the program.

"When I asked him why, he told me he couldn't stop thinkin' about me. I found out later that I was the seventh woman he'd rescued from human traffickin'. But I was the only one he couldn't stop thinkin' about.

"Four months later, Fred asked me to marry him." Stacey rubbed her red swollen eyes and looked at her sisters for the first time since she'd begun to answer Mary's question. "The most Fred did after we started datin' and even while we were engaged was hold my hand. I couldn't believe that someone could want me for more than what I could give him sexually. With a lot of counseling and by God's grace, I healed and embraced this gift of a new life I had been given.

"I never told Fred about my past and he never forced me to talk about it. All of these years, he's loved me in spite of who I'd been and the secrets I've been holdin' onto. The year I came back to Ireland with the letters, he never even questioned me when I told him I needed to make the trip and lay some things to rest.

"I left the letters tellin' you everythin' but, more importantly, I wanted Brendan to know I loved him enough to give birth to him, and then give him to the person who could love him the best." Stacey looked at her sisters and waited. There were no more tears for her to cry, but how she ached from the pain of it all.

"Lauren said that you kept that picture I took of you and Brendan on your mantle," Shay finally spoke.

She nodded. "Christopher, my son, looked like him as an infant. I knew I could put the picture out and no one would know it wasn't him. I could look at the picture and remember how happy he looked with you and Quinn that day when I saw you. It made me glad to know he was with you. When I lost Christopher, I thought the grief would push me over the edge, but because of my faith, because of Fred, and," she paused, "because of Lauren, I stayed strong."

Shay placed her hand on hers. "I lost my daughter too."

Stacey's eyes grew round with surprise and dismay. "The baby you were holdin'?"

Shay nodded and told Stacey about the boating accident that had taken Katelyn's life.

Stacey reached for her sister and held her. There were more tears.

When they pulled apart, she looked at both Mary and Shay. "I'm sorry I hurt you. If I had known you never received the letters, I would have tried again." She swallowed hard. "I can never ask you to forgive me, but after I found out where Lauren had traveled to and the people she had met, I knew none of this was by chance. I don't expect anythin' from either of you, or from Brendan. I only wanted to tell you how sorry I am."

Mary was the first to speak. "I forgive you, Glenna. Over the years, when Brendan would talk about you, we always reminded him of your struggles. I understand better now how deep those struggles ran. I'm happy that you were able to find peace and to build a life for yerself. And I'm sorry for your loss."

Stacey hugged her and then Shay told her she forgave her too.

"You need to talk to Brendan," her older sister encouraged.

Stacey's eyes grew wide with dismay. "He can't know about how he was conceived. It was one of the reasons I left. I wanted to spare him the pain of knowin'."

"He's strong, Glenna, and a good man, a man of faith. He deserves to know everythin' because he's angry."

Her face fell. She wasn't surprised to hear it, but it made her sad all the same. "If he'll talk to me, I'll tell him." She would find the courage.

Mary and Shay looked at each other with a silent message between the sisters who had remained together all of these years.

"I'll go talk to him and let him know you're here," Shay said.

"I'll drive you," Mary said as she stood from her seat to help her sister up.

Stacey stood too, her heart filling with dread.

"Quinn has a late meeting tonight, and we won't be gone long." Shay nodded to the bookshelf in the corner of the room. "Brendan's photo albums are over there. Help yerself while we're gone."

"Thank you. Thank you, both."

The three sisters hugged one more time before Shay and Mary left.

Chapter Forty-Four

Brendan was on the phone when his aunts arrived. He motioned them into the office and finished his conversation, worried because he could tell they had both been crying. When he hung up, he asked, "What's wrong?"

Shay and Mary looked at each other. "Glenna is here," his mom answered.

He felt instantly cold, but he wasn't surprised. He'd been expecting this—they all had. He was just glad she'd waited until after Ellen and Donal's wedding.

Brendan sat back in his chair. "I won't talk to her."

Shay nodded. "I understand, sweetheart, and you don't have to. But I do want you to know that she did come back when you were three, and tried to tell us everythin'." Shay told him about the visit she'd made and the letters she'd left at the bakery—the ones they'd never received.

He shrugged. "Well, good for her, but it wasn't enough."

"No, it wasn't, but there are reasons." Shay reached across the desk to place her hand on top of his. "You're my son, and I love you more than anythin'. I will support you if you choose not to talk to her. We just felt you needed to know that she is here, how she had tried, and does have a reason."

Shay made a move to get up, and Brendan stood to

help her. When she was standing, he wrapped his arms around his mother and squeezed his eyes shut before opening them again. He kissed Shay's cheek and then hugged Mary.

When they left, he closed the door and sank into his chair. He thought of the photos hidden in the box at the top of his aunt's closet. They didn't know he knew they were there. How many times had he secretly looked at the pictures of Glenna, the longing to know her welling up inside of him. All of that had stopped when he'd grown older and realized that she was truly dead or that she wasn't interested in coming back, the latter being the worse. When the longing had stopped, in its place a seed of resentment had taken hold. He'd not allowed himself to nurture it too much. She hadn't been worth it... until a few weeks ago when the worst of the two options had become a reality.

Overnight, the seed of resentment had bloomed and it seemed to be growing larger and larger. It felt like it was crowding him out. He and Lauren didn't talk about it, and they pressed on with their plans to build a life together.

Even now, he was desperate to run next door and lose himself in her. She would hold him, and she would tell him she understood and how it was okay if he didn't want to talk to Glenna. But the shadow of resentment seemed to stalk him, and he didn't like the way it felt.

He heard a tap on his door.

"Come in."

Ellen popped her head in. She and Donal had been back from their honeymoon for two days.

"I helped Mum walk Aunt Shay out. They told me what happened. Are you okay?"

He was about to say he was fine, but found himself saying instead, "Do you know what Donal is doin'? I need my pastor." Not his friend, his pastor.

She thought for a moment. "It's his afternoon to study, but if I call Shona and tell her it's urgent, she'll put me through. She knows I wouldn't say it if it wasn't true. Donal would consider this important."

He nodded.

Half an hour later, he was sitting in his best friend's office, and knew he needed to be here. He wouldn't like what Donal would have to say, but he needed to hear it.

"So, what do you want to do?" Donal asked, after Brendan had recapped the conversation he had with his aunts.

"Forget she exists."

"That's definitely an option, but a little hard to pull off, don't you think?"

"Yeah, especially since she gave me a brother, one I never had the chance to meet." Brendan ran his fingers through his hair in frustration. Christopher was the part of the whole sad story that hurt the most.

"Let's talk about Glenna. From what you've told me, she was an addict. Yet she cared enough about you to stay clean while she was pregnant with you. What if she'd stayed around for six months, tried to remain sober, and then failed?

"Or what if it was two years later when she fell apart

again? Think about it. She's livin' with you in Dublin tryin' to make ends meet. The world is weighing in on her. The responsibilities of being a single mother are bearin' down on her and she breaks, starts using again. No one knows except you and the people she's gettin' the drugs from. One day, she's out of her mind, high as a kite, and you wander out of the house and get hit by car. Or worse you're abducted, abused."

Donal continued painting the possible scenarios. "Now, let's pretend you're five and all of this happens. You've seen her strugglin', know it's been hard, but you love her because she's the only mother you've known. She relapses and you lose her. You're taken away from her and given to one of your aunts. You're devastated because all you know is that you love your mother, more than anythin', but she's gone, separated from you because she can't stop using."

He leaned his arms on his desk. "But none of that happened, Brendan. Instead, your mother left you with two loving aunts and an uncle who she knew would love and care for you far better than she could, that they would love you like their own, actually. And she also made sure she wasn't around for you to see her self-destruct.

"Which of the three scenarios would you rather have happened?"

Brendan knew he wouldn't want to hear what his friend had to say next. But he was here for a reason, and so he answered, "None of the above."

Donal raised his eyebrows but didn't say anything.

"I would have wanted to stay with my aunt and *when* Glenna was clean and sober, I would have wanted her to come back into our lives and make things right."

"But you told me she tried to deliver some letters."

He was right, and Brendan kept circling around that little detail. She had tried to reconnect in some way. It may have been a cowardly way, but she had tried.

"Brendan, forgivin' doesn't mean you have to let her into your life. Forgiveness doesn't require a relationship. You can forgive... and move on. The forgivin' is for your sake Brendan, not hers."

Brendan thought about the crowding he'd begun to feel because of the resentment and how it was creeping into his thoughts, and he knew Donal was right. Listening to what Glenna had to say and then learning to forgive her was what he needed to do—for *him*.

"You're right, Donal. Ever since I found out she'd left for America and started a new life with another family, I've been angry and resentful. I won't resolve that until I know why she did it. I'll talk to her."

He left Donal's office then went to lose himself in Lauren.

Brendan found her in her flat playing on the floor with Noirin.

He bent down, kissed his daughter, and said, "Noirin, I need to talk to Lauren in the other room, okay."

"Okay," she said as she went back to playing with her kitchen set. "Biscuits and tea will be ready when you're done," she added while holding a plastic teapot.

447

He helped Lauren to her feet and led her into her room. They kept the door open so they could hear Noirin in case she needed anything.

Brendan pulled her into his arms and held onto her for a long while.

"What's the matter, Brendan?"

He was thankful she had waited to say anything— just sensed he needed to be held for a moment.

He pulled away to look at her. "Glenna is here, Stacey, I mean."

"What!" Lauren's hands fell to her side. "I don't know why I'm surprised. Dad kind of indicated she was trying to work things out. She's here? Did you see her?"

"No, she went to my Mum's first. Then Mary joined them. The two of them came by the bakery to tell me she was here. I needed to talk to Donal, because I knew he would tell me what I needed to hear."

She gave him a nod. "I understand. I've felt so guilty about everything. I feel like I've been treading water when it comes to my mother-in-law. I would have said that you didn't need to talk to her, but that's not what you needed to hear, is it?"

He nodded.

"What did Donal say?"

Brendan told her.

She sat on the bed and pulled him down beside her. "You'll talk to her then?"

"I have to. I've been so angry."

"I'm glad, Brendan."

CHAPTER FORTY-FOUR

"I'd like for you to be with me."

She gave him a hesitant look. "I don't think that's a good idea. I think you need to talk to her by yourself."

He didn't agree and was about to tell her, when she added, "This is all about you, Brendan. It's not about me or even about your aunts: it's about you. I know you want me there because I love you and because Stacey and I have a relationship, but I'll only be in the way. Don't you see?"

He leaned his elbows on his knee and thought for moment. The idea of talking to Glenna was only tolerable if Lauren were by his side. But like Donal, she was right.

Brendan reached into his pocket and pulled out his phone. He pressed a button and placed the phone to his ear. "Hi, Mum, tell Glenna I'll talk to her." He paused. "Yes, I'm sure. Tell her to meet me at the bakery after it closes. I'll talk to her there."

Chapter Forty-Five

"Thank you for stopping by, Ellen," Lauren said as she worked on the salad she was making for dinner. Noirin was in the living room watching a television show while she prepped the meal.

Ellen washed her hands so she could help.

Lauren had called her and asked if she would come over. She explained how Brendan was next door talking to Glenna.

"What can I do?" Ellen offered.

Lauren handed her two heads of lettuce, one romaine and one butter. "How about shredding these. I have two bowls, one for us and one for you and Donal. Is he home yet?"

"He'll be home in a bit. That sounds really nice to say," Ellen remarked, her voice a little on the dreamy side.

Lauren looked up from the zucchini she was chopping and smiled. "It is really nice. I remember how it felt with Christopher, coming home from our honeymoon and getting into the routine of living together. It's different with Brendan; we live next to each other, so we see each other every day, multiple times a day. In some ways, it already feels like we're in a routine. But I've enjoyed it no less."

"Has he told you where you're goin' for your honeymoon?"

"No, it's a surprise."

"He sure does like his surprises. I never knew that about him."

Lauren turned to look at Ellen. "Is that right?"

She nodded. "He has always been thoughtful at birthdays and Christmas time, but I've never known him to want to surprise people. It's nice to see this side of him."

"Was he ever that way about Eva?"

"I don't know. I only met her twice—well three times if you count Katelyn's funeral. She didn't seem too interested in visiting Tramore with Brendan."

They were quiet for a moment, working on the salad. Ellen finished the lettuce, which she'd placed in two bowls. "Are you doin' all right, Lauren?"

Her friend shrugged her shoulders. "I am. Just worried about what they're talking about, and I'm afraid. I love Stacey. I've only ever known her as Christopher's mother, Fred's wife, and a really terrific mother-in-law. But she's hurt her family, and apparently, there are reasons for that. I hate to think what they might be, and I'm struggling with that. I know I'll forgive her, but I'm worried that things won't be the same. I'm sure she'll want to see me before she leaves. I'm not sure how to act, knowing what I know."

"You'll know what to do when the time comes. You always do."

"Thanks, and enough about me. I asked you here to comfort me, but I also want to know how your honeymoon went. It was kind of weird talking about it in front of Donal and Brendan when you two were here for dinner last night."

"Yeah, a bit, but it was glorious." It truly had been the best ten days of her life, getting to know Donal even more than she knew him before.

"Tell me what you saw," Lauren requested.

Ellen shared with Lauren all the touristy things they'd done. "We spent one day in Tivoli, rented a car and drove there. Stunning. Part of me wished we had booked the whole trip in that one area, away from the crowds. Oh, and the views, they were incredible, rollin' hills with vineyards as far as the eye could see. If we had gone to Tivoli earlier in the trip, we probably would have canceled our hotel in Rome and stayed out there."

"You'll have to make that your next vacation," Lauren offerred.

"We should plan a couples' trip together. Your parents will be here by then. I'm sure they wouldn't mind watchin' Noirin. Has your father heard about that job?"

"Oh, I forgot to tell you he had a Skype interview, and if he makes the cut, they'll fly him in for a face-to-face."

"That's grand. I'll keep my fingers crossed. Wouldn't that be terrific?"

"Yeah, it would be really nice. My folks weren't ready to retire, but they'd already been assessing their finances and felt they could sell the ranch and make the move. Dad said they'd be eating potatoes every night and living in a one room house, but they'd make it work. If he gets this job, it would make the move easier. As a professor, he could work a lot more years to come."

"What would your Mum do?"

"She'd probably enjoy working in a shop or doing some bookkeeping. She kept up the business end of the ranch."

Ellen was done chopping the red onion. "I'm really glad you're staying in Ireland, Lauren."

Her friend looked at her. "Does it seem strange for me to feel so connected to a place I've never been to, only dreamt about? When I started this journey in the spring, I never imagined that I'd be making this place my home. But it feels right. And to think how things are opening up for my parents. All I need now..." her voice trailed off.

"All you need now is for things to be better with Brendan and Glenna, so it won't be difficult to continue to be a part of their lives?" Ellen finished for her.

Lauren nodded. "Brendan would never begrudge me a relationship with her, but if it's only me and them, it will be hard. I'm afraid, over time, the distance will settle in and we'll drift apart." She shrugged. "But I won't let it come to that."

"If things don't work out, you can still maintain a relationship with her. And, who knows, maybe at some point Brendan will come around."

"Yeah, maybe."

Brendan didn't feel anxious about talking to Glenna. He was still too angry to feel apprehensive about confronting the woman who had abandoned him and her family. He sat at the table nearest the fireplace and checked his emails on his phone while waiting for her.

He looked up when he heard the front door to the bakery open, the jingling bell announcing her arrival. He remained in his seat and gave her a blank look before nodding at the chair across from him.

Brendan assessed the way she clasped her hands tightly as she made her way to the table. Her eyes never left his as she took the seat he offered.

"Hello, Brendan." Her voice trembled slightly. "Thank you for agreeing to meet with me."

He simply nodded and waited for her to continue. He wanted her to get to the point and to be done with this conversation.

"I don't really know where to begin..." She paused but never broke eye contact with him. "My sisters indicated that you knew about my past both as a little girl and teenager, when I started using, and how I'd run away from home."

"I've heard." They were the first words he'd spoken to her since she arrived.

"It was so difficult for me while I was pregnant and after you were born. It wasn't just because of the drugs. Yes, I was cravin' them, but not in the way that you think. I was hurtin' and damaged, and the only way I knew how to cope was to turn to what had numbed me for so long." She paused and a flash of uncertainty filled her eyes. "You see, Brendan, my pregnancy wasn't because I hadn't been careful, or ignorant. I was—I was raped."

Brendan hadn't expected to hear those words. He was stunned,

When she saw the look on his face, she quickly added, "I didn't want to tell you about that part, but my sisters said you deserved to know. Was it right to tell you?"

He didn't know how he felt about it, from both angles. He understood the difficulty she would have had raising him as well as being around him, a constant reminder of how he'd been conceived. And then, on a personal level, he struggled with knowing he was a product of such a violent act, having to carry that bit of truth around with him for the rest of his life. What he did know and was truly confident in is that his conception had no bearing on who he was as a person.

"Tell me the rest," he replied to her question as to whether telling him was the right thing to do.

For the first time she looked away. When she finally looked back at him, she began to tell him everything. How she'd begun using in the first place. How her addiction and the need to escape her pain had returned her to her old lifestyle. How that return soon led her to be sold to a human trafficking ring in New York. She then told Brendan how Fred had saved her with his offer of a new life.

"When we were first together, I wanted so badly to tell him everythin'. But I was afraid. He knew what I had been, but I had spared him the details. The thought of losin' him terrified me." She paused. "Imagine that you've been given the most precious thing in the world and then losin' it because of mistakes you'd made."

Brendan did imagine it: it was Lauren. The day she had told him the woman sitting in front of him was alive and well, he had a taste of what it would be like to lose her. But he wasn't feeling very understanding. "You should have trusted Fred. From everythin' that you and Lauren have told me about him, from what I learned when I met him, he would have understood. He actually would have helped you reconnect with us—the right way. You should have done more than come back to give us letters."

She nodded. "I thought it had been enough. My return address was on the envelope. When my sisters never contacted me, I thought I had my answer. But you're right. I may not have felt like I could share everything in person, but at least I could have hand delivered the letters directly to them. But I was a coward, ashamed, and..." her voice trailed off. She looked away again. "I was afraid of wantin' you so badly in my life that I would hurt my sisters in the process. My life was in Tacoma. Your life was here and you were so happy. I could tell when I saw the three of you together." Stacey shook her head. "But it's no excuse, and I was wrong. I only wanted you to know how sorry I am for everythin'."

Brendan felt cold and a little more than weary. "I love Lauren, and we're spendin' the rest of our lives together. I won't ask her not to be a part of your life. And I won't ask it of my mother and Aunt Mary." He paused. "I'm strugglin' right now with our Maker to find it in me to forgive you. If I do, it will be for my sake. But forgivin' you, Glenna, doesn't mean I want you in my life."

He stood from his chair and glanced down at her bent head. He saw her shoulders shaking and knew she was crying. Brendan felt nothing. "I'll lock up later, after you leave."

"Thank you for seeing me, Lauren." Stacey stood hesitantly inside of her entryway. "I've made a mess of things."

Lauren nodded at her.

"I'm sure Brendan told you everything."

"He did." It had distressed Lauren to know the truth about Stacey's past. It was hard to believe actually, almost impossible. When Brendan recounted the details to her the night before, after he'd spoken with her mother-in-law, she had been at a loss to accept what she had been told. Lauren had been equally stunned to learn about the rape. Her heart had ached for her mother-in-law.

When Brendan came back to her flat, he didn't seem as angry, merely accepting. When he had told her about his parting words to Stacey and not wanting her to be a part of his life, she'd felt the first stirrings of loss and had grieved at the possibility of losing Stacey forever.

Lauren told Brendan she understood, and she did. She also told him that, like him, who hadn't asked her to give up her relationship with her mother-in-law, she wouldn't ask him to change his mind about wanting Stacey in his life. And while she meant it, determination not to lose her, someone who had meant so much to her over the years, rose up inside of Lauren.

Stacey shifted and looked away from Lauren. "I'm glad he told you everything. What he didn't tell you, because I couldn't bring myself to tell him, is that a day of my life hasn't passed when I didn't love and long for him." Her voice broke over the last few words.

"That's why you put the picture on the mantle?"

Stacey nodded, her eyes welling up with tears.

Lauren reached for her mother-in-law whom she loved very much, regardless of all she now knew.

They held onto each other and allowed the tears to run their course.

Eventually, Lauren led Stacey to the couch. "We will make this work, Mom. I love you and nothing has changed. I know you're sorry for what you did, but we can't go back. We can only move forward. And I don't want to lose you."

Stacey sobbed and reached for her. She lifted her hand to cradle Lauren's face. "I love you too, sweetheart. Thank you for wantin' to make it work. You're everything to me not just because Christopher is gone. I've felt that way about you from almost the beginning. You're the daughter I never had, and I want you to be happy. I know Brendan will give you that."

Lauren gave her mother-in-law a tender look. "He has Christopher's smile."

Stacey lifted her hand to her mouth, a fresh rush of tears coming to her eyes. "Really?"

Lauren nodded. "When I first met him, I thought it looked so familiar and comforting. It wasn't until everything happened that I realized why. You know," she paused, "in spite of all this, I feel as if I have a part of Christopher back. I know Brendan didn't say much to you last night, but do you know what hurts him the most?"

Stacey shook her head.

"He had a brother and never had the chance to know him."

Her mother-in-law covered her face with her hands. "I'm so sorry, so sorry."

Lauren held her. "I didn't tell you that to hurt you but to give you hope."

Stacey pulled away and wiped the tears from her eyes. She looked at her, expectantly.

"Before we realized who you were, he told me he wanted to know all about Christopher. He even asked if they would have been friends. Of course, they would have. In so many ways they're alike. Their kindness and compassion. The loyalty they have for their loved ones." Lauren told Stacey about Katelyn's death and the sacrifice Brendan made, choosing to raise Noirin. She even told her about Eva. "The reason I told you about his anger over never knowing his brother, is that you, Mom, you are the only one who can tell him everything about Christopher. You were there for every one of his moments. I wasn't and neither was Dad.

"I won't pressure Brendan into changing his mind, and he will never pressure me or make me feel bad for wanting a relationship with you. But I'm not giving up hope for him or your sisters. How are things on that end?"

"Okay. I spoke with them this mornin'. I told them I'd be leavin' tomorrow. Everyone needs time to deal with everythin'—and then we'll see. We exchanged phone numbers."

Lauren reached for Stacey's hands. "I need to tell you something. I love Shay. She asked me to call her mother. I want to, and I will. But it doesn't change anything between you and me."

Stacey nodded. "She's a good woman. I don't know how I would have survived our childhood if it hadn't been for her. I don't know what went wrong with me. I got older and found people outside of my wrecked family who didn't know my circumstances, and they accepted me. It was liberating. With them, I could leave the pain behind. With Shay and Mary, the pain of our past was ever present. I could never escape it.

"Unfortunately, my friends' acceptance of me influenced my decision to do things I should never have done, and it put me on a far more terrible path." She sighed. "But like you said, we can't change what's happened. I'll hold out hope too, Lauren."

Lauren squeezed her mother-in-law's hands tighter and then they embraced. *Hope.* It too was ever present, and instead of being a burden, it was a gift.

460

Chapter Forty-Six

"I can't believe this place will be ready in a week!" Ellen exclaimed as she stood in the center of the new bakery with her arms outstretched, a dust rag in hand. She loved the carved, stone wall they had built into the space. The hues of natural earth tones gave the room warmth and reminded her of having tea in a medieval castle. Large hand-hewn wooden beams ran across the ceiling.

The construction had been completed earlier that week, and the four of them, Ellen, Donal, Brendan, and Lauren were there working late on getting the last of the cleaning done.

Ellen's replacement at Cups and Cakes in Tramore had been hired and trained for a few weeks now, freeing up Ellen to move full time into the new tea room in Dunmore East. A week ago, she and Lauren had finalized all the hiring of the staff. The servers started this week to help with the cleaning, and the bakers would start next week, training and learning the recipes. They were scheduled to do a test run of the tearoom the following Sunday with their family and friends, the day before their first service.

Ellen walked over to Lauren and hugged her. "You have worked yerself to the bone helpin' me while plannin' your weddin'."

Lauren kissed her cheek. "I didn't plan the wedding

by myself. I had Brendan. And you, *you've* been working yourself to the bone opening this bakery and helping me plan my wedding. Besides, I'm a full-fledged employee now."

Lauren had received her work visa, and after she was married, she would work on her permanent residence status.

Ellen chuckled in delight. "Yes, you are! And I am so happy we will be workin' together."

They heard the guys shuffling in from the back. They had finished hauling out the last of the boxes to the dumpster.

"What's all this delira about?" Donal asked as he and Brendan entered the room and stared at them.

Ellen made her way to Donal and threw her arms around him. "The delira is about how happy I am. You, my love, make me extraordinarily happy. And," she turned to look at Brendan and Lauren, "they make me really happy too. This place makes me really happy!"

Donal kissed her, and said, "Well, I'm pretty delira too. And I'm famished."

"Me too," Brendan agreed. "But I think all of us are too knackered to do any cookin'." He looked down at his watch. "Lanigan's should still be open—wanna go there?"

"Sounds great to me," Lauren agreed.

"We'll catch up to you guys," Ellen said, still holding onto her husband.

When Lauren and Brendan left, she gave Donal a kiss. He deepened it and lifted her higher into his arms so her feet were no longer on the ground. "I can't get enough of you," he said when he pulled away.

She lifted her legs and wrapped them around his waist. He placed his hands underneath her to help support her and then kissed her some more. "I don't want to go dinner," he said in a ragged breath.

Ellen's own breathing was coming in fast spurts "Well, we can't abandon them now. Besides you were the one who said you were hungry."

"How do you know I was talkin' about food?"

She kissed him greedily and her hands were everywhere. "I know you were talkin' about food," she said in between kisses, "but you're entitled to change your mind. They'll understand, won't they? After all, we're newlyweds."

Ellen didn't have to ask him twice. Donal abruptly put her down, and after holding her gaze for a moment, he reached for his phone and texted Brendan to let him know they wouldn't be joining them after all.

When he put the phone back in his pocket, he reached for Ellen and instead of devouring her like he wanted to do, he cradled the sides of her face with his hands. With his thumbs, he stroked the soft delicate skin of her cheeks. "You make me feel so crazy."

"It won't always be like this," she whispered as she pressed her lips to his.

"No, it won't. It will be better." He pulled away to look at her. "It will be so much better."

Business at Lanigan's was winding down. Brendan and Lauren took a quiet table in the corner. Instead of sitting across from each other, they sat side by side.

They didn't need to look at the menu and gave the waiter their order. Lauren always ordered the meatballs, and he ordered the bales of hay. Lauren had laughed the first time she'd realized it meant spaghetti. They always shared.

"You know, one day we're going to have to try something different when we come here," she said before taking a sip of her water.

"We could always do the fish and chips."

"Nope. It has to be Fiddle Faddle's."

"Is that right? So, I've spoiled ya for all other fish and chips, have I?"

"Yep, it's all your fault."

Brendan kissed her.

"You know why they didn't join us right?" Lauren asked.

He raised his eyebrows at her. "I really don't want to think about that, you know. She's like my sister."

Lauren's cheeks flushed.

"Besides if they were here, I couldn't do this." He leaned down and kissed the smooth delicate skin of her neck.

"You have a thing for necks, don't you?"

"Just yours." He kissed her there once more before pulling away. "You're really good at what you do, Lauren. Have I told you that?"

"What do you mean?"

"You're a good businesswoman. I've known from the beginning what a grand artist you are. The recipe cards turned out superbly and the retail display that you two set up today will be a big hit. But I didn't know how you would be at runnin' a business."

"Feeling more confident about letting go of some of the work so you can focus on the investing?"

"I wasn't overly worried, but it's nice to know you have it."

She smiled at him. "I'm glad you approve. By the way, am I going to have to wait until we board the plane to find out where we're going on our honeymoon?"

He nodded. "Ellen is helping me pack your suitcase."

"Seriously?"

"Dead serious. If I tell you to pack swimmin' suits, you'll know it's somewhere tropical. If I tell you to pack hiking boots, you'll think we're stayin' in the mountains somewhere. If I tell you to pack a snow suit, you'll think we're plannin' to ski."

"Skiing while it's still summer?"

"Of course, places like Switzerland or Chile have skiing all year round. I'm sure they even have places in the U.S. where you can ski during the summer."

"I guess I never thought about it. Is that where we're going? I don't even know how to..."

Brendan silenced her with a kiss.

When he pulled away, she said, "I could coax you into telling me. I have ways."

His pulse quickened. How tempted he was to carry her playfulness through, to see how far she would go, but he wouldn't. "I'm a man of conviction, a *chuisle*."

She looped her arm through his and laid her head on his shoulder. "Yes, you are, Brendan, and I love you for it."

"Are you ready?" Lauren asked Ellen.

Her friend looked at the staff who were waiting for her final instructions. Their family, the employees at Cups and Cakes in Tramore, and their closest friends, sixty in total, would be here for the dry run of their first high tea.

Everything was in place. The lights were polished. The windows shone like beams of light dancing off the ocean, and the tables were dressed impeccably with white tablecloths, Laura Ashely china, and a fresh bouquet of flowers for every table. They had chosen pale pink tea roses and lavender crocus for the arrangements, adding tufts of fern leaves for the greenery.

The dining room was stunning.

Ellen took in a deep breath. "I'm as ready as I'll ever be."

Their men were out front greeting their guests.

Soon, service was in full swing. Lauren and Brendan helped in the front of the house with seating and delivering tiered trays filled with Ellen's lavender biscotti, tomato tartlets, Irish rarebit, and several other painstakingly thought-out options. The previous week, they had

taste tested all the employees' training runs and everything was delicious.

After delivering a fresh pot of tea to Rachel and
Matthew from the book club, Brendan came up behind
her. He placed a hand at the nape of her neck, and said,
"Why don't you go and take a break for a minute in the
back. I've got things."

Her feet were killing her. "Are you sure?"

He kissed her briefly. "I'm sure."

She made her way to the kitchen.

"Lauren, how are things goin'?" Ellen asked, her
head bent down, a pastry bag in her hand. She was piping
white icing fleur de lis on her chocolate-covered short-
bread cookies, a nod to her French training.

"Great! The Blue Brew tea is a hit. Everyone who
ordered it is raving about it."

Ellen looked up at Donal who was helping her dip the
shortbreads. "Can you write that down, darlin'."

Donal was acting as sous chef and note taker on things
that were going well and things that needed adjusting.

Lauren walked over to the counter. "Brendan sent
me in here to get off my feet for a few minutes, but I can't
take a break while you two are so hard at work."

They had staggered the reservations just as they
would when they opened for business. Most items could
be made ahead of time, but not everything. The stag-
gering allowed them to keep a steady pace, but nothing frantic.

"Here, wash your hands and take these dried

shortbreads over to the prep station and start plating the stands."

Lauren did as Ellen directed and studied the charts she had made for the plating, showing exactly how everything was to be placed on each tier. Earlier that week, when Brendan had seen the charts, he had said, "See this is what I'm talkin' about. You have a gift for this kind of thing."

She smiled at the memory. As soon as she was done plating the cookies, she heard Brendan say, as he walked into the kitchen, "I thought you were supposed to be resting your feet."

She looked over at Donal and Ellen who were working away and said, "While they're going full blast? Not a chance."

"Understood, but break time is over—you're needed at table twelve. That's the one in the corner by the retail section."

"Isn't that where ours and Ellen's parents are seated?"

"Yeah, they said they needed you."

Lauren wiped her hands on a towel and followed him out.

She didn't see her until she got to the table. Seated next to her mother and Shay was Stacey.

Tears filled her eyes as she looked at them, smiles bright on their faces, and then she looked at Brendan, her brows raised in question. "I love you, Lauren." He turned to look at Stacey. There was a small smile on his face, but it was genuine. He then gave her a nod.

The woman that had given her a son to love, the first man she'd ever adored, rose from her chair and walked over to her. Stacey reached for her hands.

Lauren's voice quivered slightly when she said, "I can't believe you're here."

Stacey looked at Brendan, and Lauren could see the love in her eyes for the child she had given up so many years ago. Unknowingly, the woman she loved, like a second mother, had given her another son to love. Two beautiful men to have and to cherish for however many days she had with the older one.

A year ago, she wouldn't have believed it was possible to be so happy again. In her deepest moments of despair, she had believed that the happiness she had with Christopher only came once in a lifetime. And yet today, she was realizing how wrong she had been.

Stacey's voice was also slightly shaky when she turned back to Lauren to reply. "I was invited to come early for the wedding. Brendan thought it would be nice to have me here with your mom these last two weeks to help you. Fred and your dad will fly up together next week."

Lauren hugged her mother-in-law. She then kissed the man she loved before moving to her own mother to give her a hug and kiss.

"Okay," Lauren said, feeling replete with happiness, "this is going to be a little challenging when the three of you are all in the same room." She looked at her mother, then Stacey, and then Shay, and said, "Mom, you will always be Mom." She then looked at Stacey and said,

"You are Mama Stacey, and," she looked at Shay, "you're Mum Shay. Do you think we can manage to keep my three mothers straight?"

There was laughter and some bantering as the table agreed they could make it work. While they chatted, Lauren moved over to Brendan's side and reached for his hand. She led him outside of the bakery so they could be alone. When they reached the side of the building, she drew him to her, her hands cupping his face.

"What made you change your mind?" she asked.

"*Ar scáth a chéile a mhaireann na daoine*," he said. His gaze was intense, and she could see the depth of feeling behind the words he spoke but didn't understand. That strong, wonderfully lyrical language was mysterious and such a part of who Brendan was. It melted over her like a warm summer.

"It means, 'under the shelter of each other, people survive.'"

Lauren buried her face into his chest and squeezed her eyes shut. The intensity of what she felt was close to grief. It was then she realized there was a fine line drawn in the landscape of one's soul. A slight shift in one direction landed you on the side of grief and pain. A slight shift in the other direction landed you on the side of complete euphoria. Only a clear hard line separated the two emotions, but the intensity of both were the same.

He placed his finger under her chin so she could look into his eyes. "I did it for you, *mo chroi*." Brendan caressed the side of her neck. "But somehow, with time, I believe it will turn into something for me too."

That intensity of emotion. It made itself known again, but this time, instead of closing her eyes she held the gaze of the man she loved and said, "You are my shelter, here in our earthly dwelling, and I will take great pleasure in being covered by you."

Epilogue

Nine Months Later

It was the first chance they'd had to travel to Tacoma together. Lauren had been back on a couple of occasions to meet with the property manager who would run the Airbnb and to pack up and ship the items she wanted to take back to Ireland with her, including all of Christopher's personal items. She wanted Brendan to learn more about his brother through the things he valued, and because she couldn't bear to part with them.

They weren't able to spend the whole summer in Tacoma, just yet, but on this trip, they had made plans to spend two weeks. It was mid-June. Their hope was that by the following summer they could work remotely and spend more time in the home she and Christopher had made together.

Brendan experienced his first baseball game, an early afternoon starting pitch time between the Mariners and the Oakland As. Fred and Stacey had joined them. It had been wonderful to see him so excited, like watching a kid in a candy store for the first time.

Her husband's prediction had been right about his birth mother. Brendan's decision to invite Stacey to Tramore, before their wedding, had turned into something for him too. Shay would always be his mother, the one who had loved and raised him selflessly, exactly like he'd done for Noirin, but there was an affection growing between Brendan and Stacey. And it was obvious Fred loved him like a son. It would've been impossible for him not to develop such feelings, for after all, Brendan was his son's brother. Fred too saw the similarities in their smiles and it felt as if he had a part of Christopher back.

Lauren and Brendan had married in Adare at the Dunraven Arms, a two-hundred-year-old hotel with flower-filled gardens and olde-world charm. The ceremony and reception were both held there with a small gathering of friends and family for an elegant but intimate wedding.

For their wedding night, they had rented a small thatched cottage, nestled in a little woodland area right outside of the small picturesque town. For as long as she lived, Lauren would never forget their first night together.

She discovered that her husband loved romance. His desire to do such things was more than just believing she would enjoy it. He did romantic things because he liked how it made him feel—the yearning, the intimacy it created, and how it opened one's soul and spirit.

"When I feel like this," he'd said after they'd made love, "I believe I could write poetry. The way it moves me, the thoughts and the emotions that are churnin' inside of me. It's like they're beggin' to be let out, and I'll die a little if I don't find a way to express them."

She had looked around the bedroom with the

candles he'd lit, the fragrance of hyacinths filling the air, and she'd felt it too, the wild, untamed emotions. Those feelings combined with the way her body felt after being loved by him, not because of a physiological response but because of the heart and soul behind the person doing such wonderful things to her, were deep and vast. There was a wonder in the exchanging of selves, weaving the parts of two halves into all of the recesses of their persons, a connectedness that was hard to put into words.

In the morning, they'd stopped at the same gift shop they'd visited the first time he'd taken her to Adare. As they waited in line to purchase a journal, one she'd picked out for him for their trip, a journal for his poetry, she happened to look at him and caught the intense way he was gazing at her.

Lauren remembered their first time in that shop and how they had looked at all the couples and Brendan had guessed what their lives together were like. There had been the couple he was certain were newlyweds because of how the man had looked at his wife, like he could devour her on the spot.

Remembering that moment, and seeing the intense look on her husband's face, Lauren reached up and drew Brendan's head down so she could whisper into his ear, "You look like you could devour me right about now."

When she pulled away, his eyes grew bright with the intensity he felt.

They quickly paid for their purchase and barely

made it through the front door of the cottage before the devouring began.

Early the next morning, after checking them in at the airport kiosk, Brendan handed Lauren her boarding pass.

"Bruges, Belgium?" she asked, looking down at the words and then quickly back up to Brendan. "I've never heard of it. I want to pull out my phone and start Googling pictures right now."

"Wait, *mo chroi*. I want it to take your breath away when you see it for the first time, live and in person."

"Have you ever been?"

He shook his head. "I wanted to go someplace with you that neither of us had ever been."

Bruges had been a magical place, in the northwest part of Belgium, distinguished by its canals, medieval architecture, and cobbled streets, with thirteenth and fourteenth century buildings still standing.

In the heart of that romantic city, Brendan had written his first poem. That night, after making love to her, he held her and read her the words that had been begging to come out, and they were beautiful. When she dried her tears, she said, "Forget the real estate business, you're going to make your fortune as a poet."

He'd rolled her onto her back and covered her body with his. His eyes intense. She could feel the wild beating of his heart as his chest laid pressed against hers. "I love you, so much, Lauren, my beautiful wife. Do you feel it?"

He'd raised her hand to his chest so she could

feel the fast-steady rhythm of his heart. It was an outward showing of the intense emotions coursing through his body, that clear hard line that separated pain from euphoria.

"I feel it," she said, and then lifted his hand to her heart. "I feel it here, mirrored beats. Do you feel it too?"

Brendan had kissed her in response, a sweet tortuous kiss that ignited into something magnificent. A moment they would always remember.

"What are you thinkin' about?"

Brendan's voice brought her out of her thoughts. They were sitting together on the couch in their Tacoma home, resting after a long day of sightseeing and the baseball game. Noirin had fallen asleep on the way home and Brendan had carried her to her bed.

"I was thinking about our honeymoon," she replied.

His eyes lit up. "Oh, you were, were you?"

She smiled. "Christopher once told me he loved our honeymoon, but how he loved our life afterwards, even more." She reached up to run her fingers through his dark hair. "I felt that way then, and I feel that way now, with you."

He kissed her. "Do you think we have some time before Noirin wakes up?"

"We might. Instead, I have something I think you'll be more interested in doing."

Brendan ran a series of kisses along her jaw line and down her neck. "You think so? I don't think so."

"I'm late," she said a little breathlessly.

Her words got his attention. Brendan pulled away with his brows raised in hope. "You're late?"

She smiled. "I bought a pregnancy test."

It was the first time she'd been late for her cycle since they married. Shortly after their return from Burges, they had seen a fertility specialist who said that everything was fine with both of them. Lauren wanted to put her concerns to rest, and they were so happy with the news. But every month since, when she started her cycle, she began to wonder if the tests had been wrong.

Brendan stood up from the couch, dragging her up with him. "Well then, what are you waitin' for?"

She gave him a seductive smile and ran her hand slowly down his chest. "I thought you had other things in mind?" she teased.

He kissed her a little hard, and then said, "You're somethin' fierce, woman." He turned her in the direction of the bathroom. "Now go get in there and take that test," he ordered while adding a pat to her bottom for good measure.

A short while later, Brendan heard the water running in the sink and his heart began to race in his chest with half dread and half excitement. He had meant what he told Lauren and how he would be just as happy to adopt, but he couldn't deny the joy of knowing that the two of them had created a precious life. And that out of their deep and abiding love for one another, they could give a part of themselves back to the world.

When she opened the door, and he saw her face, he knew. They rushed toward each other, and he held her in his arms circling with her in joy. Words weren't necessary—only the love they felt and the kiss they shared.

Suddenly, they heard rain pouring down from the heavens and onto the roof of the house. They pulled apart and looked out the bay window, surprised by the downpour, because it had been sunny all day.

Brendan looked back at Lauren. "And it was a such good day."

Her eyes grew wide as she remembered her first day in Tramore, broken and angry, as she recalled her grandmother's words. How different life turns out— the twists and the turns, the bend of a road and where it leads you.

Lauren beamed a bright smile at him. Suddenly, she grabbed his hand and ran out of the back door and onto the lawn, in the pouring rain. Without question, Brenda followed the woman he treasured and knew he would follow her to the ends of the earth and back, if he had to.

In the middle of the emerald green grass, so much like the grass of his homeland, she said, "Haven't you heard, *mo chroi*, rain on a good day is never wasted. It's a reminder that the pain in life is necessary. It gives us perspective. A perspective that reminds us to hug our children a little longer and more often." She placed his hand on her womb. "It reminds us never to go to bed angry with the ones we love." Lauren kissed him there and then in the pouring rain.

When the kiss ended, Brendan blinked away the rain and the tears from his eyes and translated in perfect Gaelic, "*Ní chuirtear báisteach ar lá maith amú.*"

"That's right, Brendan, rain on a good day is never wasted."

THE END

About the Author

At the age of twelve, Anne Comfort discovered the joy of reading. The worlds and places she found herself being transported to through the careful crafting of words and phrases inspired her to create her own stories.

In her world of fiction, you will find characters who have joined in the fellowship of human suffering but have managed to hold onto the beautiful moments in between. Her hope is that the stories she writes will inspire all of her readers to embrace the sacred moments of their lives, lifting them high up so they may help light the way.

Anne shares her beautiful moments in between with her husband, son, and all of her other family members and friends whom she loves dearly.

She would enjoy hearing from you at AnneComfortWriter.com.

Serves new and emerging authors
to help them write, publish, and promote their books.
Are you ready to share your story?

Visit us!
www.silversmithpress.com

www.ingramcontent.com/pod-product-compliance
Lightning Source LLC
Chambersburg PA
CBHW011400010726
47495CB00009B/2713